Tony Deane is a retired Inspector of Taxes and amateur musician. He is married and lives in Kent. He does not own a smart phone, an I-Pod or a set of adjustable spanners.

*Erotic mania. Gluttony. Lust.
Bitter rivalry. Murder. Intrigue.
Political ambition -
don't let any of them distract you
from reading*

The Gnostic Frying Pan
by
Tony Deane

A Farrago with a Prolegomenon,
69 Chapters,
and a smattering
of informative footnotes.

Text copyright © Anthony R Deane
All Rights Reserved

This novel is a work of fiction. The names, characters and incidents portrayed therein are the product of the author's imagination or are used fictionally. Any resemblance to actual persons, living or dead, events or locations is entirely coincidental

Prolegomenon

Intimates of noted mediums and lovers of the esoteric will have been inattentive indeed if they have escaped all knowledge of what followed, to use a term as loose as last year's underpants, the disappearance of the S'nang üll H'notorem, the *lapis exillis* of old lore, the Wandering Stone, from the temple of the Archerons of Atlantis.

Now it is time for the rest of the world to hear of the events, or quasi-events, or ex-events which wrought such an appalling transformation upon the cosmos in which everyone, from the greasy realms of Trang to the overestimated empire of the Hoop People, lived and moved and had what they liked to think of as their being (except for the Hoop People, who liked to think of it as someone else's being). But let us not be sad for so trivial a cause. For what is the foundering of Atlantis, compared to that of which the universal immolation of 1922 deprived us all?

We refer, of course, to Helena Phipps, the most sensuous netball player in anybody's team.

It was after learning from an indescribable source of the loss of the spotless Helena that the writer embarked on the lengthy course of self-discipline, exercise and meditation which eventually enabled him to penetrate the cracks in the shell of the collective illusion with the fine tempered tea-spoon of his psyche and at last in a silent blaze of trumpet coloured perfume to burst from the Maya-bound constraints of Things As

They Seem and to enter like a swimmer into a glassy sea the void of That Which Is As It Is.

During his exaltation the writer learned many things. He saw the reason for heliotrope and the purpose of the squid. He heard the true name of W G Grace and understood his role in the eternal war against the Drupidarian. He foresaw the name of the winner of the Derby but it was not his own and, anyway, he had no interest in a Women's Institute hat raffle.

But more significant than any of these was the supreme awakening of his perception which allowed him finally to become aware that all spaces and times, potential and actualized, all – all were finite embodiments of That Which Is As It Is, none of less value or materiality than any other. He knew then that, having cast off the illusion of separate reality, he could recede into That Which Is As It Is and emerge again in some other state of being – a figure in your dreams, an episode in an unfinished film by Orson Welles, six or seven pages of closely reasoned eschatology, or a wet Tuesday in Pontefract. He chose, of course, for he was in some manner still entrained by the oscillation of his finite self, to reconstitute his being in the universe which once gave life and loveliness to the wonderful Helena Phipps, most desirable creature in this or any other dimension of the All.

And now you have before you the results of his intratemporal jaunts, dear reader, while an elderly gentleman, who had thought himself safe from the machinations of life, stirs in his sleep and protests against the implacable Will which sends him back to the world of joggers, muggers, naggers, doggers, Spupoes, and all who seek to make life irritating for him: Captain H. 'Geronimo' Sparesbrook, of Sparesbrook Manor, Amblebroth, Herts.

Part One

The Rape of the Stone

1

When Captain H. 'Geronimo' Sparesbrook awoke that morning, he had barely got his slippers on before he established that it was to be no ordinary day. During the night, someone had sawn a hole in the floorboards under his bedside rug. He discovered the trap by the always reliable method of stepping into it.

If he had been looking forward as he fell to dying of injuries received on the oak table in the refectory below, the Captain must have been disappointed. Instead, he found himself abruptly dangling next to the neo-classical chandelier. A net had been slung beneath the hole.

"You will regret this horseplay," he growled, as impressively as a man can who is hanging from his own ceiling like a winceyette parsnip in a string bag. "The Governor of Stalebreath Academy sits on the General Commissioners with me. I suggest you release me now, while your punishment will be reasonably light. In any case," he added, "it's no use you trying to pull these charity stunts here, you fellows. I'm a ruined man. Penniless. Look in the newspapers. It's all there. Every last sou embezzled by a chap I trusted. You'd better just let me down and go and kidnap a cabinet minister or something."

Shamefaced ragsters from the school, suddenly aware that their jape had misfired, did not edge from the shadows.

The Captain began to shiver.

At the time whereof we speak (to follow the custom of describing a being by listing all the things it has ceased to be) the Captain was the survivor of two and seventy years: a former military man whose exploits are still too shameful for inclusion in the history books. A long but not at all successful career in the Business Efficiency racket ended with the notorious Duck Engineering Scandal of '02, after which the Captain had retired from public life to that loyalest of havens, Sparesbrook Manor, Hertfordshire, where he now lived quietly, supplementing his pension by acting as a casual bostelman[1] for Messrs Nasty, Brutish & Short, a firm of solicitors, who had recently sacked him for being too damned casual.

Nowadays the Captain had declined and suffered sadly from subsidence, his shoulders drooping, his eyes rheumy, his superb moustache wilted at the tips. He wore that air of disappointment most often seen in people who are able to quote their National Insurance number but have never been asked to. You expected to find mice in his pockets, signs of wet rot in his underwear. He was old, not merely in years, but aged by some ruinous experience.

And yet, until this morning, the greatest disturbance of his retirement had been the screams of busloads of inmates passing his gates en route for what advertised itself as the Violet Pring Hebbenthwaite Sunset Memorial Home for Diseased and Lunatick Gentry further up the hill.

---

[1] A bostelman, of course, is someone who corrects wannops.

A wannop is any sentence in a Will or other legal document which means what it appears to say.

He felt that it was hardly fair to ask him at his time of life to cope with nets.

But who could have played this trick on him, if not scamps from the school? Some member of staff with a grudge or a deformed sense of humour? No, what with the temptations of the Benefit Office and TV Talent Shows, it was impossible to attract staff, with or without deformities. Apart from an elderly manservant, Edward Thring, who was bound to his master by ties of gratitude, and Thring's lovely young wife, Juliette, there was no-one left to scrape the moss off the statuary or raise the blinds on rooms of shrouded furniture. The kitchens, which in his father's day had thrummed with the obscenities of spit-boys, now produced only the hissing of an economy gas-stove and the whimperings of the child of Deirdre Horne, the scullery maid, also bound to the Captain by ties of personal gratitude, which comes a lot cheaper than the Minimum Wage and doesn't attract National Insurance contributions.

In the gloom below, nothing stirred.

But suddenly, from the hole in the ceiling above his head, there came a dreadful cough. If the Voynich Manuscript had a nasty go of bronchitis, it might sound like that. The Captain strained to peer up through his netting and shuddered to see the eyes that smouldered in the glow of a candle through the hole in the bedroom floor. The crusty lips peeled apart. A liverish tongue licked long fangs. It spoke.

"Good morning, sir," it croaked. "Do you require your shaving tackle?"

"Thring!" the Captain cried. "For Magotte's sake, help me, man. They've come for me," he whispered. "After all these years, the bastards have tracked me down."

"Customs and Excise, sir? A little early in the morning for those gentlemen, I fancy."

"Not the blessed VAT, Thring. Even worse. It's – the Spupoes."

Half a century ago, when the Captain was a merry sun bronzed lad, he had gone with a band of like-minded men, uncomplicated, hearty, mercenary souls, into the jungles of the East to hunt down the unspeakable tribe of Spupoes, a race whose distaste for rates and taxes had caused an annoying backlog of paperwork up at the Government offices in Gunpur. Access to official documentation of the massacre has been consistently denied both to the narrative and to one of its lady acquaintances, Miss Lola Lalashe, an academic researcher, who happening by lucky accident to be on the same football special as Mr. Brian Zenfoot of the Archive Security Service, attempted to persuade him by rational argument that revelations of the Spupo Incident would be in the national interest, and also no small embarrassment to the government of the day of whom, she surmised, the Swastika arm-banded Zenfoot was not the most committed of supporters.

Sadly, there are limits to what the railway companies will tolerate in the way of rational argument and Miss Lalashe was forced to abandon her enquiry, along with a lot of her clothing, at Castle Bromwich. The narrative is therefore obliged to rely on evidence from a supporter in Croydon who is ever so good at foretelling the weather and has this really amazing knack of ringing you up just when you were thinking of going down the pub.

Anyway, she maintains the high point of the Captain's career was as follows.

Cunningly waiting till the entire male population of Spupoes had departed for the Ornamali Ceremonies in the distant Hollows of Brern, the Captain and seventeen handpicked cavalry men rode into the night. Who shall blame them? Even today there are those who cannot forget the infamous occasion when the Spupo hordes swarmed into the British Library at Prajnaputra and defaced all the J B Priestleys. And who, indeed, shall fault the 14th Goatshires for taking matters into their own hands, after Lieutenant-Colonel Monkley-Biscuit's twin daughters were abducted by the creatures and held for more than three weeks while one after another the tribesmen insulted the Empire and English maidenhood by fastidiously declining to lay a finger on either of them?

Armed only with their burning indignation, the British flag and seventeen machine guns, the Captain and his men victoriously liquidated every woman, child and anthropologist in the village, which they afterwards burned. He could still recall the thrill of pleasure as round after round of good English lead punched through the hides of whimpering academics.

After that, things had not gone entirely as per the programme. The dynamiting of the Hollows of Brern, though technically immaculate, failed to distribute the male Spupoes over the surrounding landscape in the form of a meaty gravy because all that stuff about Ornamali Ceremonies was completely bogus. Actually, they'd gone down to Wahkore for a dirty weekend. Returning to the village on the Monday morning with their arms full

The Gnostic Frying Pan

of Bingo prizes and Javanese whisky, they discovered what carnage had been wrought while they frolicked in Wahkore. At once they swore any amount of very terrible oaths and vowed revenge upon the khaki devils, outlining a number of plans for their khaki extremities that would have brought a twinkle to the eyes of the Marquis de Sade. They chanted and danced for five days and nights, then seized their war spears, daubed their bodies with clay and feathers and, whooping and shrieking, headed back to Wahkore for another dirty weekend. The Spupoid sense of urgency was about as intense as that of the average Council Highways Department.

But fifty years went by, and of that carefree little band who had braved the nasty looks of the Spupo women, only their leader, Captain H. 'Geronimo' Sparesbrook, remained. As he dangled in the net, he remembered them all, Tiny Fellofian, Greg Latch, Methy Dropwheel, Vig Wake, Pinxy Dollop, Bagwash McTurk, Laky Vince Hoptuft, the Bauby Brothers, Tinplate Zebby Dolenz, Little Johnny Nates, wicked old Vinny Poles, Bogg the Kisser, Jack Larvis and his lizard, and the nameless ones, day labourers and mechanicals of his band, that Geordie with the limp ears, the chap who lost his toes, the little old fellow who spoilt the wheelbarrow, more and more filed through his memory as he spun slowly widdershins by the chandelier. All dead, dead for years, and now there was only one left, Captain H. 'Geronimo' Sparesbrook, and he wasn't feeling very carefree.

Vinny Poles went first. They said a chip-pan caught fire as he nodded over the News Chronicle but the coroner never explained why Vinny should

The Rape of the Stone

have been cooking chips in a telephone booth. Next to go was Bagwash McTurk. They found his remains inside the mattress which broke the fall of Jotelunde Craagnuut, the Finnish megasoprano, in the last minutes of The Flying Dutchman at the Garden in '57. Greg Latch perished on the beach at Bournemouth when a person or persons unknown forced him to swallow a self-inflating lilo and then pulled the ripcord. The ambulance service completely let him down. Well, they had to, you see, to get him through the doors. Within forty years of the massacre, all dead, all buried, all except the Captain.[2]

"Have no fear, Captain," Thring wheezed. "I shall be at your side in two shakes." The gaunt features withdrew. And returned. "Or perhaps three," he amended punctiliously.

All in all, it seemed an appropriate moment for a witless scream. The Captain was about to put one together when with a sound like the drawing back of a rotting curtain, the rotting curtain at the windows of the dining room drew back. Immediately the Captain saw that his fears of the Spupoes had been nothing but a pointless digression. The cold morning light which hobbled into the refectory disclosed no clay smeared bodies, no green feathers.

The room was infested with boggarts.

---

[2] And Vig Wake. No-one ever found enough of the shreds of Vig Wake to make burial worth the bother.

2

It was, in some sense of the word, the first of May in Amblebroth and as usual the hills cowered under the assault of wind and rain. Down in the valley, fir trees tossed over households in which the little community prepared to celebrate the Rites of Spring. At the Strict Chapel of Bestiality in Lobelia Lane two elderly drapers struggled with an unenthusiastic goat. Just across the way a virgin sacrifice slumped on the sofa and watched Breakfast Television while her mother daubed rune signs on her bust. In the Stone Circle round the back of the Fast Food cafe the Sisterhood of Fog prepared to dedicate the latest in a long line of stolen infants to the service of the Pit, with coffee and Bring & Buy to follow. Only Captain Sparesbrook seemed unable to enter into the spirit of Beltane, which given his current predicament was not all that surprising.

"So," he said at last, glaring down from his net at the boggarts which had overrun his dining room. "It's come to this, has it? Boggarts. And which of you pigeon-toed half-heads is the leader of this scrawny crew?"

A particularly squat and shaggy boggart lumbered forward. He swept off his feathered cap in a discreditable bow. "It is I," he crowed. "Speak up, nunkle. What would you say?"

"Got a name, have you?" the Captain demanded.

"I am Snotcursni," the boggart barked. His red eyes rolled in a frenzy of self-esteem. "Mightiest of hunters from the boggart packs of Torfelbarma."

"And what precisely are you doing in my house?"

"We are waiters, nunkle."

"Waiters? I don't need any waiters. I'm not thinking of opening a blasted bistro."

"No, no, we are waiters," the boggart explained unhelpfully. "We await."

"Await? Await what?"

But further explanation was rendered as otiose as it would have been inaudible by a galeforce wind which blasted suddenly out of nowhere. Soot fell into the fireplace and the entire east wall, including the black bean panelling and the painting of Gunmetal Hall by Moonlight, vanished in a swirl of silver flame. The boggarts yelped and bayed and scampered excitedly over the furniture, ignoring Snotcursni's cries of "Heel!"

The silver fire intensified, the molten lambency at its heart assumed a shape which to the Captain's eyes more and more resembled a warrior woman mounted on a self-important charger as rendered in irritating flickeriness by a prize winning Eastern European cartoon. Horse and rider leapt from the inferno, knocking several not particularly valuable items off the sideboard, and halted, rearing, in the centre of the room.

The rider removed her helmet and shook out a tangle of auburn tresses. The Captain recognised her at once.

"Charlotte!" he gasped. "You've – you've come back!"

Yes, Charlotte de Maupassant had certainly come back. But from the way she sneered at him as she sat astride her iridescent steed, splendid in armour with a glow of rancid mackerel, her great curved sword like something for gutting elephants, he guessed she hadn't come home to finish off that game of Scrabble.

"But – why the net? Why the boggarts?" he squeaked.

"Why?" She laughed brazenly as she leapt from her steed and kicked aside the fawning hunters. "Why else, but to thank you, gallant Captain, for allowing me to sample the comforts of Terenthor, prison of doom? To whom else do I owe my last four years of torture and micro-waved dinners?"

"But – but my dear Charlotte. Charlie. It was – I never – it was all a dreadful misunderstanding."

"A misunderstanding? Oh, I see. You didn't mean to accuse me of falsehood and deceit. You didn't intend to denounce me to the Council of Severe Discord. It was quite by accident that you summoned the Pordent Guards from Sorcery House to drag me screaming from this world into that pit of lingering despair which is Gatwick Airport and thence to the grim fastness of Terenthor, house of correction for those who offend against the laws of Witchery."

"Well, yes," said the Captain. "I just meant to report you to Gyles Brandreth."

The Captain did not lie. He could hardly fail to recall that awful night when a simple game of Scrabble had degenerated, as they almost always do, into a fracas of accusation and denial, largely centring on a certain eight letter triple word score. He had indeed put in a call– but how was he to know that all calls in the mansion were being monitored for his own protection? Or that his report had been diverted to an authority more potent than even the illustrious Brandreth?[3] "I take my Scrabble dashed seriously," the Captain protested. "No doubt it's highly quixotic of - "

"Quixotic!" shrieked the witch.

Captain Sparesbrook winced. "Unfortunate choice of words," he mumbled. "Look, why don't I fetch the good old Scrabble board and - "

"Scrabble me no Scrabbles," Charlotte de Maupassant howled. "Snotcursni! Cut this wretch down. Captain, prepare to be drawn."

Sparesbrook sucked in his stomach and tried to show his best side. Then he realised she wasn't talking about charcoal and a sketchpad.

The mightiest of hunters leapt onto the table and, wielding his scimitar with more luck than skill, severed the cords of the net and allowed Captain Sparesbrook to finish off his tumble. With a thud that knocked the breath out of him, he fell upon the oaken board which the merry boggarts at once upended, tipping him at the feet of the offended sorceress. Winded, terrified and in imminent danger of losing touch with a set of bowels which had seen him through many an adventure, the Captain was nevertheless trying to look up Charlotte's skirt.

"Seize him, my boggarts!" she cried. "Oh, and somebody shift the horse. Take his arms! His legs! Expose his belly to the shining vengeance of my sword!"

"Stop!"

It was not the Captain who had spoken. He was busy trying to crawl up his own pyjama legs.

---

[3] Unless Brandreth is himself a member of the Council of Severe Discord, as events at certain Halloween party near Oxford in 1968 might suggest. An ambiguity never to be resolved.

Charlotte peered beyond him, over the heads of the boggarts, to the figure who emerged with indecent slowness from the shadowy hallway. Its eyes gleamed like drums of boiling tar. Its smile was brown and deadly. It wore an old blue dressing gown.

"Surely, madam," it rasped, "you do not imagine that Captain H. 'Geronimo' Sparesbrook would allow himself to fall into your clutches unprotected? Call off your boggarts, or suffer the consequences."

Charlotte sneered. "I see no warriors. I see no trained Bestialities. Where is this protection of which you speak?"

"Here, madam," croaked the ancient. "Know, then, that I am none other than Edward Pausanias Thring, the most dangerous man in the universe."

The silence which ought to have followed his revelation was spoiled by the cackling of boggarts. The Captain, who had looked up hopefully at the mention of protection, muttered, "Come off it, Thring. I know you're a dab hand with a weighted sock but that's drawing it a bit strong. You're about as deadly as a semolina pudding," and went back to searching for a crack in the floorboards big enough to crawl through.

Snotcursni had recovered sufficiently to point at Thring and jeer. "That bag of chicken bones? That relic of something a rat unearthed by moonlight in a forsaken graveyard? We eat his sort from dinky little dishes while waiting for the barman to whistle up the Eig'nor fluid and soda, don't we, lads?"

"Silence!"

The boggarts yelped and scuttled into corners. Charlotte regarded the aged servant thoughtfully. She stepped over the quivering body of the Captain.

"There is something more than human about you," she allowed, "and I don't mean just your admittedly impressive dangly bits."

Thring drew his dressing gown together with dignity and confronted Charlotte de Maupassant, Empress of Witches, radiant in her amour of unnatural light.

"There are indeed unusual traces in your aura," Charlotte said, "hints of a kippery gold, an acidulous pink." She pried with all the artistry at her command into the brain behind the deathly face and found her probe rebuffed by the psychic equivalent of a double layer of Neoprene undershorts. "Whence came you, Thring?" she whispered. "C'ndefhla? The Wrath Schools of Novafosca? Master Xherane's retreat above the lakes of Gaubold? Whence?"

"Swindon, actually." Thring drew himself proudly up and bared his teeth in a long brown smile, in which pain exceeded gleefulness. "My story, madam, is long, involved and largely irrelevant."

"That's it, Thring," sighed the Captain. "Brilliant. We'll bore them to death."

The boggart pack, which loved a tedious life story almost as much as they loved the hunt, shuffled forward and curled up at the old manservant's feet.

"Say on," the witch commanded coldly.

"What does it matter to you, cruel mistress of covens, that my dear mother was a zinc-knitter from

Falmouth, or her husband one of that brave band of engineers who defied blizzards and worse to drive the railway down from Bucharest to Szczecin in the latter days of the nineteenth century?"

"Not much." Charlotte yawned into her gauntlet. "Skip the formative years, Thring, and cut to the gristly bits."

"As you wish, madam," Thring sneered. "I turn then to the moment in 1922 when I entered the most secret order of the monks of Do-Zen."

"So!" Charlotte hissed.[4] "Now we come to the nub. And what did you learn among the snowy fastnesses above Kul-Hwu'ng, Edward Thring?"

"Not a lot," Thring said, "since I took the correspondence course, as advertised in the Exchange and Mart. However, ensconced in my bed sitting room over the coke office in O'Biggins Street, I came to know the mysteries of their most holy order."

"Is there much more of this?" the Captain groaned. "I think if it's all the same to you I'd like to be torn limb from limb now."

The boggarts shushed him crossly.

"Proceed, Thring," Charlotte commanded.

"In the mountains above Kul-Hwu'ng," Thring continued, "there lay a certain monastery where dwelt the twelve monks of the order of Do-Zen, greatest and indeed only exponents of the art of – tachomimsa!"

There was a silence.

"Tacho what?" whispered a boggart.

---

[4] Those who are working their way through the narrative backwards may have picked up a certain resemblance there to the Khemmenoi of Lunt. More conventional readers will just have to wait.

Snotcursni shrugged. "Some sort of potted plant, is it?"

Charlotte kicked at Sparesbrook's flank with the toe of her sandal. "What secret is he hiding, Gerry?"

"Search me. I always thought the most deadly thing about him was his halitosis."

"The art of tachomimsa," shouted Thring, who was beginning to enjoy being the centre of attention, "is the ascetic practice which instills in its devotees the ability at last to achieve the – the- " His voice broke suddenly. The boggarts frowned at each other and searched automatically for the remote control. Something rather strange seemed to be happening inside the elderly manservant. His lips mouthed at syllables which refused to be spat upon the air.

He swallowed, belched and tried again.

"To achieve, gentleman and lady, the state of – of - "

His bony fingers clawed at his pate, his mouth writhed in throbbing terror.

And then, with a final effort, bracing himself against a cabinet of curiosities, his brow knotted as though someone was drilling concrete one inch from his left ear, probably from the inside, he snatched a word from silence and flung it into the room.

"Glu'ng!"

Charlotte and the Captain stared at him.

The boggarts pulled uncomprehending faces at each other.

No-one in the refectory of Sparesbrook Manor had the slightest idea what he meant.

3

But in a hidden place unknown to mortal eye, on top of the Tesco Building in the Edgware Road, a man clad only in a loin cloth and Johnson's Baby Oil, whose calm had blossomed for an untold time in stillness, now started, and gasped and dragged his attention from the glow of a Bergamot & Patchouli Candle. Such was the psychic force in the utterance of Edward Pausanias Thring that it rent the veil of his meditation and returned to the continuum, to reality, Eric Maresbreath, Guardian of the Earth.

In a moment, he was all action. Casting aside his loin cloth, he quickly bound the Cord of Power about his temples, uttered an Unseen prayer, slipped on the identity which would enable him to pass unnoticed among the crowds whose very lives, did they but know it, were entrusted to his care, and descended from his eyrie by secret paths to the car park at the back of The Hanging Queen, where he kept his trike. Leaping astride the saddle, he patted what appeared to the casual eye to be a familiar blue and yellow teddy bear in the basket on his handlebars, slipped a glucose lolly into his mouth, and pedalled down the street, drawn by imperfectly understood forces towards the tors and moors of Hertfordshire.

Eric Maresbreath, Guardian of the Earth, Wielder of the Cord, perfectly disguised as a three year old girl with a lisp and a squint, was on his way.

4

"In other words, lady and gents," Thring elucidated, "explode."

The boggarts looked embarrassed. One of them coughed. Finally, their leader said, "Load of tosh. I'm a religious man myself, Presbyterian actually, but even I don't believe in all this supernatural codswallop. Right lads?"

Thring shrugged carelessly. "Suit yourselves," he said. "But attempt to lay one finger on the Captain and I warn you, I shall go to critical mass in under one nano-second."

Bemused by the scientific jargon, the boggarts swallowed, licked their lips, tried to see faces in the damp stains on the wallpaper, or picked lint off their knees.

"Look, nunkle," Snotcursni said, and he sounded almost as if he pitied the Captain's white hairs and candy-striped pyjamas, "I mean, I shouldn't rely too much on this, erm, this mystic mistile of - "

"Missile?" someone suggested.

"What I said, missile, right, this, erm, missic missile of yours, you know. I, erm, I mean, I'm not one to knock anybody's faith, but well, exploding manservants - "

"Menservants?"

"Shut it, toadsucker. I mean to say, you know - " He gestured lamely. "And, if he did go off, I mean, could you get far enough away yourself, you know, to avoid, the, like, blast?"

Thring smiled dreadfully. "Little hope of that, I confess," he said. "The blast of a glu'ng explosion is quite, quite potent. I can assure you there would be little left."

"Of the house, you mean?" Snotcursni asked, looking at the fixtures and fittings with an insurance assessor's eye, which he kept in a pouch at his side.

Thring cackled. "Of the house, of the hill, of the world, of the entire universe," he drooled.

Presumably instant annihilation is a nicer way to go than what Charlotte de Maupassant had in mind, but Captain Sparesbrook looked as if he wouldn't object if a crack team of philosophy dons, psychologists and handsome media personalities came down to argue it out for a year or two.

"Gentlemen!" howled Thring, "You are in the presence of the End of Everything. Get down on your knees."

After a time of high-pitched yelping and running round in circles, calm returned to the refectory.

"I see you've overcome your scepticism, Snotty," the Captain remarked, prodding the upturned rump of the boggart leader with the toe of his Turkish slipper.

"Well, nunkle, when you're in the presence of the End of Everything," came the muffled reply, "the only safe thing to do is to worship it."

The Captain shrugged. "Suit yourself. Thring, get your things on and go and make me a cup of Bovril, will you? And show these small gentlemen the way out. Charlotte, you may stay, on condition that-"

But the witch had vanished. Of horse and rider nothing remained but a slight odour of henbane and a heap of lambent silver dung.

5

Sweating over his forge in Corporation Lane, seventeen stone ape-wrestler and amateur manicurist Herbert Jubb swore mightily as, distracted by the sudden shrill of the telephone, he mis-timed his hammer blow and crushed the hand of the escaped convict whose manacles he was even then at gun-point attempting to strike off.

"Bother!" he roared. "And after the finest bit of cuticle work I ever did, too. Isn't it always the way?"

Ignoring the whimpers of the ungrateful felon, he swept the bits of finger into his fire and seized the telephone. "Hallo? Who's this?"

Juliette Thring, who indeed it was, was taken by surprise. Of course she was used to her husband's impetuosity and managed to continue the call while he puffed and panted above her.

"Who is this?" Jubb repeated.

"Well," said Juliette, who had not expected a guessing game. "It sounds like Herbert Jubb."

"No it doesn't," said her father. "I'm Herbert Jubb."

"Yes, I know," said Juliette. "And I'm Juliette, your daughter, or rather foster daughter." Passing up the opportunity for a little more useful exposition, she plunged madly on. "Daddy, listen, something totally dreadful has happened."

"Oh, yes?" Jubb said distantly. He was rather busy, keeping an eye on the criminal's attempts to cauterize his stump with a red-hot iron from the forge. Really, the man had no style at all.

"Yes," Juliette insisted. "Daddy, guess who's been downstairs holding Captain Sparesbrook a prisoner in his own dining room?"

"No, that's too hard for me," said Jubb. "Sorry. Now, if you was to ask me about techniques of manicure in seventeenth century Spain, for example. I might be able to tell you a thing or two, but as it is, well, sorry..."

Juliette, whose patience was not the sort that would have supported Sydney Harbour bridge for two hours against a strong wind, pushed her husband off the bed, screamed, and bellowed down the phone: "Daddy! Will you listen to me? Demi-Urge, what kind of a world is this?"

"Pass," said Jubb absently. The escaped felon's attempt to seal off the spurting blood vessels in his wrist with the hot iron had merely succeeded in setting fire to his prison garb. Now, an ambulant bonfire guy, he lurched about the forge, touching off the curtains, the doyleys, the antimacassars as he went. "Hold on, I must just go and put the cat out."

The smell of singed fur was of such power that for a moment Juliette, a mile and a half away, caught a whiff of it over the telephone.

"Daddy, what on earth is going on over there?" she cried.

"Ah," responded the blacksmith, glad at last to have a question he could answer. "I'm glad you asked me that. You see -"

"Oh, never mind." Juliette foresaw hours of improbably explanation. "The important thing is, Charlotte de Maupassant's back."

There was a silence in the universe for the space of about half an hour. Pounds accrued to Juliette's telephone bill. The escaped convict looked ashen, as indeed he was. Elsewhere, Captain H. 'Geronimo' Sparesbrook patrolled the parsnip beds, on the lookout for witches and stray boggarts. Eric Maresbreath pedalled grimly down Camberwell High Street, and in Juliette's bed a centipede was crushed to death by the left knee of Edward Pausanias Thring as he clambered back onto his wife.[5]

"Daddy! Daddy? Are you still there?"

But Herbert Jubb, man-mountain, maestro of the musical saw and champion manicurist of West London did not reply. About him the tarred weather boarding of his forge flamed and sparked, timbers fell, stone work toppled like the last reel of a horror picture, but Herbert Jubb, conqueror of apes, crouched barmy-eyed in the telephone seat, his knees drawn up against his leather aproned chest, a thumb in his mouth, and when the hungry flames drove their forks into his flesh, did not move.

Such potency lay in the name of Charlotte de Maupassant.

And she, even now, in the concealment of the potting shed, was preparing to renew her assault upon the inconveniently guarded person of Captain H. 'Geronimo' Sparesbrook. She paused, naked and thoughtful among the seed trays, prettily undecided. In what form might she penetrate the defences of Sparesbrook Manor? An armadillo pedlar from distant Peru? Two midget brain doctors

---

[5] What a tragedy that would have been if, for example, the centipede had actually been an operative from the undercover service of the Archerons of Atlantis! What fates of universes might have been utterly other because of the knee of Edward Thring. Not for nothing is this man called The End of Everything. Fortunately the centipede was only a centipede, and left no family.

selling encyclopaedia door to door in their holidays? A glossy brown excrescence from the warty pits of d'Nmorbia, offering to do light housework in exchange for the blood of any newborn infant on the premises? No, none of those seemed to possess that element of the outré but familiar which alone might captivate the Captain.

Then: "Dare I?" she whispered. "Dare I? Yes! Why not? Have I not spent four years in the dungeons of Terenthor, building up a greater head of incantational power than even that of Gertrude Glamis when, o evil day, she brought into being the continent of Australia? It can be done! It must be done! It shall be done!"

And, running her fingers once up and down her pink smooth body, Charlotte de Maupassant began the greatest transformation of her life.

6

Perhaps this is the moment to remark that not even the catalogues of Poxley & Enron, estate agents to the stars, have anything to show more fair than that sport of geography, Amblebroth Hill, with its pair of residences.

A screen of conifers guarded the grounds of the hilltop asylum from sensation seekers, though for miles around it was possible on a clear day (of which in this vicinity there were very few) to catch the flash of sunlight on binocular and telescope in dormer windows.

Halfway up where, had the hill been the treacle pudding it resembled, the syrup would have started, the remains of Sparesbrook Manor clung to the weedy gardens with claws of rotting wood and brick. What splendours of ages past had shone from its windows none but the visionary or antiquarian, astray on the footpath by the Neolithic tomb beyond the remains of the northern wall, might imagine. Eheu fugaces! as someone with a little more learning than the narrative might have observed.

A driveway that must once have crunched under the wheels of landaus and Lagondas now suffered the fingerings of nettle and bell bind. Glimpsed between the rhododendrons the mansion appeared to retain something of its past glory, but that was an illusion, caused by the distortion of the space time matrices in the region of overgrown shrubbery. As the approaching mendicant quickly realised, and rapidly turned tail before anyone could pop out and touch him for a quid, the home of the Sparesbrooks was past its best.

Indeed, it gave every indication of having been raised from the earth and dropped from a height of twenty feet, an event which may have occurred at 3 a.m. on 15 August 1977, a night of which not even the local post mistress can be persuaded to speak.

Passing over the lawns and the sunken pond, dry now and haunted by the ghosts of small amphibians, we approach the portico of the Manor, where rusting boot scrapers and old milk bottles clutter the tiles...

The clocks ticked on, tocking and rocking on the rickety boards. Herds of mice, many sick from hunger, tottered about the wainscots. Night echoed like an empty cauldron over the mansion halfway up Amblebroth Hill. Captain Sparesbrook patrolled the path by the yew hedge, a loaded shotgun in the crook of his arm. Regarding every bush and puddle as a potential witch, he had already blasted into oblivion two statues, an ilex and a water-butt.

At the edge of the wood, he turned and scanned the grounds. The mass of the mansion was dark against the starlit sky. A brightness shone from one upper window and, closer at hand, the softer glow of lamplight haloed the cow-shed where Deirdre Horne smiled upon her mangered babe.

Juliette and Edward Thring stood at the upper window, watching, where the full moon shed its benison over the parsnip beds, the figure of their master as he stood, lost in thought, beneath a juniper tree.

"It's time," creaked the aged voice of the husband. "Juliette. It's time."

Wearily, Juliette hitched up her skirt and bent over the windowsill. "Hurry up, then," she sighed. "I've got the silver to polish."

"No, no," Thring rasped angrily. "I didn't mean that. I meant - " He shuddered, eyeing his wife's legs and round little bum. "I meant - Oh, the hell with it, let's fool around. First."

Awakening from a trance of memory, the Captain felt the breeze of twilight feather his forehead, smelt the perfume of the arbours, heard the night birds cry. In his old heart, a strange emotion stirred, curdled and sank in little lumps to his feet. A word almost stillborn emerged from his lips and was seized like a linnet by the hawk, silence. What word might it have been?

He shouldered his shotgun and plunged his boots through the mud of the parsnip beds towards home. Looking up at the windows, he frowned to observe the blonde, curly head of his manservant's wife bent over the sill of an upper room and bobbing vigorously.

"Everything all right, Mrs. Thring?" he called courteously.

"Yes- thank you - sir," came the oddly staccato reply. "Just giving - Mr. Thring - his - OATS!" The last word hit a higher note, as Thring went into paroxysm. He had forgotten cut his nails again.

The Captain tipped his hat to the lady, not completely understanding why Thring's porridge had to be served at an upper window, and strolled on towards the door. Lilacs rained their odours upon him as he trod the path at the side of the old manor house, filling his soul with more inexpressible longings. The image of those blonde curls, that retrousse nose, those eager lips, would not leave him. Blindly he stepped into the door, swore, stepped back, opened the door, and walked inside.

The moment he closed the door behind him, he sensed that something was wrong. It looked like his hallway, but – where was the old brass ramcobbler his uncle brought back from Lahore, where was the painting of Scratchbone Mill, said by some to be a genuine Arbuthnot? And was not the shade of the tiles a touch more bilious than was their wont? And did not the clocks tick with a deeper tone? And where were the mice?

"Sod it, I've walked into the wrong house," the Captain thought.

On tiptoe, he returned to the door. The handle refused to budge.

The Captain cleared his throat and ventured a small halloo.

For a time there was silence. Then, distantly, he heard the sound that turned his innards to string. Far away, and yet curiously near, as though from every room at once, came the coppery tinkle of laughter, a woman's laughter, wicked, triumphant and cruel.

His ears went white with fear. Memory, more insistent than a doorstep hawker, got its foot over the threshold of his consciousness and started to display the most grotesque of its wares - Charlotte, he recollected with dread, had once claimed that, should the need arise, she could transform herself into an Alternative Universe. Could it be that she had now accomplished the feat?

If she was herself the trap, then he had walked right into her.

It was not the first time that the Captain had entered a woman but it was the first time that he had not been able to get out again. He was nonplussed.

Questions like wasps assailed him. Was, for example, the blonde head at the upper window really that of Juliette Thring? Or had Charlotte in her exquisite mockery created a duplicate of the girl too? And what of Thring, his manservant and ultimate deterrent? No doubt Charlotte, if she had provided a replica of the ancient, would have taken care to defuse it first.

Defenceless, apart from his shotgun, the Captain lowered his muddy boot onto the first stair. He didn't like to set his hand on the banister rail. It might be an unpardonable liberty.

"Charlotte," he said, as he crept up the stairs. "Charlotte. Charlie. can't we talk this over, man to – man to mansion? At least put the lights on. It's black as hell's coal cellar up here."

A door opened, ripping a gash of light in the dark corridor. Silhouetted there, shapely in her liberty bodice, the wife of Edward Thring leaned easily against the door post, toying with the knob.

Even in the days when he marched with the 14th Goatshires, even then, when women were as scarce as a decent chop-house and a good deal dirtier when you found them, even then, Captain H. 'Geronimo' Sparesbrook had not enjoyed such a fully developed pang of longing as that which overwhelmed him when the dark eyes of Juliette Thring smiled upon him.[6]

"Ah, good evening, my dear," the Captain stammered. "Is, ah, your husband in?"

Juliette felt her groin. "Not at the moment, zur," she said winningly and with a good deal more Tess of the D'Urbervilles about her than usual. "Would 'ee loike to come inside for a moment, zur?"

The Captain grew hot and flustered. If this was Charlotte's doing, then the woman was wasting herself as an arch-villainess. She should be on the telly. He would put it to her. With an experienced man, a commanding type, as her manager, she would sweep the trophies of Talent shows.

His dreams of glory were curtailed by the hand of Juliette, tugging at playfully at his Old Crumdovian tie. Since it was presently serving as a belt, his cavalry twills fell down. The woman leapt upon him, her strong arms about his neck, her feet locked behind his knees. The Captain wondered if it was his birthday.

But his birthday was months away and Juliette did not come in an amusing wrapping with natal congratulations on her bum. When her gasps of desire modulated artfully into the howling of a transpolar wind and the house melted into a night of blizzard and ice, and the body clamped to his own swelled into something huge and furry that stank of fish, he knew that Charlotte de Maupassant had finished toying with him.

---

[6] If it is she, and not some infernal doppelganger.

The animal, formerly Mrs. Thring, appeared to be hesitating between crushing him to death with its immense forearms or chewing off his head in small morsels with its fangs. The Captain realised that he would have to rid himself of this inconvenience first and then set about persuading Charlotte to don the gold lame swimsuit, fishnets and white gloves for her career as an illusionist. Yes, first, the bear, which had already devoured the wings of the moustache which decades of growth and waxing had brought to their recently foregone splendour. Wrenching his arm from its jaws, the Captain snatched an Imlishan dagger from the wall and unseamed the beast from the nape to the chaps, causing several hundred weight of steaming hot tripes to tumble over his frost bitten legs.

At which point the transformation unwound and he found himself in the corridor of his mansion clutching the disembowelled body of Mrs. Thring. And her husband, Edward Pausanias Thring, glu'ngtoka and End of Everything, stood before them, aghast.

7

Meanwhile, for through this sorry vale none may wholly free from trouble wend his daily way, Eric Maresbreath too had run into difficulty.

Difficulty in Eric's case had manifested itself on the footpath through the public gardens at the back of D & B (Moleskinners) Ltd. Although with consummate skill he had woven his trike between the heaps of dog dirt and the crumpled beer cans, he had failed to notice up ahead the moonlit presence of Big Dennis Wipers, lay reader and paedophile, who had observed the approach of what he construed as a three year old sex-goddess with a squint and a blue teddy with considerable delight. Wipers was delighted, that is, not the teddy.[7]

"Hallo, little girl," leered the mad lay reader.

Not for the first time, Eric found himself envying Superman the Clark Kent persona.

Big Dennis, his enormous corduroys blocking the path, extended a bag of disgusting comfits. "Would 'oo like a sweetie, den?" he crooned. "Would 'oo like to come and see the little bunnies in the bushes?"

Egrah'nca cautiously moved a paw and touched the growly place on his tummy. He got a

---

[7] Who is, this time, an undercover agent for the Archerons of Atlantis and who is viewing the forthcoming proceedings with alarm and a Mark VII Prognosticator disguised as a lump of toffee stuck to his fur. His name is Egrah'nca and he is the James Bond of six inch high, blue fur covered cuddly toys.

buzz from that sort of thing – a low frequency buzz, in fact, a couple of octaves below the hum of a bumble-bee. Eric, simultaneously unwilling to blow his cover or anything else, back-pedalled furiously, collided with a gas-lamp and, alas, fell off his trike. Egrah'nca, whose buzz had travelled via a wormhole in time and space to the halls of the Archerons, and was about to summon The Nidro Force, shot out of the basket and plopped into the adjacent tadpole pond. The Nidro Force, which had lowered its newspaper and half reached to remove its slippers, decided that it must have imagined the summons and returned to the illustrated interview with Andruta Tiservi on page 23 of the Basileian Bugle.

"Leave me alone, you nathty old pervert," Eric shrieked, as Dennis' massive fist closed round his ankle and began to haul him towards the darkness among the rhododendrons. "I shall summon the police. I mean, poleeth."

"Cor, I really go for you, darlin'. You're a right little stunner," Dennis enthused headily. "And don't call me a pervert," he added. "Little girls like you didn't ought to know such language. If you was my daughter, I'd... " He paused thoughtfully. "In fact, I think I will anyway. I'll take off your little knick-knacks and..."

Dragging Eric into the laurels took all his concentration for the next couple of minutes. Alone at last in the cheesily foetid cavern of leaves, Dennis reached for the Magotte Saves buckle of his corduroys, wetly chuckling.

What happened next caused him some astonishment.

The Rape of the Stone

The little madam whose purpose in life Big Dennis saw as the satisfaction of his desires untied her golden hair band and flicked it at him.

The Battle of Bosworth, 1485, during which the fortunes of Small Dick III declined, was spread, fighting wise, over a considerable area, but there was a certain point on the field which occupied at the co-tangential moment all those years ago a vector space linked by axial forces to the laurel bushes in which Big Dennis Wipers would, half a millennium later, attempt to have his carnal way with the Guardian of the Earth. That this may have been an unwise move, Big Dennis readily conceded after the crack of emerald fire lashed from the tip of the cord and seared the space about him like a fall of wet light. The night went a sort of mustard colour with vermillion accessories, there was a smell of envelope glue, and then grass before his eyes, and a burden of some sort across his back, and a rather painful rock under his right offside hoof. Big Dennis shifted angrily and was ordered to 'Be still, you jade'. He felt the cut of a whip across his rump.

And so, Big Dennis Wipers, by a small kindness of fate, achieved a place in history as the horse which bore Richard's naked body from the field that August day in 1485.

Eric Maresbreath scrambled out of the laurels, leaving nothing behind him but a slight tang of scorched leaves, and ran to fish his teddy bear from the tadpole pond.

But Egrah'nca had gone.

8

In one of the upper corridors of Charlotte de Maupassant, what may have been an effigy of Edward Pausanias Thring, wielding a very substantial croquet mallet, advanced upon what felt to its occupant like the real and mortal bulk of Captain H. 'Geronimo' Sparesbrook, while what he devoutly hoped was a replica of Mrs. Thring dripped blood and effluvia over his Wellingtons.

None of that minimally concerned the blue and yellow teddy bear with the lump of toffee stuck to its fur which at that moment was being hauled by a thousand tiny ropes attached to straining tadpoles towards a murky opening at the bottom of the pond. Consciousness came and went. Once he felt himself born on frog back through watery labyrinths. At another time he was lowered in a rime-encrusted cage through a sub-zero updraft. Later he knew that he was bound to a stake in the centre of an empty darkness. Try as he might he could not reach his growl and he felt that on the whole he would rather not consult his Prognosticator.

Absolutely and impeccably unconcerned by either of those events, the ashes of the late Herbert Jubb mingled with those of the former convict in numinous union among the ruins of the forge. Thunder rolled through the heavens, clouds obscured the moon, the air was ripped by a bolt of lightning, brighter and more terrible than the gleam from the wing of a Ford Cortina. Striking a passing owl, it hurled the feathery mass into a puddle into which, by a billion to one evolutionary accident all the chemical elements necessary to the formation of life had happened to conglomerate in exactly the correct proportions, many of them supplied by the mingled remains of Jubb and the (as yet) nameless felon.

Activated by the electric charge, which mad old Mr. Sniffwind preposterously insisted had come not from the thunderclouds but from a window of the Violet Pring Hebbenthwaite Sunset Memorial Home, the enzyme soup heaved and writhed, frothed and spumed, sparkled and groaned and then, under the sudden stars, began to solidify, and mould, and rise, until it stood at last erect beneath the howling sky, a man.

Well, sort of.

With a sound like the flushing of a municipal lav, the oozing miscegenation took wing. It circled twice the smoking ruin of the forge, soared over the roofs of Corporation Lane and uttering an eldritch screech began its clumsy flight towards the benighted mass of Amblebroth Hill

In His own realm, the Demi-Urge may well have chuckled something along the lines of "Let's see the buggers sort that one out."

"Thring, wait, for Magotte's Sake, wait!" the Captain screamed, as what may or may not have been his manservant raised the mallet high into the air. "This is not your wife."

Thring, at the word 'wife', snarled with crazy ire. The Captain, with a soldier's gift for sizing up the situation, sensed that Thring, real or not, had acquired no sudden capacity for reason, so having felled the old loon with one blow of his late spouse,

The Gnostic Frying Pan

he fled downstairs three at a time and hurled himself through the hall window.

Distantly he heard Charlotte's scream of pain but his laugh of triumph, like a motorbike starting up, was cut short when the emerging moon beamed upon the thing that had touched down before him on the parsnip beds.

Ten feet high, and composed of mud, feathers and protoplasmic ooze, the owl-headed quadrumanual biped gazed upon him hungrily with a great green eye. Then it turned its head through the best part of a circle and gazed at him with the other eye, which was blue. Then it spoke.

"I know him," it croaked. "My daughter's boss. Hieronymus Sparkbolt or some such moniker."

The head swivelled, allowing the green eye to examine the prostrate figure in its nest of glass shards.

"Bless my soul," observed the Owl-thing, "I know him too. This is the soi-disant Captain, H. 'Geronimo' Sparesbrook. So, we meet again, Sparesbrook, and radically altered circumstances, I'd venture."

"That voice!" gasped the Captain. He raised one lacerated palm and held it out before his face. "It cannot be. You! The embezzler! The fiend who stole all I worked for, schemed for, lied for. I thought you incarcerated forever."

"Oh, yes," said the Owl-thing. "I'm very much afraid it is. Alive and well and living in a rather unusual body, I grant you, with a somewhat obnoxious co-tenant - "

"Thanks very much," it interrupted itself with hoarse irony.

"Do shut up," it recommended itself sweetly. "Yes, old boy. It is I, your erstwhile accountant, young Malcolm. Now, you unutterable swine, what have you done with my mother?"

Before Captain Sparesbrook could reply, if the witless gibber he had in mind could be construed as a reply, the universe screamed.

Imagine what your own mother might say, should she rediscover the child she thought lost forever, but rediscover you in the person of a schizophrenic Owl-thing with bad breath and a tendency to leave slime trails on the flooring. Then magnify this mixture of joy, grief and sheer disgust by the size of a complete universe. Small wonder that Sparesbrook rolled himself into a ball and tried to bury himself among the parsnips.

The immeasurable wailing rose and fell, the entire continuum of alternative space and time reached down upon itself, trying to enfold the Owl-thing to its bosom, whether in attempt to mother or to smother it, who shall say? But the strain of grief upon its illusory foundations was too much and, like an overstretched corset, the universe of Charlotte de Maupassant split asunder.

9

Meanwhile, further from the eye of reason than Frinton or the programming department of the BBC, Egrah'nca knew the taste of fear. It reminded him of tadpoles. Some distance away, across the dark subterranean plain, a gong had sounded. In answer, a pair of livid red eyes had clicked open. It was dinner time.

Desperation had overcome his terror. Blinking thrice, he activated the Prognosticator, and looked to see what dreadful end awaited him. But the water must have got into the works because all he saw was himself, neat and brushed and tidy, with a pink ribbon around his neck, sitting on a shelf in a smart London toyshop.

Egrah'nca closed his eyes and, screwing up his courage, began to recite the Psalm of Byfurth (Revised Modern Language Version) as recommended in the novels of Timora Garpatheny, the Atlantean best seller. The red eyes inched appreciably nearer. Soon they would bring up whatever they used for a mouth and turn him into minced morsels.

He could hear the scrape of the creature's armoured belly on the rocks, smell its salty breath. He realised that he had gone wrong somewhere in verse 205 and with a curse (which, being Atlantean, itself ran to close on eighty lines) began again.

But it was too late. The thing was upon him, flaring its oily black nostril and creaking open its fearsome jaws. Damning the technician who had forgotten to waterproof his Prognosticator,

The Rape of the Stone

Egrah'nca made the gesture of self-abolition and ceased to exist.

"Oi," said the monster. "Who's nicked me bleedin' din-dins?"

Now, when Charlotte de Maupassant's universe came apart at the seams, the stresses and strains involved were of such magnitude that, not unnaturally, they warped the present universe in numerous places as well. One of the places, for example, was eighteenth century England, which accounts for *Pride & Prejudice*[8], and another was the Muggoth Pit on the shores of the seas of Scaliselarga.

That is why, having a good many years later ceased to exist, Egrah'nca was rather amused to find himself back in business on the shelves of Howles, without doubt the shop of all the shops in London for toys of distinction, games, and everything which delights the childish mind. Here you may marvel for hours at the whirring of clockwork trains, or wonder at the beauty of dollies, or browse among volumes of Canaris the Educated Fox, or the delightfully naughty Soffits.

And here, if you are Miss Amelia Madeleine Pismire (which is fairly unlikely, on the whole) you may be brought by your nanny one bright afternoon in the late summer of 1922 to chose for yourself a present to commemorate the fact that this morning, though aged only four, you answered all the integral calculus questions in your elder bother's

---

[8] The harrowing story of bigotry and social rejection suffered by Ngina Wanyoike, the Kikuyu lion tamer.

school book. You are, of course, a child prodigy of unquestionable brilliance.[9]

Egrah'nca gave up trying to fathom the implications of what had happened to him for his Prognosticator, which had somehow foreseen the past, or perhaps remembered the future, an achievement which had so bewildered its delicate circuitry that it now did nothing but mutter something about the 1981 Miss World Contest and a Miss Venezuela, whatever that was.

However, strength had returned. It was the moment for action. He touched his growl.

Yes, this was the big one, no doubt this time. The Nidro Force, which had been doing a little window box gardening, threw down its trowel, donned its atomic cape and sped like a tachyon through a time warp to reassemble itself as a natty pink ribbon around Egrah'nca's neck. Pausing only to dismember a dolly with a rather unpleasant look in its eye, Egrah'nca leapt astride a toy dog and galloped away.

(Which, incidentally, is how Amanda, who dearly wanted a blue and yellow teddy bear with a pink ribbon round its neck, came instead to buy the box of lead farm animals which poisoned her two months later. Thus perished one who, had she lived, might have made the world a sweeter and more peaceful place. On the whole, you're probably glad now you're not Amanda Madeleine Pismire, right? Or is it better, do you think, to have been about to be great than to have been but never have been great at all? Can we, justifiably, maximise the

---

[9] Or you would be, if you were Amanda. Pity you're not, in some ways, isn't it?

The Rape of the Stone

intrinsic value of a potential, qua potential, while minimising that of the actual, qua actual, or would it not be more proper to value that which is, however lowly, above that which might have been but which, by the nature of things, can no long be?)

It was not a problem of that sort which occupied the mind of Eric Maresbreath as he paddled down the moonlit river Unar, behind the pickle factory. Certain neural modifications on the oily underside of his cortex ensured that the retrieval of his stuffed companion would automatically take precedence over other duties. Misled by an impeccable process of reasoning, he had deduced that his beloved teddy bear must have floated away from the pond so, following the stream from the park and through a grim culvert (where he had been forced to pause in order to prevent an attempt by the multibrained Sargoids of Pompanooza to manifest in this universe for the purpose of crushing all matter into a tiny cube to provide fuel for their masters' in-car music-centres: such tasks are daily routine for a Guardian of the Earth, of course, and scarcely worth mentioning in the same breath as Eric's search for the blue and yellow teddy bear) he had come at last to the mighty river Unar, whose grease rich foam surged down through the dark back streets towards the pleasure beach. Of course, he knew nothing of the bear's narrowly averted fate at the jaws of the red-eyed Muggoth.

He had almost reached the point where the Unar tumbles into the chasm beneath the sugar beet factory when, many miles away, just down the hill from the Violet Pring Heppenthwaite Sunset Memorial Home, the arch-villainess of the cosmos,

The Gnostic Frying Pan

Charlotte de Maupassant, was reunited with a fair amount of her prodigal son, Malcolm. The resulting phenomenon, which made Vesuvius look like a pimple on a teen-age bum, had flung Egrah'nca back to 1922, which is why there wasn't much point in looking for him under the factory, and now the grief wave shocked its way through Eric Maresbreath. His fingers lost their grip on the old pram chassis he had just excavated from the river bed, his hair went puce, his entire being divided into seven separate sections and, in a twisting red hysteria of terror, he, he, he, he, he, he and he spiralled away on the crest of the wave, and the sun was in the sky, and his eyes were on the distant horizon, while his ears on the other hand (one between the thumb and the forefinger, the other on the palm) hurtled at the speed of light towards the uninteresting planet of Wo'nku. Three of the Maresbreath sub-sections circled round and, emerging in the mid twentieth century, became the Andrews Sisters, stars of stage and screen and Victrola, while another appeared (by way of a curious annunciation in a conservatory) in stone age Macedonia and was worshipped for a year as the Goddess Sclit, whose images have caused such frowns of abhorrence on the brows of archaeologists. Of the remaining three allocations, one became the Kingston By-pass, one was trapped in a space-time hiccup and hung eternally on the point of being about to get his leg over Helena Phipps, and the last, by some freak of cosmic reverberation, found himself in a hidden place unknown to man, on top of the Tesco building in the Edgware Road, clad only in a loin cloth and

Johnson's Baby Oil, gazing into the flame of a Bergamot and Patchouli candle.

"What the hell am I doing here?" he said aloud. "Blimey, is that the time?"

Well, there's a question indeed. Mighty brains might have brandished intellectual spears for millennia over that one. Eric merely snatched up the traffic warden's uniform neatly folded in the corner, dressed and consulted his watch. "Time I wasn't here," he said, setting the academies humming again. "Mustn't be late for my date with Helena," he told himself, going all strawberry milkshake at the thought of her.

And so Eric Maresbreath, Guardian of the Earth, cast aside the cord which had bound his brows, put on his black and yellow cap and sought to pass from the knowledge of history.

And if you'd ever seen Helena Phipps taking a shower, or playing netball for the Lyminge Under Twenties, or modelling undies in the Harlotella catalogue, you would say he'd made the right decision.

When a woman like Helena is waiting for you, the Earth can go and guard itself.

10

The intertemporal grief-wave generated when Charlotte de Maupassant recognised in the Owl-thing her only child, Malcolm, accountant and embezzler, had spared neither Egrah'nca nor Eric Maresbreath and did not pass the Thring family by.

Juliette, the real and indefinable, not that unstable simulacrum soon to be disembowelled in the likeness of a polar bear by Captain Sparesbrook, had endured the queasy ministrations of her husband's ardour at the bedroom window for as long as was necessary. Then, when he had suffered his usual infarction, tripped over his trousers and cut his lip on the edge of her aluminium briefcase, she smoothed down her skirt, fastened her bodice and said, "That's very strange. The Captain's burying himself in the parsnips. I wonder what's the matter."

"Nrrgh," said Edward Thring, trying to staunch the bleeding with a strip torn from his wife's petticoat.

"Eddie!" Juliette screeched. "How many times have I told you, don't keep ripping bits off my underwear. Magotte, you make me so mad! One of these days, I'll – I'll – "

For a moment Juliette looked as if she was about to explode. Then she did.

Edward, by chance, avoided the worst effects of the grief-wave and received no more than a blow in the mouth from some passing fragment of Juliette which cracked his false teeth and opened up his lip again. At least there was no-one now to object: he crawled to Juliette's drawer and, selecting the most expensive of her designer knickers, with immense satisfaction tore off a strip for his bleeding mouth.

Down below, in the parsnip beds, the muddy Captain huddled his head under the shelter of his arms and waited for Armageddon, or Ragnorok, or anything less terrifying than what was going on about him now. A light red rain, formerly Mrs. Juliette Thring, spattered over his shirt, the scribbled leaves of *Love's Labour's Won* tumbled about him, bursting into flame as they fell, a rat nibbled his boot soles.

Eventually the Captain peeped out.

From the yew hedge across the dark and cooling garden, the delicate song of a night-bird filled the air with lovely melancholy. Further away, the mail train rattled over the bridge by Hopwood's Swamp. And in the distance the clock of Blessed Benifons struck the hour. Of the Owl-thing there was no sign. Nor of its mother.

The Captain waited for twenty minutes to be certain, then staggered to his feet.

"Charlotte?" he called softly. "Charlie? Are you there?"

He was alone, alone in the real if now slightly warped universe he had always known. Could he dare to hope that Charlotte and her unspeakable offspring had remained behind in that other cosmos, where Juliette Thring was a cannibal's offer of the week and her husband, dear faithful old Thring, a maniac thirsting for blood? He resolved to get a good deal closer to Juliette in future, not realizing that the sticky patch on his back was as close as he could reasonably expect to get. He would be more decent to Thring, too. Especially as the man was a dangerously advanced mystic. He would start now.

The Captain crept into the house.

Where everything seemed to have returned to normal. Apart, that is, from the aged manservant tottering down the stairs with the remains of a pair of blood-stained satin knickers hanging from his jaws.

"Oh, my stars," the Captain said faintly. "He's only gone and eaten her."

Long though it has been since we last saw Egrah'nca, hurled back to 1922 and mounted on a dog, it is nevertheless not yet time to return to his side. What, after all, is the fate of a special agent of the Archerons of Atlantis, with or without the Nidro Force round his neck, compared to the cosmic upheaval caused by the magnificent grief of Charlotte de Maupassant? Its effects upon most of our characters we have already observed, and no doubt learnt many useful lesson should the like befall ourselves. The initial grief-wave, which bore Egrah'nca back to 1922, and caused not only the multiplication of Eric Maresbreaths, the Andrews Sisters, the Kingston Bypass, the goddess Sclit, the infant misnomer of Deirdre Horne[10], and the dissolution of Juliette Thring, but also as it travelled back down the aeons the 100 Years War, the Grey Death, Cynewulf and Cyneheard (the Saxon Songbirds), the Synod of Whitby (664), the fall of the Roman Umpire, Babylonic cuneiform, parts of the Gobi desert, and the Jurassic age. Arriving at the

---

[10]See Chapter 13

The Rape of the Stone

beginning of time, it head-butted the singularity at the generation of the cosmos and began to travel back again, this time snatching a disturbingly inscribed stone from the Great Temple of Atlantis, turning the first page of *The Battle of Maldon* into carpet tiles, catching up a horse from what looked like a promising site for a car park near the field of Bosworth, and finally breaking in a shower of time froth over the mansion on Amblebroth Hill, an event which coincided with the return to consciousness of Captain H. 'Geronimo' Sparesbrook, who opened his eyes in time to see a horse drop out of the chandelier and smash the slavering Thring to the ground.

He felt himself then in the clammy grip of the time froth, a sensation rather similar to being tied up in a brown paper parcel and sent second class to Daventry in a badly sprung coach and four. For a moment of horror he thought he saw the Owl-thing before him, oozing in feathery coils about his body. Then it dissolved into a snowstorm of tiny dinner plates and he found himself back on the tiles. But not alone. A tightening sensation in his shirt and cavalry twills suggested that someone else was trying to occupy his clothing. Twisting, he sought to find out who was the cuckoo in his Lux-soft nest. The strain on his garments was too great. Like an alternative universe, the seams ripped apart, tumbling himself and Juliette Thring, both stark naked, onto the floor.

The Captain, whose sense of self preservation had not entirely deserted him, looked wildly round for his manservant but was relieved to see the hazardous ancient lying very still beneath a stertorous palfrey.

"Juliette!" he whispered urgently. "Juliette, the world may never permit us to meet again. At any moment you may turn into a dishcloth or we may both be interred beneath the Patio of Oblivion. Let us seize the moment. Let us at least leave a little fleeting taste of joy behind us in the mouth of this appalling, meaningless world."

"Captain!" she said, nudging his fingers off her thigh. "Desist. Not here. Not now. Not in front of the child."

He followed the indication of her mystifying eyes. The door of the servant's quarters had swung open to reveal a three year old with a squint and a green lolly in its mouth.

Neither of them could understand why, when the horse saw the child, it whickered in terror and disappeared at high speed up the stairs, leaving a great mound of dung on the hall floor.

11

From the Tudor chimneys and desolate moors of Hertfordshire to the Great Atlantean Temple of Basileia is not a journey that the average commuter expects to take, unless the points have iced up again at Dover Priory, yet taken it you have, sliding with the narrative down the shales of the centuries to that wondrous era when Atlantis ruled the waves.

Climbing down from the pedestal which until our arrival displayed the elephantine statue of G'nifferon III, inventor of the Prognosticator™[11], we are in time to see no less a personage than the Magnarch of Verox himself, as he approaches the polished granite steps of the great ziggurat.

The narrative apologises for springing that on you. Misled by popular romances, you no doubt imagined the Atlanteans to be a race of godlike beings, tall, blond and above all human. Unfortunately (or fortunately, depending on your species) apart from the slave races of modified anthropoids and other creatures who acted as experimental material, erotic playthings and in extreme cases minor civil servants, the inhabitants of Atlantis were distinctly reptilian.

To human eyes the Magnarch is undoubtedly a disturbing sight, though any saurians among the readership will be wondering what all the fuss is

---

[11] In accordance with Fincham's Third Law of Equivalent Mass, the equilibrium of the universe has been maintained by the displacement of a corresponding amount of matter. It will turn up in our own time in the form of crumbs down the side of sofas.

about. The Atlantean race, for all its intellect, looked for its ancestors down a very different evolutionary tree.

Guards who had hurried from their stations at the sound of the Magnarch's approach dived for cover when they saw the look on his face. In fact, diving for cover was widely recommended as a suitable response to a sighting of the Magnarch, whatever mood he happened to be in.

The Magnarch despatched a brace of modified leopards with two flicks of his tail and bounded up the hundred steps.

Within, to ceremonial trumpeting more hideous than anything in a 1930s Hollywood musical the incense bowls exuded their miasmas of stinking smoke, darkening the already tenebrous atmosphere of the Temple, whose confusion of cloisters, clerestories, apses and chancels was today crammed with devoted worshippers, trying not to flinch when hot fat dripped on them from the torches, especially as the torches were mainly composed of worshippers who flinched last time.

A concealed choir gave tongue to some primal dirge but a sudden shift in the crowds was not the response of affronted music lovers. The great bronze doors had been flung back. Heads cowered quickly, anxious to avoid a glimpse of the Magnarch of Verox as he strode, or rather loped, down the great central aisle, stalked up the altar steps and, belatedly remembering the protocols, prostrated himself sarcastically before the opal throne on which sat the great high priest of Atlantis, the Magnarch's father, The Serene Principle of Goth.

The Principle looked down on him with a red and sardonic eye.

"My son!" breathed His Serene Highness. "This is an unexpected pleasure. The guards were under orders not to let you in."

"I persuaded them otherwise, Father."

"Tsk. No doubt that means another deputation of grieving widows to buy off with pensions. And does this happy surprise imply that you have decided to return to the flock of the faithful?"

"Don't bet on it. I didn't come here for five hours of self-abnegation and psalm singing. Listen, you old mammal - "

"Now, now," reproved the Principle. "By the way, tradition expects that I extend a hand to be kissed." No fool he, it was the hand of a specially selected servant.

"Hear me, o reverend father," the Magnarch said. He spat out some fingernails. "Which you might do rather better, by the way, if you removed your foot from my head. Thank you. Now: what does the name 'Amblebroth' mean to you?"

The Principle made a curious gesture. The congregation moaned the appropriate response.

"Do you know," he beamed, "you're just in time for the high point of the religious calendar? I am shortly to Inspect the Forbidden Drains. My son, I have long wished that you would take an interest in these matters."

"How could I fail to do so, Serene Father, impressed as I have been by my recent discovery of your office's charitable ventures. The Holy Sage Trepoch must have foreseen good cause to be very pleased with you."

The Serene Principle frowned. "I am not sure I catch your drift, dear boy. To the best of my knowledge charity was not highly recommended by Trepoch, may his name be praised."

"Really? And yet you have personally authorised the outlay of millions of diams on what can only be described as an act of charity. Have you not?" He tugged a selection of rather battered record slates from his pouch and flung them at the Principle's feet.

Nimbly dodging the sharp edged slates, the Principle smiled serenely. "Excuse me, my son. The ceremony calls for me to perform a ritual disembowelling at this point. Feel free to join in the chant if you wish." A hideous liturgical wail resounded in the shadowy domes of the temple as the Serene Principle called upon the Demi-Urge to accept this, their sacrifice, and spare them from catastrophe and death, in the name of Trepoch, the wise and all-seeing, and so forth.

The scream of the communicant brought the anthem to a close.

"Remind me to write and complain about the quality of the altar offerings this month. If that raddled old trout was a virgin of seventeen summers, then I am a Sumerian ox-worm."

"Perhaps," said the Magnarch, "if you spent more on virgins and less on disgusting Captain Sparesbrooks, you might enjoy your services more."

"Oh, I see, now we come to the nub, do we?" the Serene Principle sighed. "I should have guessed that sooner or later some modified mole of yours would find out about Sparesbrook. Which was it, by the way?"

"The human, Egrah'nca," the Magnarch said. "Disguised as a small stuffed toy."

The Rape of the Stone

The Principle raised what might have been an eyebrow. "An interesting choice," he murmured.

"Forced upon me," the Magnarch said, "when I learnt that the Master of the World[12], may his boots turn to carnivorous plants and devour him from the feet upwards, had installed a Guardian of the Earth in the guise of a small child right up at the forefront of time. We managed to tweak the little brat's neural circuits to give it the illusion that the toy had always accompanied it on its missions and shot Egrah'nca into the basket of its tricycle. I was rather pleased with that, actually. Egrah'nca has reported back to me that this so-called guardian had been summoned to the side of one Captain H. 'Geronimo' Sparesbrook, for what purpose I do not yet know. However, Serene Father, I know it exists, and where, and when. A search through the clandestine archives has revealed to me that your office is shelling out cash like madmen at modified hippo hunt to maintain a time and motion study team in twenty-first century Hertfordshire with the object of keeping the foul creature alive, and - "

"And, naturally, you wish to know why."

"Why?" the Magnarch screeched. "No. I don't care why. I want it to stop. I want that money put to decent, publically beneficial uses. A hyper-expressway to the erotic pleasure-houses of P'nor'n, an extensive new torture complex with viewing plazas - "

---

[12] The Master of the World – ruler of the mystic city of Shambhala and Chief of the Serene Unseen Brotherhood (send for free introductory pamphlet, The Universe & You, a short Unseen prayer, a blessing, and predictions for the next half century.)

"Impossible." The Principle flapped his cape irritably. "The outlay is vital."

"But why?"

"I thought you didn't care why."

"Of course I care why. Come on, what's it all about? Why are we bankrupting ourselves to keep this Sparesbrook thing in being?"

"Hush, my son. You are distracting the acolytes."

"Hang the acolytes."

"Later, dear boy, later. Now, listen: what do you know of the 143th quatrain of the prophecies of the sage Trepoch?"

The Magnarch shrugged. "I am a scientist, not a credulous fool," he snapped. "What have I to do with quatrains?"

His Serene Holiness opened a jewel encrusted tome.

"In the land of rain and pasties," the Principle sang, "Shall arise the keen-eyed Sparesbrook, And with his explosive weaponry device, Annihilate the great (or, possibly, enormous, the meaning is unclear) enemy of Atlantis, who seeketh the Stone of Power." He closed the missal with a slam that echoed round the domes of the Temple. "Clearly," he said, "this Sparesbrook object is to play a vital part in the matter of the S'nang üll H'notorem."

"S'nang üll H'notorem?"

"Of course."

"That little Mayan restaurant in Sekuba Street?"

"Mayan restaurant!" The Principle struck the marble floor with his ivory staff. "My dear Verox,

The Rape of the Stone

the S'nang üll H'notorem is the very hub and centre piece of our religion."

"Really. And?"

"S'nang üll H'notorem is its name in the ancient tongue of our forefathers. Had you paid more attention at University, my boy, no doubt you could have translated it for me."

The Magnarch nodded eagerly. "I can do that," he said. "Erm, don't tell me. S'nang. Yes, well, we'll come back to that. Üll: preposition. Of, for, by, from, with, in, under, above, down, to against, through, without. Right?"

His father nodded bleakly.

"H'notorem. Tricky. Something to do with a hole. Starts in a hole. H.' – that connotes blackness. I remember that. Something something a bit black that starts down a hole. And S'nang, of course, means stone. The stone which commences a portion of blackness down a hole." He considered the information revealed by his efforts. "Just what I thought. More religious rubbish."

His Supreme Highness sighed. "Where would you be today," he wondered, "if I had not eaten the wife of the chief examiner? The correct translation, my child, is stone which contains a fragment of the original black hole, source of the multiverse. Now do you see?"

"Where do you get 'multiverse'?"

"Üll. When taking the ablative it expresses the content of everything which could possibly exist. Hence the useful neologism, multiverse."

"Stretching things a bit, I'd have thought. Still that's religion for you."

"Religion!" snapped His Supreme Highness. "A load of dressing up and bad poetry. I'm not interested in religion. Do you think I fought and devoured to be where I am today just so I could drape myself in yards of musty lace and chant dirges all day?"

The Magnarch was a little shocked. "Really, father. I'm surprised to hear you say that."

"I'll surprise you, my boy. The S'nangstone, my princeling, is a good deal more than a chunk of rock. It contains, as I told you, a tiny molecule of the black hole from which all that exists sprang into being at the beginning of time itself. Need I elaborate?"

"Yes."

"Ultimate power," whispered his father. "The source of all that exists or might exist or may have been about to be on the point of having existed – locked within that cube of vibrating rock. What do you think powers our civilisation? What ensures that we remain at a cultural apogee while around us savage nations gibber and war? Why is our shepherd's pie always crisp and brown on the top?"

"The S'nang üll H'notorem," said the Magnarch.

"Now he sees," sighed his father.

"But what," the Magnarch asked reasonably, "has the fabulous source of our wealth and power to do with a retired military personage in what some outlandishly call the United Kingdom of England and Various Other Bits?"

"It's vanished," said the Serene Principle.

"It's what?"

"Gone. Disappeared overnight."

"Don't be ridiculous. Great blocks of primeval rock don't just evaporate. You're joking."

"I never joke. A sense of humour is not compatible with the practice of any major religion."

"I know what it is, you've had some blasted Valk merchant with a barrow round the back door of the Temple and flogged it, haven't you?"

"Your audacity is, fortunately for you, exceeded only by your powers of self preservation, my son. No, I have not sold the Holy Stone of Our Forefathers. It has, I repeat, gone missing. Utterly. And my sages cannot be deflected from the opinion that the Sparesbrook creature will be instrumental in preventing its falling into the wrong hands. For if we fail to recover the stone, we're looking at the end of our entire civilisation. Already we are forced to rely on conventional power plants. And we're running out of modified hamsters. How annoying, of course, that the heathen fornicators of P'nor'n are still practising their blasphemous perversions with the full benefit of modern technology, while those of us who have always remained mindful of the commandments of the sage, Trepoch, have not so much incantational power left to us as a 12 volt battery or a small personal generator."

"A fascinating theological reflection," the Magnarch said. "You imply, do you, that the blasphemers of P'nor'n in their heretical employment of non-S'nang power sources will still able to enjoy a full range of communication and other devices as efficient as ours were, before this catastrophe?"

"As efficient?" squealed the Serene One. "As efficient? You speak, my dear boy, of a mob of self-seeking licentiates, dedicated wholly to the pursuits of bodily ecstasy and enormous wealth. Their equipment makes ours look completely shrivelled. And floppy."

"How unfortunate," the Magnarch observed, "that you have forbidden us to mingle with the unorthodox mysteries of P'nor'n, on pain of small but exceedingly uncomfortable mutilations."

"Were the moment more appropriate," the Principle said, "I might usefully be reminded now to call upon you to elucidate a small matter which has been troubling the Serene security department for some time. Absurdly enough, the records seem to indicate that you are not as unfamiliar with the heathens of P'nor'n as I am sure is the case. These suggestions that you are a personal friend of the Khemmenoi of Lunt, for example, would be quite mistaken."

"Naturally," lied the Magnarch. "But let us not trouble ourselves with these trivialities," he went on quickly. "Our concern today is not with P'nor'n. Bearing in mind that we're talking culture, power and civilisation here, the finger of suspicion points in one direction only. East."

He made a dramatic gesture at the wall. Wearily, the Principle waved his crozier at the window. "East," he said.

"East," the Magnarch repeated firmly, switching forelimbs. "Shambhala, fastness of the self-styled Master of the World." He paused to allow a gang of servers to strut past with a wary looking bull and a grinning maiden. "It can be none other than that bastard Sheppenic and his pseudo-monks."

The Principle shook his head, caught his triple tiara and replaced it carefully. "The holy books make no mention of Shambhala in this context. Or any other, come to that."

"Of course it's Shambhala." The Magnarch's roar almost drowned the ululations of the choir.

"But the sage Trepoch in his quatrains -"

"Quatrains!" The Magnarch sneered with such fervour that half the congregation went into psycho-analysis. The other half applied for assisted suicide. "You know as well as I do that the quatrains are translations of hugely imperfect texts prepared by monks selected especially for the dimness of their wits and the ambiguity of their handwriting. People still haven't forgiven the Temple for that twaddle about concentric canals. Months we spent digging them, not to mention the expense and the traffic chaos, on the basis of something you people claimed to have read in the quatrains. Then someone thought to check the original papyrus and found it wasn't concentric canals at all. He was actually talking about electric candles. It'll be exactly the same here, Your 'Sparesbrook' will turn out to be a sparkplug. Or a sperm bank."

"Perhaps you're right," the Principle mused. "My first thought was that the execrable Valk-people, criminally asserting some imagined right of ownership on the factitious grounds that the Stone had been misused for centuries as part of their primitive and obscene religious ceremonies before we providentially liberated it, had somehow contrived to steal it back. But, yes, perhaps the inane Sheppenic and his crew are behind it all. Though I confess I am unable to imagine how he managed it."

"Well, you somehow managed to send a crew off to whatever is meant by the uncouth term,

'Hertfordshire'. I suggest - " He broke off, frowning. "How exactly did you do that, by the way?"

"We reversed the polarity on a cerbo-snatch and propelled a team of insurance salesmen thousands of years into the future. It seemed to work all right, so we assembled a crack unit of time and motion people, equipped them with all the necessary gear, and inserted them in a secure location where they could keep an eye on Sparesbrook."

"Then why not simply send another such unit to Shambhala[13] and kipper Sheppenic over one of his disgusting scented candles until he tells you what he's done with the Stone?"

"You have no conception of the power drain involved. When we had the Stone, we took it all for granted, the power, heat, light, energy, the whole package came free and without side-effects. So long as we kept up a regular supply of sacrifices. Now that it's gone, we can just about run to the very occasional use of a reverse cerbo-snatch to supply

---

[13] And where is Shambhala? When Marco Polo asked that question of the great Khan, he was directed to a place called, in Russian, 'Belovodye' which may be translated as 'Interminable Thrush'. It may also be translated as 'white waters', it depends how good your Russian is. The Khan's Russian was downright wicked, which is probably why he sent Polo off on a fruitless trek through the Kokushi Mountains, across Bogogorski and over Ergor, and thus to Tibet. Shambhala lay, in fact, or as near to fact as a mystic city can get without being too polluted by it, in the other direction. When Polo, after a good deal of knee bruising and fingernail tearing, finally made it to the monastery on top of Ergor, he was told by the abbot of 'the red path to Shambhala' which put the entrance in Mongol country. But, of course, the abbot added, if any man should attempt to enter the land without first having been 'called' he must surely die. Marco Polo, who knew an excuse when he saw one, decided it was time to have a really good look at Persia.

our T&M people, as outlined in the manufacturer's guide, but any tricky stuff is right out of the question. Plus it would void the warranty. I tell you, things are so bad, I'm afraid to open the fridge in case the light comes on for once. Whoever has taken it, the fact remains," concluded His Serene Highness, the principle of Goth, "that the mystic Stone, the S'nang üll H'notorem, is no longer in the Holy of Holies. And unless we get it back pronto - "

"We're history," the Magnarch whispered.

"Worse than that," the Principle sighed. "We're myth."

12

Not quite so far back in the realms of prehistory as the fabled and loquacious continent of Atlantis, Egrah'nca, moving by night to avoid observation, had made his way to Hyde Park and, choosing with the aid of his Prognosticator a suitably unscathable tree, ensconced himself in a hollow under its roots. The time was 1922. He seized the Nidro Force and commanded it to return him to the present.

Unfortunately the Nidro Force had spilt most of its energy during a bumpy bit around 1931, probably something to do with the Dogger Bank Earthquake, and needed to recharge.

Egrah'nca made himself comfortable and settled down to wait.

Outside there was a General Strike, a depression, a lot of men came and dug trenches, another lot came and dropped explosive things on the first lot for a while, then stopped, a succession of summers and winters passed during which the skirts on the legs visible from Egrah'nca's hidey-hole got longer, then shorter, then a little longer, then very short indeed – concurrently his hidey-hole became considerably more noisy because people started playing loud electric instruments just outside it. He had a very good view of the bands, though, and particularly enjoyed the bit when the man in the frilly white dress released a lot of very tasty butterflies. Then things quietened down and after a few more decades he knew that he was at the very forefront of time once more.

The Rape of the Stone

At three a.m. on a May morning, he edged from his hiding place and darted across the wet grass to the shadow of a waste bin. Egrah'nca was back in business. His first task was to report in to his Master. The Nidro Force had failed to achieve full capacity, having exhausted a lot of energy obliterating inquisitive squirrels, but there was enough for messaging. Composing himself in the correct manner, he took an end of the ribbon in each paw, closed his eyes (which of course involved lying on his back with his legs in the air) and tuned into the current informational parameters.

There were a lot of amateur parameter tramps on the ether waves that night and it took him several hours to get through, what with cruisers from Mu asking to wig it with a manxo-panaxo any night after Tuesday, and a foul-mouthed entity from Kadath in the Cold Waste who kept snapping in to ask if any little tu-bup wanted to groil his magger, but Egrah'nca made it as the sun rose and settled back to integrate his control into the structure situation.

Outside, the gates of the park swung open and the first humans of the day appeared, some hurrying on missions of what they imagined was importance, others simply dallying, some too whose place of work the park was. Here comes the jolly little man whose purpose in life is to ensure that adequate amounts of broken glass are strewn about the swings, that the slides have a good coating of mud, and the correct sand is injected into the bearings of the roundabouts. And here is the lugubrious old stick with the peaked cap and the stout staff tipped with a spike of steel with which he will ensure that all the items of value lost in the park, all balls, watches, teddy bears, bits and pieces of underclothing and jewellery shall be properly mangled before submission to the park's Lost Property Department in Aberdeen, replacing them with fresh pieces of dog mess, which he bears hygienically wrapped in cling-film in a sack at his side.

Teddy bears?

Oh no, no, say not that fate has saved this cruellest blow till now. Our little furry chum, last hope of Atlantis, is he to perish at the end of a park-keeper's prong? After uncounted decades in a tree stump, has he returned to life only to be skewered and sent to Aberdeen? Better to have perished in the Muggoth Pits of Scaliselsarga, better to have been filleted and smoked by a pothead, better not to have been born at all, than to be sent to Aberdeen...

The park-keeper draws nearer on the morning fresh grass, snatching up a handbag here, and there a copy of Algonquin's *Treatise on Intestinal Lacunae* (the year's runaway best-seller) and leaving behind a glistening trail of foot-prints which move ineluctably towards the small bundle of blue and yellow fur beside the waste bin.

Hear us, Egrah'nca! Awake! Flee! For the dogs of doom, in the shape of Ronald Henghist, 63, confirmed bachelor and 32nd Degree Masonic Gate Master, are upon thee! Wake! Wake!

Oh, wake!

13

The reader, relieved no doubt to have escaped from the narrative in expostulatory mood, although reasonably concerned about the imminent impalation of Egrah'nca, will have reserved the main force of his or her intellectual passion for consideration of another matter which, perhaps not of such immediately penetrating a nature as the steel spike on a park-keeper's prong, is nevertheless of a nature at once unique and imperative.

We refer, of course, to the beautiful tale of the birth of the child of Deirdre Horne.

Deirdre Horne, as portrayed in Ken Russell's splendid biopic by the late Sir Max Adrian in surely the greatest triumph of his posthumous career, was a maid, in the occupational rather than the gynaecological sense, employed by Captain Sparesbrook in the relatively affluent days before Malcolm de Maupassant simplified the Captain's finances.

The circumstances of the wondrous birth were these. Dismissed from Boots the Chemists for persistently drinking the disinfectant hand gel, Deirdre (a personable creature when she took the trouble[14]) applied for a job as assistant stable lass at the Permanent Stud, an establishment maintained by Charlotte de Maupassant (q.v.) on her estate near Amblebroth. She soon grew to like the work. She would rise at 6 a.m., muck out, feed, water and

---

[14] 'The trouble' - users' argot for disinfectant hand gel

groom the magnificent beasts in their stalls. Then, having eaten, she would polish up the leathers and harnesses, lead the troupe out for their exercise, and perform the many other tasks allotted to her.

It was one mild Wednesday afternoon in early April, two months after she had joined the Stud, that Deirdre, idle for a moment, leaned on the door of the stable belonging to Uncle Tom, a proud black beauty with eyes of fire and, stroking his sleek neck, whispered, "I tell you what, Tommy, a girl can get really bored round this place, you know that?"

Uncle Tom snorted and nodded wisely.

"I believe you understand me, Uncle Tom," the girl cried with glee.

"Well, of course I can understand you," Uncle Tom said in the rich tones of All Souls, Oxford. "Good Grief, child, the fact that I hail from Stoke Newington doesn't make me a dumb animal, you know. I have a degree in Sociology."

"Then what are you doing here in this – this flesh market?"

Uncle Tom shrugged.

"What else can you do with a degree in Sociology? And, anyway, giving old ladies a good time, what's so ignoble about that? Better than planning to rule the universe by cruelty and deceit, like some I could mention."

Uncle Tom refused to explain what he meant by that. "No, I've said too much already. Want to come in for a quick ride?"

She shook her head. "No," she said, "let's do it out here. It really turns me on, thinking of all the people on the number 72 watching us while they wait for the lights to change."

The Rape of the Stone

She exercised Uncle Tom quite often after that and eventually, as inexperienced young riders often do, she fell. The news quickly reached the ear of Charlotte de Maupassant who, enraged by this cheap, indeed gratuitous, immorality, had the girl dismissed and Uncle Tom sold at the next auction to a northern university who wanted someone to clean out the toilets and teach a little sociology on the side.

Pregnant, homeless and with nothing to fall back on but her bum, Deirdre tramped the leafy lanes of Hertfordshire. At last she came to the gates of a mansion whose name, she deciphered from a lichenous board awry on the rusty iron, seemed to be Sparesbrook Manor. With barely enough strength to wrench apart the iron gates, she passed between the pilasters and limped up the weedy drive to the front door, which is where she was discovered an hour later by Malcolm de Maupassant, returning in his motor car from a scout hunt on nearby Stalebreath Moor.

He had failed to notice her immediately because he had inadvertently parked his car over her and it was not till he called for Thring to help him unload a fine brace of sixers, as well as a Brownie which should have been thrown back, that he spotted the pair of shapely legs projecting from beneath the back axle.

"Damn' hitch-hikers!" he snorted, lashing at the shins with his hunting crop. The girl crawled out, large bellied and streaked with sump oil, which is just how Malcolm liked them.

"Well, well, well," drawled the haughty accountant. "Here's a pretty co-incidence. Do you know me, girl?"

"Yes, sir," said Deirdre. "I used to work for your old ma, up the Stud."

His brow darkened. "You'll speak respectfully of Mrs. de Maupassant," he snapped. "Thring, fetch your wife and tell her to attend to this young wanton. Scrubbed up, she will make a suitable replacement for the scullery maid we fired last week."

Deirdre soon found that Malcolm de Maupassant's position of accountant to the Sparesbrook Will Settlement and Indiscretionary Trust agglomerates conferred on him rights and privileges beyond those of ordinary men. She guessed as much when she came across him one evening, eating a slice of roast scullery maid in the conservatory.

"Oh, I beg your pardon," he said, bobbing a curtsey, but Malcolm waved a tibia at her in a friendly manner and bade her cheerfully to sit down. A carnivorous S'narg plant at once seized her by the throat but, chuckling, Malcolm clubbed it into snivelling submission with the scullery maid's orthopaedic boot, then resumed his repast, occasionally tossing a tit-bit to Fangfest, his Great Dane, who sprawled on the floor writing a letter to his aunt in Kobenhavn.

"So," said Malcolm. "The little mother-to-be looks healthier now. How long is it?"

"Another month, sir," Deirdre said.

"Good, good." Malcolm wiped his greasy chin on a white frilly apron. "What are you hoping for, a roast or a pudding? I mean, a boy or a girl?"

"I don't mind," Deirdre said. "So long as it's healthy and happy."

The Rape of the Stone

When the momentous day arrived, some three years before the Night of the Alternative Universe, she had been alone, enjoying an idle minute in the conservatory, feeding voles to the carnivorous plantlets, so we have only her word for what happened.

Anyway, the way she tells it, a sudden and alarming light fell upon the conservatory, filling it with the stench of frying vegetation and casting suggestive shadows on the matting. It passed, but left behind a curious glow among the rubber plants. Hypnotically drawn, Deirdre parted the leaves and found herself in a one-to-one situation with the goddess Sclit.

The goddess was twelve feet tall, radiant, puce of hair and smelt of Johnson's Baby Oil and Bergamot & Patchouli candle wax.

The divine being stared down at her as though across the aeons. Immortal lips parted. A faint, far-off voice cried, "Guardian of the Earth!" and "Help!" and "Save!" and "Mother!" and "Eric Maresbreath!"

Then the brightness faded, and Deirdre was alone.

Some say that Deirdre had been at the handgel again, and that it was stretching things a bit to interpret the message as "Hail, Deirdre, Mother of God, thou shalt bear a child, Saviour of the World, the Guardian of the Earth, and the child shall be called Eric Maresbreath." No other construction has ever been put forward, however, so there the matter rests.

The visitation of Sclit brought on her labour, and Deirdre Horne gave birth to a chubby little child whose name, she dutifully announced, was

Eric Maresbreath. Juliette Thring tried to dissuade her, Malcolm de Maupassant was openly derisive, but Deirdre was adamant. Sclit had spoken: the name was Eric Maresbreath. It probably meant King of Kings or similar, in whatever language Sclit spoke at home.

"Poor little creature," Juliette murmured, looking down on the tiny figure in its manger.

"A mortal shame," agreed Edward Thring, as he pulled at his wife's clothing.

"Here," barked the Captain. "I've brought the little bastard a present." He tossed a bundle of dishonoured cheques into the manger, nodded admiringly as Juliette's bosom burst from its ungirded foundations. "Lucky man," he murmured to Thring, patting his old head, and departed in a gentlemanly fashion.

And there, gurgling and farting in the manger, dribbling over a bundle of dishonoured cheques, we shall leave little Eric Maresbreath[15] for a while. It will be four years before we meet again, although before we go, it impossible to refrain from remarking that if what Deirdre Horne had encountered in the shrubbery was indeed a manifestation of the Omniscient, then it could at least have got the little bastard's sex right.

---

[15] played in Russell's work of genius by Peter Cook and Dudley Moore on a tandem.

14

Percipient students, if such there be, will have remarked in intervals between rioting, ingesting illegal substances and recovering from the Allcomers Graffiti Championships, that a small time dilation has occurred somewhere in the recent stages of our history. It will no more have escaped them than it had escaped the hidden eyes behind the mullions of the Violet Pring Hebbenthwaite Sunset Memorial Home, whose minarets glimmered in the moonlight over Amblebroth Hill, that where the agent Egrah'nca lies in the imminent, if suspended, danger of a fate much expected by guests of Vlad the Impaler it is already dawn, whereas in the Captain's ancestral pile night continues to echo like an empty cauldron, whatever that means.

Here we may observe another of the side effects of Charlotte de Maupassant's appalling anguish. For an area of approximately two hundred square metres, centred upon that spot in the parsnip beds where gripped the claws of Malcolm, her son and Owl-thing, the space-time continuum is running five and a half hours slow.

The immediate result is, now that the Captain and Juliette Thring have stumbled hand in hand to consummate their passion on a suite of garden furniture in the conservatory, and Deirdre Horne has whisked her sleep walking infant back to her manger in the cowshed, and Edward Pausanias Thring continues his repose under a sweet, steaming mound of horse droppings, the narrative finds itself with nothing to do. Pointless to nip back to Egrah'nca, for he lies on his back by the bin listening to the ether tramps spark their naboth longo-parongo across the milliard finite abstractions of the cosmos. Before we can thrill to his peril in the park, another idiot sun must haul itself in a drool of light over the eastern hills, unwitting that before the day is through it will, like all the suns before it, commit lemmingish suicide over the western edge of the world.

Into the private emotions of Charlotte de Maupassant and her boy, the narrative, which has some scruples, is disinclined to intrude, especially as to be honest it has completely lost track of the Empress of Witches. What it would really like to do is pop along to a certain flatlet in Goitre Lane and peep at the pre-auroral ecstasies of Eric Maresbreath and his beloved, the unbelievably delightful Helena Phipps.

The narrative sometimes fears that it is becoming a dirty old manuscript.

Time (as someone or other would have us believe) passes. Only the sleepless eyes of the inmates of the asylum on the hill are unlidded as the queenly moon is deflowered by the dawn. Stars in swathes are mown from the ebon fields of night. The narrative expires in a swoon of violets and kid-gloves.

All is still.

Incapable of much in the way of thought or feeling, and running on the spot to maintain some kind of life in his withering limbs, the vicar of Blessed Benifons held his morning communion with the Ineffable, which had manifested as a year-old copy of Mayfair on the window-sill of his crumbling summer-house.

Donning his pale-pink spectacles, he wrapped a lacy cape about his otherwise naked limbs and pranced forth across the dewy grass, allowing the long level beams of the morning sun to lash his hairless thighs. His skimpy lips writhed like shrimps wrestling as he burst forth into a song of praise. His whole being throbbed to the splendour of the light.

When the ten foot Owl-thing dropped on him out of the monkey-puzzle tree, he assumed at first that it was the Most High, taking umbrage at certain passages in last month's parish newsletter, but a glimpse of the horny claw which had clamped about his upper arm and the strange sensation as the beak stripped a ribbon of flesh from his back convinced him that he had been in danger, in very real danger, of heresy.

Struggling like a mouse, which is a very silly thing to do when in the grip of an Owl-thing, he screamed a prayer to the Demi-Urge, begging it to reward his years of worship by transforming the raptor into a line of jam jars, or a basket of useful tools, or the seven volume set of the Philosophy of Alfred van der Junta, the Dutch antinomian and polymath. The Demi-Urge, no doubt busy with other matters, did not respond. Neither did the vicar of Blessed Benifons, after the Owl-thing had plucked off his head and commenced to ingest his bodily innards, like a tit on a crimson milk-bottle.

"Oh, Magotte," wailed the voice of Herbert Jubb, as the creature paused to turn the remains of the vicar up the other way, "must you? I mean, what's wrong with a nice crème caramel, for

Magotte's sake, or a few grape-nuts? Why do we have to go about eating vicars all the time?"

"My poor, sensitive Jubb," it replied, having gulped down the vicar's shins with gusto. "I assure you, it won't be vicars all the time." It nibbled at the knees. "Sometimes," it said, "I enjoy a good bishop."

When the woman now known as Mrs. Aramintha Gristle, the vicar's housemaid, arrived an hour later with her carpet beater, she was surprised not to find her employer in his study, bent over his books, the position in which he generally preferred to receive his first thrashing of the day.

Mrs. Gristle, a former filing clerk in the Ministry for Unfulfilled Prophecies, had resigned from her post after purloining an aeons-old prediction which foretold the birth of the Saviour to a black gigolo and a maid in the domestic rather than the gynaecological sense. Locating a potential sire was simple, thanks to Charlotte de Maupassant, and the Sits. Vac. furnished the job. But, alas, Charlotte had then made what Mrs. Gristle would always think of her one gross error, and wrecked the scheme. The ministry having declined to re-employ her, Mrs. Gristle found herself fretting in a life of flagellant servitude, light housework and -

Something, it may have been the sound like the flapping of wings in a cess-pit, interrupted her self pity and drew her to the window, in time to see what for a ludicrous moment appeared to be a ten foot agglomeration of sludge and feathers take wing from the roof of the summer house and disappear in a splatter of slime over the tree tops.

A brave, if overweight lady, Mrs. Gristle thundered down the stair, breaking a number of the treads, and dashed though the kitchen to the garden door. She ran into the garden and peered about her.

"Vicar?" she called. "Vicar?"

Taking a leather whip from her thigh boot, she cracked it sharply, a sound which usually brought her benefactor running. Nothing stirred, save where a weasel scurried over the mound of skulls which had served the vicar for a rockery.

Then she saw it. Lying in the centre of the lawn was a tight roundish bundle about the size of a laundry bag. Curiously she approached it across the grass, the tall palouva flowers leaving sticky threads on her naked belly. For a moment, spying the lacy cape and the black velvet biretta, she thought that the object was indeed a laundry bag.

Then she made out the shapes of bones and recognised the skin which even in its present state still bore the signature of her whips, and knew that what lay before her was no less than the world's largest and most holy owl pellet.

Compelled by a never before experienced awe, Aramintha Gristle prostrated herself upon the grass, which absolutely soaked her leopard fur G-string, and worshipped the relics. And thus at this dew-soaked, sun-blessed moment, did a new and deadly cult come upon the world. Possessed, its first priestess raised her whip towards the skies, straddled the pellet, and screamed out the words which would echo from Ramsgate to Buxton.

"Behold! The Demi-Urge is with us! The great Demi-Urge is with us! Bring out your first born, that He may feed his fill!"

15

Somewhat belatedly, the narrative mounts an allegorical moped and roars from the garden of Blessed Benifon's vicarage, where it was detained by the unlikely emergence of the high priestess Aramintha Gristle, and slices across time, space and the M25 to Hyde Park, where it arrives covered in smuts and has to sit down on a bench for five minutes to pull itself together. Wobbling over the grass, it reaches the bin which it left so many paragraphs ago, only to find that, as you might have expected, it is too late.

Egrah'nca has gone. Of the blue and yellow teddy bear with the pink ribbon round its neck, there is no sign.

Having wiped something nasty off its foot with a copy of the New Statesman it carries for the purpose, the narrative shrugs its shoulders and goes off to ogle the secretaries sunning their limbs by the Serpentine.

However, what really happened to Egrah'nca was, fortunately, recorded in the Central Observation Office of the Archerons of Atlantis.

On the crazed and flickering screen of a failing Omnipert, the action unfolded before the gaze of T'nemporg, duty officer and underling, as he chewed his lunch.

His eye widened as the park-keeper with his prong scampered across the grass towards the recumbent body of Egrah'nca, special agent, close friend of the Magnarch of Verox and temporary teddy bear. T'nemporg, who knew which side his bread was buttered, wiped his greasy fingers and hastily thumbed the long-range organic modifier, zeroing in on a glimpse of skull under the brim of the park-keeper's sweaty cap. Calibrating intuitively, he slammed a couple of rounds into the man's synapses. Sticky with the residues of non-incantational energy, the Behg-Mg'notomor relays finally seized up and died in an ordour of rotting oranges. T'nemporg sat back, anxiously gnawing a mrylla. Trepoch alone knew how they would cope when the next crisis occurred. But he didn't seemed to have knocked out any useful quatrains on the subject.

"Good work, T'nemporg," murmured a voice.

Dropping the mrylla, which scuttled away and disappeared into the circuitry, the duty officer leapt from his seat and humbled himself.

"Clear that up, T'nemporg," the voice said coolly. "I may be the Magnarch of Verox but that's no reason to soil the furniture."

"No, your Insatiableness," whispered T'nemporg.

"Of course, I do have an appetite the size of a Colubrian rog-thumper's dick, and you are a delicious looking little modified gibbon, but – well, you're a lucky boy today, because I've just eaten that pig-shaped thing doing the crossword in the guard-room down the corridor."

"Thank you, your voracious majesty," whimpered T'nemporg.

"No-one important, I trust."

"Oh, no, no, your Unconstrainableness. Goodness me, no."

"That's all right then. Now, tell me, what exactly have you done to the human?" the voice enquired politely.

T'nemporg scratched his privates and began shudderingly to explain. Magotte, how he loathed these Royal Visits.

The park-keeper, having gleefully spotted a teddy by the bins, had skipped forward, prong erect, when a sudden thought entered his mind. Oddly enough, he felt it come in, just under the brim of his cap. It struck him suddenly that the teddy, whose furry breast quivered a millimetre beneath the grim ministration of his spike, would make a cheap but acceptable gift for the daughter of his niece, Deirdre, whose birthday it was this very morn. He snatched up the furry toy, hid it in his sack of glistening dog turds and carried Egrah'nca away.

"Good, good," oozed the voice of the Magnarch of Verox. "Very neatly done. Perhaps I detect a modicum of insubordination -"

"No, your Jawship!"

"Of insubordination in the manner of transport. Perhaps not. Now," the voice went on, with silky undertones, "tell me, T'nemporg, what reward do you wish for this deed? You have, my dear gibbon, saved the life of the favourite of the Magnarch of Verox. That calls for special recompense. Let me see. Would you like to see my holiday snaps?"

"Er," said T'nemporg, hubris and greed overcoming his sense of self-preservation, "if it's all the same to you, I'd rather have another pig-shaped thing. That was my wife. Oh, sod."

Even before the words had ceased to echo on the Immediate Reprint Screen above his head, the hapless T'nemporg realised that he had said the wrong thing. It was small consolation to know that he would never make the mistake again.

"My dear gibbon," the voice sighed, "you have turned down the opportunity to view myselves clad in copper lurex on the sands at Gorpul dül Mimpoth. You have rejected the unprecedented offer of a chance to observe the Verochian limbs disporting in the Alkali-Chutes in the Vi'npocalmogolom Pleasure Gardens. You have refused the ultimate goal of the thrill-seeker, a glimpse of my superbly ambivalent body luxuriating in the cat-houses of P'nor'n. All this you have spurned, in your gross and materialistic desire for a pig-shaped wife. T'nemporg, you are a gibbon of very small vision."

T'nemporg widened his eye again at once but it was too late for that. With a sound like a vacuum cleaner sucking up a basket of kittens, the Magnarch of Verox engulfed him in absolute otherness.

As Ron Henghist, the park-keeper, cycled though the late afternoon across the wind lashed moors on his way to Sparesbrook Manor, with Egrah'nca now gift-wrapped in his saddle-bag, he had thought himself merely peckish. But when he had passed through the gateway at the lower end of the track which led via the Neolithic tomb in its circle of muttering pines to the opening at the end of the yew alley, he gasped suddenly at the importunity of the hunger which racked his being. (He could not know, of course, that he had just ridden into a pool of time-froth polluted with the carnivorous tendencies of Malcolm de Maupassant. A good deal of this froth had splashed about during the cataclysmic reunion of the ogrish youth with his mother in the alternative hours of the previous night, some of it travelling back with the grief wave and, mixing with the evolutionary process, giving rise to the Tyrannosaurus Rex, the piranha, the human race, the S'narg plant, the Magnarch of Verox, veal and the Mosoto Tribe of Southern Dagor, who no longer exist, having devoured themselves at the climax of a Pignott ceremony in the spring of 1762.)

    Henghist tumbled from his cycle, clutching his rumbling guts, and groaned for food. A couple of beetles and a mole did nothing to ease the ravening of his maw. A struggle began between the artificial brain pattern inserted by the luckless T'nemporg in Henghist's neural pathways and the feral appetite possessing his body after its immersion in the glob of time-forth. Crackling and fizzing, his synapses urged him ever onwards, commanding him to deliver the teddy to little Eric Maresbreath in her manor on the hill below the lichenous walls of the asylum. Churning and aching, his stomach told him to eat a sheep. He wept with frustration.

    The sun was low in the western sky when Captain Sparesbrook crept from the conservatory and, hiding his nakedness with a copy of *Chick's Own*, went to answer the knocking at his door. He stepped around the inert body of Thring in its tumulus of horse manure, unchained the security bolts and peeped out. Not unnaturally he tended to suspect any stranger of being Charlotte de Maupassant in new guise but somehow, when he saw his visitor, he doubted that even Charlotte could invent a mad-eyed park-keeper with a gaily wrapped if grease-stained package and half a sheep draped round his neck.

"Not today, thank - "

But Henghist had already thrust his way into the hall.

"I'm afraid we're all Buddhists," the Captain said.

"I brung this," the intruder grunted. "For the nipper. Little Miss Eric."

"Well, it's deuced kind of you, old chap," said the Captain, "whoever you are, but, well, her mother's only just got her onto porridge. I don't think she's ready for dead sheep quite yet."

"That's my tea," Henghist explained. "This here - " He waved the package, "is for the babe."

Captain Sparesbrook peered at the present suspiciously. Now this was much more the sort of disguise in which to seek the concealed lineaments of Charlotte de Maupassant. He leaned over, prodded the package, and said, "All right, Charlotte, come out of there."

Nothing emerged.

"'S a teddy," Henghist explained. "Nice one, blue and yellow, with a proper pink ribbon."

Without taking his eyes off the parcel, Captain Sparesbrook walked backwards to the bell-push, picked himself up, brushed the horse dung off his legs, and touched the button. A moment later, Deirdre Horne appeared in the doorway. She looked rather harassed.

"Captain Sparesbrook," she said, "if you must keep horses in the house, that's your prerogative, of course, but do you think you could

The Gnostic Frying Pan

find one that doesn't crap all over the carpet every time it sees my daughter? It's hardly in keeping with her dignity as - " She lowered her voice in reverence, "the Saviour of the World."

The Captain turned, frowning, to his visitor."Are you related to the goddess Sclit at all?"

Henghist ignored him. "Hallo, Deirdre my duck," he crooned, thrusting the parcel into her unwilling hands. "Here, I brung a little something for the nipper, with Many Happy returns and all that. I bet she's a size now, eh? Always growing out of everything, ain't they, kids. Not that I never had – never did – of me – what?" He stared about him, open-mouthed, bemused by the baronial hall, the naked military gentleman, the ancient under a heap of dung, the scullery maid with a present in her hands. "What was I saying? Where am I? Who are you? Where's me spike?"

The moment that Egrah'nca passed from the hands of Ron Henghist, park-keeper and unwilling messenger of the Archerons of Atlantis, the synthetic neurons in his brain had begun to decay with a volatile fizz, leaving him with a sight headache and a permanent tendency to hear sitar music if he tilted his head to the left. It also left him without the faintest idea of where he was, or who this buxom dolly might be, or why there was a naked military man with *Chick's Own* round his loins. In such a situation there was only one thing to do, so Ron Henghist did it. He sat down on the stairs and begun to worry his sheep.

Burbling prettily, up the cellar steps came chubby smiling Eric Maresbreath. Seeing her mother and the gift-wrapped object in her mother's clutches, the squinting infant dropped the cat and the adjustable spanner, and trotted up to her parent, one covetous hand extended.

"Present!" she cried. "Pleathe! Prettie Pleathe!"

Before Deirdre could object, the child ripped the package from her mother's hands and, chucking aside the boring blue and yellow teddy bear, began to study the colourful pages of "All Action Photo Sex Fanciers Weekly" in which Ron Henghist had wrapped it. But a glance showed her it was nothing out of the ordinary so she skipped over and, pulling the teddy out of the pile of manure, entertained herself by poking its paws into the staring eyes of Edward Thring, as he lay silent under the congealing dung.

"Masterly," thought Egrah'nca. "Absolutely masterly. What a loss it was to the amateur stage when, halfway through *River of My Dreams* Eric Maresbreath received the call and knew himself to be Guardian of the Earth. How skilfully he imitates the ways of a three year old girl-child. And if he does that again I'll eviscerate the little sod."

Unplugging his left foot from his nose, Egrah'nca (blind fool) lay back in the comfortable illusion that he had been reunited with his target, and went to sleep.

16

Another day burnt out in Valhallas of flame in the sky above the haunted gables of the Violet Pring Hebbenthwaite Memorial Home, and the faint clang of the iron doors came down the dusk to the windows of Sparesbrook manor, which reflected the sunset to the sky, as though burning among the yews.

Juliette Thring, shovelling the last spadeful of dung into the dustbin, paused to retrieve her husband's glass eye, then straightened up and stared thoughtfully down the hillside to the meadows, where the mists were rising and the first of the poisonous moths were already flitting between tall grasses. Strange, that the bells of Blessed Benifons had not rung this night, as they ever had before, summoning the faithful across the fields to evening worship. But, then, it had been a strange day all round, what with panic-stricken stallions refusing to come out of the airing cupboard, and a man in a peaked cap devouring a sheep in the gazebo. Though she had to admit, little Eric seemed very taken with Henghist's present, especially since she had discovered that by tugging at his pink ribbon she could melt steel like candle-wax.

Juliette knew now much of what had transpired during the previous twenty four hours - for the Captain, after their ardours had been slaked on a swinging garden seat in the conservatory, had slept fitfully and cried out much in his sleep of boggarts and Charlotte de Maupassant and her eldritch son.

A thin voice creaked down to her from a bedroom window. Looking up, she saw her husband, revived but monocular, squatting on the window seat and waving at her. Faintly she heard the words, "It's time, my dear, it's time," and, unloosening her bodice with a sigh, returned to the house, leaving the garden to the mist, the moths, which had caught a nightingale, and Charlotte de Maupassant who, in the guise of a dustbin, which was the best she could manage after exhausting her incantational reserves on her thwarted attempt to destroy Captain Sparesbrook, vowed vengeance on the woman who had just filled her with horse-shit.

With rueful anger, she began to vent imagined scoldings upon Malcolm, her sole issue, for ruining everything by allowing himself to be turned into a terrible and disgusting Owl-thing. But the effort nigh extinguished her.

Shaking off clumps of nitrogen rich manure, Charlotte coagulated into a shape more nearly her own, tottered through the shallot beds and collapsed, weeping with weakness and frustration, beneath an apricot tree. No question of pursuing either Captain Sparesbrook or her foolish son, not now, not in this state – she barely had the strength to stay real. Without several months of rest and recuperation, she knew, she might at any moment turn into anything from a reckless tuba player from Ankara to Derek Bishop, Arch-Warlock of Liverpool.

To leave the abominable Captain triumphant in his mansion was disagreeable indeed but Charlotte was insufficiently robust for further assaults on his person or his sanity. Just thinking about it caused her to flicker in and out of existence as successively a beach towel, a tulip and a wheatear. Catching a loose thread of her own self, she managed to haul herself back into being as a wraithlike shadow of Charlotte de Maupassant, Empress of Witches and would be Mistress of the Universe.

Shivering with feverish grief, she stumbled away from Sparesbrook Manor, and made her faltering way to the boarded up premises of the Permanent Stud, where she cocooned herself in the hayloft of an abandoned stable. Many months would pass before she would once more be in a fit state to wreak any sort of havoc, never mind rescue her unfortunate boy from his hemi-stringiformic predicament. But when that day came, she vowed, as she sank into a year-long slumber, to make a proper job of it.

Well, it seems that *The Rape of the Stone* has finished a little earlier than planned. So here is a recording by the Christadelphian Orphic Choir and Orchestra, with Dame Gladys Fishwick on Euphonium, playing Pandromian Caprotchevsky's symphony number 42, *'The Great Bowel'*.

We shall have time for only the first movement.

[Cue a ghastly atonal soup of ululations, clangs and fartings which lasts for over a year, unlike most modern music, of course, which only feels as if it does...]

Mercifully, the Great Bowel movement is at last interrupted by the arrival of:

PART TWO

The Stone Unturned

17

In an incense fuming corner of the New & Reformed Church of the Demi-Urge, round the back of the goods yard in Deptford, the high priestess Aramintha Gristle massaged her thighs with perfumed oil and nodded as the Bishop of Dunwich spoke earnestly of the need for less tolerance in religion.

"Yes, yes, I do so agree," she murmured, retying her scarlet sarong. "I find myself that nothing counteracts the tendency to heresy more powerfully than the threat of being ripped apart by a ten foot tall Owl-thing. It seems a shame that you have no such convenience in your own church, Dr Dawkins. And yet," Aramintha continued, borrowing the reverend doctor's hand for a moment to hold her suspender in place while she adjusted her knickers, "you know, sometimes I feel that an owl-pellet is not a very inspiring object of veneration. There are moments, and of course I fight against them with my strongest prayers, when I could wish for something a little more – distinguée."

"Of course, of course," sighed the bishop. "We are all sincere and devout servants of the Supreme Incompetence, that cannot be denied, especially if the Inquisatorial Office has got our phones bugged, but we are all of us prey to doubts. I, too, have sometimes caught myself - " he lowered his voice – "unable to endorse entirely my own tradition's rejection of human sacrifice. The aroma of roast infant - " He licked his drooling lips, " - is simply delectable."

His words betrayed at once, although not to the megalomaniac housemaid who had anointed herself High Priestess of the Demi-Urge, that the temple had been polluted with time-froth, a large gob of which had slithered off the wings of the Owl-thing one evening as it crouched in its filthy nest in the steeple which it had made its home. Even ten-foot abominations find that constant adulation does wonders for the self-esteem and there were always juicy little tit-bits to peck up after the services.

Sixteen months had passed since that dreadful night in the mansion on Amblebroth Hill when Charlotte de Maupassant's attempt to destroy Captain Sparesbrook in her alternative universe was frustrated by her rediscovery of the son whom she imagined to be a prisoner in Hexteth Gaol. The most noteworthy events of the period were those surrounding the extraordinary rise of the New & Reformed Church of the Demi-Urge which within a year had ousted Bingo, Tanning Salons and Roller Skating Rinks as the favourite occupations of the nation, and now looked like out-classing the monarchy itself.

Below stairs, little Eric Maresbreath had by sheer determination managed to age a year and a half, while Egrah'nca, numbed by hours of head banging and cuddling, and suffering from gangrene in his chewed ears, felt as if he had aged by about 110 years which, being on the Atlantean time foundation, he had. Thring and his young wife continued on their tirelessly erotic way, simple souls, unperturbed by the series of hideous attacks upon the bodies of bank managers, lawyers, clergy and members of Parliament which sometimes appeared in their newspapers and which were attributable to the greed of the Owl-thing, who was now peering down at the bobbing bum of the Bishop of Dunwich, as he convocated with the Arch Priestess on an electric vibro-altar™ in the temple below.

"D'you ever get, you know, lonely?" Jubb was asking, blinking his share of the eyes as though a tear had clouded them. "I do. I miss my forge. And I had a daughter, you know, well, foster daughter, I won her in a game of Crown & Anchor off a Nepalese gentleman whose hearse broke down outside the forge one night in August, fifteen year ago. I give her the name Juliette, like, though by birth she was called Dur - "

"Jubb," interrupted Malcolm de Maupassant. "You have bored me with this witless tale at least a hundred times since I had the ill fortune to be intertwined with you in this thing of slime and feathers. Have the goodness, sir, to hold our tongue. I am intent on securing our breakfast."

The Owl-thing sighed Jubbishly and with half its brain brooded on the dear past. The other half observed the plump primatial flesh as it rolled off the priestess to lie on its back while she bent over him in some ecstatic ritual. The bishop's eyes opened in glad surprise, which transformed by way of curiosity and disgust into unambivalent terror when he saw, perched on a ledge high above him, between a pair of misericords representing the mother and father of the Director of the Royal Opera House, Beirut, the slimy bulk of a ten foot Owl-thing, watching him with one greedy and one inconsolable eye.

The bishop shrieked.

"Like a bit of that, do you, dearie," Aramintha chuckled. "You clericals are all the same, suckers for a - "

The sound of the bishop's screams shook chunks of plaster from the wall beside them, rather spoiling the effect of the mural, and brought the Owl-thing swooping down, which rather spoilt the effect of the bishop. Aramintha Gristle, who no more wanted to meet her Deity than anyone else does, gathered up her clothing and fled through the vestry to the pantry, and thence to the corsetry, where she hid among the swaying lines of stays and listened with horrid fascination to a sound more dreadful than a test commentary or a record of authentic Lincolnshire folk music - the sound of her lord at his breakfast. Soon she found herself being sick all over a black satin basque with red roses round the cups and pretty purple suspenders. It wasn't all garden fetes and chats with the Young Wives, the work of a priestess in modern Britain.

18

It was a haggard and chronically apprehensive Captain Sparesbrook who emerged from his hiding-place in the hold of his cousin Mithras' cabin cruiser that morning. He crept up the ladder to the rotting deck and peered nervously out at the day, which had sat down on the river bank like a fat lady on a dirty deckchair. A smell of washing flapped in the air. Dogs ran races down the towpath. Not far away a train scoured under the foot bridge, showering the river with gravel and beer cans. Presumably none of them was a magically transformed Empress of Witches but he could not be entirely sure. Often enough in the depths of night he had heard what in his abjection he thought to be the baying of boggarts echoing between the warehouse walls.

The Captain wriggled across the planks, inserting eight or nine splinters into his legs en route, and gained the shelter of the gunwales, where at last he felt sufficiently at ease to unwrap a slab of old cheese from his pouch and fall to breakfast.

Sixteen months, more or less, the Captain had lived in this fashion, more a hunted beast than a human being. For a few weeks after the night of the Alternative Universe he had clung, defiant, to his niche in the ancestral home, but after three successive days of a howling sand-storm in which thousands of rabid goat fleas buzzed and penetrated every corner of his clothing, and which since such weather was not usual in Hertfordshire he attributed quite mistakenly to the machinations of Charlotte de Maupassant, the Captain had been forced to quit. Packing a supply of cheese and some fire-lighters into a bag, he had abandoned Sparesbrook Manor by night and taken the old way by the Neolithic tomb to the main road and safety.

His path had led him through the dregs of the pool of time froth which had caused Ron Henghist to annoy the local sheep. Its potency was not so diminished that the Captain did not find that he had thoughtlessly consumed most of the cheese and all of the firelighters before he reached the village.

Clutching the residue of his slithery packet of Camembert, Captain Sparesbrook had passed silently between the cottages, concealed from prying eyes by the expedient of mingling with a nomadic band of goose fletchers, making their way down to Islington for the annual Thrump Fair. Indeed, so well did he hide himself that the Captain entirely forgot that he was anyone other than Master-Fletcher Symington McQuash, and spent three unwashed weeks in an open cart with a black-eyed wench named Lady Carolyn Mabletrees, and what fun it was, too. But the other fletchers had their doubts about the quiet stranger with the nervous tic and the smell of cheese, especially when, putting him to the test, they found he had no skill with the glimpot, and didn't even know into which hole to insert his doody.

And so it transpired that one night in the depths of old Fanglake Forest, the Captain was rudely dragged from his sleeping bag and tied to a giant oak tree in the Fletchers' Clearing, a place so dreadful that even in daylight only tourists and salesmen in search of somewhere to pee would come near it.

With the ropes biting into his flesh and the stench of stale urine in his nostrils, the Captain remembered himself. Sadly, the fletchers had by now worked themselves into a frenzy and could not hear his shouts as they danced and leapt through the flames of their great Moll-Fire, in which the irons of their craft lay heating. And when the sun came up, commuters on the Birmingham line and the eight lane motorway, as well as sundry devil worshippers, cabinet makers and part time livery men who dwelt in the council estate across the road all looked with amusement on the sorry figure roped to a stump in the central reservation, his trousers round his ankles, the long white neck and orange beak of a gander dangling limply from the fly in his Y-fronts. About his neck hung a placard on which was inscribed in letters of goose blood the single word: 'Y-fletched'. Those who understood, and there were many, ceased to smile when they read that forbidding message, and drew their loved ones a little closer, and passed by on the other side.

It was Ms Ally Zonfurth, a travelling bag saleswoman from Uttoxeter, who freed the Captain. A braver or more fool-hardy lady than her peers, she parked her bright red Alfa Romeo on the fast lane and strolled easily up to the parched figure tied to the tree stump. She was a tall, devil-may-care woman with eyes like chips of garnet and a mouth that could talk its way out of a Chinese wrestler, but as she drew near to the Captain her cigarette dropped from her lips, her hands trembled, she whispered, "Merciful Powers, it's – it's you, Llewellyn."

But, of course, it wasn't, as she realised when the goose neck came away in her hand. having recovered from that shock, and then the disappointment of finding it was only a goose neck, she freed the Captain from his bonds and, lifting his light body, bore him to the Alfa. Gently she laid him down, smoothed his ruffled wisps of hair and, starting the engine with a smile, drove over his legs and disappeared down the road towards Stanmore.

A thunderstorm revived the Captain in the mid-afternoon. Brown with tyre-tracks and the spray from passing lorries, he crawled to the hard shoulder and, some hours later, managed to hide himself under the tarpaulin of a Dutch wagon which had parked up for a moment to give the driver a chance to get his hand out of a hitch-hiker's elastic. Nestling down among the crates of dead gorillas consigned to the Kiddyscoff Babydins Factory, s'Hertogenbosch, the Captain relaxed at last and fell asleep.

Awaking to the scream of seagulls, he peeped outside. The lorry was parked on the dock at Felixstowe. The seagulls were screaming because it was parked on their toes. Breaking off a piece of dead gorilla, he leapt from the trailer and hid himself in a customs shed, gnawing hungrily. He was thus perfectly positioned to hear the following exchange:

"Good morning, madam. Have you anything to declare?"

"Yes. I am Mithras Sparesbrook. I am not a woman. And I have a cargo of Seprophantine art treasures in the hold of my cruiser outside."

There was a crash and a riffle of pages as the customs officer looked up Seprophantine art treasures in his tariff book. The nearest he could find was Septipopus B (a space virus) which bore a duty of 22.5% plus VAT, so he charged the importer a round £1000 to be on the safe side and, having placed a large chalk cross on the seat of his purple trousers, permitted him to pass through.

The Captain dithered, anxiously watching the departure of his cousin from the shed, when fortunately a disturbance in the dock, where it seemed that several of the gorillas were not sufficiently dead, distracted the customs men and gave him the chance to leap after the figure in the velvet suit.

"Mithras!" he cried. "Cousin! Wait!"

The portly art dealer whirled around. Captain Sparesbrook found himself staring into the barrel of a Coleman & Puxley .44 repeater with self targeting sights and automatic groin smasher.

"Charlotte de Maupassant, I presume," drawled his cousin.

And pulled the trigger.

The Gnostic Frying Pan

19

It was Juliette Thring's turn to mount guard with the machine gun in the turret on the northern elevation of Sparesbrook Manor that evening. Ever since the Captain's flight sixteen months before, they had kept an armed look-out at the post. Since the inconvenience of Charlotte de Maupassant's supposed attacks had coincidentally ceased with the departure of the Captain, they had resolved not let him back. In the first weeks, trigger happy, they had gunned down two post men, a meter reader, a coach load of old age pensioners on their way to the panda baiting at Leatherhead, a TV licence inspector and a serial murderer on his day off. None of them had proved on inspection to be Captain Sparesbrook so, a little conscience stricken, they had sent anonymous postal orders to the deceaseds' next of kin with a note promising to be more careful in future.

Juliette, who had been dreaming of the days when she was simple Miss Jubb, checkout girl and assistant roach scraper at the local supermarket, was startled when little Eric's teddy, which was leaning against the wall of the turret, leered at her and said, "You know, you're a real sexy kid, Juliette. You and me could have a good time, if you played your cards right. Say the word, Julie baby, and I'm yours."

"Strewth!" gasped Juliette.

"That's the word!" cried Egrah'nca, leaping.

There followed one of the most curious scenes in the whole of this curious history and the narrative, which fancies it can hold its own with a Muggoth Pit or an Alternative Universe, is frankly out of its class and doubts its capacity to do the affair justice. Picture yourself in a four foot by three foot turret, most of which is cluttered up with machine gun belts, not to mention the weapon itself. According to your taste, invest yourself in the person of an eighteen year old beauty with radiant eyes and a mystic husband, or a six inch teddy bear that hasn't seen the interesting side of the cathouses of P'nor'n for over two years, or even a machine gun if that's what turns you on. Now do your best to imagine what came next.

Half an hour later, Juliette opened her eyes, smiled and whispered, "Oh, that was beautiful."

The teddy bear eased himself up and sat back against the wall. He lit a cigarette, blew smoke into the dusk and murmured, "You weren't so bad, yourself, kiddo. Anytime you want an introduction to Andruta Tiservi, you let me know. I'll give you a reference."

"You're no ordinary teddy bear," Juliette whispered. She frowned through the darkening air at the glowing tip of his cigarette. "Who are you?"

There was no reply. Crawling closer, she discovered that the cigarette was resting on a window ledge. The teddy bear had gone.

Juliette began to sob.

So did Egrah'nca, when the effects of the prototype cerbo-snatch wore off and he reassembled on the table top before the gleaming smiles of the Magnarch of Verox.

"Explain yourself," invited the voice of his protector and friend. "I am sure you are anxious to enlighten me. I quiver with anticipation of your reply. What, I wonder, could be so desperate that it forces you to engage in carnal fol-de-rols with a native woman? Come, your message. I am all ears."

Egrah'nca refrained from casting that lie back at the Magnarch. Far from being all ears, his patron was largely teeth. He decided that now was not a good time to remind him.

Stealthily he reached for an end of the Nidro Force, with which he stood a chance of a sort even against the Magnarch, but the ribbon had gone. Several thousand years away, the charmingly tousled Juliette was tying it garter-wise around her upper leg, in memory of the supreme half hour of her life in the machine gun turret on top of Sparesbrook Manor.

"Of course," breathed the glutinous voice, "I accept that you are not wholly to blame for the fracas. A certain modified gibbon whose name I forget, indeed I remember him only as a tooth-ache, must take a posthumous share of the responsibility. In fact, I have a good mind to return through time," the voice quivered with rage, "and eat him again, the drivelling fool. But you, O Egrah'nca, you – Words fail me, my little friend. Tell me, what masterly plan had you in mind, when you allowed yourself to be separated from Eric Maresbreath? The real Eric Maresbreath, I mean, not that idiot child you've been hanging around for the last sixteen months, local time."

"Sixteen months?" Egrah'ca glass eyes blinked in bewilderment. "Never! A couple of weeks, at the most."

"Sixteen months," repeated the voice stickily. "No doubt you will claim that the severity of temporal relocation has scrambled your sense of duration. But that does not explain why you have allowed yourself to become the plaything of a witless infant."

"Now there I must beg to differ," Egrah'ca said. "She's at least eighteen."

"Not the trollop," snarled the voice of the Magnarch. "I refer to the female bratling who has usurped the name of Maresbreath."

Egrah'nca gulped nervously and wished he hadn't. Swallowing noises of any kind tended to cause unpleasant juices to flow from the Magnarch of Verox. Edging as much as the steel bands would allow from the river of treacle on the table, he said, "You mean, that's not the Guardian of the Earth? Well, that does explain quite a lot actually. But where's the real one, then?"

"Where, indeed?" sighed the voice. "While you were teasing that poor beast in the Muggoth Pits – incidentally I do apologise for our failure to informationalise you supply-wise on that one – your target defilleted and disintegrated." The Magnarch sighed. "We have modified virtually every creature known to science and still we seem unable to perform the simplest of tasks without error."

"It's like something out of Timora Garpatheny," said Egrah'nca, licking his lips anxiously as he tried to change the subject. Another mistake. Several oozy drops splattered his fur which begun to smoke. He whimpered bleakly. "Only instead of modified marmosets or whatever, she has these mechanicals things, what's she call 'em, 'confusers'?"

"Computers."

"No, I'm sure they're confusers. Anyway, one minute her characters are congratulating themselves because they've invented a confuser that can cock things up a million times faster and more thoroughly than five hundred humans, the next they're wondering why the unemployed are looting the streets of their cities."

"Well," said the voice, "I'm sure there will be other crises we can ignore for a nice literary discussion, so just now I see no need for us to situationlise confrontationwise over your mistakes. You just go back fieldside, sort things out and when you return we can, shall we say, chew the whole thing over? Hmm?"

"Mmm," said Egrah'nca. "Glug," he added, as a thick tide of juices overwhelmed him. Fortunately he was saved from immediate digestion by the reactivation of the cerbo-snatch. Hoorah!

20

Night fell over the river. Another day safely endured. How fortunate it had been when his cousin's gun had exploded and neatly severed the art dealer's head without damaging a shred of his clothing! It had been the work of a minute for Sparesbrook to strip the corpse of its white sweater and purple suit, to assume the garments, steal the cruiser and moor it here, the hold still packed with Seprophantine art treasures, on the banks of the Thames just below Stepney, at the wharfs by Goitre Lane.

Something too silent for a jet passed between him and the moon as he climbed the tarry steps to the catwalk and vanished over the roofs of Goitre Lane, leaving only the aroma of slime on the air. A moment of wet brown fear smeared over the Captain. He wiped it bravely aside. Why should the Owl-Thing be here? No doubt what he had seen was a glider, or a kite, or - He shook his head and, reaching the street, set off into the dark, wharf encumbered alleys in search of a bit of fun.

Egrah'nca was flung out of the cerbo-snatch and catapulted across Goitre Lane to fetch up with a horrible smack against an advertisement for Fluffo Wonder Tyres. Before he passed out he thought he saw for a fleeting moment what looked incredibly like Captain Sparesbrook in a filthy purple velvet suit chasing a rather common looking young woman in a plastic mac up a side alley, but that must surely have been a side-effect of time travel.

The number 11 bus pulled up at the stop outside the funeral parlour in Goitre Lane. When the bus doors opened, the morticians dropped their work and rushed to the windows, the bus conductor almost strangled himself with his satchel, and even the corpse on the embalming table twitched eagerly. Helena Phipps, for it is she, being accustomed to such tributes, smiled coolly and drifted away, leaving only the trace of her perfume on the grateful air.

She crossed the road and, suddenly, stooped down. Men in vests and braces at their parlour windows forgot the smell of sausages and their wives' complaints for the moment and suffering soul wrenching pangs of longing as they gawped at Helena stooping down. When she rose, not a man of them would have surrendered sausages, wives and pension for the chance to be the blue and yellow teddy bear which she had lifted from the pavement and now, with a tender smile, tucked into her bucket bag with her netball shorts.

Forty feet above her, on the roof of Weldon's Wharf, attracted by the golden brown gleam of Helena's knees, the Malcolm de Maupassant division of the Owl-thing swivelled round, clicked its beak in appreciation, and drooled.

Herbert Jubb, on the other hand, was weeping.

What, you may be wondering, was it like, really, to be Herbert Jubb, part-owner of the Owl-thing?

Imagine yourself, towards the dark end of a November afternoon, slightly overdressed and with bags of shopping in your hands, struggling up a hill while lorries roar past you in clouds of muck and old ladies keep getting in your way and abuse you when you try to sidle past them. You are wind tossed, damp and a little hot, and the top of your head prickles, and your knees ache arthritically. Then, as you stumble round the corner by the Temple, you glance up as usual at the lighted windows in the upper storey of the terrace in Goitre Lane and see, in the very act of struggling out of her tightest netball vest, Helena Phipps, the loveliest woman known to mankind. Just as the straining material is about to slide from that magnificent bust, a fool on a moped comes out of the alley by the dentists, blacks out from delayed shock, and smashes straight into you, hurling your shopping one way and you the other, till you fetch up with one leg either side of the bus-stop. For a moment, feeling the hard pole, you think that a miracle has happened. Then you lose consciousness and awake in an ICU, only to learn that by a bureaucratic error you have been transplanted into the body of a migrant filing clerk from Abyssinia with cold sores and an interest in frogs.

Imagine all that and you will have the beginnings of a glimmering of how Herbert had felt that evening, as with a belly full of indigestible bishop, he had flapped across the moony sky over the eastern reaches of the metropolis. Whereas Malcolm de Maupassant seemed reconciled to his embodiment in the Owl-thing, and positively enjoyed the dinner arrangements, poor Herbert as the months wormed by had grown more and more despondent, yearning for the vanished pleasures of feet, and a warm forge, and the occasional rude phone call from his foster daughter. Trapped in the monster with a cannibalistic and disenfranchised accountant, his future seemed desolate indeed.

A change in the miasma had brought him back to the present. He found himself huddled on the roof of an east end wharf. De Maupassant had brought him there before. It meant another night dining off immigrants. Herbert Jubb, who hated foreign food, had begun to weep.

Malcolm gave him some sort internal nudge and drew his attention to the woman in the street below. He stopped weeping. Now that looked a good deal more tasty than some bloody curry flavoured docker with too much pomade in his hair. On hushed wings, the Owl-thing leapt from the roof and swept down, down, down towards the unguarded back of Helena Phipps, loveliest Owl's supper in the universe.

Separated from the forthcoming excoriation of Helena Phipps by the thickness of a wall and an obscene mural, the acolytes of the Demi-Urge, convened as always in the Goitre Lane Temple, hurriedly tucked away their Maltesers and copies of Women's Weekly as the house lights dimmed and, in green satin French knickered splendour there appeared on the dais before them the bulbous shape of their visiting Arch Priestess, Mrs. Aramintha Gristle. Very different indeed from the days when the old building had been a humble mule skinners was what followed, and in the interest of economic security the narrative has agreed to draw a veil over the early part of the proceedings.

Tugging aside the veil, we are in time to see the assembled sisters put away their prayer mats, razors and PVC anoraks, and resume their seats. Above them, her two magenta tassels still twirling,

Aramintha summons a pair of servers, who drag away the used and twitching remains of the communion supper, a retired naval officer from Stoke Newington who had misguidedly enquired of Mrs. Gristle whether she could direct him to Victoria Coach Station. Then, commanding silence with a flash of her spectacles, she announced:

"Gentlewomen! Tonight we have the special joy of inducting a new sister into the priesthood of our order. It is not necessary, I am sure, for me to dwell on the heart warming response of the women of England to the call of the Demi-Urge. You all know the extent to which the good news of His Coming has captured the hearts, and in many cases the liver, kidneys, spleen, entrails and gonads too, of this great and blessed people. And now it is my pleasant duty before we celebrate the Rite of Gorum with a squadron of Icelandic marines specially blinded by Miss Wordsworth -" a slim lady in a silver tabard blushed and nodded to her beaming sisters "- it is my duty, I say, to welcome into the fold our new sister!"

With a clap of her hands, which caused sparks to fly from her many rings, Mrs. Gristle ordered the opening of the great bronze door at the rear of the stage. Pausing only to sacrifice a naked youth at the ceremonial owl-pellet, now jewel encrusted and ensconced in a sandal wood coffer on a bed of squirrel skin, she stepped back and assisted into the glare of the spot lights a figure wrapped from head to foot in a white sheet.

"Gentlewomen!" she cried again. "Fresh from the mysteries, sanctified and pure, I rejoice to give you -" She tugged at a hidden cord "- our newest convert, Empress of Witches, and Mother of Owl-things, the blessed Charlotte de Maupassant."

The sheet had dropped to the lino, revealing the proud lineaments of the woman whose efforts had single-handedly reduced the once celebrated Captain Sparesbrook to a life of cheese and art treasures on a cruiser in the Thames. An unusual woman, she was, strangely enough, not tellingly beautiful, nor did she wear erotic undies or play netball. But Charlotte de Maupassant had passed through the Mysteries of the Demi-Urge in the basement of the second hand clothes shop across the road, and would never be the same again.

Wrapped now in a gold shift, Charlotte stood to attention before the assembly and intoned after the Arch Priestess the words of the oath, ending with the awesome cry, "May the Owl devour me!"

"And may its talons strip our virginity!" responded the congregation fervently.

"Gentlewomen! Salute our new sister!"

A shrill hurricane of applause, whistles, screams and ululations filled the echoing vaults of the former mule skinners. Charlotte de Maupassant received their congratulations with a reserved smile. After all, it is not every mother who has the chance to observe the deification of her disgusting son. But she smiled, too, because with the power of the Church of the Demi-Urge behind her, she knew that her plans for the annexation of the universe, not to mention the destruction of Captain H. 'Geronimo' Sparesbrook, had grown a little nearer to maturity.

21

In the machine gun emplacement on top of Sparesbrook Manor and, though she did not know it, in full view of the infra-red telescopes bristling from the windows of the Violet Pring Hebbenthwaite Sunset Memorial Home, the deserted Juliet had dried her tears on the Nidro Force and then, in an excess of pretty emotion, tied it garter fashion above her left knee. Having quickly pulled on the clothing which her encounter with Egrah'nca had scattered about the turret like the result of a dog's encounter with a tax return, she lifted the intercom and said, "Turret to hall, turret to hall. Come on, you lazy pigs, it's someone else's turn to roost up here in this bat infested nook."

The intercom crackled faintly, like a roasting altar boy, and by some atmospheric freak picked up a snatch of parameter tramp doxo, so that the surprised Juliette found herself being addressed as a mingolo and invited to a spag-hogger in Lemuria next Wednesday week (dress optional). Before she could reply, the wave-lengths drifted with the swirl of the galaxy and silence returned. A chill finger of dread inserted itself down the back of her blouse and playfully twanged her bra strap.

Frowning, she hefted the machine gun. which weighed only slightly less than the dead horse on which they had been dining for the past few months, and crept down the spiral steps to the manor house below. The Nidro Force, unaccustomed to finding itself tightly bound about

The Gnostic Frying Pan

the warm flesh of a lady's upper leg, began to get very hot under the collar.

Darkness and silence greeted her like an old friend. The house appeared to be deserted. Even the grandfather clock in the hall had stopped. Her finger on the trigger of the automatic weapon, she crossed the green tiles, crept to the door, which stood open to the dying day, and checked the surroundings. The parsnip beds, overgrown now, and rank with S'narg plants from the crumbling conservatory, whispered in a late breeze hurrying from sunwards over the decaying yews. No-one moved, not a mouse, not an aged manservant, not so much as a little Eric Maresbreath. In the shadow of the rhododendrons, Juliette edged down to the potting shed and confirmed that it was clear. Encrusted with brilliant red flies, the carcase of Dennis Wipers hung from hooks in the ceiling. Most of the good meat had long since gone through the mincer but Juliette did not fail to observe that the haunch Deirdre had been saving for Blessed Magotte's Day had recently been severed. So – they had gone, all of them. Deirdre Horne, her child, and even her own husband, Edward Pausanias Thring, slinking off with the best cut of horse meat while she mounted guard (among other things) in the turret. The wicked ingratitude of it!

With a sudden yelp, she dropped the machine gun and tumbled to the ground, writhing like a woman with a ferret up her petticoat. In fact it was no ferret but the Nidro Force which, enflamed beyond endurance by its latest position in life, had attempted to have its ribbonish way with her.

Quickly recovering her composure, she managed with some difficulty to extract the pink satin and transfix it with a garden fork. Snake-like, it coiled, thrashed and then, not quite so much like a snake, emitted a bolt of hadronic ire which vaporised the fork, a passing tern, a DC10 on its way to Sri Lanka with a cargo of plastic potties, a Stealth Black Space Shuttle, a spy satellite belonging to the Duchy of Lancaster and, proceeding vertically across the immensities of the cosmos, some several hundred thousand years later winded the Goat-horror of Vharg as it prepared to crush First Lieutenant Tamsin Boucher of the Dyzlene Security Force between its giant mammeries. In this universe, nothing is ever wasted, except perhaps the Goat-horror of Vharg.

Recognising that there was more to the ribbon than eighteen inches of pink satin, Juliette overturned the rainwater barrel on it and, cleverly taking advantage of the ensuing billows of steam, leapt over the hedge and made it to the lane which ran alongside that corner of the Manor grounds under the wheeling bats and trees whose twigs seemed to clutch at her like her husband's hands.

Behind her, on the hillside below the asylum, Sparesbrook Manor stood cold and creaking in the dusk. There was no sound, except where a S'narg plant devoured a partridge in the vegetable garden, and nothing moved. Nothing – except, yes, there, a mouse is dragging something long, and pink, and damp, and ribbonish towards a hole in the wainscot. The Nidro Force is about to become a home improvement to a family of rodents.

And Juliette? She ran through the night to the river Dymph, a stream and tributary of the mighty Unar, where she found the punt that was to bear her during the next three days away from Amblebroth to the great waters of the North Sea, and from thence into that unknown land beyond the fiery waves where the sun goes down, those black peaks the old sailors tell of at nights in the safety of bingo halls and library reading rooms, the three sharp peaks of that island you may glimpse, if your eyesight is twisted enough, silhouetted against the red disc of the sun as it slides into the sea - but on which, sail they never so far in conventional craft, none but the elect may set a venturesome foot.

Back in the silent Manor, the door in the front of the grandfather clock fell with a sudden clatter to the tiles.

"It's all right, she's gone," said a voice, and a moment later creeping from the hidey-hole behind the clock came the smutty figure of little Eric Maresbreath, playing with a haunch of horse-meat, followed by her mother, dragging the quivering form of Edward Thring, his body bound with bell ropes and his mouth sealed with duct tape, his rheumy eyes writhing independently with some furious emotion.

"I'm sorry we had to restrain you. But it was for your own good. Will you promise to behave yourself now in front of the infant deity?" Deirdre demanded.

Thring made some noises behind his duct tape. They didn't sound a lot like a promise to behave. Deirdre banged his head on the floor until he felt better, then uncovered his mouth. "She's gone now, the shameless hussy," she murmured soothingly.

"And good riddance," snarled the aged manservant. "How could she? How could she cuckold me with a blue and yellow teddy bear?"

Raging again, he burst from his bonds, leapt up, ripped the intercom from the wall and smashed it to pieces with an antique brass ram-cobbler. "Juliette! Juliette!" he wailed, sounding for moment uncannily like a four man pop band from Blackburn. "Oh, Juliette! Why didn't you switch the bloody intercom off?"

With a desolate wail, he whirled the ram-cobbler about his head, showering the terrified mother and her child with lumps of chandelier. "I'll find her yet," he screamed. "I'll hunt her down and destroy her! One week, that's all." He turned and glowered at them, as though Deirdre and her precious babe were responsible for his misfortunes. "One week," he promised again. "And if I haven't found the deceitful strumpet at the expiration of that period, with this - " He smacked the ram-cobbler into a marble statue of Dame Brenda North of Kircaldy which bumped on three stairs, then smashed on the tiles, "I shall compose myself into the state of tachomimsa, and – Glu'ng!"

And having uttered a frightful snarl, the aged loon dashed into the night, with about as much chance of tracking down Juliette to the nameless isles of the sun as Captain Sparesbrook, after a year long diet of cheese, had of catching the female in the plastic mac in the alley up the back of Goitre Lane.

So the universe has one week of existence left to it. One more week in which to read Proust, hear every note of the Ring of the Nibelung, really get started on that play about playboy adventurer Hugh Gaitskill, learn the shawm, come to grips with quantum physics, and then – boom. The whole lot, Proust, Bach, Gaitskill, quasars, quarks, mesons and you, turned into a smear of intergalactic Ready-Brek around the gob of eternal nothingness.

"Eric! Holy one!" Deirdre Horne screamed at her infant saviour. "It's the end of the world. Come on! Do your stuff! Save it! Save it!"

Little Eric Maresbreath, who was sitting on the floor crunching bits of the statue of Brenda, the celebrated Scottish Leg Artist, gave her mother a glance of shrivelling contempt.

"What makes you think this lot is worth saving?"

The Mother of the Messiah fainted.

22

Unaware that the Universe had just seven days left of its run, the BBC screened episode one of its new ninety-eight part drama serial, *Mobcaps over Middlesbrough*. The advertising agency Bender Calicut Frères launched their campaign to make dead gorillas the Gift for the Discerning (they'd had a consignment hanging about for nearly eighteen months, after some trouble at the docks) and Helena Phipps, hearing the whoosh of a falling body in the smoky gloom, turned in Goitre Lane, looked up, and smiled.

The smile of Helena Phipps makes the Mona Lisa look like a leprous tart smirking at you from an upper window in Old Compton Street. The smile of Helena Phipps makes of a dim brick Gehenna like Goitre Lane a fresh meadow in Illyria, where daffodils dance, and white stallions race the wind, and slime-feathered Owl-things overshoot their target and fetch up with a squelching wallop against the side of a derelict warehouse two hundred yards further down the road.

Tossing her lovely head, Helena Phipps ran up the steps of number 143 and let herself in. The door closed behind her and at once the meadow turned back into tarmac, the flowers became dog turds and fag packets, and the stallions a couple of rabid mongrels getting stuck into each other under a lamp post. The derelict warehouse remained a derelict warehouse and the Owl-thing, sliding in a sticky glob down the wall, a faintly whimpering casualty. But of course it hadn't heard about the end of the universe yet, either.

No more had Egrah'nca and, quite frankly, he wouldn't have given a bog-scrotcher's fart if he had. Any week that includes the delights of Juliette Thring and a trip in the bucket bag of Helena Phips might just as well be the last, because anything else would be an anti-climax. For a moment the thought soured his ecstasy – it was all downhill from now on. Then a soft and beautiful hand closed about his furry middle, riddling him with thrills of authentic bliss, and placed him gently on a perfumed pillow. With difficulty Egrah'nca prevented himself from squeaking manically with joy.

Helena Phipps was taking him to bed with her. He doubted that his nylon and kapok frame would survive the incomprehensible pleasures to come but there was no-one on earth who would have exchanged them for the promise of a hundred years added existence in the tedious world.[16] When he felt someone else slide into bed on the other side of him, his confidence in his luck was so great he knew it must be Juliette Thring.

"My dear Mrs. de Maupassant," the Arch Priestess, Aramintha Gristle roared, for it was difficult to make herself heard over the groans of the spent marines as they dragged themselves towards merciful extinction in the river, "do let me offer you another posset."

"Most kind." Charlotte nipped a candied eyeball in her crimson nails and popped it between

---

[16] Particularly if they knew that the world in question was down to its last 168 hours.

The Stone Unturned

her lips. "Delicious," she murmured, wiping a tickle of syrup from her chin. "I can scarcely believe, your Holiness, that this is the normal treatment for a new member of your, I mean, our auspicious order."

"Indeed not, my dear," the Priestess crooned. "Usually you would be hurled naked into a pit of boiled rat droppings for twenty four hours and then flagellated with blackthorn twigs to drive the error out of you. But I am quite sure that in your case, my dear Mrs. de Maupassant, nothing of the sort will be necessary. Another jellied winkle, my dear?"

While Charlotte nibbled what had, prior to its immersion in gelatine, been the pride and joy of Regimental Sergeant major Alban Foxe-Terrier, her mind assessed the words and, more importantly, the tone, of the woman who sprawled on the divan beside her. And arrived at a disquieting conclusion.

Despite the flattery and tit-bits, there was iciness, there was more than a hint of suspicion. Had she perhaps intuited that Charlotte de Maupassant had joined the order, not for love of a supposed Demi-Urge which she knew to be effectively nothing more than two men in an owl suit, but as part of her plan to rule the cosmos? Oh, and to destroy Captain Sparesbrook, his staff and all of his relations on the side?

"...with a duck and a small tin of enamel," concluded the Priestess, and burst into hideous laughter, in which Charlotte was quick to join.

Invisibly, intangibly, sticky ropes of time froth draped themselves about the former flensing pit of the muleskinners in Goitre Lane, now transformed into a luxury boudoir with en-suite sacrificial flame for visiting Arch Priestesses. The two ladies on the Regency style divans loosened their silver tabards and gorged themselves on exotic military delicacies. For a while only the crunching of crackling and the slurp of grease filled the reeking chamber.

Then the Priestess, casting aside an unfinished slice of Senior Aircraftsman, belched and said, "And now, Mrs. de Maupassant, if you are replete, perhaps we can get down to business."

Charlotte hauled herself into a sitting position and belched even more effectively than her hostess. "What business is that?"

Mrs. Gristle chuckled. Her thumb carelessly brushed a concealed switch in the belt of her harem trousers.

At once titanium vices clamped on the wrists and ankles of Charlotte de Maupassant, spread-eagling her on the divan. In the same moment, with a grinding of rather badly maintained gears, the room began to descend into the depths of the earth. The Priestess's laughter rose like an hysterical loco entering a tunnel.

"Did you imagine I do not know you?" she shrieked, slapping the captive cheeks with a piece of WAAF. "Wasn't I your best customer once, at The Permanent Stud,[17] before you made the one gross error of your life?"

"Of course," groaned Charlotte. "I know you now. You went under the name of – Mrs. Rosemary Maresbreath."

"Do not breath that foul nomenclature in this sacred fane," the woman bellowed. "I do not wish

---

[17] The high class establishment for the entertainment of enervated business women formerly kept by Charlotte de Maupassant (vide Chapter 13).

to be reminded of him, the despicable Eric, the most faithless creature ever to steal a maiden's heart and feed it to his whippets. He deserted me, you know, the graceless swine, left me one dreadful night, halfway through *Danube, River of My Dreams*, as we sang together on the stage of the Henbolt Theatre, Herne Bay. Later I received a divorce petition with, scrawled on the back, some nonsense about being elected Guardian of the Earth. Guardian of the Earth!" she chortled through her tears. "Eric couldn't guard a bag of dog vomit. That's why I've brought you here, Mrs. de Maupassant."

The room had stopped descending now.

"Together we shall instigate the most monstrous reign of terror since the devil-possessed Stephenson inflicted British Rail upon the unsuspecting world. My faithless spouse shall learn how powerless he is to Guard the World from our terrible visitations. I need your supreme incantational powers, Mrs. de Maupassant. Either you bow to my demands and become my assistant and love-toy, or - " She smiled horribly as she opened the door of the chamber – "it's the Muggoth Pits for you. I'll leave you, now, to think it over."

And so saying she stepped through the door and fell two hundred feet to the bottom of the lift shaft in which the room had unfortunately chanced to jam.

Jam was the word which came to Charlotte de Maupassant's mind when, having oozed out of her bonds and re-constituted herself at the doorway, she peered down at the mortal parts of Aramintha Gristle on the concrete below. Still entangled in the webs of time froth, she found herself longing for a few cream crackers and a very long spoon.

Meanwhile, she was stuck in an odorous room several hundred feet below the surface of East London with perhaps enough provisions to keep a person alive for eight days, and another 159 hours to go before glu'ng, not that she knew about that, yet.

Helping herself to one of the late Priestess's *Disques Bleus*, she sat down on the divan and began to think.

23

After smashing at full throttle into the wall of Stimboom & Corkmat's Herbal Tobacco repository, as was, in Goitre Lane (and for the chance of a smile from Helena Phipps, who would not gladly have done the same?) the Owl-thing dripped down the brickwork and collapsed into a soggy senseless mess on the railway line below.

Awoken by the drumming of the rails which presaged the passing of the midnight cadaver train to the Fenchurch marshes, the Owl-thing crawled in the nick of time off the line, losing a few slimy feathers, flapped erratically into the night air, and hid itself away in what used to be the directors' washroom, where it sustained itself by nibbling at the bones of Messrs Stimboom & Corkmat, who had committed joint suicide in 1966 after the asset strippers failed to take over their business.

It was not long before Herbert Jubb, fortified by a couple of crunchy skulls, realised that the Malcolm de Maupassant areas of their joint brain remained void of consciousness. The possibilities of the situation immediately struck him, unless it was a section of rusty pipe falling from the roof. Using one of the arms which remained under his control, Herbert smashed open the window and looked down through the stench of a London night at the oily Thames far below. Now was the chance to do the decent thing. Painfully, he hopped onto the window ledge, folded his wing across his eye and, with a whispered, "Forgive me, Juliette" hurled himself and the cataleptic Malcolm into the void.

On the way down he changed his mind and began to flap frantically but with only one viable wing he might just as well have retained his self respect.

Egrah'nca lay, burning with shame and fury, on the carpet in Helena Phipps's bedroom. His slight disappointment on discovering that the third occupant of their bed was not, after all, the radiant Juliette Thring but only his target and former Guardian of the Earth, Eric Maresbreath, had turned to a more nearly fatal emotion when the naked fool had cast him from the pillow and begun to tear Helena's Smith & Wesson's brushed nylon from her body with the finesse of an aroused gorilla.

"Swine!" raged Egrah'nca silently. "Oh, would that I had not allowed Juliette to remove the Nidro Force from around my neck. I could have subjected the sod to a blast that would turn him into a cloud of putrid electrons and fanned him up the chimney. Oh, the unutterable beast, look what he's doing to her now. It's no good. I can't stand it."

When the fangs of the small blue and yellow teddy bear met in the flesh of his buttock, Eric Maresbreath dropped Helena with a scream and then clutched in terror at his privates, perhaps fearing that his willy had been wrenched off as she fell. Fortunately, it had not, which was some consolation when Egrah'nca got him in the Atlantean cjebus grip and hurled him into the wardrobe. Flailing, he emerged seconds later festooned with the various bits and pieces picked up by Helena on her various modelling assignments, including the interesting item illustrated on page 17 of this year's Harlotella catalogue, whose red latex cups impeded his vision so that he feet, already hampered by a tangle of stockings, became trapped in Helena's discarded nightie. He toppled forward, cracking his head on a bed post, and rolled heavily against the dressing table, which fell on him. Still, endowed with some of the superhuman strength of his former calling, the hapless amnesiac ripped his way out of the pretty bonds of satin, silk and latex. He glared across the room at the bed, where the astonished but ravishing figure of Helena Phipps knelt on the sheets with an eiderdown covering the less interesting bits of her nakedness.

Eric reached behind him and produced a bronze statuette of Helena, an award from a grateful committee in Southwold.

"Now," snarled Eric Maresbreath, "I don't know who you are, but let's see what you're made of."

Egrah'nca, who knew very well what he was made of and had no desire to see it blowing about the bedroom, licked his lips nervously and tried to make contingency plans as, bronze figure upraised, the Guardian of the Earth (retired) advanced upon him.

When the Owl-thing smacked into the warehouse wall, a good deal of time-froth impregnated slime sprayed off its wings and showered, among others, Captain Sparesbrook in the alley below, immediately altering his intentions towards the plastic-mac'd siren who fled giggling before him up the steps of the railway bridge.

At the top, she turned and called, "Hey! Wanna eat some pussy?"

The Captain's eyes glowed crimson in the dark alley.

"Oh, yes," he slavered. "Oh, my word, yes. Oh yes, indeed."

The siren, an American student on an exchange scholarship at the Shadwell Stair College of Temporary Appliantology, who supplemented her grant by selling herself to sailors, slinkily descended the iron stairway towards the whiskery old guy in the stained purple suit who awaited her.

"Hi, there," she breathed. My name's Betty-Sue K. Fry Inc.[18] What's your name, honey-lamb?"

Restraining himself from devouring on the spot the peach and candyfloss meal-on-a-stiletto which pressed so mouth wateringly against his old limbs, the Captain gave his name as Mulciber Tang. "I have a cabin cruiser moored nearby," he said hoarsely. "Would you care to come aboard. I have a collection of Sepraphontine art treasures unequalled in East London."

"Baby," breathed siren, running her fingers up the front of his cheese streaked sweater, "I ain't interested in no old art treasures. Guess this little pleasure boat of yours might happen to possess a bunk, though?"

"It might," the Captain agreed. "And a dining table," he added.

The siren squirmed. "Oh, I ain't fussed none where you do me," she purred, "just so long as you do me nice. And hand over the cash afterwards," she added quickly. "Oh and, hey, you got any food

---

[18] The 'Inc' was on the advice of her accountant, who specialised in bodies corporate.

in there, I'd sure be glad of a bite. I'm kinda starving."

"A bite?" beamed the Captain, leading her back towards the jetty. "Oh, I think that can be arranged. Oh, my word, yes. Oh yes, indeed."

24

Admirers of that great free nation, the U S of A, will be gratified to learn at once that Betty-Sue K Fry Inc is not scheduled to perform the office of light snack to the ravening Captain Sparesbrook. Statophobes, however, should find something to please them in the manner of her deliverance, when the narrative has steeled itself sufficiently to recount the details. Until that happy moment, the narrative slips back to a certain boudoir suspended nearly a quarter of a mile beneath the sewers of Goitre Lane, where we left the bewildering Charlotte de Maupassant, attempting to her plot herself back into business. The narrative, which may have allowed its obsession with underwear and plump sirens to get the better of it lately, will perhaps feel a little healthier in the presence of this commanding but refreshingly unerotic woman.

The trap that could hold a Charlotte de Maupassant had not yet been invented. It was the work of a moment for the matchless witch to transform herself into eight hundred tons of buttered crumpets, the weight of which snapped the room's rusty cables like uncooked spaghetti, and then to become for a few seconds the sound of a combine harvester in order not to be mangled when the plummeting chamber dashed on the rocks two hundred feet later. Reconstituting herself, Charlotte peered about her and discovered that she stood at the mouth of a white-tiled tunnel which led either into a public lavatory or the unknown precincts of the subterranean city beneath the streets of London.

The Stone Unturned

Generating her own lambency, Charlotte moved warily into the tunnel. Empress of Witches though some had acclaimed her,[19] Charlotte de Maupassant confessed to the taste of fear (a mixture, she found, of dirty pond water and tadpoles). She edged stooping between the wild shadows on the walls into the nameless dark.

Or rather, as she discovered when her glow illuminated a large blue and white signboard, the named dark.

"Scaliselarga-on-Sea," she read, "Welcomes Careful Divers."

A poster had been nailed to the bottom of the signboard. A rather poor quality photograph of a blue and yellow teddy bear surmounted the inscription: "Wanted: Boiled or Stewed. Two thousand mivvels will be paid to any person submitting information to the Keepers of the Muggoth Pits leading to the capture of the above illustrated snack." It was signed by Heg'naar'n Stag'naavrk, Company Secretary, Muggoth Pits of Scaliselsarga Ltd, Registered Office, 33, Caxton Avenue, Eastbourne.

Charlotte flickered in and out of existence for thirty seconds, unable to control her own being, so horrible were the emotions which the notice had struck from her heart. Not half an hour ago she had been congratulating herself on her own superiority, on the subtlety and certainty of her schemes, of her grip upon the reins of chance and necessity.

---

[19] The exception being the Edith Grove coven which favoured a dissected toad in a glass case in Sydney Museum, who they said was Tintinabula Smoyles, the great Maori conjuress and mistress of Beelzebul, caught in an unfortunate moment of inattention by an amateur amphibilogist from the University of Queensland.

And now, o irony, she trembled alone upon the frontier of Scaliselsarga, land of doom, while winds blew like the fingers of customs officers about her body and the mingled scents of the sea and the Muggoth Pits assaulted her nostrils. What, she wondered fearfully, was the connection between the late Aramintha Gristle and Heg'naar'n Stag'naavrk? And how would Heg'naar'n Stag'naavrk react when he learnt that Aramintha now took the shape of a reddish jelly on the underside of her own boudoir? Was there any possibility that he might be grateful?

Tucking her robe into her knickers, she waded forward through the pool of water that reeked and swashed about the floor of the tunnel. When, some minutes later, she heard, quite close at hand, the whoop of tiny horns, she found herself wishing devoutly that she was back in the Chamber of Mysteries. At least that didn't smell of rotting camels.

Before we accompany Charlotte de Maupassant any further into the murk of Scaliselsarga, and to be quite honest the narrative is not at all sure that it wants to go, it is time to stop and sort out the implications in the distortions of the temporal frame which have occurred in Goitre Lane tonight.

Had we the benefit of an Atlantean time-window, like the one in the airfield next to the Magnarch of Verox's holiday flatlet in Gorpul dül Mimpoth, we could pop back to the moment when the Owl-thing hit the warehouse like a high velocity cow pat and measure from there, for it was at that moment the dilations and contractions began. One consequence is that, although for Herbert Jubb the night has advanced to the moment when he leaps suicidally from the directors' lavvie on the top floor of the Herbal Tobacco repository, it has for Captain Sparesbrook and the plump plastic-mac'd Betty Sue K. Fry Inc. not yet reached the identical moment when they tumble giggling into the galley of cousin Mithras's cabin cruiser, moored at the Goitre Lane jetty. Egrah'nca has rudely awoken from his dream of bliss in the bed of sensational Helena Phipps, an event which in an unwarped universe would have been roughly coterminous with Charlotte de Maupassant's discovery of his portrait a quarter of a mile away, as the dead crow drops. Far enough away from Goitre Lane to be unaffected by the labouring womb of time, Deirdre and little Miss Eric Maresbreath sleep fretfully under a bramble bush, tired out by their pursuit of Edward Thring. Thring, though, has without realising it stumbled into an eddying time phase and is being sucked inexorably towards Goitre Lane, although he thinks he is on a train bound for Euston Station.[20]

Now, to rejoin Charlotte de Maupassant, in the watery maze below London.

When the first thin strains of horn-voices sounded, she had begun to run, slipping and reeling through the shin-deep pools. Her brain sought among spells for a suitable response to the situation. She had just remembered a really snappy one when her brow came into contact with an iron girder, quite invisible in the shadowy passage, and without a sound she slipped senseless into the water. The

---

[20] It is just possible that Thring has been diverted not by an eddy of time but by Eddy O'Thyme, the points operator at Finsbury Park junction.

horn-voices whooped triumphantly. Waves began to break over the floating body of the Empress of Witches as something huge surged up the tunnel towards her.

Also tumbling towards water, the Owl-thing flapped its one good wing and wailed pitifully. Malcolm de Maupassant, regaining consciousness, was for a moment aware of rushing air, then he and Jubb and their feathery carapace smashed with a noise like a soup kitchen falling into a bath through the roof of the cabin cruiser moored at the jetty below the warehouse and, with the confusing glimpse of a man in a shabby purple suit shaking tomato ketchup over the belly of a plump siren in a plastic mac to entertain them, departed via the bilges and plummeted into the depths of the Thames.

So did the cabin-cruiser, which left Captain Sparesbrook and his little pudding in a tricky position. Washed clean of time-froth, and a trier when it came to matters erotic, the Captain, undeterred by the extreme difficulty of the position, made a splendid attempt to have her anyway, and might have succeeded, if a crate of Seprophantine art treasures hadn't bobbed up between his legs, negating his interest in sirens for some time to come. Drowning magnificently, he wallowed in the muddy waves and might have cheated Charlotte de Maupassant of her revenge, had not the porpoise like Betty-Sue borne him on her back across the river to the house boats moored against the opposite bank. Having heaved him up onto the deck of a deserted hulk, she kicked his stomach until he brought the assortment of indescribable things he had swallowed, relieved him of his wallet and,

The Stone Unturned

shaking the dregs from her plastic mac, slipped away into the night in search of sailors.

Some time later the Captain arose and took a few faltering steps. The wormy deck gave way and tipped him into the hold beneath.

In order to understand why an antique brass ram-cobbler now flashed from the shadows to crumple with a hollow clang on the Captain's head, it is necessary to paddle back up the time stream yet again to the moment when the Owl-thing connected with the warehouse wall at the end of Goitre Lane. Once more the Captain's crimson eyes observe the descent of his plump siren down the steps of the railway bridge, under which roars the train with its macabre load for Fenchurch marshes. On a heap of carcases in the third van from the back the snoozing Edward Pausanias Thring is jolted awake as the driver, sure that he can see a loathsome glob of slime and feathers crawling on the track, slams on the emergency brake and screeches to a stop in the cutting just the other side of the warehouse. By the time he has finished being accused of gross negligence by the guard, whose tomato soup has spilled all over his new Mothercare catalogue, the sleepy Thring has mistaken the grime and slag covered embankment for Euston Station and reeled dozily away with his ram-cobbler under his arm, looking for the buffet.

While the Owl-thing shuffles up the stairs towards the directors' facilities, from which it must yet again hurl itself in Jubbish despair, Thring realises his mistake, but is too late to reboard the train which is already snarling out of the cutting and picking up speed as it thunders away into the night. Goitre Lane, that whirlpool of incompletely explained cosmic forces, has sucked another wanderer into its toils.

Aimlessly now, for he doubts his Juliette will be here, though he had hopes of finding her at the buffet in Euston Station, the cheated Thring mopes away into the night, crosses the river by the Hillier Parry bridge and is surprised to encounter a rather squelchy siren in a plastic mac, leaning against a lamppost at the corner of the street. Enquiring of her the nearest way to a bed and a clean handkerchief, he is startled to hear her tale of the crazed gentleman in the purple suit who has just attempted to make her his main meal of the day and now lies on the deck of a house boat half an alley away.

Swayed by her tearful pleas, Thring went in search of the cannibal lunatic and, observing him in the act of apparently eating his way through the deck of the house boat, sprang into the bowels of the vessel and cobbled him as he dropped through.

Even as the musical clang died in the foetid air of the bilges, Thring recognised the alleged anthropophagus as none other than his beloved employer, Captain H. 'Geronimo' Sparesbrook. Tears burst from his eyes as he cradled the groaning man in his arms and spilled on the wounded cranium but they had no medicinal properties whatsoever and within a few minutes, hugged and possibly stifled against the blue pin striped jacket and jade green shirt of his old retainer, the Captain ceased his unequal tussle with the blood clots in his brain, gasped an indistinguishable word (which might have been 'Geronimo!') and died.

25

"Wait!" was the clearly distinguishable word which Egrah'nca bellowed as Eric Maresbreath did nothing to conceal his intention of reducing the teddy bear to fluff and stuffing with a statuette of his beloved. "Eric! Don't you know me? It's your little teddy! Don't you remember?"

For a moment, Eric faltered, a short-lived memory of green lollies and tricycles and Bergamot & Patchouli candles rippling in his amnesiac brain. It didn't halt him, but it did give Egrah'nca a chance to jump over Helena's legs and scuttle up the chimney.

"Come down from there, you little furry bastard," Eric roared. Soot smothered his next remark. He backed away, coughing.

"Helena!" boomed the greatly magnified voice of the bear, "make the fool put that pricelessly beautiful work of art down and tell him to listen to me."

Eric dropped the statuette and slumped weeping down on the bed. "That little viper bit my arse," he sobbed, as Helena soothingly wrapped her legs around him and kissed his ear.

Encouraged by the absence of rage, Egrah'nca summoned up his now inconsiderable powers and said, "Eric, listen to me. Don't struggle, don't get upset, don't panic. Just listen to me. I want you to cast your mind back, Eric, to the days sixteen months ago when you and I were chums, Eric. Do you remember? Those days in the secret chamber on top of the Tesco building in the Edgware Road, our

The Gnostic Frying Pan

plans to guard the Earth. Those stories you used to tell me, that time you descended into the extinct volcano to defeat the Goible Mercenaries who had entered our space time in order to kidnap Norwich City Council – surely you haven't forgotten that, Eric? Eric, the Earth depends on you. The Empress of Witches is abroad, and things have been seen walking in the woods above Perivale. Can you sit by and let the menace triumph, Eric? Eric?"

Lifting his lips momentarily from Helena's bosom, Eric Maresbreath murmured, "What's that row in the chimney? Somebody dropped an i-Pod from an airliner, do you think?"

Helena did not reply, which was hardly surprising, so occupied was she with more pressing matters, and soon the room was silent, apart from gasps of pleasure from the pair on the bed and the hollow boom of Egrah'nca up the chimney.

Another of the world's last hours, and then another, slipped off like a stripper's stockings. The day stood before Goitre Lane in the nakedness of dawn, the sun a great red nipple pressing against the spire of the temple. Light explored the crannies of the street, touching the still gently twining limbs of Helena Phipps and her love, skimming the surface of the Thames which this morning has a slick of slime and a feather or two in addition to the normal traffic, and even wriggling into the decaying hulk of a house boat on the opposite back, where a glazed eyed manservant cradles the corpse of his beloved employer and reckons up the hours before he can compose himself into the state of tachomimsa. Unfortunately he has forgotten his calculator and gets the answer hopelessly wrong.

The Stone Unturned

The narrative apologises in advance to all readers and especially to the Owl-thing, which has surely suffered enough, but regrets that it is once more necessary to clamber back up the rusty rungs of time to that familiar moment in the middle of the previous night when the Jubb-de Maupassant partnership, blinded by the smile of Helena Phipps, totally mistimed its pounce and sailed at close to the speed of sound into the side of the warehouse by the railway line. Train spotters may be glad of the chance to observe the passing of the midnight goods to Fenchurch marshes, especially as the locomotive at the front was a pre-war Pillager class 0-4-0 still in the livery of the LNER, the dear old Attila the Hun. More numerous, perhaps, if no more enthusiastic, fans of plump siren Betty-Sue K Fry Inc will seize the opportunity to gloat again through her plastic mac. And the millions who enjoy a good suicide will be brought cheering to their feet as we find ourselves, not for the first time, at that turning point in the history where the plummeting Owl-thing interrupted captain Sparesbrook as he, an artist in condiments, prepared his supper in the cabin cruiser by Goitre Lane jetty.

Having punctured the hull of the house boat without a second thought, the great bulk of the Owl-thing cart-wheeled down through the murk of the Thames and came to rest against a muck-encrusted prehistoric stone on the river bed. The stone at once upended itself and the Owl-thing, accompanied by a large number of hand guns tossed into the waters by actors in long running police sagas, at once slithered through the gap, which closed above it as though on springs. Tumbling in a wash of river water down long forgotten channels, it surged some time later through a white tiled corridor and came to rest at last in a brackish pool, where strange to relate there already floated the figure of a woman with her robe tucked into her knickers and a nasty bruise on her forehead.

"Mother!" screamed the Malcolm de Maupassant party to the monster.

While not even the eruption of Krakatoa could compare with the violence of the grief-wave generated more than a year ago by Charlotte de Maupassant when she encountered her lost boy in the grisly manifestation of an Owl-thing, it would be ungenerous to deny that the emotions which exploded from Malcolm in his turn when he discovered his mother's body floating in a pool several hundred feet below the city of London had a power all of their own. Concentrated by the tunnels, the psychic vibrations slowed in their upward thrust until at one point they entered the visible range and alarmed commuters on Green Park station by rushing through in the form of the 9.42 to Cockfosters. Looping and twirling along the earth's magnetic grid, the shock waves burst from the bed of the Thames, tossed aside the sacrificial stone, and climbed nearly forty feet into the air before dissipating in a glittering shower of Seprophantine art treasures over a square mile of East London.

26

It will not have escaped the reader's notice that the universal wall paper has worn somewhat thin in the vicinity of Goitre Lane. The constant dilations of time, the tendency of events to repeat themselves, the peculiar attraction of the place for the personae of this chronicle, all indicate not so much that the narrative is out of control as that in Goitre Lane we have a Node Of Power.

And the cause? We have observed it already, on two occasions. We refer, of course, to the prehistoric sacrificial stone which now rested upside down on the roof of a sunken cabin cruiser on the bed of the river near the Goitre Lane jetty. Not for nothing had forgotten wizards by their arts selected that of all the lumps of faintly greenish rock[21] from the sea-shore at Brighton and thrashed a gross of slaves with twigs of the sacred moleweed to encourage them to haul their prize overland to the construction site at Sgg'n (in some universes now known as Milton Keynes) where the contractors were erecting another multi-storey temple of the sun and shopping plaza. The stone, however, proving rather too heavy for the wooden precursor of the modern crossing by Hillier Parry, tipped in a sudden crackle of limbs and timbers into the waters of the river Drog along with a prize team of slaves, whose odds at next year's Salisbury Dolmen

---

[21] Venerated by the Saxons as the 'Bright [beorht] Helm-Stone', from which the name of the modern seaside resort is said to be derived.

Hauling Championship suddenly lengthened. There the stone settled on the river bed and was never seen again, at least until the entry of the Owl-thing and the exit, sometime later, of its shock wave.

The stone's unnatural power is not attributable to the chance resemblance of the weathering on its side to an effigy of Crom Ten Pogol, genital God of the Valk people, for which the wizards had selected it, but to what some insist is a tiny fragment of the original black hole, source of the multiverse, which lies embedded in its centre.

Yes, dear reader, you gaze at last upon the very stone which maintained the theocracy of Atlantis in its illusion of eternal power – at least, until that day of dread when, piggy-backing upon the grief-wave of Charlotte de Maupassant as it recoiled into the future, the object of the Serene Principle's veneration was lost to him forever.

For some reason (perhaps busily trying to design a really nifty flu virus or attempting to keep up with the physicists' ceaseless demands for more hypothetical sub-atomic particles) the Demi-Urge failed to notice immediately that the continent was no longer under the protection of the S'nang üll H'notorem, so it was a couple of weeks before the prophecies were fulfilled and the earth for hours on end shuddered and tore, knocking millions of diams off the resale value of the Temple of Goth, and the entire continent rose from aeons of lethargy and after a couple of attempts to turn itself counter clockwise began to slip sideways into the ocean, opening up exciting if temporary opportunities for chintzy little seafood eateries in what had previously been the august business district of Basileia. Quaking and spewing fire, the plain of

The Stone Unturned

P'nor'n sank into a sudden magma-filled abyss, while the uplands of the Valk country tried to justify their name and rose fifteen hundred feet into the air, a feat which not even the seer Dacha Ten Rogan had foretold. Finally the entire surface of the continent tattered, all the countries of Atlantis were torn asunder and vanished along with their 64 million inhabitants beneath the waves.

And what further sonorities of cataclysm the stone conjured as, buffeting the banks of time, it made its way to Now! What rude interferences with the dress of history for academics to ponder in the manse of a wet weekend in February! Perhaps the least among which may be counted the incident on a battlefield near the Valley of Elah when the stone, swooping low over the plain, accidentally deflected a pebble projected from the sling-shot of a young shepherd lad, sending it some feet wide of its target. The target, a hulking NCO in the First Philistine Bruisers, Lance Corporal Cremmo Troch, thus failed to be enshrined in myth as the notorious textual variant and giant, Goliath, but as recompense achieved with his battle-cleaver a more radical re-editing of the psalms than even the boldest nineteenth century German critic would have countenanced. The S'nang üll H'notorem, meanwhile, surfing on its grief wave, had passed among the Israelite army, doing them no good at all, which is why the Philistines scored so resounding a victory and the children of Abraham disappeared so irretrievably from the pages of history.

Subjected to the peculiar stresses of the primeval rock, the vicinity of Goitre Lane, as it would be in years to come, became a shunned and ill omened place from which the Roman legions themselves drew back with a Latin gasp of dread. Legends accumulated like dirt under the fingernails of history. During the reign of Richard II an old woman was tortured to death on the 'smale fowles' for having concourse with a tribe of demons and a similar fate befell one Mistress Moll Digbone some two hundred years later, after she had been observed dancing by moonlight with, it was whispered, a partner who 'was not of this earth nor yet of the heavens above us'. Most of Mistress Digbone was nailed to a cart and driven about the country for the edification of the poor but a small portion may be seen to this day in a glass case in Foots Cray museum labelled 'fragment of early Saxon stone-ware, c. AD 834.'

It was not until the early 1800s that folk began to forget their fears of the old site. William Blake is said to have poured forth a number of verses warning his countrymen to keep their distance, for 'in the grain-presses of Goiter cries many a soul, That kissed the blind Druidical stone of Udan-Adan' but no-one paid any attention to the old rat-catcher of Clerkenwell Street. For the next hundred years the area might almost be said to have thriven. Modest streets of slums arose, and gutters plentifully stocked with typhoid bacteria, and factories where children might labour for 16 hours a day. Yes, the old superstitious fears were at last swept aside, except on the eve of Blessed Magotte's day, when even the sellers of face-grinders retired early from their rounds, and apprehensive eyes watched through the night hours for a glimpse of Mr. Ingram, as the local bogeyman was known. In 1830, and then again in 1886, panic spread among the populace on Blessed Magotte's Eve after the remains of a young woman were discovered in a cellar in Goitre Lane but calm was restored when someone pointed out that (a) they were the same remains and (b) they were a good 250 years old and bore a label reading 'A moiety of Mistresse Moll Digbone. For Mago's sake, forbear...' The remainder of the label had been eaten by rodents, but the whole thing was donated to the Foot's Cray Museum, as you know. The twentieth century, alas, brought nothing but decay to the area, and the once prosperous street of brothels, money-lenders, smart opium dens and thieves' kitchens declined into nothing more than a row of lodging houses, small businesses and flats.

Thus it was that the relatively low strength convulsion of Malcolm de Maupassant's shock was magnified to a point where the world, however brief its remaining existence, was obliged to take notice. Among those directly affected were L. Silentius Bos, legionnaire first-class and unashamed Celt feeler, who was disgraced after failing to explain to his centurion precisely why he had risen forty feet into the air, turned a somersault and voided his bowels copiously over the officers' mess one evening in 55 AD. Also, Mistress Moll Digbone, gathering the curative seeds of the marsh viol one moonlit night, bemused by the iridescent Fred Astaire who appeared before her and with a twinkle of spats begged her for the pleasure; also Mr. Alexander Ingram, gent., a simulacrum of whom murdered several hundred children in the summer of 1788 and who was thereafter regarded with some coolness by his married friends; also Captain H. 'Geronimo' Sparesbrook, who returned to life like a hermit crab slipping back into an old, uncomfortable but nevertheless very welcome shell.

"Captain!" gasped his manservant. "I thought you were a goner."

"So, did I, Thring," the Captain croaked thoughtfully. "Thring?" His gaze sought among the shadows for grinning horrors. "Thring - do you know where I can find a good book on devil worship?" He struggled free from Thring's pin-striped embrace. "Are there leaflets a chap can send for? Or does one just turn up at a Black Mass and introduce oneself to a verger? Or do I mean virgin? I assure you, Thring, my late experiences have taught me that these questions are not academic."

Thring shuffled away and skewered a cobbled rat on an iron rod. He shook his head. "I regret, sir," he murmured, "that I have never had occasion to investigate the matter. It would scarcely be seemly, for a man of my calling."

"Oh, yes, tachowhimsy and all that. And yet, Thring," he continued earnestly. "I assure you, I have seen perdition, and it works. I beg you to join me now in a prayer to our Demonic Father. Otherwise - " He nodded at the roasting rat meaningfully. "- you may have a vision of your own future before you, Thring."

Thring licked rat juices off his fingers and smiled thinly. If he didn't find his wife by Friday it would be glu'ng. He doubted that the Fiend himself would come out of that one.

And what of Egrah'nca and Eric Maresbreath, whose astrethic bodies are so finally tuned to the whispers of the time winds – surely they did not escape? Well, yes, they did, because when the shock wave smashed the windows of the flatlet at 143 Goitre Lane and sucked Helena Phipps' portfolio of glamour shots up the chimney, Eric and Egrah'nca were miles away in the wondrous woman's pale green A40, en route for Byfleet, surely on a mission of intergalactic importance. Well, no, actually they were motoring down to spend the week-end at Helena's mother's cottage, where the loveliest of women would join them later in the day.

Eric Maresbreath was trying to listen to the football results as he slouched behind the steering wheel, while a small black teddy bear lying morosely among the tissues and toffee papers on the passenger seat, muttered, "You're supposed to be Guardian of the Earth, not a bloody knocking shop doorman."

"So you keep saying," Eric admitted, frowning over the fortunes of Fulham. "And I agreed, didn't I, that I couldn't account for the years between the moment when I was giving my *Danube, River of My Dreams* and the one when I found myself with a daft bit of gold string round my head in that building up the Edgware Road. I did admit that, didn't I?"

"Took you bloody long enough, though," Egrah'nca observed. "Three and a half hours I spent up that rotten chimney while you – you - " He gritted his fangs and bit back the words. "Anyway, the point is, we haven't got time for weekends off. We've got to get you back in training." Hearing Eric's soul-racking cough as he lit his fifteenth cigarette of the day, Egrah'nca sighed. "Frankly, I'd rather try and get the Magnarch of Verox to eat a cheese salad."

The main problem, though, as Egrah'nca saw it, was that they hadn't the faintest idea how to locate Charlotte de Maupassant, whom they believed to constitute the main threat to the life of Captain Sparesbrook. He had telephoned the Atlantean time and motion team from a call box at Putney but they had completely lost track of her. "Some flap on a glu'ng," he grumbled, "whatever that is. They kept trying to tell me about it, but I told them, I said, you sod about with your glu'ngs, I said, whatever it is, it's not the end of the world. I told 'em, I've got more important badgers to bait. They got a bit shirty after that, so I hung up on them."

He prodded at his Prognosticator which might just as well have been a lump of toffee for all the response he got.

"That looks rather tasty," Eric remarked. He pulled the beige construction from the bear's fur. "Mmm. Steak & Kidney. Very exotic."

"If only," said Egrah'nca, trying to provide a bit of continuity, "we knew where Charlotte de Maupassant had got to."

27

Captain Sparesbrook's religious enthusiasm, like so many others', was misplaced. During the unquantifiable period which he spent in death, his astrethic body had not, in fact, been cast into the realms of darkness visible where rules the Appalling One. It had merely sunk through the earth and come to rest in the bedroom of Heg'naar'n Stag'naarvrk, which anyone might easily mistake for The Pit.

Charlotte de Maupassant, awaking to find herself tightly bound with unspeakable 'ngyyl ropes, certainly seemed to think so, for when the minions flung her though the door to grovel on the baby-skin bedside rug, her first word was, "Hell!"

In a horrible stench of dead fish, a number of which he had taken to bed with him to practise some unnameable Scaliselsargan perversion, Heg'naar'n Stag'naarvrk opened one froggy eye and stared down at her.

A bestial parody of human speech gibbered from his flapping lips as she attempted to rise. The sound was repeated. Suddenly, she understood.

"You mean – *you* are the Demi-Urge?" Charlotte whispered.

The toadish mouth vomited up a chuckle of guttural malignancy and said, "Not personally, madam, though I do serve on its board of directors for a small annual fee and expenses. You are not, as I first thought, the Arch Priestess, Mrs. Gristle. Whom, then, do I have the honour of addressing?"

"My name is Charlotte de Maupassant. Some call me Empress of Witches."

"Ah, yes. Too bad about the Edith Grove coven. And that bedraggled lump of slime and feathers in the lobby?"

"Is my son, and also a foolish blacksmith, both somewhat blended after an accident with an owl and a bolt of lightning. Incidentally, is there any possibility of your removing these bonds? They are uncomfortably tight."

The great batrachian head shook regretfully. "Unfortunately," it gurgled, "they appear to 'ngyyl ropes, which I am sorry to say have a disappointing tendency to insert millions of tiny filaments into the flesh of the captive and, after a quite unreasonably short time, become so indissolubly knit to the bone structure that any attempt at release would rather ensemble the peeling of a very ripe orange." He made a sucking noise, possibly illustrative. "A nuisance for you, but I am powerless to intervene."

"Then it seems I must help myself," cried the matchless witch, transforming herself at once into a reading from the works of John Masefield. The 'ngyyl ropes writhed across the floor, seeking a new victim.

By the time Charlotte had got back from the sea again, the lonely sea and the sky, and resumed her customary shape, the depraved toad entity on the bed had begun to scream quite gratifyingly. The 'ngyyl ropes, their ill-temper aggravated by the verses of the Poet Laureate, had lashed themselves about the warty body of Heg'naar'n Stag'naarvrk ACA, businessman and blasphemy.

"Madam," it gurgled. "Please, I beg of you - I'll give you anything. Shares in the Muggoth Pits.

The deeds to some land I own in the shadow haunted fields beyond Thorpe-le-Soken. Anything. If you'll - " A n'gyyl rope, tightening about the bulbous throat, put an end to his drooling entreaties.

Charlotte de Maupassant's education at the Blessed Tracy School for Girls, Wickhampstead, had failed to include a course in the works of minor American authors, so she did not recognise in the creature expiring on the bed before her the reality which poisoned the fictive powers of H. P. Lovecraft, who would have delighted the juvenile world with many a wonderful tale of Yog-Sothoth the pink giraffe and his hilarious adventures in Rl'yeh, the land of sweeties, with his cousin, the grey felt elephant, Cthulhu, had not a fume vent from the Muggoth Pits been positioned directly beneath the cellar of his Providence home.

Their fibres burrowing ever deeper into the late Stag'naarvrk, the 'ngyyl ropes ceased to thrash at the eiderdown. Charlotte de Maupassant did not hesitate to conduct a thorough search of the many drawers and bureaux in the hellish chamber, secreting now a National Savings Book, and now a copy of the terrible Application Form of Ghed'nechi in various parts of her robe.

It was beneath the mummified corpses of a number of rat-like creatures with tiny human hands that she made the greatest of her discoveries. Lifting the lid of a cardboard box which had once contained a Chinese music centre, and tossing aside the expanded polystyrene, she felt her entire being freeze in a moment of glorious horror.

Scarcely daring to breathe, she stopped and ran her fingers over the contents of the box.

Was it?

Could it be true?

Almost fainting with glee, Charlotte de Maupassant hefted the box and stumbled from the room.

On the bed, the remains of Heg'naar'n Stag'naarvrk crumbled suddenly into dust.

28

It was just after the green A40 had passed Richmond Park that the accident happened.

The government of the day, alerted by several of its members who were on day release from the Violet Pring Hebbenthwaite Sunset Memorial Home for Diseased and Lunatick Gentry, had learnt of the imminent threat of glu'ng and responded with untypical alacrity. Having carefully defenestrated those minions who had chanced to overhear the whispered tidings in the corridors of power, the cabinet and a number of its lady friends loaded the more portable of the nation's art treasures into the back of the Chancellor's ice cream van and set off at high speed for the Seat of Regional Government beneath the Cotswolds, where Dame Glynis Farmer, the brilliant quantum physicist and manageress of a chain of pork butchers, had in record time constructed what the Magnarch of Verox would have recognised as a Time Window of a somewhat quaint and antiquated style.[22]

It was sheer bad planning on the part of the Minister of Transport that put Mrs. Winnie Sacks on the lap of the Lord Privy Seal. He should have realised that sooner or later the old goat would try to get his hand up the leg of her bloomers. The Minster for Women's Rights in the front passenger seat, startled, kicked out wildly, and smashed the

---

[22] Much as, say, a Victorian attempt at a lap top would look to you.

Chancellor of the Exchequer's rose tinted glasses, blinding him at a stroke. As he was driving, it was something of an inconvenience.

Wildly swerving, the van crashed through the central reservation and collided with a consignment of deleted 78 rpm records coming up from Glastonbury. Eric Maresbreath stamped on the brakes of the A40 and skidded straight into the back of the ice cream van among a shower of art treasures, obsolete recordings and segments of parliamentary democracy.

The halls of the Archerons of Atlantis hummed with activity, so filled were they with minions that a modified mantis might not adjust a Ro'nim vector without committing sodomy on half a dozen elk mutations. After the discovery of the loss of the stone of power, all leave had been cancelled, all staff called in, which accounted for the unusual silence in the cat-houses of P'nor'n, and even the Magnarch of Verox had taken to sleeping on a camp bed in his office with his secretary. Or rather with a succession of secretaries, not so much because of promiscuity as on account of feeling a bit peckish towards three a.m. At the moment, though, no-one in Atlantis slept. For the astounding stone, the source of light and heat and power, the S'nang üll H'notorem had vanished like that library book you really, really wanted to read. No longer did it nestle in its wondrous Holy of Holies, glowing faintly and emitting a sound not unlike a washing machine on eco-cycle. And, with the S'nang üll H'notorem wrenched from their grasp, the Archerons of Atlantis were staring cataclysm in the eyes.

And they didn't like the look on its face at all.

The Magnarch of Verox, who had slipped away from the Temple and changed into something less slimy, appeared in the foyer of the Prognosticator's Department and smiled at the Receptionist, who appeared to be almost witless with terror. Whether that was because of the dreadful secrets known only to the Prognosticator's Department or a perfectly rational response to the Magnarch's smile, who shall say?

"Greetings, your Jawship," quavered the Receptionist, who seemed to be a modified quagga. "I trust your Jawship is full. I -"

"Enough," snapped the Magnarch. The Receptionist flinched but refrained from counting her hooves. "Who have you got here that can tell me about the Stone?"

"Erm, we have a Press Release," said the quagga.

"Just give me a quick summary. The Stone has been stolen. What consequences do your people foresee?"

The quagga gulped. "Holocaust, cataclysm and flood, sire."

A sigh escaped the Magnarch. "If I wanted generalised forecasts of doom," he snarled, "I would have stayed at the Temple."

The quagga began to cry and was soon quite unable to continue. It disappeared suddenly under the counter and was replaced by a creature of somewhat sterner stuff, who might at one point in its gestation have been a water buffalo.

"Sorry about that, sir," it boomed. "We thought you ought to know, sir, that our surveillance team reports that the Shambhalese agent has been activated. They've heard some talk, sir, of a glu'ngtoka."

The Magnarch inclined his head in a way intended to convey complete and certain knowledge of everything to do with glu'ngtokas while at the same time wishing the buffalo to demonstrate his own grasp of the subject.

"The only information we have, sire, was obtained from Bynha, the maligned genius of Porseja Bo, who believed the glu'ngtoka to be an adept in tachomimsa."

"How very enlightening," the Magnarch cooed. "And what did the infernal sage of Posejna Bo think he meant by tachomimsa?"

The buffalo cowered. "He suggested it might be something to with potted plants."

"Potted plants?" screamed the Magnarch.

"Is it entirely inconceivable, I wonder, your Unconstrainableness, that given the enormous number of potted plants existing in the Twenty-first Century they may be part of some hideous vegetative plot to conquer the cosmos? And we have lost the Stone! We are powerless. And doomed!" the buffalo thundered, as screaming drunkenly, a modified female stumbled out of an elevator and, treading heavily on one of the Magnarch's favourite toes, began to weep into a tub of porgisvra plants in the foyer. Morale was beginning to plummet. The Magnarch turned away and loped off down the corridor to the Control Centre.

"I see," he said, having heard the technicians offer their explanations. They knew their master well enough to feel no reassurance at the silkiness of his reply. "We are plunging head first down the log-

The Stone Unturned

flume of doom, and now you tell me that our top agent has effected a discontinuance, has he, and can no longer, parametrically speaking, be contacticised. Dear, dear, how very unfortunate. Perhaps one of you delightful creatures (forgive me, your modifications are so extensive that I regret I cannot begin to guess what you might have been) can tell me why we are not activating the cerbo-snatch? Ah, the Guardian of the Earth has eaten the Prognosticator, without which the cerbo snatch has nothing on which to lock. Yes, I see. And which of you was it that suggested the toffee business? Well, if you won't own up I shall simply have to discipline the lot of you, and that will give me indigestion for days. Oh, it was, was it? Step up here, Tegr'nta'ng, dear boy."

Call it sentimental if you like, but the narrative has decided to return to the foyer for a few minutes, rather than observe the chastisement of Tegr'nta'ng. But precious little of interest is to be seen there, for the queue of engineers, servicemen, off-duty G-ramp operators and the like waiting for their turn on the modified female is now so extensive that none of the action can be seen.

Rejoining the Magnarch in time to glimpse him picking a shred of lab coat out of his teeth, the narrative records the following event.

"A thousand pardons, your Mawship! I crave your ear!" cried a messenger, dutifully severing his own ear and offering it to the Magnarch who, as custom dictated, took a tiny bite before returning it to the messenger. "News from the - " He lowered his voice, murmuring a few words which only the Magnarch heard. "They report, o unappeasable one, that a shock wave in the target area has caused a large number of indeterminacies to erupt. Glamour photos of a lady - " His words caused a perceptible stir of interest among the technicians " - have been absorbed into the temporal stream and are falling out all over the time, with unpredictable results. Already a six by nine colour print of the female, clad only in a somewhat disarranged burgundy bra-slip and white stockings, on the point of entering into an unusual relationship with a tennis racket, has caused the entire crew of a schooner in the China seas to throw themselves overboard in an excess of grief and joy. While another of the same incomparable woman, now to be observed popping out of a strategically ripped peacock nightshirt with mandarin collar and ankle strap courts with four inch heels and scalloped vamp, has caused Pope Matilda XIV to resign and turn the Vatican over to the mob. The effects upon the time structure as these marvels flutter down from eternity into the course of history - your capaciousness, they may not be easily reckoned."

The Magnarch sighed wearily. What was the course of history to him? He was about to say something rather ironical and witty on the subject when the messenger said, "Oh, sorry, your Appetence, almost forgot, what with the excitement of the lady and all. They also told me to ask you about something called "glu'ng". They wondered if it might be important."

Grimly, the Magnarch digested the message. "Glamour shots," he said. "Wandering stones. And now this. Glu'ng - a word that smells to me of yaks butter and yeti droppings."

And, lifting a telephone, he spoke the words that no-one thought to hear him say again.

"Operator." His voice whispered like a burgundy bra-slip riding up over white stockings. "Get me the Master of the World."

29

Up at the forefront of time, the world's last week was proving to be a dull one. The newspapers, driven bull-mad by the lack of events, took to setting to fire to each other's offices to generate copy. The BBC news team went on holiday to Bournemouth and when it arrived found Sky News waiting to interview it.

Those members of the government who had not been party to the escape attempt, and so avoided the carnage on the Kingston Bypass, having first voted themselves a massive pay rise, passed their last days in debating the Slaughter Act, which was designed to reduce the crime rate, cut the police force, slash public expenditure and control the population at a stroke by making murder legal. The case was well put by the Lord Matthias Prudentz, Pontiff of Newbury, who pointed out that humans were a meaningless congeries of chemical reaction, thrown together by random forces in a universe without value or purpose; that free will was an illusion; that consciousness has never been observed to exist, and that therefore no moral or spiritual significance could attach to the termination of their being.

The Bill might have been passed, too, had not a slightly intelligent MP who had been elected by mistake, Jock Spoyled-Pipres, for Amblebroth, risen to point out that, should the Bill receive the Royal Assent, the first candidates for the elbow would undoubtedly be the honourable colleagues at present at ease in the chamber around him. The Pontiff screamed and stamped and hit people with his crosier but the Bill was as good as garrotted. Someone suggested an amendment, restricting the victims to females, but fearful of the feminist backlash (a nail-studded leather instrument wielded by Ms Candida Lange as a symbol of equality with Chief Whip) the Commons threw the whole thing out and instead voted themselves another massive pay-rise.

"Mm," yawned the Captain politely, as Thring finished reading the article to him. "No doubt. Very regrettable. Are you going out again today, by any chance?"

"Oh, yes, sir, as always."

"What is it that you are searching for," the Captain demanded, somewhat formally, "on these interminable expeditions of yours? Believe me, however vital it may seem to you, it cannot compare to the significance of Union with His Malefic Highness, the President of the Infernal Regions."

Thring's fingers knotted on the acacia wood grip of the ram-cobbler. "I seek my errant other half," he croaked. "Faithless, adulterate beast that she be. And when I have tracked her to whatever greasy love-nest she has made her own - "

"Adulterate?" the Captain queried nervously, memories of garden furniture tumbling through his mind. "Er, surely not?"

"Most surely," Thring rasped. "She betrayed me. Me, her only husband. Me. In front of an audience including the Saviour of the World. And her mum."

As far as Captain Sparesbrook could recall, his adventure in the conservatory had been witnessed by nothing more sentient than a tray of S'narg plants.

"Over the intercom," Thring said, clarifying things a bit. "The whole filthy exhibition of depravity, broadcast like the infamous August 1986 edition of Gardeners' Question Time."

"I had no idea," the Captain confessed, "that there was an intercom in the conservatory. Thring, my dear old retainer, these noises can be most misleading. I thought myself one June that the TV was screening some extreme type of pornography but when I looked up it was only the final of the Women's Singles at Wimbledon. My dear old fellow, let me assure you - "

"Conservatory?" Thring shook his head. "I know nothing of conservatories. I speak of the machine gun turret atop Sparesbrook Manor, where the base and degraded female stooped to couple with, of all things, a blue and yellow teddy bear."

Conflicting tides of relief and bewilderment shook the Captain. "Teddy bear?" he echoed.

"The child's toy, possessed no doubt by some mad demon - "

"Mind your language, old chap. They can be very touchy, demons, so I'm told."

"Possessed, I say, by some slavering peculiarity of the Pit - "

"That's better."

"The toy came to life. And she, Juliette, the wanton harlot, she yielded lubriciously to its seductive wiles. I have permitted myself one week in which to locate the strumpet, and teach her the error of her ways." He patted the ram-cobbler. "If I am unsuccessful, then it's the end of the world."

"Oh, no, no, no, surely not," the Captain crooned. "Plenty more fish in the sea and all that. Go on a Saga holiday or something. You'll soon get over it."

"Literally the end of the world," Thring said grimly. "If I do not find my runaway wife, it'll be tachomimsa. And glu'ng."

"Glu'ng, glu'ng," went the telephone in the Magnarch's ear, unless he was imagining it. Then: "Master of the World's Office[23], Sadie Q Tourmaline speaking. To whom am I talking to, please?"

"This is the Magnarch of Verox," the voice said. "Put me through to the Master. As a matter of extreme urgency."

A longish silence was terminated by the bewildered voice of Miss Tourmaline.

"Sorry, caller. You did- you did say the Magnarch of Verox?"

"I did," said the Magnarch.

"But – you can't be. I mean - "

"While you are attempting to induce in myselves a serious identity crisis," the Magnarch snapped, almost severing the phone wire, "Atlantis is spiralling towards devastation. Now, seize that Master of yours by the collar of his disgustingly vulgar kimono and drag him to the telephone, before I order in a squadron of suicidal drum-flies to irradiate him forthwith."

---

[23] The Master of the World, unseen ruler of the mystic city of Shambhala and Chief of the Secret Brotherhood of Initiates of the Occult Sciences, dwelt (it is said) in a hidden tower to the north of the city. Quite how you hide something as obvious as a tower the narrative cannot say and assumes that esoteric wisdom must have something to do with it.

"Hold, please, caller," trilled Miss Tourmaline.

A moment later the atmospheric whiffling of the ear-piece[24] gave way to a voice at once hearty and oleaginous, and the Magnarch sneered to hear after so long the unprepossessing tones of the Master of the World.

"Shambhala 26 double 6," he creamed, pretending that he had not overheard every word of the exchange between his secretary and the incoming Magnarch. "Master of the World speaking. How may I please you today?"

"Not in the slightest," the voice of the Magnarch said waspishly, "unless you are contemplating one of the more agonising forms of self-destruction."

"Verox, you old son of a h'nmago!" cried the Master. "Hey, long time, no see. Listen, I was just talking about you, no, really, telling little Sadie here about that time we took the vacation trip together to your place at Gorpul dül Mimpoth. You remember, sure you do."

"I could scarcely forget," the Magnarch said, "since I have still not entirely succeeded in getting the bits out of the carpet."

"Oh, well, yeah," the Master said. "Listen, you never sent me the bill for that."

"And if I did," the Magnarch retorted, "where would you have found eighteen hundred dwarf children plus VAT? In your establishment devoted to peace, love and - " His sneer threatened

---

[24] Nothing to do with background noise from a Big Bang, by the way, but like all such sounds a permanent echo of Charlotte de Maupassant's maternal grief.

to dislocate at least three of his jaws, "universal brotherhood," he retched, "I imagine that blood-sacrifice is regarded as something of a no-no, is it not?"

"Well," said the Master uncomfortably, "you know how it is, we got standards to maintain, we got mahatmas here in delicate stages of training, you got to be careful to what kind of vibes you expose these guys to, you know? I mean, what happens if you let a potential Buddha watch Match of the Day or listen to local radio for half an hour? You get yourself a Hitler, that's what happens, you get Stalin, you get - " He named one of the Invisible College's greatest failures, a very popular star of weekend television whose name the narrative has been handsomely bribed not to reveal. "Though how they expect a guy to rule for 1000 years and maintain telepathic control over World Leaders and such, plus make personal appearances every 25 years or so without so much as week off or membership of a recognised corporate incentive scheme, beats me. So, anyway, enough of my little problems. To what do we owe the honour of this call to, Verox, old boy?"

"Glu'ng," said the voice of the Magnarch.

The Master cleared his throat. "Sorry, old buddy," he said. "Guess we had a snarl-up there. Sounded like you were imitating a telephone."

"I said glu'ng," the Magnarch repeated.

"Oh. Well, sure, yeah. I mean, what's glu'ng? Some new wonder herb that increases your sexual potency and kills head lice or what?"

The Magnarch sighed and covered the mouthpiece with a claw. "Invisible college," he groaned at the technicians around him. "I have jam doughnuts at home that know more about the esoteric history of the universe than this collection of Siberian spit-worshippers. I swear they get all their secret doctrine out of the public library." Returning to the Master of the World, he said, "I am sure, my dear fellow, that the term falls within your purlieu."

"Oh, well, just hold on there, Verox," the Master said. "I got my girl-Friday here checking the shelves right now. Rings a bell with me, that glu'ng, sure as a fart it does. Just a matter of Sadie shinning up a few ladders. Yeah, here she comes, sweating like an old sow. Great, Sadie, honey, what did you find?"

A riffling of pages came over the line. It was followed by laborious sound of the Master of the World reading an arcane transcript.

" – *described in the last journal of Lord Farish Huckstep-Pole, the nineteenth century explorer and amateur gynaecologist, discovered interred beneath a cairn of stones on top of* - " He turned a page " – Sevenoaks Public Library."

The Magnarch sighed again.

"No, delete that," the Master of the World said. "That's been kinda stamped on. I shoulda said, *"on top of the furthest flung of the mighty peaks of Himalaya, Mount Pankarfeng*. He tells of being led, blindfolded, by clandestine paths, blah, blah, all the usual celery, rocky tunnels, valley of warmth and flowers, you know the old clichés, ancient priest, yeah, yeah, daughter with child, blah. Then a lotta horse-radish about, uh, contractions and, uh, afterbirths, and, uh, excuse me a moment."

While the Master of the World threw up in his filing tray, the Magnarch sighed yet again and pulled a face at one of his technicians, who instantly died of horror.

"Yeah, hey, sorry about that, always a might delicate, you know. Where was I? Oh, yeah, hidden valley, all that salad. Ah, here's the bit: *'Later that evening the aged elder conducted myself and my companion to a chamber deep in the heart of the monastery. Here, to our amazement, we were permitted to observe some twelve monks in the traditional beige head-scarf and leather trews, seated at what must have been a primitive attempt at the circle, each one intoning some blasphemous word of prayer to their heathen deity. How I wished for a good English revolver and a few rounds with which to purge the place, though I knew it would be impolitic to express my desire to our tottering mentor. Instead, I was obliged to hear him through the set-piece which he no doubt inflicts upon all passing strangers.'"*

The Magnarch began to hope that the cataclysm would hurry up and overwhelm Atlantis and spare him any more of the Master's voice.

"'In which he makes some extraordinary claim to be maintaining the world in being against the devilish power of what he in his outlandish tongue called' - here it is, Verox - *'the 'Glu'ng. Observing my ill-concealed scepticism, he burst into some filthy dialect, from which I was able to gather either that his grandmother had poisoned her toe after wrestling in mud with a badger, or that his intestines turned to powder every evening at nine, or that those who mocked the monks of I'nt'nishgoia suffered horrifying deaths in the cages of Gasherkang. Easily smoothing the senile sage's ruffled feathers'* - some sorta ceremonial cape, I guess - *'I enquired as to what might cause this glu'ng to come about, and was advised that there existed certain adepts who after many years of a life that certainly did not recommend itself to*

yours truly, especially when he thought of little Gertie Dibbs preparing pheasant and onion duff for supper in her lamplit rooms behind Jolly Street, could achieve a concentration of being known as 'tachomimsa' and so align themselves with the cosmological underpinnings that by exploding they could bring about the End of Everything. When I naturally enquired, if that were so, how should anyone prove it, since when the state was achieved the evidence along with the experimenters must of force be subsumed in the general catastrophe, the wizened headman began to scream about his grandmother's toe again, or it may have been the powder in his loin-cloth, and we were with scant politeness conducted to the somewhat damp and odorous quarter in which, by the light of our last atlas, I write this journal.

"A deep feeling of unease touches me. Shall I see Harley Street again? Shall I assist into the world even one more scion of a noble house? Or am I doomed to perish, alone (apart from my companion) here on the roof of the world? If the greatest trial comes, let me face it as a true Englishman. And, Gertie, do not be ashamed if your name is on my lips as I-. Here the journal ends. It was found beneath a mound of stones together with the frozen remains of Sir Farish and his companion, Miss Margaret Boot, only daughter of Nat Boot, a sadler from Droitwich.' Hey," said the Master of the World, "that's quite a story. Maybe I could interest someone in the film rights."

"And beautifully read," the Master said. "I liked the way you did the italics. So we have nothing to fear from this business of the glu'ng then. The monks are, I trust, still at their posts, keeping us safe."

"Could be a problem there, Verox," the Master said. "Sadie's just handed be a report. Says the monastery of I'nt'nishgoia was converted into a lamp factory in the autumn of 1930. Nobody's up there praying, Magnarch."

"So," said the Magnarch. "While Atlantis faces its own cataclysm, Everything on the other hand seems destined to perish hand in hand. It would appear that we are doomed."

The Master of the World stared down the lamp lit length of his vaulted office to where his secretary, Sadie Q Tourmaline, sat shredding the tax demands.

"Fear not, Verox," he announced. "Tonight the Master of the World shall ride!"

"And a fat bloody lot of good that'll do," the Magnarch said, as he hung up the phone. "Still, we've scared the pants off the jumped up little sod, that's one consolation."

Considering that Atlantis perished years ago in a cataclysm caused when the time travelling grief-wave of Malcolm de Maupassant's mother abducted the source of their wealth and power, the S'nang üll H'notorem, it may be difficult for the ordinary intelligence to grasp the reason for their distress. Why, after all, should the Magnarch of Verox now pick up the phone again and cancel three days in Gorpul dül Mimpoth just because in a few thousand years time the entire universe would come to an end in a moment of glu'ng?

Need you ask the question? Surely you realise that the forces unleashed by the exponent of tachomimsa are entirely without limit? When the glu'ng event occurs, as Thring had explained to the Empress of Witches so long ago, it means the End of Everything. Glu'ng, being both illimitable and omnitemporal, will end everything, everywhere. And, more significantly, everywhen. Not only would Goitre Lane and environs disappear in a great whoosh of impalpable cosmicide: so would the entire past history of the universe as it happened, or rather as it failed to happen. Every second of the lives of stone age Macedonians at their worship, Atlanteans, Romans in their circuses, Greeks in their academes, Borgias and Plantagenets, you name it, the lot would perish in a moment of exquisite agony. No wonder the Magnarch of Verox was off his food.[25]

---

[25] Only one secretary a night, remember.

30

From the echoing vaults of Shambhala, that beleaguered city of light and culture in the gloom of the world's corruption, to Kingston-on-Thames is a journey so fraught with peril as to be almost sacrilegious, but the narrative has made it virtually unscathed and now draws your attention to the soft glow in that window on the sixteenth floor of the Ozzy Preen Infirmary, Tumblers Road. There, on the night following the accident on the Bypass, in which the entire Cabinet was demolished and, more significantly, Eric Maresbreath reduced to a comatose length of gristle and tubes, pretty nurse Timperley's face blushed deeply in the light of the lamp on Dr. Ruffyan's desk as the surgeon's eyes gazed with frank appreciation at the contours of the nurse's uniform.

Dainty chin defiantly tilted, Nurse Timperley said, "- and in my opinion, doctor, the patient in bed 13 is definitely not receiving the most beneficial treatment."

Dr. Ruffyan's face hardened but the nurse plunged bravely on.

"I mean to say, tests have shown that Mr. Maresbreath has two four inch slivers of 78 rpm gramophone record embedded in his hypothalamus and a fragment of stone dating back to the prehistoric Middle east lodged under his skull above the corpus callosum."

The doctor's strong fingers toyed suggestively with a specimen jar. "I know all this," the rich voice drawled. "In what way do you imagine his treatment might be improved, nurse?"

Nurse Timperley gulped and said, "I think we should take his legs out of traction, stop the hourly enemas and call off the injections of female hormones. I've let him have his teddy back," the nurse added defiantly. "He would cry so whenever he regained consciousness."

The surgeon laughed sardonically. "Emotional little creature, aren't you, my dear? We're going to have to teach you to toughen up that soft heart of yours, if you want to stay in the Ozzy Preen, my sweet." Rising, the doctor slid an arm about the nurse's trim waist and drew their bodies closer together, so that for a moment they were not doctor and nurse, but man and woman swept up in the age-old whirl of passion and hearts that pounded like an accountant's on Budget Day.

Finally, with a little cry, nurse Timperley broke free.

"Come, you tease." The doctor's voice was urgent, demanding. "Don't you understand? I want you. I need you. Damn it, do you want me to go down on my knees?"

"No, thank you," the nurse said primly. "I'm not into that sort of thing. And, besides, you're married. You're not really interested in me. It's all just a bit of casual fun in the sluice room for you, isn't it? But I want something finer than that."

"Wedding bells," sneered Dr Ruffyan. "And a plain gold band on your ring finger. You insufferable little romantic. Shall I tell you what marriage is? Marriage is coming home after a hard day in casualty to a home like a pigsty and the stench of gin. It's having to clear up puke from the bathroom floor because your beloved has been on a bender again and at present is lolling unconscious on the roof of the garage. Marriage isn't orange blossom and happiness ever after, my dear little Timperley. It's heart ache, and ugliness, and year after year of soul destroying, life murdering scorn."

Wiping away the tears evoked by the revelation of the despair which lay behind the mask of cheerful amorality, the nurse seized the strong, warm hand impulsively and whispered, "I'm sorry, Dr Ruffyan. Truly I am. But – the patient – poor Mr. Maresbreath – couldn't we at least cancel the hydrotherapy? At least until the wounds have healed?

"And if we do," the doctor murmured, close to the nurse's black curls. "What then? What of us, nurse Timperley? Or may I call you Roger?"

"You can if you like," the nurse said shyly. Greatly daring, he looked into the doctor's titanium grey eyes. "I don't mind – Eunice," he murmured, smiling.

Eunice Ruffyan held the slim, warm body of nurse Roger Timperley a moment, then reluctantly released him. "Very well," she said, with a tolerant laugh. "You may tell the auxiliaries to cancel three of Mr. Maresbreath's ice plunges tomorrow. Will that satisfy your tender little heart?"

Roger Timperley nodded his black curls, too full of joy to speak. Allowing his lips to be pressed once against the firm mouth of Dr Eunice Ruffyan, he freed himself from her questing fingers and turned back to the ward.

"Roger," said the voice behind her, quiet, authoritative and calm. "Roger. I – it's not easy for me to say this, Roger, but – Roger, I believe I love you."

Head bowed, the nurse did not turn to face her. "And I love you," he whispered, warm tears of joy on his cheeks. "I've loved you since the day you first rode your Lambretta into ear, Nose & Throat."

"Then – may I be allowed to hope - ?"

"But your husband, Eunice." Roger Timperley whirled round. "I know he - he's an alcoholic and a model railway enthusiast, but – "

"Oh, that's got out at last, has it?" Dr Ruffyan said grimly.

Roger quickly protested. "Oh, no, no, it's not general knowledge. It's just that I – I saw him one day, sidling into a back street exhibition of N-gauge layouts. I promise you, I'll never breathe a word to a living soul. And I can't tell you how sorry I am."

"I don't need your pity, nurse," said the proud surgeon. "Oh, yes, it's hell, of course, being married to man who thinks you don't know he has copies of Railway Modeller hidden in the garden shed, or who thinks you suppose he's just hunting for wasps' nests up in the attic, despite the excited little gasps of 'jickety-can, jickety-can' and the smell of ozone. It's hell, yes, but – if I have your love to support me, Roger, I believe I shall be able to bear it."

"Can it be right?" whispered Roger. "No. Don't touch me now. I must think. I must – Eunice, I must be sure."

Stepping aside to allow an orderly to wheel out a number of patients who had died while the fore-going went on, Roger Timperley hurried to the bedside of Eric Maresbreath, accident victim.

The bed was empty. Next to it, the window hung wide open.

With a little cry, the nurse summoned Dr Ruffyan to the vacant sheets. "Look," he gasped. "He's gone. Mr. Maresbreath. Gone. And the window – "

"It's sixteen storeys to the ground," Eunice Ruffyan said. "No-one could survive that."

"You realise what this means?" Timperley stared wildly at the empty bed.

"Of course. You get undressed. I'll fetch the screens. Darling –"

"What's that bally row in the corner?" old Mr. Day enquired a few minutes later, looking up from his pillow.

"Just Dr Ruffyan, as usual," croaked the colonectomy in the next bed. "Pulling that bloody model railway routine again."

"Fifth this week, ain't it?"

"Sixth," said the other. "You were out cold when she dragged that visitor of him with the dodgy hooter into the sluice room the other afternoon."

"She's a girl, ain't she?" Mr. Day chuckled as he snuggled down again.

"Not much doubt of that," the other agreed.

31

The narrative apologises for having been so entranced by the romance of Dr Eunice and her curly headed darling that it entirely failed to spot Eric Maresbreath apparently hurling himself from the window on the sixteenth floor of the Ozzy Preen. Already late for its appointment on Stalebreath Moor, it regrets that it cannot now pause in Byfleet to satisfy the craving of Helena's many fans, nor can it spare a moment to explain why Juliette Thring was consuming doughnuts at a deli counter in Queens, while glancing through last week's New Bunsen Malt Mart and Lard Swappers Weekly, her only concession to her former existence the length of pink ribbon (not, we hastily add, the Nidro Force) which she always wore garter fashion about her left leg, a few inches above the knee.

Passing by way of Juliette Thring, we have avoided another visit to the rarefied halls of Shambhala, and now fetch up on the floor of a certain houseboat, where Captain H. 'Geronimo' Sparesbrook lay, weak but recuperating, and waited for Thring to stagger back from Joyce Crowley's Occult Book Shop & Tea Rooms with another pile of Demonic literature. He had been waiting for a day and half and had begun to fear that his aged retainer had been driven into gibbering lunacy by his failure to locate his adulterous spouse.

As fail he must, for Thring's chances of retrieving his errant wife had grown no better, though to her disappointment she no longer lolled, stripped to the massage of the breezes, on a couch of rosewood beneath the trees of the nameless isle, while glittering youths attended her with spicy chalices of wine and dishes of exotic cremes and the various other conveniences of life on a lost island. But one day, slipping out of an invisible letter box three feet above the golden sand, in a litter of free nail vouchers, football pools and offers of double glazing, came the nine-by-twelve polychromatic blow-up of Helena Phipps, toute entière from toes to brow. The glittering youths, driven mad with desire, immediately forgot about Juliette and devoted themselves to snatching passing ships and planes in the hope that one of them would boast the name of Helena Phipps on its passenger list. Juliette, piqued to find herself no longer cynosure of the month, had flung herself into the sea. No-one so much as glanced up at the splash. A strong swimmer, she somehow survived the sharkish perils of the ocean to crawl some days later, exhausted, onto the shores of Bimini Island. The truth, she was not too tired to recognise, would have been treated as evidence of insanity by the party of holidaying archaeologists who found her on the beach when the sun came up, so she had told them some rubbish about magnetic clouds and white sea and the compass tying itself in knots, at which they all nodded and started babbling about triangles.

What did surprise her was the discovery that the year was now 1987. Time, for some reason, had run backwards and rather faster on the lost island. Strange to think that somewhere across the indigo sea, on a small green island, her infant self would one day play prettily among the ashes and discarded hooves of her foster father's forge. She

The Gnostic Frying Pan

soon found that on the whole she preferred life as the mistress of Professor Mordred T. Schneiderhauser, of the University at Catamite, New Bunsen. At least she was safe from the ram cobbler, though in deadly peril, like everyone and everything else there ever was, from the time consuming effects of glu'ng.

With some straining at the seamy side of its undergirding, the narrative manages to tear itself away from the magnetic attraction of Juliette Thring and returns to the vicinity of Goitre Lane. The Occult Bookshop, discovering fairly soon in its career that there was very little profit in the business, since unsuccessful customers tended to be swallowed up before the end of the month by the Infernal Regent, while successful ones sent back Final Demands with the Rune Sign of Widmore scrawled on the back, had quickly diversified into pornography, and was doing very nicely. The owners of the shop had invested heavily in various editions of Readers' Wives, and it was that which had proved the undoing of the gasping Thring.

At first it had been no more than the odd glance at the covers as he tottered past with another load of mouldering volumes, their purchase financed by the sale of the ram cobbler. The next trip had seen him stop and thumb hurriedly through Hampshire's Mrs. Sheila McMosley in her bulging undies. On his third visit he had hurried directly to the racks of porn, his attention trapped at once by a glossy edition of *Wives of Our Ancient Retainers – Candid Snaps*.

On page twenty-three, twenty-four, fifty seven, fifty eight and one hundred and three, he found what he had been seeking: a total of eight

The Stone Unturned

pictures of his lovely young wife in various stages of undress in and around Sparesbrook Manor by means of a high-powered telephoto lens aimed, he realised, from somewhere in the direction of the Violet Pring Hebbenthwaite Sunset Memorial Home.

It was the photograph on page 103 that sent him screaming from the shop. An advertisement for a sister publication, *Sensational Adulteries of the Wives of Our Ancient Retainers*, the accompanying taster had been shot through the window of the conservatory on the ground floor of the Manor, where the garden furniture lay. It showed his own dear wife, enjoying a few moments of recreation and relaxation with none other than his employer, Captain Sparesbrook.

Passersby, used to the spectacle of demon haunted figures fleeing in a gibbering frenzy from the Bookshop, took no notice of the man who hurled himself onto the back of the coal lorry. Perhaps they tutted once before they forgot about him, little knowing that the spindly figure with the mixture of froth and coal dust on its lips was the reason why there was no longer much point in paying the deposit on next year's holiday in Benidorm.

Away from his shame, his master and the coils of Goitre Lane, the lorry bore him, crouched among the sacks of Welsh Small Nuts. When it pulled up a zebra crossing, Thring leapt onto the pavement and scaled the walls of an abandoned brewery, where he hid himself among the rusting vats.

Observe him now, gentle reader, a tragic, angry figure, his pin-stripes torn and begrimed with coal dust, his shirt stained with drying froth. He combs back his few remaining hairs, removes his shoes and braces, and extracts from a secret pocket in his vest a faded parchment covered with diagrams and arcane symbols, which tells him how to assemble the portable monastic chamber concealed in a compartment in the back of his pocket watch. Three hours later, sweating and out of breath, he collapses cross legged within what quite convincingly resembles a rocky cell in the heart of a Tashkent monastery, complete with MDF altars and electric candles (as foreseen all those millennia ago by the sage Trepoch) places the tips of his little fingers in the corners of his mouth and his thumbs up his nostrils, and begins to keen the opening syllables of the Dirge of Aalistorgi.

Edward Pausanias Thring has begun to compose himself into the state of tachomimsa. Glu'ng status will be achieved ahead of schedule. Hit the panic button, ladies.

32

A sound like an LP of the opening bars of *Rheingold* played at 45 rpm swelled into a deathly wail and died away, then repeated itself again and again, freezing for a moment the technicians of Atlantis as they traversed the great halls of the Archerons.

Time and again the siren voice howled up and down the audible scale, completely drowning the shrilling of the alarm bells. A modified beaver had gone 'bari'nk' and, howling like an air raid siren with a stubbed toe, charged up and down the foyer with a wombat clinging to her front like an infant ape accompanying its mother down an avalanche.

"Here is a glu'ng update," a synthesised voice purred from the speakers on the walls above the workers. "I repeat, here is a glu'ng update. Glu'ng has been brought forward to G minus twenty-eight. Glu'ng has been brought forward to G minus twenty-eight. Please resubmit your work plans for revision to the central planning department. Resubmission dockets can be obtained by application to the Common Services Section. Thank you."

The Archerons, gathered in their serpentine enclave, stared at each other in wild alarm. Since none of the Archerons would trust any of the others for more than half an hour after a heavy dinner, that was quite normal, of course.

"So the Master of the World has ridden," concluded the Magnarch of Verox unexcitedly.

"Given the fastest horse in Siberia, it will still take him six and a half years to get from Shambhala to the city called London where, our time and motion people have at last condescended to tell us, the adept has been traced. I think, dear colleagues, we may as well discount our friend, the Master."

The heads of the other Archerons nodded gravely over the great stone table. After a heavy dinner they all had the greatest difficulty in staying awake. Since, as has been said, it was only after a heavy dinner they could trust each other enough to meet face to face, it is small wonder that the affairs of Atlantis were in such confusion.

"What of Egrah'nca?" asked one who, suffering from an indigestible cousin, had remained a little more alert than his peers.

The Magnarch shrugged noisily. "Contact remains broken," he said.

"Then we must summon the Nidro Force."

At the dreadful name the drowsy Archerons stirred nervously and began to manufacture excuses to leave but the Magnarch silenced them with a lash of his tail. "I regret that classified information status has not yet reached disapplicization re the Nidro Force situation," he informed them. "All I can tell you is, the Nidro Force is not here."

The Archerons relaxed slightly.

A stomach rumbled. The Magnarch, years of experience in evidence, rose from his seat and vanished down one of the many tunnels. Distantly, behind him, he heard roars and screams and the rending of scaly flesh and wondered idly which vacancy had come up today.

In some ways, he thought that the devoured one was lucky. Five minutes perishing in the ripping jaws of the Archerons would take his mind off the forthcoming glu'ng.

Meanwhile, in the bowels or, at any rate, the gullet of the earth, the Owl-thing drifted back from dreams of manicure and human flesh to a divided consciousness in the backyard of the palace of Heg'naar'n Stag'naavrk, late of Scaliselsarga-on-Sea. It soon found that its movements had been restricted by a heavy chain which someone had thoughtfully riveted about its neck. For the moment it was content to lick out the bowl of blood which had been provided for it by someone wise in the ways of Owl-things.

"Crikey," said Jubb at last. "Now what do we do?"

"Your speculations on that topic, Jubb," said Malcolm de Maupassant, "are of equal weight with my own. Dash it, the last I remember is a vision of the infamous Sparesbrook about to devour a plump young person in a plastic mac. The man evidently has his good side after all. How is it that I now awake to find myself here, fastened up like some common cur on this unattractive patio? What is your opinion, Jubb? Note the oozing stalactites, the fat white fungi and the stench of decaying octopi. Do you suppose it might be Grimsby?"

Jubb shook their head. "Beats me," he admitted. "I never was much good at answering questions."

"If only my dear mother were here," Malcolm began, and then froze, as a memory iced up his befuddled brain, a memory of his dear mother draped in the garb of an acolyte of the Owl-thing, bobbing up and down in a pool somewhere among the myriad tiled tunnels of Scaliselsarga. Another, much weaker wave of miserons glanced from his wing and dissipated among the alien geometries of the sunken city, its only noticeable effect on the sub-lunar world being the closure of a two mile stretch of the M25 for half an hour the previous Thursday.

"No," whimpered the Owl-thing. "It cannot be. It must not be. No mother of mine would ever be seen dead in the toad holes of Scaliselsarga. For that, Jubb," it added, "is where we find ourselves. I should have known it, when I saw the tortured body of that old warlock dangling from the rotary clothes line. My mother has spoken of this dread place many a time, crooning me to sleep with tales of its blood-beslubbered post offices and unspeakable pubs. Jubb! My mother – say she is not dead."

"She is not dead," said Jubb.

"What? Are you sure?"

"I don't know," Jubb said. "I just did what you told me. Say she is not dead, you said. So I said it, didn't I? I don't know if she's dead or not. I don't know your mum."

"Jubb! Why, what a mannerless hound you must think me! Here we are, bound together by a fate more horrible than any devised by a television game show producer and I have neglected all this time to introduce myself. Forgive me. I imagined that you had learnt my identity that night at Sparesbrook Manor, when the universe tried to clasp us to its bosom."

"Funnily enough, I had a number of other things on my mind at the time."

"Naturally, naturally. You recall, then, the clumsy felon whose inflammatory mishap relieved you of your forge? That was I. In the early hours of the previous night I had, by a delicate combination of bribery and gelignite, exploded my way from the grip of Hesketh Gaol, where Sparesbrook had caused me to be immured, the ungrateful swine, merely because I had done something creative with a few million pounds from his ridiculous Will Trust. Had our little accident not supervened, I was en route to Sparesbrook Manor, to discover firstly the whereabouts of my mother, and secondly the flavour of the Captain's liver. My name, dear Jubb, is Malcolm, and my mother is Charlotte de Maupassant."

If you have ever been imprisoned in an airing cupboard with a rabid pigeon, you will know something of how it felt to be Malcolm de Maupassant when Herbert Jubb heard the name of Charlotte de Maupassant come hooting from their beak. Imagining a brick wall, he did his best to smash his skull against it and, when that didn't work, went screaming through the waves of his brain in a futile search for some corner that was not polluted by terror.

With difficulty Malcolm wrested control of the beak from his gibbering companion and put a stop to the stream of witless too-whoos. "Jubb, Jubb," he said gently. "Mother would be very flattered, but please - Our task now is to obtain liberty from our bonds. Uncontrolled panic will, I fear, be of little assistance there." In the Owl-thing's present circumstances, what would?

33

Coincidence, that imperfectly understood force without which life, consciousness and television soap operas might never have evolved from the random spawn of the elements, had pulled out all the stops. Nothing of the sort had been attempted since the late Charles Dickens began to traffic in fiction. That, at any rate, was Egrah'nca's opinion, as he crawled with Eric Maresbreath, searching among the packing cases in the former secret room on top of the Tesco building in the Edgware Road for the golden cord.

That a lorry load of deleted gramophone records should contain several pressings of the Andrews Sisters, effervescing their way through *Boogie-Woogie Bugle Boy of Company B* was not, he accepted, unreasonable, and that two slivers from one such disc should have penetrated Eric Maresbreath's forehead and lodged in his brain only to be expected. But that mere haphazard selection had included among the art treasures in the Chancellor's ice cream van an effigy of the Macedonian goddess Sclit, carved from her own shin bone, and that nothing more than gravity and various laws of thermo-dynamics had co-operated to ensure that the tiny sculpture had lodged in Eric's cerebral organ Egrah'nca could not bring himself to credit. And that both of these events should have occurred, of all places, on the Kingston Bypass, so that a representative sample had been absorbed into Eric's system when he was dragged along two thirds of its length by the out of control governmental escape vehicle screwed up the laws of chance and blew its nose on them.

The result of the accident, if the word may be used without irony, was that, after a brief coma during which the various atoms of the records, the bone and the Kingston Bypass were united with his own corporeal substance, Eric Maresbreath had awoken in the Ozzy Preen infirmary, restored (almost[26]) to his former magnificence as Guardian of the Earth and Wielder of the Cord.

"Well, I just don't believe it," Egrah'nca said, not for the first time. "I mean, all those factors coming together at just the right moment, it's not credible. There's got to be a Mind of some sort beneath it all."

Breaking off from humming a three part harmony rendition of *Rum & Coca-Cola*, Eric Maresbreath laughed. "And do you think," he said, "I find it any easier to believe that my old blue and yellow teddy bear is really a top operative of the Archerons of Atlantis? No doubt my cuddly hyena, Duncan, will prove to be an emissary of the Vhartem dwellers of Leng."

"Who's behind you, Eric?" Egrah'nca asked.

---

[26] Almost — because one seventh of him still hung forever in some mirrored dimension eternally almost but not quite getting his leg over a phantom reflection of Helena Phipps, loveliest creature in any universe you care to name. That accounts for a certain look of distraction and pain which occasionally clouded the dedicated features of the Guardian of the Universe as he scrabbled among the boxes of Kiddidins, searching for the lost cord.

The look of distraction and pain on the faces of commuters to Esher, on the other hand, were caused by the sudden disappearance of the highway from under their wheels.

The Guardian of the Earth whirled lethally and with a single blow felled the looming stack of fruit jellies.

"Oh, don't be so bloody literal all the time," Egrah'nca sighed. "I meant, do you remember now who you represent? Who's your boss? Who dishes out the luncheon vouchers? Eh?"

Eric smiled proudly. "I serve but one master," he said, "and he is Master of the World."

"Yes, it's that shower, isn't it." Egrah'nca said glumly. "No wonder we've had so much trouble."

Evening stars pricked the sky over Stalebreath Moor[27]. Manacles tinkling in the frosty air, a work party from the Violet Pring Hebbenthwaite Memorial Sunset Home shouldered their picks and, panting mistily, began the weary trudge from the mine in Stunnard's Valley to the asylum, dragging the ore-wagons behind them, their spirits no doubt lifted by the thought of the therapies which awaited them – electro-convulsions, psychotropic drugs, or for the very worst cases music therapy with a patronising middle-class flute-playing blonde. From the concealment of an abandoned troop carrier, Deirdre Horne watched their departure, her heart sinking to recognise again the familiar ragged uniforms of sack-cloth and hairy string.

"Eric," she said crossly to the toddler who squatted at her feet. "You've brought us round in a

---

[27] At last. This chapter was supposed to begin several hours earlier. The narrative is sorry you missed all the deeply moving events of the afternoon.

circle. I can see the roof of the Manor, not half a mile away on the hillside."

"Good," said little Miss Eric. "Now I can finish my book."

"You're far too young," Deirdre snapped, "to be writing your memoirs. And who's going to believe all that nonsense about the North African Campaign? You weren't born in 1943. I wasn't born in 1943."

"I told you before, mother - "

"Yes, I know, all that twaddle about reincarnation. Well, if you think I'm stupid enough to fall for all that claptrap, my girl, you've got another think coming. What kind of superstitious cretin do you think I am? You just forget all about your silly memoirs and get on with saving the world."

Little Eric stamped her foot. "Shan't," she said.

"Don't you talk to me like that," Deirdre snapped. "And don't start grizzling, or I'll give you something to really cry for."

Little Eric looked at her mother challengingly.

"Want a carry," she said.

For a moment Deirdre grasped the arguments in favour of deicide. Then, recalling that the world really did need saving, she stooped down and hoisted the child in her arms.

At that moment, slipping erratically out of the firmament like a single oversized snowflake, came a six by nine sheet of glossy card which, when trapped in the eager fingers of little Eric, proved to be a monochrome photograph of an astonishingly beautiful woman in the uniform of a school girl with crumpled tie and hockey-stick (but lacking, of course, any form of knickers).

The mother and child stared at the apport in the fading light of the moorland sky.

"When I go to school," Eric said, "will I have to dress like that?"

"Yes, dear," said her mother, lost in conjecture.

"Well," said Eric, "my bot won't half get cold."

"It's a sign," Deirdre said. "It must be. Don't you realise who this is?"

Eric tilted her head and sucked her thumb thoughtfully.

"Is it the Queen?" she asked.

"The Queen! Of course not. This is Helena Phipps, the one they put on page 3 that day they had to recall the entire print run because nobody turned up for work. We are being told to seek her out. But where?"

"Flat 2B, 143 Goitre Lane, London," the precocious child suggested.

This flash of prescience following on the miraculous apparition of what Deirdre had already begun tentatively to think of as the Blessed Helena delighted her so much that little Eric hadn't the heart to point out the printed label stuck on the back of the photograph which gave Helena's name, address, statistics and various specialities for the benefit of potential employers.

Turning her back once more on the Manor's hulking shape, she cuddled the child to her bosom and set off across the freezing fog-bound moor for London and Goitre Lane.

And so the time-webs rope in another couple of wanderers.

"Here, I tell you what," Egrah'nca said. They were taking a break from their search for the cord. Eric had opened a box of Newberry Fruits. The teddy bear had found some vanilla tea. "It's been bothering me ever since you ate my Prognosticator."

He waved aside Eric's apologies with a blue paw.

"What do you know about something called glu'ng? Eric? Eric, come out of that crate and stop trying to bury yourself in tins of Kiddidins. That's no way for a Wielder of the Cord to carry on. I only asked you what a glu'ng - Eric! Stop it! You'll do yourself a mischief."

Seizing the bear by the throat, Eric Maresbreath stared into the beady orange eyes. "What do you know of glu'ng?" he demanded.

"Nothing," Egrah'nca wheezed. "That's why I'm asking you. I'm sorry I mentioned it now. Look, put me down, we'll find the cord, foil Charlotte de Thingme-bob's evil plans and be back home in time for Blessed Magotte's Eve. What do you say?"

"Charlotte de Maupassant?" Eric's scorn curdled a consignment of evaporated milk. "What's she, to an adept in glu'ng? Do you mean to say that while I've been frittering away my time with that Phipps woman - " A spasm briefly wracked his being and his leg jerked urgently - "somewhere in the universe a glu'ngtoka is wandering free? Yes, I faintly recall, it was the psychic alarm bell of one such which awoke me from my mystic slumber in this very room, before the dreadful forces spread me across several universes in a number of eerie forms. And while I have been dragging up in the uniforms of American female military personnel, an adept has been preparing to destroy us all! Curse the day, Egrah'nca, that ever you were born. Curse it, I say."

"All right," said Egrah'nca, and did so, at length. "Though actually," he added, "I wasn't so much born as cut out, stitched up and stuffed."

"Much as we all will be," Eric said quietly.

"Well, I just don't see what all the Sturm & Drang's about, that's all."

So Eric Maresbreath explained to him about tachomimsa and glu'ng and, having persuaded him to come out of the boxes of bath bombs, together they returned with a new sense of urgency to their quest for the lost cord. It was the only thing in the universe that could help them now.

34

For further information on Mrs. Gloria Gannet, the reader with time to spare is directed to Volume 1, number 27 of *Nude Wives of our Great Union Leaders*, where a number of regrettably poor quality polaroids and a text which makes up in content what it lacks in grace, charm and syntax will provide all that even the most curious could wish to know about the Tesco supervisor who found the golden cord.

And well might she wish she hadn't, if Mrs. Gannet, after the third flail at her husband's blushing rump, had been in any condition to make wishes. As the auric flagellation really began to heat up, there came a blossom of blue and silver light and a roar like the explosion of a gas-main and, in a shower of china mice, miniature liqueurs, ash-trays and Don Williams LPs, the Gannets' flat in Canon's Park exploded. Half the roof and the whole of the spare bedroom, including the geranium plants and the bondage outfits, hurtled through the air and demolished the granny flat on the side of the converted abattoir across the street, while the bathroom descending in a haze of ice crystals from a great height derailed the 19.27 to Burnt Oak and thus brought about the divorce of Mr. & Mrs. Victor E Montgomery.

The blast was visible for miles around, not least from the window of the former concealed room on top of the Tesco building in the Edgware Road.

"Another space shuttle down," remarked Egrah'nca. "They've hardly finished digging Lords Cricket Ground out of the remains of the last one."

"That's no space shuttle," Eric gasped. He stared between the racks of chocolate pixies at the chrysanthemum of atomic fire swirling in the sky over Stanmore Marsh. "By Sweet Helena, I do believe someone has activated the cord."

He seized Egrah'nca by the ear and raced down the stairs.[28] Fearlessly boarding a red bus, he made his way swiftly to Locatelli Gardens, where a couple of fire engines had run into each other and now burned fiercely beside the wreckage of an upturned police car. At the furthest corner of the road an ambulance was parked. Its driver, having observed the fate of the previous emergency services, had refused to come any nearer. In that he was wiser than he knew. The cord had special built in processors for handling attempts to spoil its fun.

Spectators almost choked on their popcorn and overpriced cans of gaseous drinks when they saw the man in the duffle coat with a teddy bear in his pocket leap the smouldering firemen and dash into the flaming mock Tudor property. One or two enterprising souls offered odds on his chances of coming out again but found no takers.

Tracing the source of the improbable light by following the scorch marks on the wall paper, Eric Maresbreath bore Egrah'nca to the inferno of smoke and horror which had once been the bedroom and love-nest of George H. Gannet, leader of the

---

[28] Let us scotch this myth right now about his superhuman leap from the sixteenth floor of the Ozzy Preen. He left by the lift like anyone else. The open window was the result of a loose catch, nothing more.

The Stone Unturned

Amalgamated Wind Estimators Union, and his now flame haired spouse, Gloria.

They saw the cord at once, lying in a circle of unburnt rug, surrounded by tongues of flame, still clutched in the hand which on page 47 of *Wives* is wielding the size 11 vibrator "Boilermaker's Lunch".[29] Of the remainder of what occupies the centre-fold like an invitation to speleologists, there was no sign.

Resolute and resourceful now, Eric Maresbreath lost no time in bravely leaping into the room and hurling his furry companion through the wall of fire.

"Grab the cord!" he shouted.

Egrah'nca, fuming splendidly, and already beginning a smoky cough, swore a good deal but did as he was told. The slope of the floor terrified him and he expected at any moment to fall in a collapsing waffle of timber and fire into the depths of the house. He had no way of knowing that such slopes are standard in properties erected in the 1950s.

"Chuck it to me!" Eric commanded. "Ouch," he added, as the partly barbecued fingers of Mrs. Gannet poked him in the eye. "Be a bit more careful next time," he complained, untangling the cord from his neck.

"Next time?" coughed Egrah'nca. "How often are we going to do this, for Magotte's sake?"

His face alight with exultation, or possibly fire, Eric Maresbreath bound the golden cord about his hair and, as the Magnarch of Verox would have

---

[29] Available at your own risk from the Joyce Crowley Occult Bookshop and Tea Rooms. Quote Dept GFP for a special discount.

The Gnostic Frying Pan

put it, attainmented a refilletization status, although the word fillet would probably have released enough high-enzyme fluids from his ducts to digest the British Museum and extinguish the fire in Locatelli Gardens.

Egrah'nca stared through the encroaching flames at the transformation which came upon the refilleted Maresbreath. His stature increased as though by insertion in his desert boots of Dr. Weir's Patent Lifts, and his body converted fat into more rippling muscle than butcher's slab in an earthquake. The Guardian of the Earth, complete again, raised his divine eyes and smiled across the room, a Siegfried (as Wagner imagined him, not the usual bandy-legged barrel waddling about Bayreuth going Hohei! Hohei! in a bearskin rug or, given a director suffering from a touch of the concepts, a rose pink tea gown) among dwarfs. As an incarnational effect, it had a lot more going for it than the facade of a three year old girl.

"For Magotte's sake, stop admiring yourself in that mirror and get me out of here!" Egrah'nca screamed.

The Guardian of the Earth wrenched himself away from his reflection in the former ceiling of the Gannets bedroom and leapt from the window,[30] snatching up his teddy bear on the way, to the roof of the potting shed below. Having extricated himself from the ruin of seed trays and old bicycles, he clambered back through the hole in the roof of the shed, cast aside his ragged duffle coat, and said:

---

[30] Yes, now he can leap from windows, see?

"Now, my friend, my little spy from the halls of the Archerons, I shall tell you our next move. We must return to Goitre Lane."

"Can't you keep your hands of Helena for half an hour?" Egrah'nca snapped. "At least until you've saved the Universe."

"Foolish Ursine," Eric laughed. "Let me explain. My enormously enhanced senses tell me, on the bed of the river, not far from Goitre Lane, there lies a certain block of stone. Ancient wizards found it, centuries ago and, drawn by the effigy on the side of the enviable genital god of the Valk People, Crom Ten Pogol, commandeered it for use in a new temple. But little did they know, the unlettered mages of prehistoric Albion, that this was no ordinary stone."

Egrah'nca yawned. His interest in comparative anthropology had not yet reached its apogee. He snuggled down in Eric's waistcoat and went to sleep.

Unaware that he had failed to hold his audience, Eric droned on: "It was a stone, Egrah'nca, which your master, the unbearable Magnarch of Verox, would instantly recognise, for it was the keystone of ancient Atlantis, snatched from under their very snouts millennia ago, and come at last to rest on our island's shore. The effigy of Crom Ten Pogol on the side resembled an inscription which appeared to read, in your barbaric tongue, *S'nang üll H'notorem*. The stone was, in fact, stolen by a team of Atlantean burglars from its rightful owners, on its way to its predestined resting place, halfway up the wall of the extension being added to his palace by my leader, the Master of the World. My mission is to retrieve it and restore it to its due setting, thus excluding the draught which keeps blowing out the Master's lighter every time he tries to smoke a cigar. Of course, I guard the Earth too, on the side. We shall uplift the stone, my little furry ferret, and with the aid of its power discover the whereabouts of the glu'ng adept, foil his mad attempt to reach the state of tachomimsa, and save the world. After that, it's ho! for the hidden paths by the abysses of Ortrevelim and the citadel of my home, the bastion of culture, Shambhala the Timeless! Away!"

The Guardian of the Earth's obsession with exposition has, though he little knows it, placed him in jeopardy. Seated within his ceremonial chamber on the roof of an abandoned brewery, Edward Pausanias Thring, now floating six or seven inches off the floor, moves ineluctably towards the tachomimsian equilibrium. His yellow eyes have rolled up into his skull, his tongue lolls over his chin like a strip of coconut matting, his breathing is shallow, almost non-existent. What hairs remain on his blotchy scalp stand erect and crackle like grass in a frost. Now he drifts a little sideways in the incense laden air and a faint but visible glow begins to shine from the region of his aged trouser seat. Gathering in brilliance, it soon lights the interior of the portable monastic cell, casting shadows of the plastic bats across the ceiling. A fearful sound, louder and more thrilling than the scream of a falling hod carrier, hisses from his lips, growing in pitch and intensity like a whistling kettle coming to the boil which, in some ways, it is. The state of tachomimsa is all but achieved. Glu'ng is all but upon us. Where is the Guardian of the Earth?

He is lecturing a somnolent teddy bear, that's where he is.

The Magnarch of Verox slumps into a chair of finely carved bone and chews miserably at a tea-lady. He knows what fate must have in its ring binder. All unaware, our other friends dance on. The Captain, muttering obscene devotions, lies in his houseboat. Juliette Thring entertains the Dean and his wives at a cook-out in New Bunsen. Deirdre Horne totters under the weight of her child, Saviour of the World (failed) as they trudge along the hard shoulder of the A20 near Sidcup. No small distance away, vertically, Charlotte du Maupassant has discovered at last the whereabouts of her mutated offspring and tugs at the chain which secures him to the patio in Scaliselsarga. Dr Eunice Ruffyan is screaming at nurse Roger Timperley, having just caught him gloating over a photograph of an explicitly sensuous woman in glitter stockings which, he swears, has just materialised in his rubber gloved hands. And the Master of the World on his stallion Strapner gallops with the wolves across the frozen tundra under a gibbous moon.

Too late now to fill in that tax return you've been leaving behind the clock till next weekend for the last eight months. Too late to build the extension or take up home brewing. Too late to Come Out, or assassinate a president, or edit the works of Alexander Pope.

In the ruins of a London Brewery, Edward Pausanias Thring has achieved the state of tachomimsa.

It is the hour of Glu'ng.

Pfft.

END OF PART TWO

As even the most sceptical of readers is bound to admit, especially if 'ngyyl ropes are involved, there is a certain indefinable difference between the expression *End of Everything*, which is said to trail along behind a glu'ngtoka when he frets himself up into a state of tachomimsa, and the expression *End of Part Two*, which stands above.

The first, for example, is associated with nothing more dreadful than universal emptiness, while the second was often wont to precede the utter horror of the commercial break.

At least we are to be spared that dismal agony. What follows reveals itself to be no less than a plausible simulacrum of

PART THREE

The Stone Also Rises

35

Corporal Wallace Dowsing, loafing his way through guard duty on the roof of the top secret anti-sedition establishment disguised as a day nursery in Pandulph Alley, dropped his fag and snatched up his laser assisted field glasses when he heard the outlandish sound, rather like a kettle coming to the boil and then falling into a box of wet cement, which emerged from the ruined brewery across the way.

"Aaaaaaeeeeeooowww – Pfft!" he scribbled on his notepad.

The lasoculars pierced the crumbling walls of the malt-house and the balsa wood sides of Thring's simulated monastery in time to see the aged manservant's skull flip over like the top of a boiled egg and a shower of golden sparks fountain from within in a moment of defeated glory before dying away in a damp hiss and a bitter looking cloud of smoke.

The empty shell of the retainer hung for a moment in levitation, then collapsed to the floor, where it toppled over, revealing to Corporal Dowsing's power assisted gaze its soot blackened interior. Shaking, and more than a little sick, the soldier lowered his glasses and lit another cigarette. Used though he was to sights of horror in the cages of the Research Laboratories several floors beneath his boots, the glimpse of a glu'ngtoka failing to achieve glu'ng had unnerved the young corporal. He stared up at the clouds and wondered, for the first time, whether he had been right to give up his

The Gnostic Frying Pan

title to the throne of Luxembourg and, under an assumed name, attempt to life the life of an ordinary citizen of The United Kingdom and Various Other Bits. At least in Luxembourg you didn't see many aged retainers going off like a faulty Golden Rain.

Well, come on, honestly, what did you expect? To have a dog's chance of achieving the state of tachomimsa, the adept must have lived a life of selfless asceticism, sacrificing every carnal desire on the altar of his dedication. He must shun the flesh, scourge his body, and take at least three cold baths a day. Thring, as you must have noticed, had been screwing the daylights out of Juliette, his wife, as well as drooling in private over the pictures of ladies like Mrs. Sheila McMahoney of Waterlooville. He had indulged in every sort of pleasure, scoffed the delicacies of the earth as though they were peanut butter sandwiches, drunk the cup of earthly delights to the lees, and hadn't taken a bath of any temperature since the day the Crystal Palace went up in flames[31]. He could no more annihilate the whole of time and space than sew on a button. He paid the price. For years his trousers kept falling down.

And, in the artificial monastery overlooking Pandulph Alley, Edward Pausanias Thring spent every last vestige of his astrethic force to no better effect than might have been achieved with a cheap foreign firework.

---

[31] No-one ever found out exactly why Thring had been in the women's cloakroom or what he had done to cause a small explosion. It can hardly have been a dummy run for glun'g.

36

From the bronze nipples and lips of nymphs who posed in baroque horror among the pools in the grounds of the Violet Pring Hebbenthwaite Memorial Sunset Home burst abrupt fountains of brownish water which sprayed high into the air, overtopping the great cupola. Inmates on occupational therapy gazed in awe, their stone-breaking quite forgotten, as the glittering caves hissed around them, transforming the mundane scene into a rainbow shimmering wonderland alive with the music of falling waters and the stench of dead octopi. Encouraged by the sound, a number of gentleman wet themselves and had to be coaxed away by the nurses.[32]

Impelled by some immeasurable pressure from below, the arcs of water swirled yet higher, like small boys competing against a lavatory wall. One by one the nymphs exploded. Bronze shrapnel burst across the gardens. A number of casualties resulted, including P. R. Finnbriker, the Oxford philosopher, felled by three hundredweight of torso whose existence he questioned right up to the moment it annulled his own, and the economic theorist Brünnhilde Stanisgrite, choked to death by a projectile in the shape of a granite breast which lodged in the mouth that nothing in the world had ever stopped before. Apart from several sociologists

---

[32] Known to the viewing public as Butcher Holdstock and the Terrible W. A. Cocks, tag team and two man Armageddon.

who had been making mud pies on the lawn and who fortunately cushioned the blow of a falling Triton, there were no further injuries.

The pools overflowed their banks. Streams of caramel coloured water gushed down the hillside, later to smash through the fences of Sparesbrook manor and ruin a number of very healthy S'narg plants before sweeping in torrents through the house, drowning several hundred families of mice and then rushing away down the drive with a loot of tiles, plaster, grandfather clocks and, curiously enough, a length of pink satin ribbon, such as might decorate the neck of a child's teddy bear, or the upper leg of a Juliette Thring.

Unless Grimwood's Theory of the Spontaneous Generation of Water is, despite the controversy, to be given that credence after all which the Editors of *Tit-Bits*, *Hi-Fi News* and *Nude Wives of our Great Military Leaders* denied it, we must ask ourselves, whence came this mighty flood, which in so short a time has created so much havoc in the grounds of the asylum, not to mention Sparesbrook Manor. Let us see if Charlotte de Maupassant and her son know anything about it.

While Edward Thring was involved in his pathetic attempt to negate the space-time continuum, the woman whose desire was to tyrannise over it knelt in the yard of the palace of the deceased toad-entity, Heg'naar'n Stag'naavrk, and wrestled with the chain which fastened her translated child and his companion to the paving stones. A sorry sight she looked, too, hundreds of sequins missing from the tatters of her acolyte's robe, her bare arms and legs spattered with mud, still bruised in places from the attentions of 'ngyyl ropes. Her auburn hair hung about her face in damp rats' tails, which she preferred to conventional curling papers, as she struggled with the iron links, her bosom heaving with anguish and exertion.

There are times, you know, when the narrative could almost fancy Charlotte de Maupassant.

"Ah, if only," she grunted, " I had – the muscles of a stoker and – the fingers of a mad dog strangler![33]"

With a final wrench, she tore the bolts from the dripping stones and rose triumphant. Choking ungratefully, the Owl-thing rose rather less triumphant and nearly sundered itself as half of it tried to flee down the nearest tunnel.

"Be still, Jubb," commanded the Alpha Male voice of Malcolm de Maupassant. "Mother, would you have the kindness to place yourself on this side of our body. It seems that my dismal confrere cannot contain his terror at the sight of you."

Charlotte sniffed and tossed her hair, to show that she didn't give a damn, but shifted round to a spot where the blacksmith's share of the field of vision did not include her.

Then she gasped. "Who did you say?" She stared open-mouthed at her son. "Malcolm? Who have you got in there with you?"

The Owl-thing shuffled a bit. Inside, Jubb was doing his best to keep the mouth shut. You will have some idea of how it felt if you recall those

---

[33] Compounded in a quart of raw cider, they make a marvellous body lotion.

The Gnostic Frying Pan

occasions when you have tried to prevent yourself from being sick.[34]

With a retching sound, Malcolm said, "Do not concern yourself, mother, he is no-one with whom you need claim acquaintance. My partner in this sorry business is a menial blacksmith, who goes under the ridiculous name of Herbert Jubb."

Charlotte's eyes glowed cat-like in the murky yard. "The blacksmith?" She raised an eyebrow. "Well, well, Herbert," she murmured. "We meet again."

"Do not demean yourself and me, mother, by acknowledging this person. He is a thing of no account."

"And speaking of accounts," said Charlotte, transforming with a click of her fingers the bag of empty beer bottles in her hand back into the box of Demi-Urgical paperwork, "just take a look at - "

Whatever revelation the Empress of Witches may have been on the point of making was unfortunately lost in a sudden crescendo of sound. A wind that stank of rotting sea beasts blew its foulness over them, tearing a blizzard of feathers from the Owl-thing's hide and sending the rags of Charlotte's dress streaming back from her body like grubby bunting.

"What's happening?" croaked the Owl-thing.

"Quick," shrieked Charlotte in the roar of the gale. "Here, catch hold of this box. Whatever happens, don't let it out of your hands. I mean, claws. It contains all we need to become Mistress of the Universe! Now, run, run, run..."

---

[34] E.G. when you caught a whiff of those dead octopi just now. And look out below.

But they were saved the bother of running. A twenty foot high wall of brownish water erupted from the tunnels and bore them away among a swirling flotsam of minions into the darkness of Scaliselsarga-on-Sea.

37

Well, we have evidently observed the Great Flood of Amblebroth somewhat earlier in its career as it churns through Scaliselsarga, but we have not yet traced the waters to their source. Perhaps a visit to Goitre Lane will shed some light on the matter.

The hours of quiet in the bilges of the derelict house boat had done wonders for Captain Sparesbrook's bodily structure, although his mental faculties had unfortunately suffered a great deal from darkness, solitude and fantasies of blood sacrifice. At last the moment came when he knew he must either die here or force himself to rise from the boards, to stand, to take a hesitant step, and another, and another...

"Beelzebul be praised!" he yodelled. "I can walk again! Praised and gloried be the name of the Arch Fiend! May his loins never be sated! May his magnificence rise above the shivering white body of the world! May he thrust his great throbbing Will into the anguished receptacle of the universe! Io Beelzebul! Io Beelzebul! Io -oh -oh -oh-oh..."

The Captain's dance of eulogy was interrupted when the hulk gave a sudden lurch and flung him back into the bilges. At once he became aware that the river's song had altered. No longer did it murmur an idle lay of reflected skies and sacks of kitten. Suddenly transformed, it began to indulge itself in Wagnerian show pieces as transcribed by Pandromian Caprotchevsky, the mad organist of Walthamstow.

Shaken, bruised and appreciating for the first time the emotions of an egg in an electric whisk, the Captain clung to the splintering boards as the wreck spun widdershins on the turbulence and gathered speed in a spiral towards the middle of the Thames, whose brownish waters were disappearing with a ghastly slurping into a whirlpool of irresistible ferocity.

The old houseboat stood up on its bows, tipping the unfortunate Sparesbrook head first into a mess of rat bones, old cans of creosote, tyres and the remains of a dead tramp, pirouetted twice, and was sucked into the maw of the river.

Now we seem to be getting somewhere. Clearly, if the word may be used of the contents of the Thames, the fountains at the Violet Pring Hebbenthwaite Sunset Memorial Home were conjured into life that day by the pressure of water which by way of the cyclopean masonry of Scaliselsarga, came originally from the Thames at Goitre Lane.

No blame attaches to Betty-Sue K Fry Inc. She was fast asleep under a Bulgarian Chief Petty Officer in the torpedo hold of the MV Drochero, anchored off Bumber Point. Nor indeed to the delicious Helena Phipps, who lay in her lonely bed at her mother's home in Byfleet and wondered what had become of Eric and his teddy bear.

In her wildest dreams (several of which, suitably illustrated, would make attractive features in *Nude Fantasies of Our Greatest Netball Players*) Helena would never have imagined what had occurred when the Guardian of the Earth and his Atlantean partner went in search of the fabled S'nang üll Hnotorem.

The Gnostic Frying Pan

Not a sufferer from wild dreams, apart from that one where glossy black limbs entwined her pliant flesh while rough lips nuzzled her flesh and whispered of semiotics, Deirdre Horne tottered on through the fog with her child on her shoulders. Her woollen dress clung wetly to her body as she stumbled through the gorse and nettles, and over the rivulets which appeared all too suddenly to be avoided out of the white chilliness. Sometimes great monoliths and menhirs loomed over her, slabs of granite which seemed to condense out of the mist itself, and sometimes she scrambled through the branches of toppled oaks, where sheep huddled, bleating in the cold.

"Not how you picture it, is it?" Deirdre said, as they stepped onto a creaking rope bridge over a rocky chasm. "I'd always thought Chigwell was more built up."

A sharp rise in the ground forced her to save her breath. A hard climb later she found herself ascending out of the fog bank onto the brow of a heathery cliff. Far below her a brownish flood poured down the hillside and enmoated what, with a cry of utter desperation, she recognised as Sparesbrook manor. Once again, she had walked the perimeter of a circle and returned to Amblebroth.

Tired and wet, she knew there was perhaps enough strength left in her body to bear her and the child down the hillside and along the bank of the newborn river[35] to the inundated walls of the Manor. In a weariness so complete that it had

---

[35] Or shall we say, in deference to little Eric's opinions, the re-incarnated river?

strength of its own, she lurched forward through the tufts and hummocks.

Her disappointment was forgotten for a moment as, emerging from the grove of trees under the walls of the asylum, she was astonished to see first of all a ten-foot, bedraggled Owl-thing, then a woman in rags of sequined chiffon, and then the battered hulk of a houseboat erupt from the remains of a fountain and soar high into the air like targets at a shooting gallery, to fall with a series of splashes into the great brown flood which hastily bore them down to the Manor below. Her surprise was compounded when the child on her shoulders suddenly began to drum her heels against her mother's breast bone and screamed, "Mamma! Mamma! Want my teddy. Nasty man's got my teddy!"

The pudgy fingers were gesticulating at the foot of a dead elm, where a stranger lay unconscious in the mud. Clad in a duffle coat, grey trousers, a blue velour sweater and a golden cord about the brow, he sprawled among the broken bulrushes with, as little Eric had spotted, the furry shape of a blue and yellow teddy bear clutched to his chest. Man and bear were both soaking wet.

Deirdre rubbed her eyes. For a second the damp stranger had reminded her somehow of the lambent vision of Sclit which had appeared to her all those years ago in the conservatory downstream.

The child's petulant screams penetrated the heroic swoon. Eric opened his eyes. A trembling hand adjusted his cord. Then, as though memory had come back suddenly from a day off, he stared about him, searching for something which evidently

The Gnostic Frying Pan

was not there. Seeing, Deirdre, he sprang up and loped towards her.

"S'nang!" he shouted. "Where is S'nang?"

Then he fell into the river, which in his anxiety he had failed to notice, and was at once swept down towards Sparesbrook Manor in the wake of his predecessors.

"He's taken my teddy away," little Eric yelled, tugging at her mother's hair.

With one backward glance at the shadowy corners of the asylum, Deirdre swung round and galloped after the bodies in the flood, keeping pace almost with the shattered cabin cruiser which had recently bobbed up from the fountain hole in a shower of Sepraphontine art treasures and tomato sauce.

The clues have been assembled. The deduction may now be made. It is quite obvious what has happened.

His disquisition on the provenance and destiny of the stone called S'nang complete, the Guardian of the Earth had returned by arcane roof top pathways to Goitre Lane. To call at number 143 and leave a note for Helena was the work of a moment.

To loiter in her bedroom checking out the contents of her underwear drawer took rather longer.

Then, fearlessly, he dived into the filthy river and swam down, down to its depths.

Steadying himself on the wreck of a sunken cabin cruiser, Eric Maresbreath peered through the murk in search of the ancient stone which a moment later slid off the cruiser's upturned hull and struck him on the head. Valiantly he attempted to catch hold of it but, blinded by the cloud of blood, allowed the stone to slip between his hands and tumble to the river bed, which it smashed open without regret. At once the river began to spiral down through the jagged plug-hole, sucking after it both Eric and his pocketed teddy bear, followed shortly after as we have heard by Captain Sparesbrook and his houseboat. Passing through Scaliselsarga, the errant flood collected Charlotte de Maupassant and her unchained monster, and spat the whole crew out from the fountains in the water garden of the Violet Pring Hebbenthwaite Sunset Memorial Home.

Not bad, Watson. Nine out of ten, I fancy. we cannot award you full marks, my dear old comrade, because you have omitted one enormous and vital point.

"What is that, Holmes?"

"You have failed to comment upon the Muggoth that howled in the Pits."

"But – but the Muggoth did not howl, Holmes."

"That is the point, my dear doctor. The flood bore more than a human cargo from Scaliselsarga, more indeed than a couple of old vessels. I trust that you have your service revolver about you, Watson?"

"You mean?"

"Yes. Unless I am much mistaken, and I never am, apart from that embarrassing business with the orang-utan in the lime-green tutu, a Muggoth has been loosed upon the world."

38

Safe (from Muggoths at any rate), the Magnarch of Verox relaxed at a table in his favourite restaurant, the Cantina di Gorpul dül Mimpoth, and beamed at his companion.

"Send me the wine-waiter," he said, closing the menu.

"Yes, sir," grovelled the servant. "On or off the bone?"

"Oh, off, C'ndunga, off. With a few petit pois and button mushrooms."

"Quite, your Unconstrainableness. And for sweet, sir?"

The Magnarch mused.

"Bunny girl?" he suggested to his companion. "No, I don't think so either. Look, what's that person over there having, the blonde woman in the frilly shirt and the surprising purple dungarees?"

The waiter peered across the candle-lit restaurant.

"Crème Brulee, I believe, sir."

"Yes? Well, then, when she's finished have her plunged in old brandy, lightly dusted with icing sugar and served at our table with a jug of custard, would you?"

For the next half an hour the restaurant sounded to nothing more than the crack of bones and the munching of eager jaws. The Cantina was a decent little place, pricy but beautifully done out, and they knew how to cater to a fellow. True, there was a minor disturbance tonight when the honeymooner at table 19 raised some objection to his bride's forming the nourishing part of the Magnarch's afters, but the offer of as many cigarette girls as he could cope with soon mollified the young gentleman.

The Magnarch's companion, Her Royal Highness, the Khemmenoi of Lunt, heiress to the platinum throne of Shemgho and general manageress of the most exclusive chain of cathouses in P'nor'n, one of whose near relatives made so sinuous an appearance in the poetry of Nineteenth Century England, pushed aside her empty plate and smiled at her old friend and customer through the candle glow.

"Quite, quite superb, as always," she hissed. The candles flickered, and grotesque Magnarchical shadows danced on the wall among the bottles of Eig'nor fluid in their nets. "I have tasted nothing so exquisite since the funeral breakfast of my late cousin, the Stagnancy of Krak."

"An Archeron whose demise while holidaying on the Isle of Ponge was deeply regretted by all his colleagues," the Magnarch assured her.

"Yes," said the Khemmenoi. "Too bad. I know you guys were all looking forward to him. And, believe me, you missed a real superooni."

The Magnarch smiled winningly, at which a number of diners fled screaming from the room, and remarked to himself that her association with the harlots of P'nor'n was having a deleterious effect upon the Khemmenoi's manners.

"Say now, Magnarch," she whispered, toying with a glass of syrop. "We at the pleasure-palaces of P'nor'n have been saddened of late. We have sought

The Gnostic Frying Pan

about us for the blissful sight of yourself and your fellow Atlanteans and our eyes have clouded with disappointment." She drained the syrop. "Also business has been shocking. What's up? Lost your gr'nooms?"

The Magnarch, who found indecency in the language of females quite disgusting, looked a little bleak.

"We have been somewhat pre-occupied," he admitted, "with a crisis of unprecented magnitude. The glu'ng adept - "

The Khemmenoi's syrop glass shattered on the mosaic floor.

"I see that the significance is not lost on you," the Magnarch observed. "However, you may relax, my dear madam - "

"Don't call me that, buster," the Khemmenoi hissed, revealing quite clearly the snake blood in her ancestry. Her body swelled and pulsed colourfully, the red cavern of her maw expanded, her tail rattled out its drum roll of death.

With a graceful apology, the Magnarch calmed her before events could surpass the scandal which hit the headlines of the Basileia Bugle a couple of years previously, when the Khemmenoi, imagining some insult in the gesture of a Lemurian Nusp-pedlar, had engulfed him whole, thus offending unforgivably against the laws of Lemuria, under which all Nusp-pedlars were reserved for the high table of the Supreme Tax Collector. It had taken a good deal of bribery and young virgins to assuage the wrath of Rogua, the present incumbent, and even then it was probably only the Khemmenoi's position as manageress of the cat-houses which saved her. Devouring a Magnarch of

Verox, while yet living and without the written permission of at least three of his fellow Archerons, ranked several points higher in the scale of social blunders.

"As I was saying, your Highness," the Magnarch continued, "there is no need to disturb yourself about the glu'ngtoka. My sources in, ah, a certain establishment whose identity I am not permitted to reveal, have confirmed that he has failed to achievementise. No, the catastrophe to which I allude is the imminent destruction of my own civilisation, as foretold by that holiest of sages, the divine Trepoch, and confirmed to me by my own male progenitor, His Serene Highness, the Principle of Goth. He tells me that the mighty Stone, source of all wealth and power, has somehow been abstracted from its sacred niche in the innermost temple, and carried off, he knows not where. Without it, the sanctified sages say, our continent is doomed, and we shall perish in flood and fire and general calamity. And he's spending the temple taxes on preserving the life of some scarcely evolved bacterium called Sparesbrook under the impression that the nasty little creature will somehow preserve us from our doom."

"You don't say! Can this be true?"

"Well," sighed the Magnarch, "you know how it is with these religious people. Everything gets whipped up into a giant meringue of fable and airy lies. My father seemed to be under the impression that the tide would come in after about forty minutes. The panic had to be seen to be believed. But here I am, and there they all still are, or they were when I last checked. My more scientifically inclined colleagues tell me we have enough stored resources to keep us going till Wednesday week. By which time," he said firmly, "I swear that I shall confirmed the identity of the thief, tracked them down, and recovered the S'nang üll Hnotorem, or my name's not the Magnarch of Verox. Indeed, that is one the reasons why I have permitted myself to relax here in these happy surroundings in the distracting company of one so delectable as yourself."

The Khemmenoi eyed him warily. "Don't get any funny ideas, buster," she said. "There ain't no Khemmenoi on the menu, here or at the cat-houses. You stick to chomping up modified females, kiddo. There's celestial blood in these veins, and don't you forget it."

"Ah, thank you," the Magnarch said, a touch of rime on the edge of his courtesy, "for reminding me, mad – your Highness. You bring me most happily to the subject I intended to introduce this evening." He leaned forward confidentially. "My specially trained scientific advisors, decent rational people, unsnarled by the delusions of religion, have consulted several first class university professors. Their entrails reveal incontrovertibly that the S'nang üll Hnotorem was stolen not, as I first unjustly assumed, by the Master of the World, but by none other than Charlotte de Maupassant, Empress of Witches."

"Empress of – ?" The Khemmenoi's skin turned an incredulous violet. "Did you say 'Empress'?"

"She appears to have come on in the world."

"Yeah," said Her Royal Highness. "Last I heard, she was a second assistant gr'noom fondler over in Andruta Tiservi's pox-pit, by the rubbish dump. Empress of Witches, huh? Next you'll be telling me she wants to rule the Universe."

"Your faculty of prevision is annoyingly accurate at times, Khemmi," the Magnarch grumbled. "She does indeed intend to rule the Universe. No doubt that is why she has stolen the Stone. The Master of the World, who one supposes is still thrashing that nag of his across half of Asia, has one of his oafs in place up at her end of the time stream, but how much he really knows I have not been able to ascertain. However, it has been reported to me that he also has orders concerning the S'nang üll Hnotorem, which could prove rather a problem, if he finds the thing first. Especially if the Valk-people get wind of it." He sighed heavily. "Worry, worry, worry. If it's not glu'ngtokas, it's megalomaniac witches, and if not them, the Fall of Atlantis. I fear I grow old before my time, Khemmi."

The Khemmenoi leaned a little closer.

"Come on back to my place," she murmured. "I got a couple of modified females there who'll do your every bidding, no charge, and if you feel peckish after, well, you can eat 'em right up, I won't mind. What do you say?"

"A very tempting offer, Khemmi. And then, perhaps, we can down a bottle of Eig'nor fluid together, and attempt to formulate a plan for retrieving our stone from the elusive Charlotte de Maupassant."

39

It is no small relief to withdraw from the iniquitous banqueting of the Magnarch and his squamous companion, especially as the narrative bears us on wings as swift as thought to a cosy bedroom in 'Tinker's Nook', the cottage of that mother among millions, Mrs. J. K. Phipps, where slept the loveliest netball player ever to slip off a pair of shorts – Helena Phipps.

A mischievous beam of light darted from the sky and, flashing past the pigeon loft of the farmhouse across the meadow, plunged through the branches of the oak tree and, without so much as a by your leave, fell upon the bosom of the sleeping model.

Lashes fluttered, lips softly parted, a sigh breathed on the morning air and, to an invisible chorus of thanksgiving from the sylphs which throng the dawning moments of the world, Helena Phipps came back from the land of dreams to Byfleet and the day.

Happily, she threw back the duvet and swung out those fabulous limbs. Her pale gold nightdress whispered to the floor and for a moment, during which several hundred invisible sylphs were crushed against the crash barriers until thrown back by invisible bouncers, Helena Phipps stood naked, her flawless skin bathed in the rosy morning light. The emotional equivalent of the finale of Pandromian Caprotchevsky's Choral Fantasia on the old hymn *Wird das Gerät aufgrund übermaßier Papiermengen gestoppt* thundered through the choirs of unseen beings, and briefly Helena tilted her lovely head to listen, as though she had caught an echo of the blissful paean.

Only the distant whistle of a cowherd and, nearer, the clatter of her mother preparing breakfast in the cottage kitchen reached her perfect ears. With a little smile of the sort that makes Owl-things beat themselves against brick walls, she draped her body with a silk robe and went for her shower.

Masterpieces of eroticism and foam though they be, not even television adverts for bath essences could approach the sensual artistry of Helena Phipps. With nothing but her own body, a cake of Coal Tar and a loofah, she performed wonders that would have caused the violin to fall unscraped from the fingers of Ronnie O'Sullivan, or Nigel Kennedy to miss a perfectly obvious black. How the water flashed on her flanks, how the suds slid over her bosom, how her hands lathered and caressed! If asked to do justice to that vision, Van Gogh would have cut off more than his ear. Dostoevsky would have taken the easy way out and knocked off a sequel to Crime & Punishment. Your humble narrative, already out of its class, will go away and watch a something calming, an upload of *Nude Wives of our Great Novelists*[36], perhaps, until the steam clears away.

"Hallo, my dear. Lovely morning," smiled Helena's mother, ceasing her clatter.

---

[36] And without mentioning any names, it recommends you see for yourselves what the wife of a certain Booker Prize winner gets up to, about ten minutes in, with a bottle of cheap champagne and a socket set. No wonder the fellow writes such peculiar books.

The Gnostic Frying Pan

Helena returned her smile and asked how she was getting on with the artificial limbs.

"Oh, not badly, not badly," the woman said bravely. "Though they do be fearful noisy, always clatter, clatter, clatter. Oh, before it slips my mind, my duck. There was someone on the 'phone for you this morning. Shocking line, sounded like she was thousands of miles away. A Miss Tiservi, she said. Now let me see, what did she say? Miss Andruta Tiservi, that was it, didn't sound foreign, but you can't tell nowadays can you, calling from The Rampant Gr'noom. Someone you know, is it, dear?"

Helena said she didn't, and reached for the grapefruit.

"Well, apparently she thought somehow she's got hold of a snap of you. It sounded like she said transparent white body stocking and red ankle-strap stilettos she said, so I said to her, I said, I don't know who you are, I said, but I can assure you no daughter of mine would have anything like that in her wardrobe. Well, to cut a long story short, she offered me – Well, I won't say what she offered me and, anyway, where I could put six mute love slaves? – if I'd arrange for you to be outside the Horse & Jockey at twelve o'clock our time where she would pick you up in her cerbo-snatch. I expect that'll be some sort of foreign car, don't you, dear?"

Helena brushed the toast crumbs off her transparent white body stocking and, gently dislodging the cat with the toe of her red ankle-strap stilettos, left her blind and limbless parent to clear away the breakfast things. Upstairs, she checked her alarm clock. 10.30. Plenty of time to pack a few necessities, get her make-up kit together, and pop down to the Horse & Jockey for mid-day.

She had never heard of Andruta Tiservi but supposed that she must be the PA to one of the big photographers. With any luck it might be a fortnight's work on a calendar for the motor trade in Borneo or Tierra del Fuego. Better than modelling knickers for the next season's Harlotella catalogue in a Braintree basement, which was what she's been doing the week before.

At mid-day, with a raincoat over her body stocking to prevent accidents, she waited at the bus stop outside the pub, watching eagerly for the arrival of the sort of low-slung sports-mobile that might be driven by someone called Andruta Tiservi.

The clock on the old Water Tower struck the first note of the hour, sending a clatter of doves from the ivy. When the echoes of the last chime had died away, the heart breakingly lovely young woman at the bus stop had vanished. Bert Coggan, landlord of the Horse & Jockey, whose trade had tripled in the last ten minutes, sighed and abandoned his plan to offer her 10% of takings to lean against the wall on a permanent basis. It would have to be his niece Shirley and her lap dancing as usual. Odd, though, he remarked to himself as he pushed his way through the crowds back to his bar. He hadn't seen the number 27 come along. It was daft, he knew, but he could almost swear that, on the final stroke of twelve, the most desirable woman he had ever seen had turned into a wisp of mist and disappeared into thin air, leaving nothing behind but a torn shred of transparent white body stocking.

The cerbo-snatch had done its work.

Absolutely typical, of course. The cerbo-snatch in the halls of the Archerons of Atlantis was a clapped out government model that could only hook in its targets if they had an active Progosticator about their persons, while even the shadiest of the cat-houses of P'nor'n (and than Andruta Tiservi's there was none shadier) boasted the latest thing in automatic self-polishing cerbo-technology. A moment later, or several thousand years earlier depending how you look at it, Helena Phipps found herself standing in Ms Tiservi's office, none the worse for her trip, except for the fact that, as she found when she unfastened her rain coat, one breast had popped out through a hole in the front of her body stocking. Since both Ms Tiservi's breasts were on display, and painted bright orange at that, it hardly seemed worth mentioning.

"Ah, yes!" purred Ms Tiservi, gazing with satisfaction from Helena to the photograph and back again. "Ah, yes. The very thing. The very bait with which to lure a certain party to my pleasure-dome. Tell me, my dear, have you done much work with Magnarchs?"

40

"Glu'ng, glu'ng," went the telephone in the office of the Master of the World, proving that the Magnarch had not imagined it.

In the absence of the Master, still acquiring an historic crop of saddle sores on the back of his steed, Strapner, discipline had loosened. Sadie Q Tourmaline, his personal assistant, clad in a silver jumpsuit with matching bootees and skull cap and wearing a ginger wig, raised green-tinted lenses from the pages of her library book, swung her feet out of the Master's in-tray, and flipped up the receiver.

"This is a recorded message," she intoned, pinching her nose between two green-nailed fingers. "The Master of the World is not avail - "

"Oh, cut that out, Sadie," interrupted the voice at the other end. "Put Sheppenic on right away."

"Why, hi, Andruta, honey," Sadie trilled. She swung her feet up again and snuggled back into the comfort of the Master's Executive Tranqui-Chair™. "Gosh, I'm really sorry, babes. The Master's not here, honestly. He's ridden again. Maybe I can help?"

Idly opening a drawer in the Master's desk, she found herself eyeing a large box of L'Autrepeche & Punz's chocolate covered Eig'nor liqueurs. Taped to the lid was a visiting card bearing the name of Andruta Tiservi, the logo of The Rampant Gr'noom, and a message in thick red ink. "To a Master — from a Mistress." Sadie's matching ginger eyebrows went upwards and her mouth made an '**O**'.

"So you're having an easy time of it, are you, Sadie darling?" said the honey and aloes voice of Andruta Tiservi. "Feet up for a year or two, I expect."

"Oh no," Sadie protested. She peeled off the silver foil from an Eig'nor sweet. "You know how it is in the Master's office, busy, busy, busy. Personalised ultimatums to the world leaders to mimeograph, typing, filing -"

"Not to mention running up and down library ladders in those fetching cream cami-knickers."

"Well, hey, I don't design the uniforms. That's the Master's prerogative. He sure likes to see a piece of tail while he's composing his sermons, doesn't he? You know," she added sweetly, "you ought to invite him over to that cat-house of yours. You'd be amazed."

"I suggest that you speak a little more respectfully of your employer." Andruta's voice was as cold as a milk bottle on a Siberian doorstep. "I may feel it my duty to report this conversation."

"You do that, babes," Sadie drawled. She opened her lips and popped in the liqueur chocolate.

"Meanwhile, you will kindly take down this message. To the Master. I have succeeded in obtaining a commodity of outstanding value and promise. Am proceeding now to the second stage of the plan which we discussed last month. Fondest love, Andruta. And put three kisses at the bottom. Read it back to me, Sadie. Sadie? Sadie? Hallo? Hallo? Hallo?"

As soon as the Master had left, Sadie had sent their copy of Esoteric Mysteries of the Unknown Worlds (Large Print edition) back to the library and ordered the latest Timora Garpatheny. The source of the splatter of green and ginger droplets on page 197, obliterating a rattling good bit where the hero, MI6 agent and world Scrabble champion, Oscar Hammerstein, who has broken into the offices of an entity known as the European Commission for Democracy Through Law in order to microfilm the secret protocols of the Annual Report of Activities, is under covert observation by officials from the EU Security Police from whom he will escape by leaping to the street via the roof of a passing Norbert D'Entressangle, commandeering a beautiful young woman's Renault Clio, and thrilling the reader with a car chase through the streets of Strasbourg,[37] is now explained.

They are all that remains of Sadie Q Tourmaline after she bit through the chocolate coating of the Eig'nor sweet. Someone had booby trapped the liqueurs.

Unaware of the effect which her little gift might have had upon the Master of the World, had not Sadie come on as substitute, Andruta Tiservi shrugged and replaced the receiver. Then from a wall-safe she withdrew the photograph of Helena Phipps in the white body stocking which had materialised in her exercise room. With a thick and sticky red pen, she scrawled a note on the back. "How would you like this little too-bup to groil your magger for you? She's fresh today at The

---

[37] And all without a single informative footnote!

Rampant Gr'noom. Do drop in," signed it with her own name and slipped the temptation into an envelope addressed to the Magnarch of Verox at his holiday home in Gorpul dül Mimpoth.

Leaving the missive in her out tray, she picked up her neural lash and hurried down to the reception area, where Helena Phipps was running through a few of her most popular poses with a silk scarf and a pair of pink stocking tights. She little knew what kind of poses Andruta Tiservi had in mind for her.

41

"Glu'ng, glu'ng," went the telephone in the office of the Master of the World, proving again that the Magnarch had not imagined it, unless it was just some sort of freak echo from the previous chapter. "Glu'ng, glu'ng, glu'ng."

With a shake of his head and a worried frown, Eric Maresbreath replaced the receiver of the telephone in the booth in the hall of Sparesbrook Manor. Egrah'nca, who had been sliding back and forth on the shiny green tiles, sat down with a bump.

"What's up?" he asked. "Can't get through?"

"It's unbelievable," Eric said. He wondered moodily out of the back door and stumped off down the path through the towering parsnip fronds. "The entire universe in peril and they can't be arsed to answer the phone in Shambhala. It's the direct line to the Master's office, too. I mean, I know your mysterious Time & Motion chappies have taken the glu'ng threat off the board -"

"Aaaaaaaaaheeeeeeeeeoooooooowwwww," elaborated Egrah'nca, skipping along behind him. "Pfft!"

"Yes, that onion soup was a bit volatile, wasn't it? Where was I? Oh, yes. Well, accepting we're no longer in danger from -"

"A tachomimsal maniacal expert's halitosis," said Egrah'nca.

"This is hardly the time for your Julie Andrew's impressions. Yes, there's no longer any risk of glu'ng, but we're far from out of the woods yet."

"Call these woods?" Egrah'nca vaulted a toadstool. "They look more like copses to me. Or spinneys. Or holts. Or hangers."

"Shut up!" Eric snapped off a stem of Crippen's Stenchwort and thwacked his companion with it. "I'm doing my best to kick start the bloody narrative. I know we're said to be safe from the raving Thring, but Charlotte de Maupassant is still very much with us (I saw her upstairs, drying out her robe over a fire of first editions), there's a madwoman here who keeps asking me if I'm related to the goddess Sclit, and during the night something mind-shatteringly vast came and rubbed itself against the east wing, doing fearful damage to the late Georgian accretions. And worst of all, I virtually had the Stone right there in my hands and I lost it. I must and shall find it again, bear it off to Shambhala, and in dutiful joy lay it at the feet of my Master. Before your bunch of scaly horrors wrap their tails round it. But you'd think, wouldn't you, that the Master could take his eyes off Sadie Tourmaline's rump long enough to answer a bloody phone."

Egrah'nca raised his yellow eyebrows. "Do I detect a smidgen of disenchantment?" he asked.

"Well," grumbled Eric, his leg twitching nervously. "It's a bit much, isn't it? I mean, they pick you up one night when you're really giving of your best in the *Gipsy Baron*, and they whisk you off to an oasis of flaming light in the back of beyond where they brainwash you till there's holes in your superego, then they boot you out of the tradesmen's entrance and tell you to go and guard the bloody universe -"

"You got Helena Phipps out of it," Egrah'nca reminded him. "More than some of us see for our pains."

"Oh, I know, I know. Though when I'll get another chance to go down to Byfleet..." The Guardian of the Earth sank down on a damp muck heap and picked at the scab on his forehead. "You know, before I became Guardian, I used to lie awake at night and wonder if I was wasting my life. My wife and I had drifted apart. We didn't see eye to eye over her career. She wanted to be the mother of the Messiah and I didn't approve. And I was stuck in a routine job, smuggling objets d'art from the Far East with not so much as an index linked pension to look forward to."

"I thought you were a traffic warden?"

"That was just a hobby. A pathetic attempt to brighten up my dismal existence. So when they summoned me before the great Buzzard Throne of Shambhala, I jumped at the chance. But now, I don't know, I find myself pining for our little flat in Bootle and the overland route to Samarkand. Do you know what I mean, Egrah'nca?"

"Look, Eric," said Egrah'nca. "You and I serve different masters, right? I'm a close personal friend of the Magnarch of Verox, you're an insignificant minion of Shambhala. In normal circumstances I wouldn't cross the road to spit in your eye. But, well, we've been through a lot together, and we've faced a common foe, so it's time to set old animosities aside and extend the paw of friendship, man to man. But if you don't stop this

The Gnostic Frying Pan

morbid wittering, I'm going to smash your head in with this croquet mallet, ok?"

"Don't care if you do," said Eric gloomily.

In the master bedroom of Sparesbrook Manor, the Captain was awoken from a dream of slavering swine-gods by a sound from outside which he instantly identified as a worm-eaten croquet mallet disintegrating over a head. Rolling over, he shook the sleepy woman by his side.

She smiled drowsily and pressed her warm body against his pyjamas.

"Oh, Gerry," she breathed. My own darling. Please – love me again."

"Not now, Charlotte." The Captain leapt briskly from the sheets. "We must get cracking on your new career. I'll ring up a few top theatrical agents. You get your togs on and run though one or two of your stunts."

And, having uttered a repulsive paean to his demonic lord, the Captain slipped on a pair of cavalry twills and a khaki sweater, and trotted in his Turkish slippers from the room.

Charlotte stretched. She smiled softly.

"Poor deluded fool," she laughed. Then, business like again, she found her spectacles, reached under the bed and pulled out the extremely damp but intact box which she had removed from the bed chamber of the late Heg'naar'n Stag'naavrk.

"Now," she cried, unaware of the lasoculars focused upon her from an asylum window, "at last I have an opportunity to study these unparalleled tomes, these works of unimaginable power! Not in the temple of Atlantis itself was there ever a set of volumes to match these for Revelation!"

Yes, there in the bedroom of Captain H. 'Geronimo' Sparesbrook, there, in her power, lay the most profound secrets of Being itself: the trading records and account books for the year ended 31 August of nothing less than the company which managed the affairs of the universe itself, the ineffable Demi-Urge & Associates Ltd.

42

In wonder we now behold the towers and pennants of the plateau of P'nor'n, land of complaisance and delight, a dream world where no fantasy of lust, mud or mechanical contrivance is without its fulfillment.

At either end of the city stand those two rival cat-houses whose pleasures sum up and transcend the thrills to be purchased anywhere else. To the east uprears the Rampant Gr'noom, where Andruta Tiservi maintains a squad of trained whores of every land to amuse her extremely varied clientele. But we are following the Magnarch to the west, where lies the house of The Khemmenoi of Lunt, the Happy Magger, this latter a confoundingly squamous building whose iridescent plates glow in green and gold under the lusty moon.

One of the few disadvantages of bring the Magnarch of Verox was his inability, because of the aeon in which he existed, to posses a smart phone. Had he been able to check one now, he might have found something to take his mind off the mixture of emotions that coursed through his glands as he accompanied the Khemmenoi of Lunt on a tour of her residence in P'nor'n, whither they had flown from Gorpul dül Mimpoth in the royal lady's private jet.

The row of modified female slaves, any one of whom employed in the cat-houses of P'nor'n would have commanded a fee equal to the lifetime's income a top sensational novelist, who grovelled in organdie when the Khemmenoi and her guest

The Stone Also Rises

swept through the marbled entrance hall had filled him with a cocktail of hunger and lust, while the sight of the muscular brown bodies of her footmen as, resplendent in their seersucker codpieces, they welcomed their mistress into her withdrawing room, stirred up a sediment of avarice which had lain for years in the bottom of his soul.

He was conducted by the gracious Khemmenoi down arched corridors of pale green and mauve quilting, where perfumes floated in the atmosphere like olfactory butterflies, and the gentle music of crumhorns caressed the air, all of which aroused in the Magnarch a fury of ecstatic proportions, unable as he was to tolerate either the colour green or the keening of a crumhorn. But when the Khemmenoi threw back the portals of the guest chamber that burning emotion was quickly extinguished by a great wave of envy.

The room was a chamber concerto for ebony and lambswool. On the wall hung the latest in Omnipercipient Peep Screens, tuned as they entered to the gymnasium on the corner of Mayberry and Feast, New York, where a certain actress-singer gave what she supposed was an entirely private performance of The World's Best Loved Form Of Exercise with her Personal Trainer across the padded top of a vaulting horse. Two fully certified harlots, who had been sprawled on the fleecy carpet in front of the screen, flicked a switch, leapt onto the bed and began to jiggle their hips in perfectly synchronised unison.

But it was the apparatus of steel and liquid herulamium in the corner of the room at which the almost speechless Magnarch could only gesture. Following his faltering forelimb, the Khemmenoi

The Gnostic Frying Pan

blushed a furious burgundy and screamed for an attendant. At once a gilded youth threw himself before her and allowed her to kick him into blubbering servility.

"I gave orders, fool," she shrieked, "that on no account was the guest chamber to be used as a junk room. What, then, is the meaning of this outrage?" She pointed an imperious finger at the machine. "Why is that heap of rubbish defiling the floor on which it stands?"

The youth gibbered and curled himself into a ball to protect his interests.

"I am ashamed, Magnarch," the Khemmenoi said. "That you should be forced to witness this scene is insult enough, but that you should find your chamber a refuse tip must, I am sure, be unforgivable. I insist that you devour this luckless lad as some form of reparation."

The Magnarch, after their intimate dinner, was not in the least hungry, especially as he had quietly ingested a jiggling harlot while the Khemmenoi's attention was engaged with the boy, but he forced himself as a matter of courtesy to swallow the servant as well.

His mouth empty, he was able at last to say, "Khemmi, that's – surely that's a Hork & Acrish Self-Targeting Cerbo-Snatch with the full dismembering facility? How can you call it a heap of rubbish?"

"You pretend to ignorance in order to spare my blushes, my courteous friend. You will surely have read this month's edition of Cerbo News. The latest model from Rvola came onto the market last Tuesday. Its automated laser intensified delouser and credit card snatcher render it indispensable to a properly run cat-house. This clapped out old heap of junk should have gone to the scrap yard this morning. No doubt my servants thought to hide it here until the chance came to sell it on the sly to some government agency or other."

"As an Archeron of Atlantis," the Magnarch said, "believe me, I well understand the emotion which the sight of such a wonder would arouse in any loyal civil servant. Why, my own office is not so technologised up to the minute-wise as your spare bedroom. Oh, we have modified females aplenty," he said, nodding at the harlot now jiggling solo on the counterpane, "and Omniperts after a fashion, though none with this interesting freeze frame capacity." He indicated the screen where the astonished actress hung in sudden paralysis upside down from the parallel bars and wondered if she had been stricken by arthritis or a disapproving Deity. "But – oh, Khemmi, if you only knew how I could use that cerbo-snatch! A certain top agent of mine would get a shock or two, I can tell you."

"Then, please, make whatever use of the machine you will," the Khemmenoi said generously. "I expect it's still working as well as it ever did." She touched a number of switches. "Let's do a test run." She nodded at the inverted actress on the Omnipert. "What about her?"

For Gelinda Palm, life had until this evening been one long free lunch. A recording star with more gold discs than a Harley Street osteopath, her performances in films as different as *Knees* and *Deirdre Horne, Man of Mystery* acclaimed by critics as the greatest since Rin Tin Tin, her succession of athletic but brainless lovers the admiration of women from New Bunsen to Tashkent, it had seemed to Gelinda that fate looked upon her as a favourite niece.

Not until this evening had she been given cause to question her opinion. The big chested guy she'd picked up on the set of *Narrow Feint & Margin* and at once employed as her latest Personal Trainer had revealed an obsession with the works of Spinoza and a taste for Mozart that repelled her even more than his underarm odour and irritating giggle. Nevertheless, she had managed to stop him twittering on about Neutral Monism for long enough to enjoy him over her own vaulting horse. She had been about to introduce him to the endless number of things you could do to a naked woman upside down on the parallel bars when she was stricken by paraplegia, followed some minutes later by what felt like a runaway rhino.

Her apartment collapsed about her ears and she felt herself sucked like a mint-julep into the mouth of eternity, which pissed her out sometime later onto a lambswool carpet at the feet of a woman with iridescent skin and a – and – Gelinda's vocabulary failed her when she saw the Magnarch. She could compare him only to the producer of her last picture but one, and even that really didn't do the thing justice.

The Magnarch applauded.

"Oh, it's nothing," said the Khemmenoi. "The real nuisance is that the rewind has burnt out, so I can't send it back again. Still, it's not that revolting. Probably fetch a few diams at the flesh market. Andruta Tiservi will find a job for her, if no-one else, though I feel sorry for any female roped into that swamp hole. She gets all the trade off the

Sess boats in there, not to mention the carriage trade from Suov."

While a slave led the still pliant from shock Gelinda away, the Magnarch familiarised himself with the controls, during which he was accidentally responsible for the mystery of Roanoke, and then with a gleeful snarl tapped in the personal DNA[38] code of his agent, Egrah'nca.

Whistling a cheerful Atlantean tune, Egrah'nca had strolled back into the Manor with the notion of seeking out a tin of Andrews Liver Salts (that onion soup had indeed been a bit on the unstable side) when little Eric pounced on him and produced a pair of her mother's pinking shears. That the room at that point turned into molasses and decanted down a funnel into a nuclear mishap, carrying Egrah'nca with it, was as profound a cause of relief as, seconds later, finding himself falling out of the ceiling fan in the Khemmenoi's spare bedroom was not. He landed heavily on a lamb's wool carpet, his arrival quite unnoticed by the pair of harlots sniggering at the Omnipert, where Gelinda Palm was just assisting the muscular young gentleman out of his jock strap.

There always was something shaky about the time location vectors on the old Hork & Acrish Mark IV: when calibrating the temporal diffusion, it was generally a good idea to lean a bit to the left.

---

[38] Distinctive Neural Activity code, not that dioxy nonsense, which wouldn't have been much use on a nylon and kapok teddy bear anyway, even if it could tell you the difference between a genetic scientist and a potato.

The Gnostic Frying Pan

Egrah'nca had arrived in P'nor'n about ten minutes in front of the Magnarch.

While his commander enthused over the obsolete technology of the Khemmenoi's Cerbosnatch, Egrah'nca lay concealed behind a cabinet of intriguing devices thoughtfully provided by the hostess for those moments when the sexual adventurer can't think of anything sufficiently bizarre to arouse the jaded appetite. He observed the ingestion of the harlot and the subsequent abduction of Gelinda Palm with great interest: at least he knew now where he was. The squamous female must be Her Royal Highness, the Khemmenoi of Lunt. He was just trying to remember the correct protocols when he heard the Magnarch say, "How very odd. I appear to have summoned a packet of processed cheese slices. Unless Egrah'nca has acquired a skill in transformation not usually encouraged in my minions, there has been some error. Luckily for him, or the fate which now befalls this rather unpleasant Gouda - " There was an indescribable sound " - would have been his."

Egrah'nca entertained a sudden whimsical notion that he might, after all, remain in dusty seclusion behind the cabinet. It appeared that he had done something to upset his patron.

The Khemmenoi quickly apologised for the incompetence of the machine but reminded her guest that it was an old and unreliable model. Why didn't he avail himself of the brand new Rvola in her office over at the Happy Magger complex?

The Magnarch dumped himself down on the bed, at which the harlot gave a very satisfying shriek, and said, "In the morning, if I may. But today has been a very -" He rubbed his stomach "- very full one. It is a sad fact of my nature that after a heavy meal, I must rest for a time. Excuse me, dear lady, if I appear ungallant, but..." With a crash that set the bed creaking, reinforced though it was to withstand the most athletic love play, the Magnarch slumped back on the counterpane. The harlot, perfectly conditioned, attempted to ply her trade and did not give up until, stifled under the bulk of the Magnarch, the wanton girl expired.

"Excellent," the Khemmenoi nodded. "A credit to your trainer. I shall certainly buy from him again."

And having switched off the light, she left the room.

Egrah'nca shifted a fraction. At once the contents of the cabinet tinkled and shook on the glass shelves. The Magnarch grumbled in his sleep and stirred. The body of the harlot slid off the counterpane but, even in death, retained its grip on the Magnarch. With a drowsy grunt of pain, he lifted his head and stared about him.

Egrah'nca froze.

The Magnarch belched, cursed and fell back into his slumber.

Now what could he do? What should he do? For whatever he did and wherever he went, come the morning, when the Magnarch got his claws on the new Cerbo-snatch in the Khemmenoi's office, he would have no choice but to drop everything and report to have his head bitten off.

If the Magnarch's wrath got the better of him, literally.

Miserably but with infinite precaution, he sank down onto the floor behind the cabinet of curiosities and, sucking at his fur, prepared to spend a wakeful night.

43

Anxious though all those devoted to the matchless witch must be to know how Charlotte de Maupassant came to the bed of her hated enemy, Captain H. 'Geronimo' Sparesbrook, and what she made of the contents of the box which she had hidden beneath his bed, their concern is as nothing compared to that of the Magnarch. Hungry as he was for an opportunity to chew things over with his lackadaisical agent, he could clearly see that his priority was Charlotte de Maupassant and the stone of power. Locate the one, and he would surely find the other.

Then, perhaps, his blue and yellow agent could do something to redeem the misspent time that's past...

Awaking the next morning with indigestion, he had at once despatched a messenger, which made him feel better, and then issued a formal requisition to the cat-house of Andruta Tiservi for all records and data uploads pertaining to former employee, Charlotte de Maupassant. A clerical harlot soon arrived, bearing a pile of mail forwarded from Gorpul dül Mimpoth which the Magnarch tossed impatiently aside before seizing the mnemodrive and inserting it into the aperture in the base of his neck constructed by a team of neurosurgeons and Kadathian engineers.

He winced in micro-agony, his brain cringing like a sentient porridge under the onslaught of the reminiscent equivalent of 500 watts per channel at full rip, and quickly adjusted the graphic equaliser beneath the hinged scale behind one of his ears. Then he rose and, flexing his digits, took up his place before the controls of the Omnipercipient screen.[39] The Magnarch of Verox was as skilled an

---

[39] In fact, 'Omnipercipient' is a wildly extravagant bit of brand naming and does not accurately describe the capacities of the medium. Intended originally as a class-room aid, it was invented by Atter Lu'naam, the great Atlantean mage more famous for his work on modified females, and had in the earliest stages of its development been a simple remote viewer. It drifted uncontrollably through the aeons and reaches of the universe sending back poor quality images of whatever it encountered on the way. By the nature of things what it encountered was generally of a mind-rotting tedium, the universe being 99% composed of dark matter even less interesting than the endless pinkish desert of Troch where the passing of a sand fly is regarded as a major news story. Sometimes it picked up men in shabby suits doing the Guardian crossword on a train from Charing Cross, or even the Saturday night output from BBC4. It was thus more than suitable for schools, where it is universally deemed important to remind the pupils that life is on the whole and very dull and pointless affair.

It was Lu'naam's great discovery of the Exponential Orgasm Wave which changed everything. Like many a major find, it happened by accident, though a good deal more intriguingly than Pasteur's dish of mouse-mould, or Sir Alexander Penis's invention of Phlegm. A by-product of his work on the orgasmic response mechanisms of the modified female, it occurred quite by chance one evening when he had connected the pleasure zones of a certain harlot, Miss Kinsella Llunge, to the monitoring apparatus of his 101 Experiments Nuclear Destruction Kit. Under the irresistible stimulus of an Atlantean love-bug, a small creature with pimply legs which makes its home in the venereal compartments of ladies where it stridulates continually causing almost uninterrupted ecstasy and a good deal of squeaking, Kinsella gasped and moaned and writhed and ran with sweat, and the uranium atoms inside the nuclear game discharged in a far from random pattern that made all the lights in Basileia flash on and off like a Magotte's Tree and generated enough interference to blitz out Omniperts from Yopps, the boarding academy for the scions of Archerons, to the Tps'ner Road Secondary Modern, Lemuria, where the budding sess-sellers were kept under lock and key until they got too big to handle.

artist with the Omnipert as any in Atlantis. Touching a few keys, he extemporised a slow introduction, in which the display drifted through the bed chambers of P'nor'n, where bodies plunged in shadows, wandering up and down the scales of time until, with a brilliant change of key, he found and introduced the main subject, Charlotte de Maupassant, serving her apprenticeship in the pleasure dome of Andruta Tiservi.

She looked different in those days, before the years of shape-changing took their toll of her. A slim girl with auburn hair and green eyes, she lay in her harlot's tunic with the half-cup top in the display cage of a hall in Andruta's establishment, and many indeed was the sess-seller or travelling salesbeing from Suov who fed the necessary coin into the slot which permitted the insertion of an arm (or similar appendage) for a thirty second feel of the harlot's attractions. Little did they suspect that they were exploring a bosom which harboured plans to rule the universe. So utterly detached was she from her circumstances that Charlotte survived her term

---

It was not long before Lu'naam's new Omnipert with the built in Kinsellometer appeared on the market. The simple device had completely transformed the machine by enabling it to home in, not on pinkish deserts or the 4.15 to Gravesend, but the greatest and most enduring arcs of sexual pleasure as they rippled in great gasping waves across the space-time continuum in an ever widening vortex of bliss. It was something of a disappointment to voyeurs, however, when snapping on the controls, they found themselves peeping at the foreplay and congress of the tortoise.

Many never recovered from the shock of discovering that on the scale of erotic pleasure the human race ranks a poor fifth after the tortoise, the jackal, Sheldrake's Frog and the Goat-Horror of Vharg. Lu'naam hastily made adjustments to the Kinsellometer, lowering its threshold of resonance, which at last permitted the owners of the Omnipert to enjoy less bestial pleasures.

The Gnostic Frying Pan

in the cat-houses of P'nor'n without mental or physical trauma (if you exclude an entirely normal hatred of sess-sellers).

The Magnarch's composition now modulated to the second subject, who turned out to be a bulky human with a hairy chest and a hammer in his fist, instantly recognisable to many of the narrative's friends as the former Herbert Jubb in his pre-half-an-Owl-thing days. The development section which followed cleverly wove in the theme of an old folk tune, as the blacksmith and the witch pursued each other in various forms across the hills and dales of England and, finally, in a recapitulation at once fresh and familiar fell together in a transcendence of passion that surpassed even that of the Goat-horror of Vharg, and very nearly equalled Sheldrake's frog.

The second movement of the Magnarch's sonata, a slow and beautiful study of Charlotte's amatory indiscretions with various local tradesmen while Herbert laboured at his forge, led without a break into the scherzo finale, a lively dance around the bed in which the Captain and the witch tumbled together on the evening following their joint expulsion from the fountains of the Violet Pring Hebbenthwaite Sunset Memorial Home. With a final crescendo of lust, torn sheets and squeezing fingers, the composition climaxed. The Magnarch, glistening faintly, reeled from the controls and collapsed onto the bed. The effort had been draining but he had at least traced the putative Empress of Witness to her current place in the space time continuum.

Not that it explains how she ended up in bed with the man most likely to be turned into a packet of dried lentils, Captain H. 'Geronimo' Sparesbrook.

When the renascent Thames had cast them up again upon the tiles of Sparesbrook Manor, Charlotte had been the first to recover consciousness. Discovering that what had immobilised her legs was not paralysis but the body of the Captain, she had cried aloud with evil glee and raised her arms in the first gesture of the Rite of the Hog. And then the Captain's eyes had flickered open and looked up into her own.

Looking into those eyes, she faltered. In them she seemed to read stories of other days, summer days when, her husband's hammer ringing in the forge above them, she and the handsome Captain from the Manor on the hill made thrilling love among the flowery hedgerows or within the Neolithic Tomb by the yew alley. She remembered his lips, his hands, his urgent desire.

And she couldn't for the life of her think of anything nasty enough to do to him.

The Captain, awaking, knew no more than that his head lay in the lap of a woman whose bosom swelled proudly above his face while her arms made some curious gesture over his muddy chest. Only half-conscious, he uttered a silent prayer of thanksgiving to his Infernal Master and, seizing the startled witch in his arms, began to press kisses upon her breasts.

The action took Charlotte by surprise but activated the behaviour patterns implanted in her neural circuits by months of modification in the training centre at P'nor'n. A pair of virtual automata, they stumbled up the stairs to the Captain's bedroom, skirted a hole in the floor, and fell together on the musty mattress in what had made the splendid coda to the Magnarch's sonata.

Sometime in the night hours Charlotte had woken up. The Captain lay beside her, relapsed again into unconsciousness. Thoughtfully, she traced the Rune Sign of Widmore on his back with her fingernail, leaving a thin line of blood on the old skin. Before he fell asleep, the Captain had broached some ridiculous scheme for putting her on TV as an illusionist or some such thing. With difficulty she had refrained from turning his toes into piranha fish and causing him to devour himself with his own feet. His kind of vileness deserved something altogether more splendidly appalling.

Charlotte snuggled under a blanket and settled down beside the sleeping man.

The thing to do, she had decided, was to string the foolish Captain along until she had become Ruler of the Universe.

Then she would really fix the old sod.

44

Pigeons and gulls wheeled in the sunlight over the bare trees. The sky, a clear wash of blue, had shed its burden of snow, the traces of which dusted the shadowy roofs of the outbuildings of the mansion and the pinnacles of the asylum up the hill.

Little Miss Eric skipped down the path, past the kennel where the Owl-thing shivered miserably on the end of its chain, the remains of a dead badger in its bowl, and over the frozen lawns to the Guardian of the Earth, who was trying to untangle a length of pink ribbon from the bramble bushes.

"Hallo, young 'un," said the larger of the two Erics.

"Have you nicked my teddy again?" the belligerent child demanded.

"It's not your teddy," Eric said. "And how many times do I have to tell you, he's not really a-"

"Is my teddy!" screamed Eric. "Is my teddy. My Uncle Ron give him me."

"You haven't got an Uncle Ron," the Guardian began, but he could see the futility of that approach. "It's pointless arguing, anyway," he said. "I haven't got him and I don't know where the little ba- baa-lamb's gone."

Eric pointed a minatory finger. "That's my teddy's ribbon," she said balefully. "You've stolen him and - and you've eaten him up. You're nasty. I don't like you."

"You're no Polly-bloody-Anna yourself," Eric snapped. "Here, take your rotten ribbon. I hope it strangles you."

The Gnostic Frying Pan

Eric snatched the ribbon from Eric's hand and scampered away. Unaware that he had just placed a Weapon of Mass Destruction in the hands of a nursery school nihilist, Eric Maresbreath kicked his way through the sprout beds and trudged aimlessly down the yew alley, still glancing here and there all the while on the off chance of spotting the S'nangstone.

Eric junior meanwhile had tied the Nidro Force in her hair and skipped off to watch a party of day trippers from the asylum being driven down the hillside by the whips of their keepers, among them a royal personage whose identity the narrative is not stupid enough to disclose. They were soon gone, loaded into what an unbiased observer would have described as tumbrels, and trundled away into the woods.

In search of further distraction, Eric climbed to the crest of Stunnard's Valley, a rocky abyss, unblessed by sunlight and fronded with unhallowed vegetation, across the road from the chip shop. Thus it was that little Eric was the very first person to witness the invasion force of the Valk-people when it thundered out of the wormhole in the cliff, galloped down the valley, and formed up around the electricity pylon.

Little Eric, almost interested in the sight of two hundred objects like giant crows in silver helmets and mounted on horseback, clambered onto a boulder and watched them sacrifice a herd of prize bullocks.

When the Valk-people had drunk their fill and the bloodless carcases had fallen into the purling Dymph, the leader of the troop raised his spear and uttered a hoarse command. It flew like

The Stone Also Rises

the cry of a rook across the frosty meadows to the ear of Eric Maresbreath, the elder, as he relieved himself from the bridge onto the roofs of lorries passing on the motorway below.

Recognising the dread sound, he whirled, spraying a glittering golden arc across the footbridge and glared heavily in the direction of the Manor. Hours of enemy recognition training in the schools at Shambhala had taught him every nuance of sound that might come from the throat, or other bodily orifice, of an alien and hostile menace. Lassitude fell from him. He ran from the bridge, leapt a fence and raced across the hummocky meadow to the yew alley, where he was seized and carried off by Detective Sergeant Leonard Bunchley and his men, who were stationed there on permanent flasher watch. Useless to protest that in the heat of the moment he had forgotten to tuck his bantam away. The policemen dealt with him in that robust but good-humoured manner which has made the name of the British Bobby respected throughout the world and he didn't recover consciousness for hours.

The Valk-people, unaware of the debt of gratitude they owed to the Amblebroth constabulary, advanced across the fields, their feathery cloaks lambent in the cold light that flashed from their silver helmets and spears and the jingling harnesses of their black mounts. Little Eric, soon weary of the show, yawned and jumped down from the boulder in search of better distractions.

In the estate office, Captain Sparesbrook slammed down the telephone for the umpteenth time and swore. Here he was, offering the world the greatest entertainer and illusionist since Harold

The Gnostic Frying Pan

'You've Never Had It' McMillan the Scottish Comedy Escapologist, and all the agents would say was, "Yes, but does she strip?"

He lit a cigar and wandered to the window, thereby placing himself in the ideal spot to observe the first charge of the Valk-people up the drive.

"Dashed peculiar outfit Monsonby's got the hunt in this year," the Captain thought. "Going to the dogs, just like the rest of the poor bloody country. Good Grief!" He had just seen the leader's sword sever the head of a villager who had been stealing twigs from the bushes at the end of the drive. "I take it all back. Damn fine shot, whoever you are."

Charlotte de Maupassant, distracted from her preliminary review of the accounts by the shriek of the murdered villager, had also become aware of the incursion of what she too recognised as the barbaric Valk-people, worshippers of Crom Ten Pogol from the craggy lanes and sand pits of the Atlantean hill country. A woman of decision, she at once transformed the remains of her chiffon robe into a sheet of strong brown paper, which she addressed after a second's thought to her former employer, Andruta Tiservi, then became a wooden chest into which she drew the ledgers and account books of the Demi-Urge, an experience slightly less uncomfortable than being raped by a crazed hippo, itself preferable to the foibles of the Valk-people, on which she had had ample opportunity to become an authority during her apprenticeship at the Rampant Gr'noom. Wrapped in the brown paper and knotted with string, Charlotte left herself on the hall table for the postman. She regretted that her magic was not yet strong enough to run to a couple of stamps

The Stone Also Rises

but she promised that she would pay Andruta back the excess charge[40].

Little Eric Maresbreath had pursued a terrified stoat into a drain and got stuck, so she missed the visit of the Valk-people, as did large Eric Maresbreath, bleeding apologetically on the floor of a cell in Amblebroth nick.

The Valk warriors urged their mounts up the drive. What sensations of bewilderment always transfix the heart of one who chances upon Sparesbrook Manor! True, as the Valk leader (a builder by trade, when not leading Valk raiding parties) immediately saw, the exterior cried out for a careful demolition of the outer skin above the ground floor window sill level from the right hand side of the main entrance door along to the projecting bay window, setting aside any sound features for re-use, and new precast concrete lintels would not go amiss with a tinted pigment similar to the existing, not to mention terra cotta air bricks, fresh rainwater stacks, redressed hopper head outlets and a rebidding of the front coping stones.

However, he was here today in his military capacity.

A booming echoed through the hall as the Valk leader's spear thundered against the door. Her hands floury from pastry making, Deirdre Horne bustled across the tiles and lifted the latch.

---

[40] By what means would the Post Office deliver the parcel to an addressee who lived in a bygone aeon? Frankly, the narrative has no idea. There are mysterious forces in play which even the narrative cannot begin to comprehend. Why do they leave 'While You Were Out' cards without even knocking? Why are the collection depots always so inaccessible? Mysteries beyond telling.

"If you're from the Social Services," she began bravely, but with two feet of Valk spear projecting from her cardie seemed lost for words. The Valk leader flipped the body back over his head. It disappeared among his followers. Only the crochet dress and sensible underwear were ever seen again, flying as pennants from the spears of several Valk warriors, who had a sense of humour, of a sort.

The Captain, who had seen this distressing incident from the top of the stairs, decided that unshaven and in his dressing gown, he could scarcely be expected to greet visitors, so to spare them embarrassment thoughtfully decided to leave by the drain pipe outside the bedroom window. Sadly, the Valk warriors were used to having that effect on people. When he reached ground level he found eight or nine of them waiting for him, spears at the ready.

"Ah, good day to you," the Captain stammered, somewhat at a loss. "Ah, yes. Fine weather. Hmm. Any of you chaps Balliol men?"

The warriors laughed like a rookery at sunset and encouraged the Captain to overcome his diffidence by prodding him with their spears. Soon he found himself kneeling on the gravel drive while the Valk leader sneered at him from each bright beady eye in turn.

"Where," cawed the warrior chief, "is the S'nang üll Hnotorem?"

Only Charlotte de Maupassant on the hall table, listening though an air-hole in the brown paper, was capable of understanding his heathen speech but she wasn't about to step forward and apply for the job of translator.

The Captain, not a man to allow calamity to dull his religious fervour, uttered a heartfelt plea to the Fiend, which meant nothing to the Valk people.

"Any of you fleabags know what the old magger-biter's gabbling about?" the Valk leader asked.

A small Valk warrior with Deirdre's knickers fluttering from his helm, was thrust forward.

"Well, Schlech?" cawed the leader, eyeing the undergarment with distaste. "You speak this eldritch lingo?"

"A word or two, honoured one," stuttered the warrior. "Just something I picked up in the cathouses of P'nor'n, sire."

A ribald chorus of squawks signalled that every member of the troop had instantaneously thought of the punch-line, so the Valk leader shut his beak and contented himself with knocking Sparesbrook over instead. "Question the scumph," he commanded.

"Er, hallo, big boy," the Valk warrior began, a little self consciously. "Er, will I groyle your magger for you?" The formalities of greeting over, he went on: "We, Valk people. We lust for S'nang. Er, that big, uh, big, uh - " He made an impressive gesture, which frightened the Captain. "Our God, Crom Ten Pogol. Mighty shagger. OK?"

"I fear," said the Captain, attempting to scrape a tunnel in the gravel, "that I haven't had the honour of meeting your Deity."

"What's he say?" rasped the leader.

"I think," said Schlech, "that he wants to look at my thingy."

"Bloody pervert," said the leader. "When we've got our hands on the stone, I'm going to take

The Gnostic Frying Pan

the greatest pleasure in ramming my spear so far up his jacksy he'll be able to use it as a hat pin. Tell him to bring out the stone or we'll burn his nest down."

"Er, big boy say," translated Schlach, "you give us stone called S'nang. We not, er – " Incendrianism being uncommon in the cat houses, he was forced to adapt his leader's ultimatum slightly. "We not, er, bite off your balls and ram them up your beak, you scumph-faced little pigeon," he finished fluently, recalling the words spat at him by the first English harlot he'd ever had, or failed to have, on his maiden voyage to P'nor'n.

The Captain covered his privates with both hands and whined dramatically.

"Look at it," the Valk leader croaked in disgust. "Playing with itself now. Dirty little tyke. They're all the same, these humanoids. No wonder their women end up in the cat-houses. Bugger the stupid stone, anyway. It's time to show him the picture."

From under his feathery cloak, the Valk leader produced a glossy photograph. Any man would have recognised the subject as Helena Phipps.

"Tell him," said the leader, "if he can lead us to this woman, we'll spare his nesting site. And he can keep the ridiculous stone too, for all I care."

Schlech stared up, aghast. "Keep the stone?" he twittered. "But, sire, that – that is Crom Ten Pogol, the great genital God of our people, to restore whom to his temple we have crossed time and space to this stinking hillside this day."

"I," said the leader, "am Secretary of the Valkan Rationalist Association. We attach no significance to the superstitions of our primitive forebears. The S'nang is a chunk of metamorphic rock, no more. As rational free beings," he cried, "we strike off the chains of the old illusions, of Gods and oaths and paranormal wonders. We shall live the life that logic dictates." He waved the photograph. "A life devoted to science, pillage and sexual adventure. That is why, having shaken off the shackles of morality, we claim this glorious creature as our own, for she belongs by right of logic to the only free people in the universe: the members of the Valkan Rationalist Association, Aiugisnia Branch."

The Captain, imaging that all the ranting concerned various permutations of his own demise, whimpered helplessly.

"That's very interesting," murmured Schlech. "Especially as I, on the other hand, am Assistant Inquisitor (Higher Grade) Hugel Schlech of the Pogol Police."

Little Miss Eric, struggling in the drain, had succeeded in freeing herself but could not manage to untangle the Nidro Force from the barbed wire. Seizing an end of the ribbon in each little fist, she tugged irritably, stamped her foot, and said, "Oh, come on, you silly thing. Oh, I wish I was with my little teddy bear again."

The flash of temporal lightning that ripped across the firmament sidetracked the Pogol Police who, having emerged from the body of the warriors, their cloaks now thrown aside to reveal the insignia of the Crimson Feather on their breasts, had arrested the Valk leader and begun to bind him with taut cords. Taking advantage of their distraction, those Valk warriors who remained loyal to their leader[41] urged their mounts forward and with a good deal of first rate spear work drove Schlech and his cronies back into the house, where they took shelter in the hall.

The leader, freed from his bonds, cried, "Warriors! The Pogol curs have stolen from us our glorious photo of the most attractive woman in the universe! Can we bear this insult and live?"

"Yes," said one or two of the warriors, but quietly.

"No!" cawed all the straight ones.

"Then we attack!" screamed their leader. "And retrieve our precious snap or perish in the attempt."

Lurching and blinded by dust, the Captain managed somehow to avoid being trampled to death in the second charge of the Valk people. He collapsed, choking, on a convenient stone and prepared to enjoy a view of the battle.

---

[41] Oddly enough, all those who had seen the picture of Helena Phipps.

45

We interrupt this account of the opening skirmish in the great Valkan Wars of Religion to bring you a special report from a chancel in the impressive halls of the Archerons of Atlantis, where his Holiness the Serene Principle of Goth awaits the arrival of his son, the Magnarch of Verox.

With bated breath, the multitudes in the congregation survey the Principle seated on the opal throne, his sceptre in his hand, a faint air of detachment on his aquiline features.

There is a stir among the crowd. As usual, eyes turn away to avoid the unpleasant chance of seeing the Magnarch himself, attended by a pair of mute eunuchs, proceed up the aisle and prostate himself on the floor of black jade before his august father.

A loathsome anthem echoes in the vaults of the chamber. When it is over, the Principle nods grimly.

"My son," breathes his ancient voice, as though the very stones have acquired tongues and speak of millennial things, "why are you farting about in the cat-houses of P'nor'n when the S'nang üll Hnotorem is almost in the hands of the Master?"

The halls resound to the volley of spitting which the audience produces at the mention of the lord of Shambhala.

"Hear me, O Reverend Father," says the Magnarch. "I have an agent who remains at the side of Eric Maresbreath by night and day. He -"

"This Eric Maresbreath," interrupts the patriarch, "is it he whom some style Guardian of the Earth and Wielder of the Cord?"

"Even so, O mighty sire of all thy people."

"He's a fake," the Principle said. "Bogus. A dummy. A decoy. Surely to goodness you ought to have spotted that by now. Good Magotte, boy, if it was up to him to save us all, from glu'ng for instance -" There was a mass shudder which shifted the entire building two inches to the left - "where would we be by now?"

"Aaaaaaheeeeeooowww - Pfft!" said the Magnarch unhappily.

"Quite." The Principle stretched out a hand and touched one of a selection of bells which stood upon a salver at his side. It emitted a musical twang. "I have summoned the Officer of Penance," he remarked, "who will allow you the joy of making recompense for the errors which your gluttony and slow-wittedness have brought upon us, foolish child. When that pleasant interlude is over, I suggest you present your apologies[42] to the Khemmenoi and advise her that you have lost your, ahem, interest in what the harlots of P'nor'n have to offer and that you have decided to concentrate in future on your career. Which happens to be, in case you have been so busy with gr'noom fondlers and magger groylers to recall it, in the field of government service. Specifically, saving this nation from a disastrous catastrophe."

---

[42] Not as courteous as you might think. The last person the Magnarch apologised to was Laurif Tcerreo'ntha, former street crossing attendant and now star exhibit in the Basileian Museum of Torture.

"I press my unworthy gratitude upon you, o father," intoned the Magnarch, rather less than sincerely, "for the opportunity to make amends, but must point out that my visit to P'nor'n was not, as you have clearly been misinformed, a pleasure trip. When you somewhat peremptorily recalled me, I was consulting with the Khemmenoi of Lunt on matters not unpleasing to your holiness - matters, I mean, concerning Charlotte de Maupassant, Empress of Witches."

The eyes of the Serene Principle of Goth flickered for a moment. He seemed to wear the expression of one who recalls youthful nights misspent in The Rampant Gr'noom, feeding diams into the machine for a chance to squeeze a fresh young harlot.

"And what of her?" he sighed, emerging half an hour later from his reverie. No-one had moved. You could never be sure that the Principle wasn't trying to catch you out. "What of her whom the laughing lads were wont to call Charlotte the Harlot, the sensation of the cat-house of Andruta Tiservi before it went downhill."

"She plans to rule the universe, lord," the Magnarch murmured, "not excluding that considerable portion of it outlined in red on this plan, at present rejoicing in its subjection to your own sovereign sway. My spies report that she had travelled in the realm of Scaliselsarga-on-Sea and returned alive, accompanied by an Owl-thing and, some say, a box of accounting papers which could spell disaster for us all. I had hoped, with the help of the Khemmenoi, to abduct her cerbo-snatchwise and applicate a neutralisal situation."

The Principle selected another of his little bells.

"I have cancelled the Officer of Penance," the Principle announced. "Elections for his successor will be held as soon as someone has been persuaded, by whatever means necessary, to run for the job. Magnarch, I trust that in dealing with Charlotte the Har-, I mean Charlotte de Maupassant, you will not lose sight of your major task, which is to retrieve the S'nangstone and save our tottering civilization before the real agent of the Master of the World -" Again the crackle of spit on stone- "can make off with it. Oh, and should you come across this young person -" He produced a photograph of a woman of undeniable pulchritude which her transparent chemise and sun-tan oil did nothing to conceal - "I wish to interview her most urgently on a theological matter. Her name, I gather, is Helena Phipps. That will be all. You may go. Good-bye."

46

"Men," drawled Andruta Tiservi, disassembling a wasp with a crack of her neural lash. "Personally, I've had all I can take. To a man you're just a collection of holes, that's all, and in the more extreme cases a light snack. You're a very attractive woman, Helena. You must have suffered their horrible attentions in your time, tearing your undies and secreting all over you and expecting you to say you like it when their unshaven bloody faces sandpaper the skin off your inner thighs. Always asking you to dress up in ridiculous bloody lingerie that takes three quarters of an hour to hook yourself into, just so they can take one look at you, come all over your sofa, and then wander off to watch the sports programmes while you spend another three quarters of an hour unhooking yourself again. Then they moan because the dinner isn't ready. Honestly, Helena, I've had my fill of men, haven't you?"

Helena, attached by leather thongs to the wooden frame of her sleeping cage, said nothing. She no longer had any hope left that all this was part of next year's Unipart calendar.

Andruta slid her arm round Helena's waist and drew herself close to the smooth body. "Please. Be a good girl," she whispered, pressing her tinted bust against the more natural shades of Helena's. "Don't make me lash you again. It's so unpleasant for me. Just promise to try on one or two teensy weensy outfits, that's all. Just try them on. There's no need to go out front tonight. You can wait in my personal office till we've got a few classy clients in, ones who won't ask you to do anything involving the loss of a limb."

Helena tightened her mouth and looked the other way.

Andruta pressed her knee against the inside of Helena's thigh. "Then I'm afraid I shall have to send you to the Modifiers," she said. "You won't enjoy it very much."

Egrah'nca, who had escaped from the Khemmenoi's bed-chamber while the Magnarch, exhausted after his artistry on the Omnipert, napped noisily on the silken bed, was lounging on a divan in the bar of The Rampant Gr'noom and for the first time in centuries felt really at ease. Posing as a door-to-door door salesman, he had gained access to the offices of the Khemmenoi's establishment and vandalised the new Cerbo-snatch to the point where a summons for a bowl of soup might deliver you anything from a million tons of wet nappies to a ravening squid from the uncharted seas beyond Doblere. Leaving half the staff choking on the nappy fumes, and the squid choking on the other half of the staff, he had crossed the city, arriving at the same time as the evening edition of the Daily Fondler, the trade rag of the cat-houses, which announced the sad news of the Magnarch's sudden recall on urgent government business. A very satisfactory arrangement, all things considered.

He offered the newspaper to a sess-seller at the next table, who took it with an ill-mannered grunt and turned at once to the strip cartoons. Egrah'nca flipped open the menu.

"Fyneer Disprot," he read. "A fluffy concoction, guaranteed to gratify the most voracious appetite, this delicious dish consists of two blonde sisters from Hyatia and a Shemlovian water-ass whose invention is without parallel."

No, he'd tried that before. Hallo, what was this?

"New! New! New! Today's Special. Fresh in from our constantly active cerbo-snatchers which scan every corner of the cosmos to bring you the most innovative sensations, comes the most sensual woman in the universe - " Egrah'nca smiled indulgently and turned the page, "Helena Phipps."

Not unused to strangled cries of horror, the customers in the bar barely glanced up from their glasses of Eig'nor Fluid. With trembling paws, Egrah'nca reread the accursed menu. No doubt about it. No 15 was Helena all right.

"Waiter!" snarled the sess-seller, his voice a melange of old underpants and paint stripper. "I'll have the No. 15. Serve it up in the Mud Room."

"Very good, sir," crooned the waiter.

Egrah'nca's horror was complete.

Acting swiftly, he ordered a number at random and dashed up the stairs in the shadow of the enormous sess-seller, nearly suffocating in the stench of raw sess which clung to man's buskins. As they approached the door of the Mud Room, Egrah'nca faked a stumble against the Lemurian's heel and, when he turned to kick the stuffing out of him, seized the cuff of his buskins in the cjebus grip and with a mighty wrench hurled them over the banister.

Unfortunate, then, that the Lemurian, anxious for the flesh of number 15, had already unfastened his buttons and did not accompany his garment to the ground floor of the cat-house several feet below.

"What's your game, then, sonny?" he snarled, his enormous tattooed limbs towering over the bear like the trunks of the hairy oaks indigenous to Upper Lemuria. "You want me to rip your arse off and pull it over your head, do you?"

"Sounds like fun," Egrah'nca lisped poutingly. "Your place or mine, handsome?"

"Urgh," said the Lemurian, stumbling as he backed away. "Urgh. Get away. No. Don't come near me. I'll scream."

"Come on, sweetie," gulped Egrah'nca, mincing after the reversing figure. "That's a lovely set of knick-knacks you've got up there. I bet they weigh a couple of pounds a-piece."

"Bleeugh," shuddered the Lemurian, tugging his coarse shirt down. "Go away. Go on. Please."

Any plans for further entreaties were abandoned at that point as the sess-seller, too intent on watching the midget blue and yellow Nancy to look where he was going, did a splendid reverse dive with twist from the head of the stairs and landed upside down in a pot of porgisvra plants with the knick-knacks so much admired of late by Egrah'nca on display for all to view.

Thanking his trainers for teaching him that Lemurians suffered from homophobia to a degree which made Valk leaders look positively enlightened, Egrah'nca dashed into the Mud Room and locked the door behind him.

It was exactly the kind of disgusting pit a Lemurian sess-seller would go for when considering sexual pleasures, Egrah'nca thought, as he waded through the slime moulds which covered the floor and declined to experience the filth encrusted sheets. A continual ooze of sludge exuded from a row of faucets along the top of the wall behind the bed. Bubbles popped in a haze of noisome gas as he picked his way across to the bench next to the pile of dung.

From a lift behind the door on the far side of the room came a whirring of machinery as Number 15 was winched up from the kennels below. The door slid back. Egrah'nca leapt to his feet.

"Helena!" he cried.

"'Ello, dearie," gurned the almost unrecognisably transformed face. "Groyl your magger for you, shall I, ducks, lord 'elp us, strike a light?"

47

As a literary dilettante, Egrah'nca knew well that best-selling novelists, e.g. Timora Garpatheny to name but one, would have cut away at this point for purposes of tension and suspense. He was therefore rather disconcerted to find the narrative still clamped firmly upon him.

"You're not Helena Phipps!" Egrah'nca shouted.

The harlot shrugged and stepped out of her knickers. "No, well, I guess not, but I'm really just as good, honey. And check the small print -" She indicated the tattoo on her bottom. "No refunds."

Gelinda Palm, darling of Hollywood, seven times winner of the Platinum Weasel of Clermont-Ferrand, the woman who taught Dick van Dyke how to speak Cockney, gave her small blue and yellow client the smile that had won her a gold star at the training centre this morning.

"The crazy dame's refusing to come out and play. Hey, dear Andruta'll teach her some sense soon enough with the neural lash." Gelinda rolled over the muddy sheets, coating her naked skin with steaks of grey sludge. "Didn't know anyone but Lemurians grooved this way, honey," she added, already wise in the ways of the cat-house.

There was no reply. She ceased massaging sludge into her bosom and peered across the room. The bench was empty. Frowning, she checked between her legs but the client wasn't there.

The blue and yellow teddy bear had gone.

And so had the Valk people, quite as suddenly as they had arrived, about a millisecond after the Muggoth, awakened by the din of battle, had heaved its horny bulk out of the salt mine across the meadow and wallowed down to the mansion to complain about the noise. There is only one thing more dangerous than a Muggoth, and that is a Muggoth which has been woken up early.

The Valk people resolved to continue their discussion of the relative attractions of Helena Phipps and a chunk of old rock elsewhere and galloped away at full speed. In their panic, they missed the wormhole in Stunnard's Valley and plunged into the salt mine.

When the little red van drew up at the mansion that afternoon, the post lady was not very surprised to observe the Captain in his dressing gown and slippers, meditating on a stone at the edge of the lawn. The fact that half the house appeared to have been sat on by something rather bigger than a Hilton Hotel caused her no alarm. She had been post lady at Amblebroth for more than twenty years now and nothing could surprise her. Having collected the brown paper parcel from the table in the hall, and stepped over the disembowelled remains of Hugel Schlech, former Assistant Inquisitor (Higher Grade) she returned to her van and drove off without a second glance at the obscenely huge beast uprooting the yew alley with its tusks.

The dews of night revived the Captain. He rose from the stone, stumbled up the path and entered the silent ruin of his home. A search from attic to cellar revealed that he was alone. Deirdre

Horne, he knew, was either dead or a plaything of the Valks. Of Charlotte de Maupassant, little Eric, big Eric, there was no sign. Only the Owl-thing remained, snuffling uncomfortably in its kennel. The Captain supposed, not unnaturally, that they had all shared the fate of Deirdre Horne.

But, as we know, they had not. The larger Eric now sat on the nasty side of the table in Detective Sergeant Bunchley's interview room and denied for the hundredth time that he was the Leominster Beast, the Sex Pest of Old Sodbury, the Faceless Fiend of Newmarket, the knicker-snatcher of Dymchurch Lane, Ely, and, thanks to a link up with Interpol, Iago el Destripador of Capillablanca.

Charlotte de Maupassant lay in the shape of a parcel in a canvas sack on Amblebroth Station.

And Egrah'nca rode down the lift that connected the Mud Room to the harlots' quarters, in search of Helena Phipps.

And little Miss Eric? Well, at one moment she was whirling with the Nidro Force across galactic immensities. The next she was where she had asked to be, in the lift that connected the Mud Room in Andruta Tiservi's cat-house to the harlots' quarters below, with what she considered to be her little blue and yellow teddy bear.

48

With an abrupt complaint to his engineer about some malfunction in the Eguuanagal Circuits, the Magnarch loped away from his flying disc and descended by private lift to his penthouse on the floor below.

"Sickening old hypocrite," the Magnarch snarled. "Not you, father," he added, in case the room concealed anything brilliant in the way of listening devices. "I was referring of course to that pus-beetle, Sheppenic."

Banned from visiting the cat-houses! Prohibited on pain of really nasty surgery from communicating with the Khemmenoi of Lunt! It was enough to make a Magnarch of Verox decapitate a row of jade jaguars with a single lash of his tail, pick up the heads and pitch them with furious precision at the portrait of His Serene Highness, the Principle of Goth on the east wall, finding no satisfaction in the way the green stones vaporised six inches from the painting in the protection screen which its donor had thoughtfully conjured round it to prevent its vandalising by any antagonistic element, such as for example his son, the Magnarch of Verox.

He flung himself down moodily on an Aztec Leather couch[43] and produced a photograph from his pouch. The creature in the picture was not, for

---

[43] Hence the disappearance of the Aztec nation, flayed alive to cover items of furniture in the salons of upper-caste Atlanteans.

once, the beauteous netball player but a baggy bald old man with a stained moustache and ginger spotted skin, caught in khaki shorts and a string vest, relieving himself into a bucket behind a potting shed. He tossed it down on an obsidian occasional table. "And that," he groaned, "is the thing hailed by my Serene Father and his Bureaucrats at the Office of Prognostication as the Saviour of Atlantis. Well, he's got his work cut out for him, and no mistake. The Stone's missing, the Master's got a covert agent in the field, and Egrah'nca has apparently decided to take a bit of a holiday."

Ripples of indignation ran through the Magnarch's scaly exterior. Droplets of angry juice exuded from certain ducts in his hide and plopped onto the seat, burning several new holes. He leapt up.

A few minutes later, trying to relax in a bath of warm goat's blood, the Magnarch of Verox stared up at the ceiling and counted the tiles. He had taken to the bath in order to unwind, his brain having almost turned to steam in the effort to fathom all the implications of his father's words. Not even the gentle heat of the blood nor the scent of essence of Pituitary bath salts had been able to loosen him up. If, as now seemed only too probable, the incompetent and risible Eric Maresbreath, so called Guardian of the Earth, was a mere stooge, set up in the furthest reaches of time for the single purpose of distracting the Magnarch's attention from the real agent, who then, and where, was that same real agent?

Tossing aside the attendant who had attempted to wield the soap, the Magnarch sighed heavily. If only his father had not banned him on pain of mutilation from visiting the cat-houses, he could have employed the Khemmenoi's Cerbo-snatch to retrieve Egrah'nca from whatever comfortable niche of the universe he was at present ensconced in. Not that the bear would have been much help in unmasking the true servant of the Master. But kicking him round the cat-house would have made the Magnarch feel better.

Comfortable was not the word Egrah'nca would have chosen to describe his current niche. Clutched so tightly that breathing was a matter of luck under the arm of the orphan Eric Maresbreath (Miss) he could not prevent himself from being carried further and further along the corridors of the back-stage area of Andruta Tiservi's cat-house. In some ways, he realised, he was fortunate, for no-one bothered to question the presence of the small child: it was taken for granted that she was just another of the dwarf princesses of Melpobria, so much in demand this year.

Attracted by the sound of screams, the child wandered down a corridor marked 'Forbidden Zone: Neural Training in Progress'. The screams grew louder. Before them a steel door with retinal recognition system and thumb print keypad under an illuminated panel flashing the legend 'Keep Locked' stood ajar. The infant Maresbreath, sucking her thumb, edged through the opening. The screams neared ear damage level.

"Helena!" gasped both the teddy bear and his transport.

Shackled to the chair with a festoon of electrodes clipped to various parts of her incomparable person, Helena Phipps sat silently, watching the neural trainer who writhed and kicked and screamed on the floor at her feet.

"What's the matter with the silly man?" Miss Eric asked.

The neural trainer looked up. "The matter?" he shrieked. "You ask me what's the matter?" He crawled over the flagstones to the child's little red shoes. "I'll tell you what the matter is, your Highness. Do you know who I am?"

Little Eric shook her head.

"My name," said the trainer, "is Attar Lu'naam. Excuse me, Dwarf Princess. May I ask yours?"

"Not a Dwarf Princess," the child began to protest, but Egrah'nca kicked her in the ribs before she get the words out. "Ow! she substituted.

"Then know, sweet Princess Ow, that I am without doubt the greatest exponent of the Neural Modifier in the whole of P'nor'n. I ought to be, I invented it. I have performed wonders with that machine, miracles of behavioural engineering. In my hands frigid spinsters with less passion than an aspidistra have been transformed into compliant whores. Feminist writers from California have become febrile nymphomaniacs. But this – this surpassingly erotic creature -" He gestured at Helena who sat calmly in her chair, studying her electrodes. "Do you realise that I have not yet inserted the love bug and already she has generated enough Orgasmic Energy to melt down seven nuclear plants? When I connected the Neural Modifier, the polarity reversed and the machine asked if it could join a monastery. I tell you, Dwarf Princess Ow, this is no ordinary woman."

The great scientist collapsed on a bench with his tousled head in his hands, weeping. Little Eric trotted across the chamber and looked up seriously at the woman in the chair.

"You're the blessed Helena Phipps," she said.

The woman smiled. Lu'naam, catching a glimpse of the smile, turned quickly to his dials and began to gibber again. Most of the relays had burnt out in a smell of oily cabbage.

There seemed no point any longer in trying to maintain his cover. Egrah'nca nudged the child again and said, "Come on, kid. Stop staring at the broad in the fuse wire and let's get her out of that chair. You unclip the electrodes. I'll take the shackles."

If Helena Phipps was surprised to find herself being released from the metal bonds by a six inch high teddy bear, she concealed the fact successfully. Little Eric, well versed in Winnie the Pooh, Paddington and such, took the situation calmly, although she would have admitted that neither Paddington nor Pooh often panted things lie, "Oh, Mercy, those breasts!" or "Knees! Just look at these knees!" as they unbolted nude glamour models from chairs in the Neural Training Rooms of P'nor'n.

Attar Lu'naam's scientific brain, already rocking on its little legs, could not cope with the sudden vivification of the toy. With a final scream, he tore off his lab coat, spectacles, red plastic jump suit and tousled wig, and before they could intervene committed suicide by reversing the controls of the Orgoniser and pumping seventeen million kilolusts through his loins.

At least he died smiling.

Helena snatched up the dead but happy scientist's discarded garments and clipped herself into them with professional swiftness, incidentally proving once and for all that if you know how to wear it properly a lab coat can be just as sexy as a see through baby doll nightie. Then, followed by little Eric and the teddy, hand in hand, she led the way out of the chamber and back down the passage to the lifts. They were lucky in that, a merchant vessel from the seas beyond Doblere having just docked, the entire staff of the cat-house were fully occupied upstairs. Lucky is not the word for the entire staff of the cat-house, of course, when you remember the exceptionally degrading preferences of the mariners of Doblere.

"Take us up to Andruta's office," whispered Egrah'nca, when a lift eventually arrived. They dragged out the throbbing remains of a chief petty officer and hurried in. Swiftly they were carried to Andruta's penthouse suite high above the cat house.

"Right," said Egrah'nca. "Now let's just see what -" He snatched the pink ribbon from little Eric's hand, who wailed crossly - "Ms Tiservi has to say to an agent of the Archerons with the Nidro Force in his paws, shall we?"

Many indeed are the possible responses which the manageress of the Rampant Gr'noom might, in normal circumstances, have made when the threesome kicked down the door and confronted her. [44]

---

[44] The narrative can think of forty seven.

What she actually said was, "Oh. Er. Gosh. Erm. Sorry. Er. Could you, er, could you, come back later? Er, gosh."

49

Why the normally self-assured Andruta Tiservi should have been reduced to inarticulacy the narrative will now attempt to report, though it feels, not for the first time, that it is about to get out of its literary depth.

The brown paper parcel which readers will recognise at once as Empress of Witches, Charlotte de Maupassant, progressed with unnatural speed through the enchanted hands of the GPO and finally arrived in P'nor'n aboard the Doblerian craft whose crew was enjoying itself with such uncouth noises in the rooms below.

Andruta's annoyance at having to cough up nearly three thousand diams in excess postage, nearly as much as a Dwarf Princess could make in half an hour with a brace of bombardiers, turned to curiosity when she removed the wrappings and discovered the flesh coloured chest within. Opening it, she removed the bundles of receipts and ledgers, accounts and balance sheets, whereupon with an immense sigh of relief the chest shuddered, expanded and sat before her smiling on the desk top in the shape of Charlotte de Maupassant, would be sovereign of the cosmos.

"Charlie!" gasped Andruta.

"Hello, Andry," said Charlotte.

For a proper appreciation of what came next, the narrative can only suggest that readers log in to a reputable pornographic web site and ask to see the Lesbian stuff. Female readers with strong stomachs could book a day trip to the Finger in the Dyke

Club, Nijmegen, and take notes any night between 7.30 and 11. The sights to be observed there, particularly when those great artistes Lotte Haderwijk and Miss Jelka Vroederstaat perform their celebrated number with the hat stand, the nest of tables and the flags of all nations, resemble in uncanny details what met the gaze of Egrah'nca and his two lady colleagues when they smashed their way into the office of Andruta Tiservi.

No wonder she said, "Oh. Er. Gosh. Erm. Sorry. Er. Could you, er, could you, come back later? Er, gosh."

"Charlotte de Maupassant!" cried Egrah'nca.

More imperial than ever, the Empress of Witches untangled herself from the limbs of Andruta Tiservi and surveyed the interrupters with chilly disdain. Andruta, blushing, ran with her clothes in her hands to an adjoining en suite.

"And you, no doubt, are an agent of the Archerons," Charlotte sneered, draping her body with a shawl. "Your lack of tact is equalled only by your lack of wits, small furry fool. What did you hope to achieve, rushing in here accompanied by a child and - and – Well, well, well, what have we here, transforming the garments of a neural trainer into something out of a Harlotella Catalogue?"

"The lady's name is Helena Phipps," drawled Egrah'nca. "This pink ribbon, on the other hand, goes by the name of the Nidro Force. Would you care to be introduced?"

Charlotte's leer congealed. Even she, Empress of Witches, shape changer and potential supreme ruler of the cosmos, even she had reason to fear what Egrah'nca now held between his paws.

"Blow her up," urged little Eric, jumping up and down in her excitement. "Go on. Shall we kill her? Shall we make her dead? Shall we? Shall we?"

Privately Egrah'nca thought the child had begun to talk some sense at last but aloud he said, "No. My master, the Magnarch of Verox, will be interested in questioning this person. You too," he called, turning towards the door through which the red faced Andruta could be seen fastening her leather halter top. "I would surmise that your presence here, Mrs. de Maupassant, has nothing to do with, shall we say, a reunion supper for old girls of The Rampant Gr'noom. Please," he added, "cease that pathetic attempt to transform yourself into the opening bars of the overture to the Barber of Seville. You should know that such tricks cut no ice with the Nidro Force."

The distant orchestra faded at once and Charlotte became slightly less insubstantial.

When Andruta Tiservi had squeezed herself back into her puffin skin tights and, rather embarrassed by the whole business, rejoined the others in her office, Egrah'nca spoke again.

"Very well, Nidro Force. Take us now to the halls of the Archerons, if you please. We'll see what my master, the Magnarch, has to say!"

50

Whimpering a little, the Owl-thing waddled out of its kennel and perched themselves on a log in front of the deck chair where the Captain sat, a plate of cold mice on his lap. Even the plumpest mouse was to the Owl-thing no more satisfying than a dolly mixture to a full grown Hun, but it gobbled the animals gratefully enough when the Captain tossed them over, its chain clanking dolefully in the afternoon fog.

"Too bad about your mother," he observed, "or wife, depending how you look at it."

"T'weren't my wife, as such," Jubb hooted, much happier since he had learnt of Charlotte's supposed abduction by the Valk-people. "Just a bit of skirt I knocked about with one time, that's all."

Malcolm de Maupassant, his spirit pale and thin after a diet of dead badger and mouse, whiffled plaintively. "Dash it, Jubb, that's my mother you're talking about. Have a care, sir. Captain, I beg of you, is there not some distant relative about the place, or travelling salesman? I do not ask for a plump housemaid, I know those days are gone, but without a decent meal I feel I shall surely perish. You need not laugh, Jubb. I doubt the consequences of my demise would be pretty for you."

"Sorry, old boy. Can't help you there," the Captain said, skimming the empty plate across the lawn, where it shattered on an old stone. "Not a soul in the place, apart from me. Unless - "

"Yes?" urged the starving consortium.

"No, I don't suppose even you could manage a whole Muggoth," the Captain said. "Is that the word? Muggoth? I think that's what your mother called it, before the Valk-people got her."

"Can't be," said Malcolm. "A Muggoth is a gargantuan beast with multiple tusks and teeth and things from the Pits of Scaliselsarga. Not indigenous to Hertfordshire."

"Well, we've got one," the captain told him. "What d'you think demolished the billiard room?"

The Owl-thing stared at him for a moment. Then:

"I don't suppose you know the Valk-people's telephone number?" it asked. "I want to be abducted."

The depths of the abandoned mine reeked of mould and methane. Black as the sheets of Hell and twice as slimy, its galleries of ragged stone rang with the crash of ice-cold subterranean waters. To the Muggoth, it felt just like home. Its belly uncomfortably full of Valk warrior, the monstrous beast heaved and squeezed its vastness through the tunnels of the mine, often bringing the roof down behind it with a lash of its barbarous tail. By some miracle of instinct, its course was taking it down and down, always in the direction of its old haunts in Scaliselsarga-on-Sea.

51

Just because the Master of the World on his steed Strapner was out of the office for the moment, galloping across the endless tundra in a now superseded bid to prevent the end of the world, the mystic city of Shambhala[45] had not shut down for the duration. Within its shimmering walls the bastion of culture and light was very much in business as usual. Tirelessly, hairless monks in lilac robes continued to transcribe the novels of Beverley Nichols and the poetry of Patience Strong. Others, trained to perfection in the skills of music, ensured that no entry for the Eurovision Song Contest would ever be entirely forgotten, while in the great galleries teams of art-restorers worked day and night to keep the world well stocked with prints of Kentish Lanes, and Tiger Cubs, and Children With A Single Tear Drop In Their Large And Expressive Eyes.

In the Philosophy Quadrant, the monk Ogvonda looked up from his précis of the works of David Icke as a messenger boy entered hurriedly.

---

[45] Shambhala, the Abode of Bliss, the homeland and source of all esoteric wisdom, has, like light, a dual nature, existing at once both in and out of time, both on this earth and in a Realm beyond it. Its inhabitants, wise beyond the understanding of mortals and skilled in the sciences of astrology, behmenism, chiromancy and other lore, are protected from the prying world by a fortress of mountain peaks, the greatest of them named Meru, which enfold great glacial valleys, barred from approach by lakes and crevasses, and entered only by way of a secret cave round the back of Yanitani's Ski Hut and Souvenir Lotus Emporium, unless that's just another decoy.

The Gnostic Frying Pan

"What is it, Drumas?" he enquired gently, as the awkward youth tripped over the collected output of Mrs. Vera Stanley Alder. "News from the corrupt and desiccated world?"

"An e-mail from our contact in P'nor'n," whispered the messenger, pulling a printout from his pouch and unfortunately tearing it in two. "Oops, sorry. It's bad news, o blissful one."

"All news is bad news," intoned the monk Ogvonda, piecing the message together. "For the attention of the Master of the World," he read. "Andruta Tiservi and Charlotte de Maupassant in the hands of the Archerons. Imperative you take action asap. Bi."

Ogvonda at once arose and, being an adept of some advancement, floated into the air and banged his head on a wall cupboard, dislodging several volumes of Erich von Däniken on loan from the Science library. "Blast," said the blissful one. "I should never have looked at that book on TM."

Like a swimmer he descended slowly by means of the bookshelves to the floor and, weighing himself down by tucking several copies of the Collected L Ron Hubbard into his robe, managed to progress in a sort of bobbing motion along the corridors to the control centre.

"Mandragora," he snapped at a radio operator. "Patch me through to the Guardian of the Earth. And make it snappy."

"The Guardian of the Earth?" Mandragora queried, her finger pausing on the toggle. "You are? I mean, he's only the stooge, isn't he? Surely you want - "

"Don't argue with me, Lieutenant," shouted the monk. "When the dung is used up, the wise man pisses on his flower beds. Get me Eric Maresbreath. Now."

"Well, I don't know," the operator said sulkily. "I mean, it's not in my instructions at all. I don't know if I can."

"You'd better," growled the monk at her ear. "Otherwise I might just find time to transfer you to the History Quadrant."

Blenching at the prospect of endless shelves of Jean Plaidy, the operator sent her fingers dancing over the switches, then handed a headset to the monk Ogvonda.

"Guardian of the Earth," the monk intoned. "Guardian of the Earth. Are you receiving me? Over."

The airwaves crackled. Multidimensional telecom lines sprang into being. A muted voice muttered. "Not now. Piss off. Call me later."

"Prisoner at the bar," said Justice Huge sternly. "If you have something to say to the court, will you have the goodness to do so at the proper time and in a good strong voice. I have had too much occasion of late to comment upon the decline in enunciation which comprehensive education and electronic communications have inflicted upon criminal proceedings. Now, Mr. Clay, you were saying?"

"Thank you, m'lud," said the counsel. "I was about to remark, m'lud, that what the jury sees before it today is without doubt the most odious, the most reprehensible, the most disgusting monster of perversion which it has been my misfortune in many years of such trials to represent."

"Ah," said the Judge. "You are talking about the defendant."

The Gnostic Frying Pan

"Indeed I am, Your Honour."

"Good. For a moment I thought you'd been reading my diaries. Carry on, Mr. Clay. Carry on."

"Thank you, m'lud. I have, for a fee, taken it upon myself to defend this despicable pervert from the two hundred and eightythree charges of rape, indecent assault, exposure, buggery, molestation and shop lifting which have quite justifiably been laid at his door, and defend the filthy little deviant I shall. But I want to make it quite clear right from the start that the fact that I'm defending the bastard doesn't mean I approve of what he's done or that I intend to go out on Tuesday night and do it myself. is that clear?"

"Guardian," said the monk Ogvonda. "I'm sorry if we've caught you at a delicate moment but I'm afraid that a crisis has arisen."

"Prisoner at the bar!" screamed His Honour, Mr. Justice Huge. "Is this really the moment to practise your ventriloquism?"

"Shut up!" hissed Eric. "Not you, your lordship," he added hastily, as the judge turned purple.

"Mr. Maresbreath," the judge said, when at last capable of speech. "It cannot have escaped your attention that during the past eighteen months a sizeable number of Her Majesty's Judges have been devoured by what the popular press calls 'the Owl-thing'. As one of the few survivors, I find myself with an ever-increasing workload and ever-decreasing patience. Nevertheless I have complied with your request to be allowed for religious reasons to retain the ridiculous length of cord bound about your temples and to take the oath on a copy of the works of Madame Blavatsky. But if you interrupt the process of this court once more with your no doubt obscene mutterings, I shall be forced to reconsider my former leniency. Is that clear?"

"Yes, your Honour," said Eric Maresbreath. "And – and I should just like to say that I really am most truly sorry to have to do this, but - "

What a boon it was to the governmental propaganda service when the Old Bailey disappeared in a flash of temporal lightning that second afternoon of the trial of the man the newspapers had dubbed, "The Monster of London and the Home Counties Except for Surrey and Bits of Essex". Evidence was soon produced to show beyond a doubt that the explosion was the work of a band of Worcestershire Nationalists whose activities had long been under official scrutiny. The series of public executions which followed did much to distract the people's attention from the latest round of parliamentary pay rises.

Among those who perished in the Old Bailey Outrage were His Honour, Mr. Justice Huge, two of his young lady friends who were watching Monty Moose catoons in his chambers, several QCs and assorted juniors, a broth of solicitors, various members of the public and relatives of those made celebrities by the ministrations of flashers, as well as court reporters, ushers, notaries, bostelmen, sweepers up and a vagabond who had dossed down in the wig room. Not destroyed, of course, was Eric Maresbreath, Guardian of the Earth, who had wielded the cord and now found himself standing on top of a PBX in the central control room of the forbidden city of Shambhala.

"Do come down," Ogvonda murmured. "Try not to tread on the switchboard girl. And get your

The Gnostic Frying Pan

direction finder tuned. Thank you so much. How lovely of you to come. I do hope we didn't tear you away from anything important?"

"All the same if you did," Eric grumbled. He had been rather enjoying the trial. He clambered down. "I might have been saving the universe for all you know."

"You were not, I take it, engaged in locating the S'nangstone?"

"Actually," Eric said. "I found the Stone. Right where you said it would be."

"And where is it now?"

Eric shrugged. "Lost it when we got swept through Scaliselsarga," he confessed.

"I am far from surprised," the monk said. "The S'nangstone, containing as it does a tiny fragment of the original black hole, source of the multiverse, warps the temporal grid about itself in such a fashion that unlike you, me or the switchboard girl here, it is unitemporal. Which means, as you are no doubt aware, that it exists in only one place at one time, instead of like the rest of us in many places all the time. That is, for example, you as I speak occupy that area of space between my body and the switchboard. You also, several thousand miles and some days away, are or have been or will be finding the S'nangstone, as you would be able to observe if you had a correctly tuned Omnipert. The stone, however, exits uniquely. Thus you maybe sure that if it is here today, it will be gone tomorrow."

"Oh, well, that's all right then," Eric said hopefully.

"No, it is not. However, I did not recall you to discuss the metaphysics of the S'nangstone, important though they be.[46] Tell me, Eric," he said, draping a friendly arm around the Guardian's shoulder, "how much have you actually grasped of your part in the Master's Plan?"

Eric shrugged again, hoping to shake off the clammy arm. "Not much. Guard the Earth, locate the S'nang, keep tabs on the Empress of Witches," he said. "The rest of the time was my own."

The monk nodded wisely. "What I am going to say may come as a shock, to you, Eric. Did you ever suspect that the Master may have had another agent in the field, besides yourself?"

"Another?" Eric stared at the smooth face. "No. Never. Why should he?"

The monk gestured gracefully. "My son," he murmured. "If the matter had been left to you, where would the universe be now?"

"Glu'ng," Eric acknowledged glumly. "Aaaaaaheeeeeooowww – Pfft!"

"Quite. Also, I cannot record, can I, that you have succeeded in annexing the S'nangstone. You have been infiltrated by an agent of the Archerons in the shape of a cuddly toy. And you have no idea where to find the Empress of Witches. Are these statements in accord with the eternal verities, my son?"

The Guardian slumped onto the switchboard girl's desk, tipping her tray of cosmetics onto the floor. He admitted that he could find no fault with Ogvonda's assessment of his prowess.

---

[46] Which is just as well, because as anyone who has taken the trouble to follow his last speech will be aware, the learned monk knew less about metaphysics than a walrus knows about crochet.

"Then you will see," the monk said gently, "how wisely our Master planned, when he sent another into the fray besides yourself." The monk's eyes grew misty as he cast his mind back. It rebounded from the cabinet of pussy cat emblazoned tea mugs and returned to his body. His eyes brightened again. "Nearly twenty years ago," he recalled, "the Master donned a suitable disguise and set forth with a specially selected infant at his side. Travelling for many a weary day, he came at last to a simple workman's home in a far country where, under an assumed name, he engaged the menial in a game of skill which, with cunning forethought, he contrived to lose. The child, a girl, was forfeit. What more need I say? The artisan was Hebert Jubb, blacksmith and paramour of Charlotte de Maupassant. The child was Juliette Jubb, alias Juliette Thring, alias Durinda Ogvonda, my only daughter. She is the agent of the Master of the World."

52

"Charlotte de Maupassant!" cried Egrah'nca. "She is the agent of the Master of the World!"

The Magnarch, whose attention had not withdrawn from the figure of Helena Phipps in her lab coat since Egrah'nca and his companions had beamed in by Nidro Force, sighed wearily.

"Hallo, Charlie," he said. "Been a while. Not got the stone then?"

"'Fraid not. Send these cretins away," smiled the Empress of Witches. "I'll show you how I used to fondle your gr'noom, back in the old days."

"Sorry," said Egrah'nca, "did I say Charlotte de Maupassant? It's jet lag. What I meant to say was, Andruta Tiservi! She is the agent of the Master of the World!"

"Good evening, Ms Tiservi," said the Magnarch. "Thank you for your invitation. I am sorry that government priorities have prevented me from availing myself of your kind offer. But how kind of you to bring the young lady with you. I should have been very pleased to enjoy her, had not my respected father, His Holiness, the Serene Principle of Goth, already put in a claim."

"Hang on a minute," said Egrah'nca.

Back in Amblebroth, Captain Sparesbrook took one look at the severed links of the Owl-thing's chain and ran for cover.

The Owl-thing itself, its beak still sore from gnawing through an inch of solid steel, perched on top of a crane on the site of the new shopping centre

The Gnostic Frying Pan

and waited patiently for nightfall. Betty-Sue K Fry, in a moment of inattention, astounded her tutor by making him an offer he thought it wiser to decline. And Miss Winifred Wordsworth, priestess, propped her tricycle against a sooty wall and hurried up a path.

She was somewhat disturbed to find that the door stood ajar. When she entered, tugging off her plastic rain hat, the sight before her caused her to gasp in amazement.

The double disappearance of the Demi-Urge (né Owl-thing) and the Arch-Priestess Aramintha Gristle had thrown the cult into serious disarray. Some maintained that Aramintha had herself been devoured. Fights broke out and in the struggle was born that schismatic sect which came to be known as the Slappers. Another breakaway group insisted that Aramintha had in fact eaten the Demi-Urge but they attracted few converts: membership was never to extend beyond Mr. & Mrs. S D Hunter of Railway Street, Dartford, despite their colourful postcards in corner shop windows.

A fairly substantial group of acolytes remained devoted to the original articles of faith. Among them was Miss Wordsworth who quite sincerely believed that the Demi-Urge and its High Priestess would one day Come Again. She was all the more offended, then, when entering the premises in Goitre Lane she found that a team of volunteers was already at work, turning the Temple into a Community Arts Project.

"What is the meaning of this?" she demanded, her rain cape flashing in the arc-lights.

A fat, bearded man in a ragged sweater put down his pot of red paint and, wiping his hands on a rag of torn chiffon, clumped beaming to her side. "Hallo, hallo, hallo," he wheezed. "What's your speciality, then?"

"I do not know who you are, young man," Miss Wordsworth said, "but unless you cease at once to deface that mural, I shall be forced to call the police."

"Oh, you're one of that lot, are you?" the bulky man sighed. "Well, you ought to be ashamed of yourself, a well brought up lady like you. Look, love, this building belongs to the Goitre Lane Revolutionary Theatre and Macramé Workshop now. All signed, sealed and delivered, with the signature of your chairperson on the contract. Powerful woman, got the whole thing through from deposit to completion in twenty minutes. So what we do with your mucky murals is our business, you naughty old grandma." He slapped Miss Wordsworth's behind and grinned. "All right, lover?"

"No, it is not all right," snapped Miss Wordsworth. "I flatly refuse to believe that Mrs. Gristle would think to profane our - "

"Don't know nothing about no gristles," said 'Mole' Baverstock, concrete poet and aesthete. He scratched his gut thoughtfully. "Lady's name was, er, Charlotte something. Charlotte Germopersaunt, something like that." He tugged a grubby envelope from his trouser pocket. "Yes. This is her. Mrs. C de Maupassant, c/o Sparesbrook Manor, Amblebroth, Herts."

Miss Wordsworth stared about her once more at the band of social workers, government sponsored teenagers and grant aided artists who were demolishing the sacrificial altar. Her cheeks were very pale. Unable to speak, she turned, weeping, on her heel and ran from the former temple.

Coughing in the smoke which blew from a bonfire in the grounds, where two dumpy women in boiler suits tended the burning remains of something in a sandalwood and squirrel skin coffer, she remounted her tricycle and pedalled grimly away to the flatlet she shared with her sister in the Vale of Health.

Half a world away, the real agent of the Master of the World relaxed with a sack of cookies by her pool and watched the sunlight gleaming from the bodies of the New Bunsen Rockets as, baseball forgotten for the moment, they sported in the water and among the pines.

"Excuse me, ma'am," said Rhonda, her servant. "There's a call for you."

"Thank you, Rhonda. I'll take it in the study."

In the central control room, Shambhala, the switchboard operator peered round the morose shape of Eric Maresbreath and said, "Your call to New Bunsen, Ogvonda."

If the hairless monk felt any pang of emotion as he took the phone to speak for the first time in two decades to the daughter he had surrendered for the greater good, he betrayed nothing.

"Good day to you," he said. "Am I addressing Mrs. Juliette Thring?"

A startled gasp came from the ear piece. The monk winced.

"Who is that?" Juliette almost choked on her muffin. "How did you get hold of my name?"

"Your name?" Ogvonda smiled. "I gave it to you, Durinda, my child."

"What are you, some kind of nut or – nut or – what – where –?"

Ogvonda set the phone down. "There," he said delicately. "I have spoken the key word. While the child was yet in her mother's womb, she was subjected to an intensive course of neural training in the laboratories of Andruta Tiservi, one of our hirelings and the manageress of a brothel much frequented by the filth of Atlantis. As well as schooling the embryonic agent in the ways of carnal pleasure, the scientists implanted a synthetic synaptic relay in her brain which would activate when she heard the sound of her true name – Durinda. That sound has by now penetrated her cerebellum and thrown the mental switch. Whole areas of memory and power are lighting up as I speak. Great though the task was that she performed in ensuring that the glu'ng-toka, Edward Pausanias Thring, should be so shagged out by sexual lusts for the body of our agent that no energy would remain for tachomimsa and glu'ng, greater yet will be the deeds which she performs this day! The S'nangstone will be ours, Eric Maresbreath. Soon it will be cemented into its predestined place. Loud will be the hymns of joy that echo through the crystal halls of Shambhala!"

"Oh, good," said Eric. "That'll be worth listening to. What do we want this stone for, anyway? I mean, I know it contains a tiny fragment of the original black hole, source of the multiverse and all that but, you know, what's the point of it all? Eh?"

53

Unaware of the imminence of the return of the babe who had passed through her neural circus so many years ago, Andruta Tiservi reclined on a lounger in the Magnarch's apartments and watched the infant Eric Maresbreath at play among the porgisvra plants. Her fingers twined idly in the auburn locks of Charlotte de Maupassant, settled on the rug beside Andruta, and saying,

"And ever since then I've asked myself over and over again: what was the 'one gross error' the Arch Priestess mentioned, just before she fell. I've puzzled and puzzled over it. It's ruining my sleep. And my analysis of the Demi-Urge's accounts is not proceeding as well as I could have hoped. In fact, I must have made some fundamental book-keeping error, for it begins to look as if the universe is - No, it's impossible." She flicked at the pages of a Bought Ledger on the rug beside her. "What did Mrs. Gristle mean, Andruta? Do you know? What was my one gross error?"

"Well, that's obvious," Andruta said, chuckling as the child destroyed another whimpering plant. "Everyone knows about that. You should have consulted me, shouldn't you, when you set up your Permanent Stud."

"I thought you'd be cross," Charlotte said. "Stealing your idea -"

"You silly thing." Andruta hugged her gently. "I was flattered. You learnt everything you knew from me, remember."

"But what then was my error?" Charlotte cried, twisting round to look into the eyes of her ex-employer.

"What do you know of the prophecies of Dacha ten Rogan, sage of the Valk-people?" Andruta asked and, when her former protégée looked nonplussed, said, "Of course, you specialised in Atlanteans, didn't you, darling. That was my error, neglecting a vital part of your education."

Charlotte de Maupassant shuddered. "Not if what I have heard about the ways of Valk-people is true. Only a few hours ago I watched them slaughtering each other in the hall of Sparesbrook Manor. It was appalling."

"There, there, my dear," breathed Andruta. "You're safe now. Eric!" she added, "put that Syncopier™ down before you hurt any more of the servants and play nicely with your teddy bear."

"Don't want to," little Eric whined. "Teddy's no fun anymore." She shook the blue and yellow body which dangled limply from her grip, then slung it angrily into the ornamental pool, where it floated face down and was pointedly ignored by the flesh-toads.

"Well, go and watch the executions then," Andruta snapped. "Sorry, Charlie, that brat's driving me mad. Anyway, I was saying, the prophecies of Dacha ten Rogan. He was a great sage of the order of Crom ten Pogol, their absurd god. You know the thing, all it does is reassure the less enlightened Valk warriors of their male potency. A ridiculous superstition, based entirely on a misunderstanding of the inscription on the side of the stone, promises the Valk people that their joy will never be complete until the S'nang üll H'notorem, as it called here, is restored to their filthy High Chapel in the hills. Of course, the more rational Valk people know that the real secret of the stone is the tiny fragment of the original black hole, source of the multiverse, hidden within and the immense power which it confers. Well, what Dacha ten Rogan foretold, in a number of rather bad verses, was that the Stone would eventually be found, not by wizards, nor by priests, not by private investigators on expenses, but by a little child, the fruit of the union of night with day, of science with art, of a black Hertfordshire gigolo with an English maid in the non-gynaecological sense."

Charlotte gasped. "Black gigolo? You mean – Uncle Tom?"

"Uncle Tom," nodded Andruta. "Clearly your ridiculous Arch Priestess had learned from her contacts in the Demi-Urge's organisation of his destiny."

"That explains why she visited the Stud so often! And, yes, she always insisted on a session with Uncle Tom. I see it all now. She hoped to bear his child. The child whom the stars foretold as locater of the all powerful Stone."

"All right, if you know so much, you tell the bloody story," Andruta snapped. We shall pass over the lengths to which Charlotte went to appease her and tune in again at the moment when Charlotte said, "So that was my gross error. Getting rid of Uncle Tom. Now I see."

"Why did you dispose of him, Charlie?"

"Oh, he'd been giving free rides to one of the stable girls. She'd got herself in the club, the silly cow, and – Oh my sweet Magotte. Andry – that means – "

"That means the predestined child may already be in being," whispered Andruta. "Assuming she didn't have it out. Eric! Will you stop making that stupid noise? Well, of course you'll get your fingers nipped if you prod the flesh-toads. Ghastly little tyke. Yes, Charlie, somewhere in that depressing little country of yours the most favoured progeny of all time may even now be lifting the S'nangstone in its chubby hands. Eric! Put that flesh toad down. Well, spit them out then. No, I don't think it looks funny without any legs. Oh, give me strength. Go on, get out of here and go and watch the hangings. The question is, what will the Master do now?"

"Not to mention the Magnarch," Charlotte added.

A door hissed open. Startled, both women turned and stared with sudden awe at the entrance into the room of a godlike being, his muscular body clad only in a loin cloth of chain-mail, his hair the colour of spun iridium, his eyes a cold and piercing gold.

He favoured them with a miraculous smile, which reduced the androgynous Ms Tiservi herself to the female equivalent of a long term convict weeping over a smuggled *Razzle*, and strode across the room.

"Who – who are you, lord?" Andruta dared to whisper.

"And where do you want us?" Charlotte added.

The godlike one laughed.

"'Tis not for you," quoth he, his voice as rich as a vat of molten silver, "that I have come this day, but for the child, my ladies, Eric (Miss)."

The two women exchanged a glance and shrugged. No accounting for taste. Or sudden lurches into iambic pentameter.

"Where is she?"

"Watching the exe-screen, I think, "said Andruta. "But - but, well, she'll be a bit on the, you know, small side, for a chap like you. I could send her down to the Rampant Gr'noom, have her stretched, if you like, or - "

The god's skin suffused with a red-gold sheen. A glance of ire flashed like the blade of a sword from his eyes, cutting short Andruta's offer. "Perhaps there are practices which we consider perfectly normal but which will one day seem as perverted to our descendants as vegetarianism does to us. Timora Garpatheny, for instance, imagines a world in which cannibalism is regarded as more than a bit of a faux pas, socially speaking. But you are foolish, indeed," he laughed "if you imagine that you can subvert me with your vicious ploys. I have overheard every syllable of your conference, your babble of Valkan sages, Ms Tiservi, and your ill-concealed admiration for the Valkan Rationalist Association. I think we may now guess who it was that directed the warrior band to Sparesbrook Manor. Incidentally, it may have been a mistake to let your favoured warrior get his claws on that picture of Helena Phipps. Alas, even the most rational of beings..... Where is she, anyway?"

"The Magnarch's father has taken her out for a ride in his carriage," Charlotte said. "Something about a ceremony."

The godlike one wiped a pewter sheen of sweat from his brow and changed the subject. "But let us not allow ourselves to be distracted from your babble of prophesied infants."

"You mean -" Charlotte pointed at the small Eric Maresbreath, currently being dragged back into the room by Andruta, and grizzling loudly because she had missed the best bit of the execution programme. "You mean, this...?"

"None other."

"But how did you find out? How did you know?"

The god laughed, a sound like platinum necklaces tumbling into a chalice of purest rhodium. "What do I not know of little Eric Maresbreath, after the hours I spent in her doll's pram, or under her bed, or buried up to my neck in her sand pit?"

"You?" gasped the two women.

The hero leaned over and, brushing aside a pair of irritable flesh toads, plucked the soggy blue and yellow bear skin from the pool. He studied it with a mixture of affection and disgust.

"A rather itchy disguise," he observed, "but a serviceable one. Yes, dear ladies, I am, restored to my normal corporeal substance, which had lain these past years preserved in ice in a safety deposit box in the National Body Bank of Atlantis, none other than your former cuddly pal, Egrah'nca."

He took little Eric by the hand, presented her with the teddy which had for so long been his other self, and led her gently from the room, pausing at the doorway just long enough to admit the platoon of guards who were waiting to drag Andruta Tiservi off to the cells. She had not clawed her way up to her exalted station as manageress of the

Rampant Gr'noom without learning how to kill a man with a single blow, which is why oral sex tended to be unpopular with all but the suicidal, but even she couldn't take on fifteen modified baboons in full armour.

"Well," said Charlotte to herself. "Tough luck, Valk people. No S'nangstone for you." Ignoring the fading scream of invective from the ex-manageress of the Rampant Gr'noom as she was dragged down the tunnels, Charlotte rose from the rug and marched across to the desk on which was spread the bulk of the Demi-Urge's account books.

"And if I have my way, none for the heathens of Atlantis either," she hissed, and fell to furious work with a calculator.

54

On the ceremonial Schemming Ground, a plateau surrounded by volcanic chimneys in the uplands of Atlantis, the High Vink of Crom ten Pogol raised his feathered staff into the smoky night air and uttered a hoarse cry. Dancing round him in a flapping of cloaks, the hooded warriors responded with a chorus of caws. The uplifted blades of spear and sword shone red in the fire light.

A sudden blaze of enchanted flame, actually produced by the surreptitious application of a cup of Eig'nor fluid to the ritual bowl, illuminated the indecent (but prefabricated) effigy of their God, whose confrontationally phallic figure overhung the dancers like a crane on a building site. Roughly where the hook would be a naked figure dangled by her ankles over the tongues of fire.

Warmly wrapped against the chill winds that blew by night among the crags of the Valkan hill country, Helena Phipps observed the interesting ritual from the relative comfort of the Principle's carriage. Gratefully she sipped from the small lead flagon of cloudy liquid which he raised to those lips to praise which no poet yet born could count himself apt.

"What do you think of it, my dear?" His Serene Holiness asked, using the old trick of wrapping another stole about Helena's shoulders to get a quick feel of her bust. "I hope it amuses you to watch these yokels wriggle. Would you care for another pretzel? Or perhaps a cup of tea?"

Helena declined both with pretty courtesy.

"Of course, what we have to ask ourselves," the Principle said, "is it really religion? Now I have no doubt that the young celebrant strapped to the, ah, the monstrance up there quite genuinely and sincerely believes that she is offering heart-felt worship to the Deity of her choice. In some ways, perhaps she is. Perhaps the Demi-Urge in his infinite negligence may accept her service to himself. Who can say? I doubt my personal bookmaker would give good odds on it. And yet I truly feel some regret at being obliged to do this."

He removed a small bell from under his furs and, leaning quite unnecessarily across Helena, tinkled it from the window.

When the Serene Laser Jet screamed out of the night and skewered the flapping warriors on beams of deadly light, even the Principle appeared a little startled. Writhing crow like bodies smoked and threshed about the Schemming Ground. The High Vink's ceremonial staff, feathered with quills plucked from the sage Dacha ten Rogan himself, or so it was claimed, had split down the middle and now protruded from each end of the High Vink. Severed by a stroke of laser fire, the enormous appendage of Crom ten Pogol tipped out of the sky and crashed into the sacrificial flame, splashing gouts of sticky burning fluid over the panicking warriors. His Serene Holiness, the Principle of Goth, grunting urgently, had worked his hands inside the furs which covered his companion's body and was squeezing anything his fingers could find.

He was rather annoyed to find his left hand covered with mustard, the fruit of his squeezing having unfortunately been Helena's packed lunch, and so did not immediately become aware of a new development in the massacre. A suicide squadron of Valk people, granted a dispensation from the vow of flightlessness until the return of Crom Ten Pogol, had soared into the air and immolated themselves in the engine of the Serene Laser Jet, causing it to explode, although the caws of triumph ceased when the battalion of Serene Atlantean Soldiery parachuted in. Finally obliged to take notice when a Valk spear flashed through the window of his carriage, the Supreme Principle gave up trying to wipe his hand in the lap of Helena's skirt and peered down at the feathery shaft which had pinned him to the leatherette. After that his attention was too much taken up with dying to observe the progress of the battle.

To remain in the carriage was to invite a share in the fate of her late host, so Helena Phipps leapt gracefully from the vehicle and dodged down the dark hillside to the edge of the burning Schemming Ground below. Crawling through the snow, she headed for the cover of what she had at first supposed to be a rock and then taken to be the body of a deceased warrior, until a closer inspection revealed it to be a dummy. A curious peep over the cardboard wings revealed that of the supposed corpses lying around her, a fair number were also dummies.

Helena deduced at once that the Valk people had prepared a decoy ceremony to lure the Principle and his air force into a trap but in that she was mistaken. These days all the ceremonies incorporated a large number of dummy worshipper. It was the Pogol Police's way of trying to cover up the decline in church attendance following the continued ascent of that logical cabal, the Valkan Rationalist Association, particularly since they had started to promise photocopies of the Snap of Helena Phipps to all who signed their pledge.

Crouched in the hellish night, laser beams, snow and black feathers falling through the smoke about her, the original of that photograph chewed a rather mangled ham sandwich and wondered if there was much chance of being rescued by a teddy bear again.

At the crunch of a boot in the snow behind her, she turned, half in hope, half in dread. Dread triumphed. Her eyes widened, her mouth fell open in a silent scream, as she saw looming out of the burning night the crow like shape of a Valk-warrior, his curved beak glistening, his feathered spear already plunging down towards her heart.

Darkness received her. She knew no more.

END OF PART THREE

Yet once more, o ye laurels, and once more, ye myrtles brown, with ivy never sere (thanks, John) the narrative with heavy heart rubs its red rimmed eyes and stares at the empty sky.

What kind of cosmos is this, that can allow the infinite beauty of Helena Phips to become a kebab on the end of a Valkan spear? The glory and the wonder of the world, now so much pet food? What kind of foul and bloated monster is it, this Demi-Urge, whose evil incompetence manufactured the sordid prison house where astrethic spirits must sully their purity in bonds of flesh? The narrative would very much like to shin down the nearest air shaft, trace the Demi-Urge to its inframondane lair and kick its bloody teeth in, if Demi-Urges have teeth, which (considering the nature of its creation, they almost certainly do).

But all the narrative can manage, so rigidly is it bound by the Demi-Urge's universal conventions, is to proceed with its forced fingers rude to unveil the breathtaking body of

PART FOUR

The Once and Future Stone

55

Yes, all right, come on, cheer up. There's plenty of photos of Helena Phipps bobbing up all the time throughout history. They'll just have to do. Do you mean to say that, against all reason, this woman now means more to you than a quick gawp at the lads' mags, the ones you personally would never dream of buying, and might sign a Mothers' Union petition against, if someone you knew brought it to your door? Well, well, well, there's turn up for the book[47].

Now, stop that snivelling. She wasn't dead. You'll just have to wait to find out what happened, but if it'll make you any more comfortable, the narrative is pleased to say that the Valk spear didn't harm her and the darkness which received her was just a fainting fit.

All right? Better now?

Good. Then let us press on at once to the cellars of Sparesbrook Manor.

On the morning in question, Captain H. 'Geronimo' Sparesbrook lay, snoring gently, next to the rather depleted stock of Chateau Murchison '78. His wiry figure, with its coating of grime and cobwebs, was quite visible, thanks to a shaft of dawn sunlight and a conveniently placed grating, to the eye of the telescope which poked from a window just beneath the eaves of the Violet Pring

---

[47] To quote Desmond Upchurch, the aspergic collector of illustrated trouser catalogues.

Hebbenthwaite Sunset Memorial Home further up the hill.

The watcher in the attic lowered his telescope and turned to what resembled an ECT apparatus beside the truckle bed. With deft fingers, he adjusted a number of switches, lifted the oxygen mask and said, "Section to leader, section to leader, come in, please."

The loudspeaker concealed behind the portrait of Dr Edith Summerskill crackled into life.

"Receiving you, strength 5, section. Go ahead, please."

"This is a GX991," the watcher said. "Target HGS remains insensible at co-ordinates TB12 12 71. No sign of target MdM/HJ. Oh, and can you get someone to send me up a packet of cheese and onion crisps? I missed breakfast."

"Noted, section. Salted or unsalted?"

"Salted. And a pickled egg, if they've got one. And a Mars Bar."

"Affirmative, section. Over and out."

In his tastefully padded cell, the chief flicked a couple of loose strands on his hand woven basket and said, "Jumbo, run up to the Doc with a packet of C&O and a pickled egg. And a Mars Bar, if Whacko hasn't eaten them all. Just patch me through to HQ before you go."

"OK, Chief. Does he want salt? Here's your line."

"Plenty of salt, Jumbo. Thanks. Hallo, Headquarters? This is Violet Unit One. Violet Unit One. Are you receiving me? Over."

"Good morning, Violet," said the fluffy dog pyjama case on the chief's bedspread. "Any developments?"

The Once and Future Stone

"All quiet, HQ," said the Chief, picking his teeth with a match. "The Muggoth's got stuck in a coal mine under Plumstead and is making a bit of a nuisance of himself but the Captain's still asleep and the Owl-thing hasn't shown up here again."

"Take a look at your daily paper," advised the fluffy dog. "Two television personalities, a popular columnist and the star of a West End musical have disappeared in the last 48 hours, your time. Word from Violet Unit 6 is that the creature's gone back to its old haunts in Goitre Lane."

"Better there than here," said the Chief. "Oh, by the way, before I forget, any joy with that order for pork scratchings?"

"Hold on, I'll check the consignment note. Yes, despatched by time-trailer last night, our time. Takes, what, about two thousand years to reach you, via Alpha Centauri. Should be there any minute."

"Thanks, HQ. Over and out."

"Hold on there, Violet, hold on." There was a muffled argument from the fluffy dog, as though the Chief's pyjama trousers had fallen out with the top, or the dog suffered from multiple personalities which evidently didn't think much of each other. Then a fresh voice spoke from its purple tongued mouth: "VU1. Are you reading me? Over."

"Reading you strength 10, HQ. Who's chatting?"

"You may address me as Egrah'nca. Now, listen carefully, Violet. I have some important instructions for you."

"Hey, hold on a tick."

"Shut up and listen," snapped Egrah'nca, who may have felt quite at home in the fluffy dog.

"Here's the latest news. You won't like it. We've established that EM is not the sole agent of the M of the W in play. There is another, and more deadly."

The Chief, who had risen to his feet, hastily unscrewed an orange crayon and pressed the concealed button. Instantly speakers all over the asylum began to play a selection from the recordings of James Last.

The response was astonishing. Within minutes the assortment of conceptual artists, cabinet ministers, disc jockeys, poets, TV scientists and stand up comedians who were kept at the asylum as a front had been executed and hurled into the incinerators. Doctors, nurses, bullyboys and the rest of the patients turned from their assumed tasks and, with what a knowing eye would have recognised as the military efficiency of a crack Atlantean Time & Motion Group, began to emergencise the drill effect situation. Communal therapy areas were, with little alteration, transformed into punishment blocks. The behavioural therapy wing became a torture chamber.

"Oops," said the Chief. "Silly ass. Should have been the red crayon. Oh, well, can't be helped."

The fluffy dog spoke again. "His Serene Highness, the Principle of Goth revealed as much to us before leaving for a short holiday with a new convert." For some reason the voice had momentarily sounded rather miffed. "However, it is up to us now to unmask and neutralise the agent as soon as possible."

"Of course!" cried the Chief. "I see it all now. It's that Charlotte de Maupassant woman!"

"Balderdash," said Egrah'nca, rather ungenerously, considering that until he recently that had been his own opinion. "Charlotte de Maupassant is under house arrest in the Magnarch's Basiliean villa, together until recently with her Valk-loving comrade, Ms Andruta Tiservi."

"What? From the Rampant Gr'noom? I don't believe it."

"The same. And conspiring with the Master of the World who, it transpires is a major share holder in Tiservi Totties Ltd, to inveigle the Magnarch into lending his name to The Rampant Gr'noom for publicity purposes."

"Never!" said the Chief. "Well, if you say so, but – Hang it all, I've had some good times in the old Rampers. Some very good times."

"So have we all," said the fluffy dog. "Nevertheless, a little persuasion in the Archerons' Information Centre has made her only to eager too reveal the whole sordid plot. The idea was to use a certain bait we need not discuss now, and then having kidnapped him hold him to ransom unless all manner of extravagant demands were met – mainly his picture in all the major news outlets endorsing the Rampant Gr'noom and closing down the Happy Magger. Barbaric! Absolutely barbaric! All civilised standards thrown to the winds. What kind of a jungle do these people want us to live in, eh? Never mind, she's being tortured to death tomorrow at peak viewing time. What concerns us now, is who is the Master's agent and how can we stop him. Get a room ready – for a little girl of five and her old teddy bear. Make sure there's plenty of gin."

"Gin? Steady on, old boy. For a girl of five?"

"No, that's for the teddy bear. Me. When I've metempsychosed into this tatty old skin again."

"But," gasped the Chief, "you can't come here. You know that sentient beings can't use the Goods Transport -"

"Because subjectively the process takes a couple of thousand years, I know. Unscientific fishbones, Violet old thing. Spit them out. I shall be with you directly."

"But – the strains on the temporal web – "

"Minimal, compared with what will happen if the M of the W gets his talons on the S'nangstone. But there, I think, we have the advantage. The child I'm bringing along is none other than the I foretold by the SDtR of V."

The Chief frowned at his padded wall, then shook his straw bedecked head. "Nope, got me there, old boy. Is it something to do with snooker tables?"

"The Infant Foretold by the Sage, Dacha ten Rogan of Valk. She whose destiny is written in the stars. You know her well, Violet. It's little Eric Maresbreath."

"What? That horrible brat from the Manor? I mean, the Target Area? Cripes, I was assigned to her my first week here. Things she did with the wild life turned my stomach."

"You should see the Magnarch's porgisvra plants," Egrah'nca sighed. "And the flesh toads have all resigned and gone back to Bletchley. Even so, she is the one. And I'm coming down there with her just as soon as I can get a connection."

"Hold on a sec," said the Chief, as a crate of pork scratchings, sixteen barrels of Guinness, some old magazines donated by the Union of Modified

Females and a snotty child with a blue and yellow teddy bear under her arm materialised in the space next to his wardrobe. "I think you've just arrived."

"Oh, good show," said the voice of Egrah'nca from the doggy. "Here, come and say 'hello' to yourself, Eric." There was a silence, punctuated by muffled urgings. Then the agent spoke again. "Little sod's gone all shy. Anyway, we've obviously made good time through the journey, so I'll sign off this end and get on our way. Over and out, Violet."

"Get someone to shift these pork scratchings," Egrah'nca added, from the teddy bear this time. "Then we'll get down to business."

"You feel quite tickety-boo, then? After your lengthy trip?"

"Of course. Our bodies, of course, were in stasis, but our minds continued to work. I don't know what Miss Eric was up to."

"I was singing Humpty Dumpty," Little Eric said proudly. "4,207,680,134 times."

"While I," said Egrah'nca, "spent the whole time trying to enumerate the beauties of Helena Phipps. Only got about halfway, then we arrived."

"At least we haven't got Charlotte de Maupassant to worry about," said the Chief. "It was a nightmare, trying to divert her attentions from the Captain. If only we knew why he's so darned important."

Egrah'nca shrugged. "The Omnipert™ can only penetrate so far," he said. Had it been convenient, he might have slipped in one of his favourite lectures, which outlined in exhausting detail his theory of the nature of the space-time continuum. He called it The Knitting Pattern. Briefly, the listener is invited to picture time as an infinite ball of wool and space as a pair of no. 10 needles wielded by the crafty fingers of the Demi-Urge as it sits in the rocking chair of infinity with its feet up on the stool of cosmic chaos. Purling and plaining forever, it ravels up the universe as we experience it. That explains why for the Atlanteans it was possible to move hither and yon on the temporal stocking stitch, or that part of the cosmic scarf available for inspection and journeys. But there is, of course, a point beyond which the future remains unforetellable: the eternal moment of Now in which the Demi-Urge sits knitting. It was easy for an Atlantean to access a time window or observe any period of history up to that point but as the wool of eternity remained disunited after that point no-one could pop any further forward into the future to see, for example, why Captain Sparesbrook was so important to their survival. [48].

"Yes, the *terminus ad quem*," agreed the Chief. "Well, as I say, at least we can forget about Charlotte the Harlot."

In the store-room, among bottles of pickled eggs and tubs of roasted peanuts, the consignment of pork scratchings gave a shudder and resolved itself into the familiar form of the woman whom everyone except the Edith Grove coven saluted as Empress of Witches, she whom the Chief was so recklessly discounting, the matchless sorceress, the free and unstoppable Charlotte de Maupassant.

---

[48] It should not be naively imagined, of course, that the Demi-Urge really sits in infinity plying a pair of needles. Egrah'nca's Knitting Pattern was simply a model in fairly comprehensible terms of an ungraspable reality.

56

Egrah'nca, admittedly a super-hero in his own right and a wonderfully cuddly teddy bear too, was no physicist, and it is doubtful that his great Knitting Pattern theory, though not inelegant, would be acceptable to many. Among those who would have rejected it, apart from the Sage Trepoch, was the Professor of Quantum Ipsology at the University in Catamite, New Bunsen, who was smoking one of Mordred T. Schneiderhauser's cigars as the deserted lover bewailed the sudden disappearance of his Juliette.

"She has a right to realise her true self," the Professor was saying. She poured herself another glass of her colleague's bourbon. "You gotta permit her this, Chancellor. No woman can be denied her absolute right to experiment with her own being. She felt the need to cut the shackles of matrimony, and you should accept that."

"Come to bed with me, Lola."

"You have gotta be kidding." She doused the dank cigar in her glass. "My old man would kill me if I pulled a stunt like that."

Juliette, impelled by the neural mechanism implanted in her brain, was about as liberated as a clockwork train set. As soon as her father, the monk Ogvonda, from his home in Shambhala, had spoken her true name, Juliette (or Durinda, as we must call her now) had gone to her bedroom, packed a few things, and driven to the airport, where she took the next jet to Europe. The airline was particularly annoyed as they had it lined up for a flight to Borneo.

Durinda ditched the plane in the ocean off Land's End and swam to Cornwall, pursued by a love-struck whale. She passed the day recovering in a hay rick and travelled by a succession hi-jacked Polish container lorries to Exeter, where she commandeered an Intercity and travelled with remarkably few major incidents to Paddington.

At midnight on the day of Egrah'nca's return to Amblebroth, an overweight and breathless figure in black, its face and hair concealed under a stocking mask, struggled along the dried up ditch below the Manor, hidden from the infra-red gaze of the sentinels on the asylum's battlements, and gained the safety of the ruined gatehouse, where Malcolm de Maupassant had once held astonishingly orgiastic seminars with his accountancy cronies. Durinda Ogvonda it was, daughter of the monk of Shambhala, her understanding alight with new powers as the dormant areas of her brain snapped one after another into life, her body obese and reluctant after thiry years of the good life in New Bunsen.

Sweeping aside the dusty remnants of orgies from long ago, the Incredible String Band records, Agarbathi joss sticks, curiously smoke-blackened tea-spoons, Dali prints and packets of Rizlas, she collapsed gasping onto the window seat from which she could keep a watch on both the manor and the bulk of the asylum which loomed above it. She placed her mobile phone on the sill beside a wormy copy of *Penguin Modern Poets: The Liverpool Scene* and with the aid of small piece of nano-technology (which if ever rediscovered will make the microchip look about as progressive as the bathing-machine) patched herself through to head-quarters where her father awaited her in his cloak of bearskin, watching the stars wheel seasonally over the frozen wilderness about the mountain called Meru.

"Father," she puffed, her eyes never for one moment drifting from their watch. "I have made a preliminary survey."

"What have you to report, my child?" the monk demanded. "Have you traced the *lapis exillis*?"

"The what?" Durinda's Latin circuits had failed to locate.

"The Stone. The S'nang. Have you found it?"

"Not yet, o my Father," Durinda confessed. "But I have established one fact. The Violet Pring Hebbenthwaite Sunset Memorial Home is a front for a team of Atlantean Time & Motion Experts. The whole place glows like Blackpool Illuminations when deciphered by my Scanector™. I had the devil of a job getting this far unseen."

"Take care that you remain so, my daughter. It is imperative that no-one blows your cover now. We have lost Andruta Tiservi."

A couple of million brain cells warmed up and provided her with a brief biography, character sketch and family tree of the manageress of the Rampant Gr'noom. "I see," said Durinda. "Well, she knows little enough. She believes she was merely party to a public relations exercise. Whatever those barbarians tear from her, it will not incriminate us."

"Depends if they see the label on that synthetic gr'noom our surgeons fixed up for her," the monk said unhappily. "I always argued against it, but they said nothing less would buy her over. Sad, sad business. Thank the stars, my child, that you are normal."

Durinda ran her finger up her plump thigh and touched the pink ribbon bound about it.

"I'll have to hang up now, daddy," she said. "Something's happening out there. A light up at the Manor. I'll re-establish contact at 0.200 hours."

"Goodbye, my child. My prayers go with you."

Durinda replaced the receiver and touched a button on the small piece of technology (it resembled a hair-slide) which had the effect of charging the call to Mr. Geoffrey Micklethwaite of Temperance Road, Manchester, then squeezed through the gatehouse door and lumbered up though the woods to the inadequate shelter of some lichenous stone godling on the lawn.

She was perfectly placed to observe the sudden appearance of Captain Sparesbrook at the French windows with a 12 bore shotgun levelled in her direction and to observe the flash of flame from its barrel.

The unaccustomed exercise had brought on stage such a double act of wheezing and throbbing, however, that the percussion she did not hear.

57

When the survivors at last straggled back from the terribly mishandled raid on the worshippers of Crom ten Pogol with the news of the Principle his father's death and the abduction of Helena Phipps, the Magnarch of Verox was so upset that he pushed aside a whole manicurist. He did not even remember to watch the highlights of the execution of Andruta Tiservi after the sports round up. From a drawer in his desk he took a photograph with a message in red on the reverse and gulped over it longingly. The messenger caught a glimpse of the woman in the transparent white body stocking and gulped too. Unnerved by all the gulping, the manicurist crawled towards the door.

"You're absolutely sure the Dickies got her?" he asked again, as the messenger backed away.

"There is no possibility of error, your Greedship," the messenger whined. "I saw her myself, awoken from a faint by the kiss of life from a Valkan beak, then carried away on a pole slung from the shoulders of two mighty Valk-warriors." Still backing, he tripped over the manicurist and flailed about on the floor.

"And you did nothing to rescue her?" roared the Magnarch.

The unfortunate messenger writhed and spun. "What could I do?" he wheedled, "with my arms torn off and a Valk spear pinning me to the side of a cart?"

"Excuses," the Magnarch raged. "Why do they send me nothing but excuses? Get out of my sight."

There was a bit of a bottleneck in the doorway when the manicurist and the messenger tried to leave at the same time. The Magnarch stared with disgust at their attempt to cheer him up with comedy clichés, then with a flick of his tail sent the pair of them tumbling down the hall and into a waiting cattle truck.

He pulled on his flying helmet and gloves, wound a white scarf about his neck and loped from the palace to his private air-field next to the sports arena, where a floodlit porgisvra hunt was taking place. The hiss of jets drowned the screams of the mutilated plants as the Magnarch's personal disc flashed up from the pad and sliced through the smoky air above the arena, much to the annoyance of several thousand fans.

No less familiar with the controls of a flying disc than with the consul of an Omnipert™, he took the machine up to twenty thousand feet and hovered, studying his instruments. Finally he selected a curious object of wood and bone, placed the aperture to one of nostrils, and began to blow, while his fingers danced over the stops beneath.

A ghastly din filled the cockpit of the saucer. Artist of the Omnipert™, maestro of the disc, the Magnarch of Verox was without doubt the world's worst musician. He had on pain of mutilation been commanded never to play again within earshot of another sentient being.

Consoled by half an hour of vicious discords, he tossed the pipe aside and took the craft down to a safe distance above the crags of the Valkan hill country. Soon his practised eyes made out the column of smoke rising in the dawn air from a canyon some miles to starboard. He banked and allowed the disc to descend like a falling leaf until it hung less than five hundred feet above the barren hillsides.

His scanners probed the darkness of the canyon, not yet laid open by the knives of sunlight, and reported a settlement of some six hundred Valk people, not counting cardboard dummies, with six pubs, a post office, a one man cobbler-cum-photographic business, a small village hall and a chapel. None of the buildings gave off any kind of resonance compatible with the presence of a human female. With a sigh and a quick burst from his altakras, which reduced the contents of the canyon to a mound of steaming grey sludge, he flung the disc round and sent it curving across the morning sunlight in search of further possibilities.

It was four hours and twelve piles of pungent sludge later that he came across a hopeful sign. His ship, cruising low over a trail whose heaps of horse dung suggested the recent passage of a band of mounted warriors, lost speed suddenly and hung like a kestrel: the scanners had picked up a fur wrap, rather stained with mustard, neither of which commodities featured in the daily life of the Valk person, as any anthropologist would happily confirm. The Magnarch sent his craft just above the tree tops, following the windings of the trail beneath him until, just at midday, he spotted the glint of silver on a hillside some three miles ahead. Quickly he took the saucer up to an altitude where no Valk lookout would spot it. It was time for another chorus.

The Gnostic Frying Pan

Roped to a tree, the midday sun kissing the skin which flashed through rents in her fur wraps, Helena Phipps watched with interest as something large and silent plunged in a dazzle of reflected sunlight out of the noon sky. A strafing of altakra fire surprised the band of Valk warriors, who had been holding a raffle. They ran for cover among the scrubby trees but were much too slow. The holder of ticket no 7 made a brave attempt to claim his prize was incinerated by a bit of marvellous sharp shooting before he could sever the ropes which held her to the tree.

Minutes later, the massacre was complete. The clearing, littered with charred Valk warriors and smelling like a fried chicken takeaway, shuddered beneath the landing jets on the Magnarch's craft as its huge oval bulk made a perfect touchdown on a soft pad of Valk ashes.

Helena had, as you know, seen the Magnarch's father at quarters quite close for observation and was familiar with most details of the Principle's physiognomy.

Unfortunately the Magnarch took after his mother.

When Helena spotted what had rescued her climb from the cockpit of his saucer and jump to the grass, she decided at once to faint again.

"Hungry work, annihilating Dickies," the Magnarch murmured as he hopped across the clearing.

58

The consternation among the Time & Motion men in the asylum when the storekeeper reported the loss of the fresh consignment of pork scratchings was equalled nowhere in history except by the consternation in Atlantis after the discovery of the loss of Charlotte de Maupassant. Since the witch had escaped (by way of a brief period in the form of a soup plate to fool the guard) in the shape of that very crate of crunchy snackettes, it is hardly surprising.

Let us stroll back up one of the side alleys of time to the moment when Durinda sat down on the window seat in the gatehouse and peep through a different window.

What may surprise the reader, as the Empress of Witches ceases to be a miasma and reconstitutes herself at the back door of Sparesbrook Manor, is her radically altered demeanour. Where is the fire of ambition? Where the fierce glow of revenge?

After a brace of millennia in the guise of a pig-based nibble, dead. Quite, quite dead. As thoroughly decomposed as the religious fervour of Miss Winifred Wordsworth who, patrolling the darkness of Goitre Lane one recent evening with the intention of razoring the youth club when it came away from its table tennis and popular music in the former Temple of the Demi-Urge, had found herself face to face with the Owl-thing on the pavement outside the Community centre. With a cry of joy, the elderly worshipper had torn open her blouse, baring her bosom or at least her winter strength liberty bodice to the chilly air as she cried, "May the Owl devour me! May its talons strip my virginity!"

"Not bloody likely," gagged Herbert Jubb.

"Like munching twigs," shuddered Malcolm de Maupassant.

And with perfect co-ordination they flapped their wings and zoomed away into the foggy air, not omitting to bless Miss Wordsworth with a well-aimed dropping as she stood on the pavement, aghast.

Many are the philosophers and free-thinkers who have rejected their god. Few indeed are those whom their god has rejected, especially having signified the fact by crapping on their hair nets. Miss Wordsworth felt as though she had been awoken from a nightmare. She stared about her in wonder, unable to recall what superstitious fear had held her so in awe of these sooty walls, this murky sky. Wiping her head with a lavender scented hankie, she turned and, with a new free spring in her step, strode away from Goitre Lane and the former Temple of the Demi-Urge forever.

If she hurried she would be just in time for the meeting of The Ministers of Gurthunt in Dungey Street. How glad they would be to see her again.

No spring at all in the step of Charlotte de Maupassant, as she crept across the kitchen and down the passage to the bilious tiles of the hall. Clad now in the dingy robes of an Atlantean convict, her hair cropped and a red brand reading 'Property of H. S Principle's Office' livid on her shoulder, she sank down in the weariness of despondency upon the stairs, her head on her knees, and wept. She wept the bitter tears of a woman who had looked into the face of despair.

Or, in her case, the account books of the Demi-Urge.

Suppose that you, in the course of your daily business, have spent years jockeying the stock markets, swinging deals and poisoning rivals, all thoughts of Canary Island holidays and new music centres abandoned in your single minded ambition to become CEO of the most powerful multi-national in the world. And then estimate your feelings as, on the very day that the board have finally voted you into the Executive Tranqui-Chair™, the Company Secretary with an embarrassed cough introduces you to a gentleman who describes himself as the Official Receiver and shows you the notice of bankruptcy in the London Gazette.

There in miniature you have a model of the emotions which ate through Charlotte's heart when, a few hours or several thousand years earlier, she had closed the final ledger and sunk down on the floor, too distraught even to shed the healing balm of tears. All those years of training in the arts of magic, all the scheming and self sacrifice, (not to mention the cockerels, goats, birth-strangled babes, livers of blaspheming Jew, tiger's chaudrons, unblemished virgins and so on, none of which were getting any cheaper or, in the case of virgins, easier to find) all that, with the sole object of one day crowning herself Ruler of – Ruler of – this.

Her sobs as she crouched on the stairs turned to painful laughter.

At first she had not been able to believe what the accounts were telling her – it must be some anomaly, some fundamental error, a transposition of figures, a confusion of debits and credits. But with every page of every ledger, every receipt, every cheque stub and bank statement, it became more and more difficult to avoid the truth.

The universe in which she dwelt was nothing more than a giant tax dodge.

It was a source of spiritual loss relief, for set off against the profits of more successful universes elsewhere.

She had tried to dismiss the realisation as a delusion but the facts were undeniable. How else explain all the pain and disease, the terror and ugliness and vivisections? The Demi-Urge had poured all its stock of Goat-horrors, celebrity game shows, carcinomous chemicals, Space-viruses, sociologists, political commentators, munitions millionaires, pop singers, guerrillas, experimental novelists, bacteria and cat fanciers into a single enterprise. The resulting universal balances of grief, terror and remorse could be used to reduce the amount of spiritual duty chargeable on the love, joy and happiness accruing to the accounts of universes unknown to this one.

The discovery, having strangled Charlotte's ambitions in the direction of rulership, went on fairly methodically to throttle her second best obsession, the one which concerned her revenge on Captain Sparesbrook. The insult which had, burning, warmed up her animosity all these years died to a blackened ash when she thought of how the Demi-Urge must have used it. What after all did it matter if he had accused her of cheating at Scrabble? What did it matter, when the universe was only a tax avoidance scheme?

The front door opened and Captain Sparesbrook hurried in, his shot gun under his arm. He did not at first notice her in the gloom of the hall.

"You're treading on my hand, Gerry," Charlotte murmured, as he set off up the stairs.

"Charlotte!" He dropped the shot gun. It fell heavily on her bare toes but she would not give the Demi-Urge the benefit of a single wince. "Charlotte! I thought the Valk people had got you."

"No, Gerry," she said, her voice tired and sad. "The Archerons had me locked up for a while, but the prison is not built that can hold - "

"What is it, Charlotte? What is it?"

"Gerry!" Suddenly a ghost of the old fire had flickered through the witch's being. Her cheeks flushed prettily. She jumped to her feet. "Gerry! The prison is not built that can hold a Charlotte de Maupassant. Don't you see? We – we can escape! We can fool him! Oh, Gerry, darling! We can be free!"

"Er, yes," the Captain said nervously. "Of course we can. Charlotte. Er, now, why don't you just come and, er, have a bit of a lie down for a while. eh? Being Empress of Witches, and planning to rule the universe, and plotting revenges on people, they do take it out of one, and - "

"Oh, Gerry, you dear, dear idiot!" she laughed. "Don't you know that I've never been more sane in my life? In all my lives? Once I was a poor old woman they tortured to death on the 'smale fowles'. Another time I recall my name was Moll Digbone. They chopped me into several pieces. But this time my name is Charlotte de Maupassant. And I shall succeed!"

"Succeed in what?" the Captain asked, stooping casually to retrieve his shot gun. "Destroying me, I suppose."

"No, no, you darling whiskered fool." She pressed a kiss upon his forehead. "Listen. Do you remember the night of the Alternative Universe?"

Captain Sparesbrook shuddered. "How could I forget?" he asked, his memory being quite choked with disembowelled Juliettes and fishy bear things. "You're not going to try that again?"

"No. Listen to me. Put that gun down, whacking me on the head with the stock isn't going to help us. Now, pay attention. I thought that what I had done that night was to transform myself into another universe. I was mistaken. My researches into the accounts of the unspeakable Demi-Urge have shown that this universe of ours is only one of many, a multiplicity of universes running in divergent strands across every direction of the unimaginable dimensions of the ground of being. I had not made a new universe. I had simply extrapolated my being as a node of transmission through which another of the multifarious cosmoi might intertessalate with our own!"

"That's easy for you to say, Charlotte," the Captain sniffed, "though I must point out that according to the tenets of my religion, what you say is capital heresy."

"Don't be silly, Gerry. I told you before the Valk-people came that your Satan was only poor old Heg'naar'n Stag'naarvrk, from Scaliselsarga. It was in his bedroom that I found the ledgers which led to my astonishing conclusion."

"And what were you doing in his bedroom?" the Captain demanded.

Charlotte giggled with delight. "Why, Gerry," she cried, "I do believe you're jealous. You know there's no man for me but you."

"What about that Jubb chappie?"

"He's half an owl now," Charlotte reminded him. "Even I don't fancy owls. Much. But let me finish. The point is, if I can do it once, I can do it again. I can take us away, the two of us, from this black pit of sorrow, this universe of anguish and interminable situation comedies, and transport us to another world, where all will be peace and light and nothing will distract us from our joy but the promise of greater joys to come. A bit like Scarborough on a Bank Holiday. What do you say?"

"Do you mean this, Charlie? Have you really forgiven me?"

"All forgiven, dearest, all forgotten, Gerry, my only true love. You were right, anyway." She blushed rosily. "I had turned the cat into an extra Q tile for that triple word eight letter score. I'm sorry."

The laughed together over the memory, which had once caused such rancour, and now seemed so absurd.

Then Charlotte said, "Now, all I need is the S'nangstone."

"The what?"

"The fabled S'nang üll H'notorem, the Atlantean Stone of Power Andruta Tiservi told me of. It took me years of brooding to generate the astrethic energy I used to switch universes," Charlotte explained. "We don't want to hang about any longer than we have to, do we? If we can get our hands on that Stone, which contains a tiny fragment of the original black hole, source of the multiverse, we can use it to change tracks right away. All parallel worlds meet multidimensionally in that stone," she explained. "Hence its tremendous power. We must get to work quickly. The Atlanteans and the Master of the World both have their agents in the field. I must just go and change into something else."

Captain Sparesbrook frowned. "Change? Into what? Not another of these nodey things you speak of so bewilideringly?"

"No, no, I just want to get out of these prisonrags and into something suitably diaphanous. As Empress of Witches, one must always – Hush! What's that?"

The Captain tightened his grip on the shot gun and followed her into the drawing room.

Charlotte pointed from the French windows across the lawn, to where a lichenous statue glowered in the moonlight. "There's someone hiding there," she whispered. "Get them!"

Years of military training activated his limbs. Captain Sparesbrook flung aside the French windows and discharged his shot gun.

An obese figure in a stocking mask reeled from cover, took a few halting steps, then toppled into the dried up goldfish pond.

"I wonder who that was," said the Captain.

59

Charlotte's explanation of the nature of the multiverse is so nearly correct that it would be churlish to discuss the flaws in her understanding. We shall instead leave her in the telephone booth in the hall of Sparesbrook Manor as she summons the Weird Sisterhood of Britain, those witches who honoured her as Empress and would leave no stone unturned in their search for the S'nang, just as we shall leave the Captain strolling over the moonlit lawn to have a look at what he has bagged. A brief call at Shambhala will suffice before we go on to learn what happened when the Magnarch of Verox came upon Helena Phipps in the clearing.

"Unusual burst of activity from the Atlanteans," Jye-Po reported to Ogvonda, who was sitting at dinner with Eric Maresbreath in the club room. "Our code breakers are at work on the intercepts now. The minute they've cracked them, I'll bring copies down."

The old monk swallowed a radish. "Very good," he said. "Eric. You're not eating your grated carrot."

The Guardian of the Earth shrugged unhungrily. "How can I eat?" he asked. "I'm worried."

"About the universe?" Ogvonda enquired.

"Bugger the universe," said Eric. "I'm worried about Helena. She'll be getting bored to tears in Byfleet."

Would it have cheered him up to know that Helena, far from enduring the tedium of Byfleet,

The Gnostic Frying Pan

was in fact getting bored to tears in the co-pilot's seat beside the Magnarch, as he flew his shining craft over the cloud base towards the peaks of the Atlantean home land? Probably not, the ungrateful lass.

"...seventeen of them came at me out of the sun," the Magnarch was saying, "cannons blazing. And me down to my reserve tanks. Bit sticky, eh?"

Helena suppressed a yawn and smiled politely.

"Don't know what all the fuss is about," thought the Magnarch as he brought the disc down through the clouds. "Sensual she may be, I suppose but, I don't know, I still prefer my lady Khemmi. Give me iridescent skin and a flickering tongue any day of the week."

Astonished though you will be to find anyone who could remain impervious to the charm of Helena Phipps, you must not lose your grip on sanity now.

Slipping from the sky like a paring of sunlight, the flying disc skimmed over the fronds of the jungle, a trail of roasted parrots dropping from its slipstream, floated across the series of concentric canals which ringed the city, scorched the masonry in the main street and finally swooped down to the roof of an apartment block overlooking the sports stadium where the Magnarch performed a text book landing on the rooftop pad of his palace.

Unwinding his scarf, the Magnarch escorted Helena to the lift terminal and descended to his private penthouse. A servant creature scurried forward with a huge tureen of some rich brew which, much to the servant's relief, the Magnarch brushed aside with a flick of one scaly paw. The

Magnarch needed something stronger than servant creature dipped in panda sauce.

No sooner has the Magnarch entered his study than a secretary hurls himself to the tarmac at his feet and cries, "Hail to Your Serene Highness, the Principle of Goth[49]. A report, your Highness, from VU1. Do you want the good news first or the bad news?"

"The bad news," says the Magnarch, "unless it's about Charlotte de Maupassant."

"Here is the good news," declaims the secretary. "The secret agent of the Master of the World has been destroyed."

"Oh, good," says the Magnarch glumly. "All right. Let's have it. What about Charlotte the Harlot?"

"She has escaped," the secretary whimpers. "And has returned to Sparesbrook Manor. The Time & Motion people testify that she is ensconced now with the creature they call the Captain."

"Reeking her horrifying revenge, no doubt."

"Well, er, no. They say she is referring to him as 'darling poppet' and kissing his ears, actually."

"Revolting," says the Magnarch. "Look, take this woman away and keep her fresh somewhere. I'll come and see what's going on."

It was the message which the Magnarch has just received which, intercepted by the phone tappers of Shambhala, had also been brought to the monk Ogvonda as he relaxed before a camphor

---

[49] An hereditary position

wood fire and poured another Altain brandy for Eric Maresbreath.

He glanced at the vellum which Jye-Po held before him, then swept it aside into the flames. No indication of sentiment showed on his face as he said, "It appears that agent Durinda Ogvonda has been rendered inoperative by a fool with a shot gun."

Eric's mouth fell open. He spilt his brandy. "Ogvonda – I – I'm so sorry – I don't – "

"Sorrow is counterproductive, Guardian," said the hairless monk. "Mop up that brandy and follow me."

"But – but your daughter – "

"I have no daughter. Her astrethic body ascends the ladder of heaven. It's all up to you now, Eric. You'll have to go back."

"Me?" Eric stared at the monk. "But I'm just a stooge," he said bitterly. "What can I do?"

"Bugger all, probably," said Ogvonda. "But when the wise man runs out of tyre levers, he does not spurn the offer of an old spoon. Come, my son. The fate of the universe, possibly, is in your hands. Find the S'nangstone, - and do it before the foul lackeys of Atlantis get their dirty fingers all over it. Tell me, where did you last see the S'nang?"

Eric recounted the details off his leap into the Thames and the block of masonry which had slid from the roof of a sunken cabin cruiser and dented his skull.

"The you must return through our time window to that moment," declared the monk. "Jye-Po: operate the projector. And, Eric – " He smiled wanly at the Guardian of the Earth. "This time, try not to drop the bloody thing."

Captain Sparesbrook was only halfway across the lawn when the small girl with the blue and yellow teddy under her arm appeared from behind the gazebo and ran to meet him with a cheerful cry.

"Eric!" gasped the Captain. "Little Eric! I thought you were - "

"Cut the melodrama, sunshine," growled the teddy bear under the kid's arm. "Let's see who you've just gunned down, shall we?"

"Astonishing," said the Captain. "Japanese, is it? Microchips and all that, I suppose."

"Stop poking my chest," said Egrah'nca.

"It's not a teddy bear really," little Eric explained. She trotted along beside the Captain as they crossed to the goldfish pond with its unusual contents. "Really he's a secret agent of the Archerons of Atlantis. I've been there. It's really good. They have these funny toads - "

"Wonderful thing, the imagination of a child," thought the Captain. "Amazes me, never know what they'll come up with next. Must be - "

He had stooped down and peered at the body which lay, clad from head to toe in black, in the empty pond. The skirt had ridden up and there was something almost shocking about the exposed thigh with its garter of pink ribbon half swallowed by lumpy, dimpled flesh.

The Captain reached down and tugged the mask from the face.

Blonde curly hair, a small retrousse nose, eyes once darkly radiant, body like a stranded dugong.

"Juliette!" cried the Captain.

"Juliette!" cried Egrah'nca.

"Oh, it's her," said little Eric.

Egrah'nca wriggled from the child's grasp, kicked the Captain out of the way and leapt into the dried up pond beside the body of the Master's agent, like Hamlet leaping into the grave of Ophelia in the top comedy of the same name[50].

Yes, the narrative is perfectly well aware, thank you, that now is the time to wring your hearts on the cheap with some Nobel Prize for Literature winning bits and pieces about politics coming between young lovers, references to Dante & Beatrice, all that claptrap, especially if it revealed that the lady was not quite dead and gave you a blow-by-blow account of her dying words with Egrah'nca.

But, quite frankly, it is a bit late in the programme to start laying on the sob stuff. And, anyway, Durinda was as dead as last month's crisis. If there is indeed a ladder to heaven, her astrethic body had long since shinned up it.

---

[50] *Ophelia Titties*, **a roistering good laugh for all** 𝑃 **family,** *The Aberdeen Orrery.*

60

"Well," said the one they called the Doc, as the off duty section relaxed over gin and bitters in the bar of the lunatic asylum. "At least we know now why we've been putting ourselves out to preserve the existence of that frightful old fraud down the road." He picked a few limp crisps from a saucer. "Bloody shame about those pork scratchings. So the gallant Captain was destined from before the dawn of time to destroy the agent of the Master of the World. Very handy."

"Ought to fetch the blighter up here," suggested Jumbo. "Might find those pork scratchings for us."

Unaware of the role he had performed in the unfolding drama of rivalry between Atlantis and Shambhala, Captain Sparesbrook hauled the remains of the late agent up to the mansion, followed by Egrah'nca and little Eric.

"You needn't think you're bringing that in here," Charlotte said, stopping him at the French windows. "Who was it, anyway?"

"The wife of my poor old retainer." The Captain mopped his brow with Durinda's stocking mask. Gasping, he managed to heave the body into a wheelbarrow. "I wonder whatever happened to him. Oh, by the way, Charlotte, let me introduce you to - "

"I know who that is," Charlotte said coldly. "We meet again, Egrah'nca. I'll bet you were surprised to see me here."

Egrah'nca acknowledged her greeting with a nod. "I had thought that by now you would be safely incarcerated in the Magnarch's anti-incantational penal complex, I admit," the teddy bear said. "I congratulate you on your escape and-"

"The prison is not built," chortled the witch, "that can hold Charlotte de Maupassant."

"And," continued the bear loudly, "offer my condolences of course."

Charlotte frowned.

"Have you not heard? Your very close friend, the manageress of the Rampant Gr'noom, perished from seven thirty to nine twenty five last night, Atlantean time. If it's any sort of consolation, I believe she achieved record viewing figures. The video rights will make her heirs rich beyond their greediest dreams, one supposes."

Charlotte turned away. Everyone stood about in an uncomfortable silence, trying to avoid noticing the unspeakable brand mark on her exposed shoulder. When she swung back, she was as composed as a Caprotchevsky nonet.

"Now do you see, Gerry my sweet," she said, "why I want to take us away from this vilest of worlds?"

Captain Sparesbrook, who had been searching in vain for the key to the estate digger and was now wondering if it would be all right to drop Durinda's body in the swamp, glanced round.

"Quite, my dear, quite," he said, already learning how to react when the woman you desire requires an answer to something you haven't been listening to.

"But first we have to find -?" she said.

He coughed. "We've got to find," he drawled, "the whatchamacallit."

"The Stone," Charlotte snapped.

"Ah, yes, of course. Jagger, was it, or that other one, looks like an Aztec mural?"

"The S'nangstone!" Charlotte shrieked. If there had been a 9 iron handy, she would have clouted him with it.

"I knew that. Any news from your witches?"

"It's no easy thing to locate, the S'nangstone," Charlotte said. "However, now that this sweet infant has returned to our side, we may be more sanguine. May we not, Egrah'nca?" she asked. With the swiftest of movements, she had succeeded in pinning the bear to the door with a toasting fork. He struggled energetically.

"You beast!" yelled little Eric, moved as never before by the impalation of her teddy. Evading Charlotte's hands, she darted forward and unplugged the fork. A little dizzy from the loss of expanded polystyrene, Egrah'nca wobbled forward and sat down on the rug. His paw touched the centre of his tummy. A low growl exuded.

"At least that still works," he muttered, in the two and a half seconds before the Nidro Force smashed through the west wall, wrecking a valuable old Portuguese armchair and a collection of netsuke. Manifesting itself this time in the appearance of a Egyptian mummy of repellent aspect and doubtful provenance in order to avoid any pink ribbon related embarrassments, it curtsied to Egrah'nca and said dustily, "You rang, my lord?"

"The child – she alone has the wits to find the S'nang üll H'notorem," Egrah'nca cried. "Listen to her words. Go where she goes. Follow her as your cynosure. Do not quit her side by night or day." He turned to the child. "Now, little Eric, sweet miss, whither shall we wander?"

Eric Maresbreath, only four, looked up at the furious eyes of the witch and the red puffing cheeks of the Captain. Quailing from their threat, she turned to Egrah'nca but could not face his mummified assistant. What could she say? What did they want her to say? Her poor frightened mind, motherless and without comfort, turned to the only other image of hope it held.

"Speak up, child," screamed Charlotte de Maupassant. "Where must we go?"

Eric blinked away her tears. "Goitre Lane?" she sobbed, remembering the picture of the Blessed Helena in a gymslip which had come to her so strangely on the frozen moor. "Goitre Lane," she repeated more firmly. "That's where we got to go."

The adults stared down at her in wonder (apart from Egrah'nca, who being only six inches tall had to stare up at her in wonder).

"Goitre Lane?" whispered Captain Sparesbrook. "But that – that's where I lost poor old Mitty's boat. Rum do, eh, Charlie?"

"Goitre Lane it is, then," said Egrah'nca. "Strange, only a few days ago I lay in Goitre Lane with the most sensual woman in the universe. And now – Ah, well. Come, then. Let us away. To Goitre Lane!"

"To Goitre Lane!" cried the others, and ran to the nearest bus stop.

"This is VU1 to HQ. Are you receiving me?"
"Roger, VU1. Go ahead."

"Reporting that targets CdM, CHGS, LEM and TNF together with a teddy bear have just left our section on a big white bus. Audio monitoring advises their destination as Goitre Lane."

"Noted, VU1."

"No news of those pork scratchings, I suppose?"

"Negative, VU1. I'm sending you a crate of cheesy biscuits as a stop gap..."

61

"Yes," said the monk Ogvonda. "Jye-Po advises me that we have intercepted traffic on the informational parameters. I think he means 'a radio message'. The child has spoken and the whole crew is apparently on its way to Goitre Lane. It is imperative therefore that you get there ahead of them and find that stone. The time window is the only way."

The Guardian of the Earth bared his forearm for the immunisation shots and, when they had brought him round, strode bravely to the back of the cavern, where the dark swirling mass of the time window sucked hungrily for his flesh.

"Well, best of luck," said Ogvonda, with little enthusiasm. "Try not to cock it up this time."

"Don't worry," said Eric. "I'll get it right, you'll see. The S'nangstone will be ours forthwith."

"Mmm," said Ogvonda. "Jye-Po! The switch!"

Jye-Po eagerly seized a whippety rod which, applied to Eric's buttocks, stung the Guardian of the World into action.

Travelling through a time window is a bit like having your corsets ripped off by a mad history don with sweaty hands and body odour. It was almost a relief when all sensation ceased and Eric found himself tumbling out of the fog above Goitre Lane.

In a leap of water, he plummeted into the Thames and sank to the bottom. Murk swirled about him, thick as custard. He tried not to wonder what the lumps were. Silent fishy beings nosed up to him, inspected the curious interloper and decided that he was inedible. They flicked away in pursuit of old library books and unwanted infants. Eric swam through the haze of suspended particles towards the Goitre Lane bank, peering through the gloom for a hint of the S'nangstone or the cabin cruiser on the river bed. A pain from his foot drew his attention down. A hopeful sign – he had cut his big toe on the sharp end of a Sepraphontine newt fleecer.

With refreshed energy, he squirmed through the muck. There! Was that - ? No, it was just some forgotten hulk, rotting in silence under the mighty Thames. He glimpsed a faded name. "...**ing Dutchm**...." and then the darkness swallowed it once more. On, on, breath turning to iron in the lungs, brain threatening to explode in a fizz of greyish bubbles. Would it never end? Would - ?

Something plopped into the water a few yards ahead of him. He flailed forwards and found himself staring at the back view of a man whose longish hair floated about his head like dahlia petals as he clung to the side of a cabin cruiser. He was unsuitably dressed for a dip in a duffle coat, a blue velour sweater and grey trousers.

"Cripes," thought the Wielder of the Cord. "It's me."

He struggled forward. Somehow his flailing arm struck a loose board on the side of the boat and caused a large chunk of masonry to slide from the upturned hull. It bounced off his other skull. Interestingly enough, he felt an echo of the pain.

Diving magnificently, he was just in time to get his arms under the stone as it cartwheeled towards the bed of the Thames while his other manifestation reeled away in a cloud of blood. Then he lost sight of himself as the stone carried him in a great gulp of water through the hole it had smashed in the fragile river bed.

A time of falling, writhing, and buffetings as the brutal embrace of the water carried him down crags and cliffs to the bowels of Scaliselsarga. At last, the right way up for a moment, he managed to transfer the stone to the crook of his left arm, wield the cord with his right, and vanish from the torrent in a crackle of atomic fire and a cloud of steam.

Seconds later the waves smashed through the palace of Heg'naar'n Stag'naavrk, gathering up Charlotte de Maupassant and her son for the thrill ride of which you know.

What with the traffic, and a lorry load of deep frozen gulls which had jack-knifed at Flittger's Corner, and the throngs of worshippers waiting to enter the shrine of the enigmatic holy woman of Westcombe Hill, the bus that carried Egrah'nca and his party to London was a good ninety minutes late when it pulled into Victoria Coach Station. It took another two and a half hours by tube and No 11 bus to reach Goitre Lane by which time night was settling down on the rooftops.

None of that was even slightly important, of course, as thanks to the Shambhalan time window Eric Maresbreath had been and gone, with the stone, several days ago.

Only Charlotte de Maupassant managed to look unsurprised when the band of whooping diminutive females in black gowns leapt upon them as they passed the billiard hall. The Nidro Force, its power neutralised by the Rune Sign of Widmore which someone had thoughtfully chalked on its mummified rump, jerked about idiotically on the pavement, unable to prevent the fearsome crew from binding Egrah'nca, little Miss Eric and the Captain in stout ropes, while Charlotte sat on the bonnet of a nearby Allegro and watched with real interest.

"Well done, girls," she said, clapping her hands, when the last of the knots was tied. "Well done indeed. A credit to your pack leader. Which of you is thirteener?"

"Me, Miss," lisped a gangly redhead. She flung up her hands in the horn salute and chanted, "Dow, dow, dow."

"Yes, yes, I'm sure you will, dear," Charlotte smiled. "And which coven are you from?"

"First Hungerford, Miss," said the thirteener. "Our Black Bat is Miss Selena Comfort."

"Of course. A fine witch and a wonderful pastry cook. Well, thank you, my dears, for your very efficient ambush."

The witch pack giggled and curtsied and blushed.

"Now, have you any news for me of the S'nangstone?"

A sudden hush.

"What is it? Come on, girl. Out with it. Tell me."

"Well, Miss, you see, before we left, Miss, after our camp cauldron sing-song, our Black Bat, Miss, Miss Comfort, Miss, she sacrificed a bunny rabbit and read the entrails, Miss."

"And? Come along, child. What did she see?"

"She saw someone called Eric Maresbreath, Miss. Finding the stone in the water down there."

"We have Eric Maresbreath here! The child with the squint. Free her from her bonds. And hurl her into the Thames!"

"No point, Miss. The entrails said it was last Tuesday."

Charlotte dragged the coil of rope which contained little Eric upright and screamed, "Well, you brat? What have you done with the stone?"

A strange sound, stranger than the muffled whimpering of little Eric, distracted her. It came from the smallest of the bundles, the one with the yellow furry ears protruding from the top. Charlotte snatched it up and shook it vigorously. The sound merely increased. It was, she realised, laughter.

At last Egrah'nca managed to speak.

"Oh, Charlotte," he coughed. "Oh, dear. Poor old Trepoch. He wasn't much good, was he? The one time he nearly got it – and he picked the wrong Eric Maresbreath." He gurgled merrily for a minute or two and then added, "Well, Charlie, I think you'd better persuade your young ladies to untie us, if you want to catch up with the S'nangstone now."

"Catch up with it now?" Charlotte was bitterly scornful. "How can we catch with it now? It was found, last Tuesday, while I was wasting my time in Scaliselsarga."

"You forget," said Egrah'nca. "We have the Nidro Force, to whom time is a meaningless convention of polite society. Release it from its bonds, scrub off that irritating bit of graffiti from its posterior, and I shall command it to transport us all at once to a suitable spot last Tuesday where Eric may be waylaid."

"I don't believe any of this," the Captain said. "How can we be in two places at once?"

"Why is it," Egrah'nca sighed, "that people only ask me to explain the nature of time when I haven't got any to spare? Just untie us, Empress. We'll worry about the metaphysics afterwards."

Charlotte nodded. "Very well, girls," she said. "Release them."

It took the First Hungerford coven a good deal longer to untangle their victims but they managed it in the end and were rewarded with the promise of an Ambushers Badge apiece to sew on their robes. Dismissed, the girls hovered through the fog and filthy air and disappeared into the night from which they had come.

"Now," said Charlotte, scrubbing at the seat of the mummified trousers with the hem of her robe. "You are free. Let us see you carry out your side of the bargain. Take us to this other Eric Maresbreath and the stone - if you can."

"Nidro Force," said the blue and yellow teddy bear. "Stop picking at your bandages and pay attention. Sometime last Tuesday the Guardian of the Earth seized the S'nangstone and headed, presumably, East. Can you establish and intercept?"

The Nidro Force nodded its mummified head, caught it neatly, and jammed it back in place.

"Take hands with me," commanded Egrah'nca.

'Mole' Butler, staggering beerily from the Goitre Lane Community Workshop, paused in mid-belch and stared at the sight which met his eyes. On the pavement outside the billiard hall, skipping round in a ring-a-rosy circle, a child, a teddy, a woman in a robe, a military gent and a horribly decaying mummy whirled faster and faster and finally disappeared in a Catherine wheel of dissolving light. 'Mole' Butler pocketed his keys and decided to lay off the sardine sandwiches. It was a resolution he would keep for the rest of his life. Not that that was any great achievement: forty seconds later the Owl-thing dropped on him from the roof of the funeral parlour.

62

Some days previously, a wet but rejoicing Eric Maresbreath found himself shivering on the cold mountain side above the mystic city. He promised himself that this time he really would get the cord's direction finder seen to.

Clutching the S'nangstone to his chest, he slithered down the icy path. Perhaps only 'Mole' Butler would have understood his emotions when, rounding a crag, he saw before him in lights coagulating a Catherine wheel which slowed and slowed and revealed a horribly decaying mummy, a military gent, a woman in a chiffon robe, a teddy and a child whirling ring-a-rosily as they skipped round on the mountain side.

His decision to run could not be criticised but as his Thames clogged sandals had frozen to the path he achieved nothing more than a twisted ankle and wound up prostrate on the ground with a mouth full of dirty snow.

The dancing crew had ceased rotating now and hastened up the footpath to surround him. Wiping a good deal of Yeti droppings from his eyes, Eric Maresbreath looked up at them unhappily.

"Oh, it's you lot," he said. "What does it take to outwit you? A Levels?"

"Cheer up, Eric." Egrah'nca stooped down beside his former companion and quickly removed his wristwatch, which he tossed over a handy precipice.

"Ah!" said the Captain. "Good work, young bear. Secret communications device, eh?"

Egrah'nca shook his head. He had always despised Eric's Mickey Mouse wristwatch. "But thanks for reminding me. Where is the secret communications device, Eric old chum?"

"Haven't got one," Eric grumbled. "Typical, of course. They never think of anything practical in that bloody mystical city. Too busy with their string trios and amateur dramatics. If I could contact my control, d'you think I'd be lying around here? Fifty besabred lay-brothers would have sprung from hidden tunnels and turned you lot into a tasty lunch for the Yetis."

"Hard to disagree," said Charlotte de Maupassant, only slightly purple with cold. "And this, I take it - " She set her sandal on a chunk of stone which protruded from Eric's snow drift, "is the cause of all our wanderings. The S'nangstone."

"No," said Eric. "No. Don't know what that is. Just a bit of old mountain, I shouldn't wonder. Never found the stone. Well, you know me, incompetent to the end."

"Look at him," Egrah'nca sighed. "He can't tell a lie without blushing, even in sub-zero temperatures. How odd, if this is only a chunk of irrelevant granite, that it should bear the inscription 'S'nang üll H'notorem' on its side." He tilted his head and frowned. "You know, it doesn't look much like Crom ten Pogol to me. What do you think, Charlie?"

"Can't see it myself," Charlotte said. "Still, to a Valk person the world may be a very different place."

"Must be," Egrah'nca agreed. "Either that, or they've got bloody funny genitals."

"That's a point that's been bothering me," put in the Captain. "I mean, I know you told us while we were stuck in that traffic jam outside Madame Tracey's corset shop in Lewisham that you and Juliette Thring, or Durinda Doo-Dah, or whatever her ridiculous name was, were, well, were, well, you know. But as a small blue and yellow teddy bear, you're conspicuously ill equipped yourself in the Crom ten Pogol department, though," he added feelingly, "no doubt you have the advantage in the present climate. Don't mind me asking, old chap, but how, you know, how did you manage it?"

"Is this really the right moment to start raking all that up?" Charlotte demanded.

"I think the old boy's jealous," said Eric.

"What're they talking about?" demanded Eric.

Egrah'nca did not reply. He just licked his ears and murmured, "Another unsolved mystery, I'm afraid, Captain. Now, if you will be so kind as to take hold of an end of this fragment of masonry, we'll – Ah!"

His cry, which was of a sort that might destroy whole fridge-freezers or shatter the walls of a multi-storey council office like sheets of flaky pastry, echoed among the icy crags, was snatched up by the wind and transformed into a ghostly chorale for altos and euphonium before it faded into echoes among the peaks and died in the piercing air.

Eric Maresbreath had wielded the cord.

Fortunately, after the severe drain on its energy cells caused by Eric's escape from the deluge, the cord needed a recharge and did no more damage to the bear than any other piece of well-aimed string might have done, if it had similarly wrapped round his neck, spun him into the air and deposited him upside down in a clump of Altain stinging mimosa.

Grabbing the stone, Eric slithered to the edge of the precipice.

"Don't move!" he screamed. "I warn you! One more step and I'll heave the S'nangstone over the edge. Then none of you will have it."

They froze. Well, they were already fairly frozen, but they tried to show that they weren't moving in any significant way. Apart from little Eric's teeth, which were chattering, all was still and silent beneath the majestic Siberian sky. Then Egrah'nca wriggled to the top of the mimosa and peered down at the tableau below him. His laughter came thin and crisp through the rarefied air.

"I don't think you should do that," he called.

"Shall I chance it and jump the blighter?" asked the Captain.

"Don't try it!" screeched the Guardian of the Earth. He slid a little nearer to the snowy lip of the abyss. It cracked and crumbled under the weight of the S'nangstone.

"That won't be necessary," Egrah'nca assured them. He jumped lightly down into a convenient snow drift, tunnelled his way out, and said, "Come along, Eric, old fellow. That's enough now. Hand over the stone and we'll say no more about it."

"Never!"

Egrah'nca spread his paws. "Well," he said, "it's entirely up to you, of course, and I wouldn't for a moment try to influence you in any way, but - "

He brushed a few mimosa leaves from his ears, "I hope you've remembered that at this very moment the most sensual woman in the world - "

Eric's leg spasmed and he seemed in some danger of sliding into the airy chasm below.

"I see," remarked Egrah'nca, "that you have not forgotten her. Helena Phipps, the woman to whom I allude, is as we speak a captive in the Halls of the Archerons."

"You lie!" Eric cried.

"Not a bit of it," said Charlotte. "I was there with her. Or I will be. Or I am. Hecate, this time thing'll drive me potty soon."

"I took her there myself," said Egrah'nca, sensing it was time for some brilliant prevarication. "As a matter of fact, I have by the aid of my assistant here -" The Nidro Force waved a clawed hand, "been in contact with my patron, the Magnarch of Verox, who informs me that he has chained your girlfriend to a damp wall in the dungeons of Basileia, where she will remain until rheumatism, mildew and senility somewhat impair her chances of employment in anything more glamorous than a local bus office. I never lie, Eric. It's not in my nature. We Atlanteans are above that sort of thing. It's a charism, a spiritual gift."

"But - but Egrah'nca, you - you love her too. I know you do. I saw the look on your little furry chops the night you found yourself on her pillow, back in dear old Goitre Lane." He sobbed at the memory. "Oh, to be there in that cosy flat once more, a cup of Ovaltine on the table, the snooker championships on the telly, and Helena draped across the sofa in a topless negligee and garters..." He brushed the frozen teardrops from his cheeks.

"These homely pleasures, wrenched from me, in exchange for – for what? A barren mountainside, half a gallon of ice up my trouser leg, and a couple of hundred weight of unlisted building that would be better off sawn into segments and turned into an ornamental fire place. Egrah'nca, I beg of you. Release her. If not for my love, then for the love I know you bear her."

Egrah'nca sucked his fur thoughtfully. Then: "Sorry, old chap," he said. "Don't think I'm not fully alive to the force of your suggestion but, well, it's more than I can do. The Magnarch wants the stone. He wants it very badly. Much more than he wants Helena."

"Impossible!" hissed Eric. "Now I know that you lie. No-one could desire a lump of old rock more than the most sensual woman in the world."

"Thank your lucky stars," said Egrah'nca, "that the Magnarch does. What the Magnarch gets up to after intimacy makes the habits of the female mantis look positively endearing. No, my old friend, I can make no concessions. If you hope to see the inside of 143 Goitre Lane again, never mind the negligee and the topless garters, then you must surrender the stone." He smiled. "Your move, I think?"

"You leave me no choice," said Eric. "But – how do I know I can trust you, you and your Magnarch? I'd be foolish to hand over the stone now and then sit back and wait for you to return with Helena. No, we must arrange some sort of swap. You tell your precious Magnarch to fetch Helena here, to me, in person, and I'll – well, all right, I'll betray my Master and hand over the stone. Word of honour. But until I see Helena, alive, unnibbled, and entirely free from mildew or any other form of fungal infection, the Stone and I remain right here, teetering on the brink of oblivion. All right?"

Egrah'nca nodded slowly. "No doubt your training makes you more able to withstand the intense cold than us." He indicated the bodies of Charlotte, the Captain and little Eric, who had frozen almost to death while the bargaining took place. "But I am not uncivilised, Eric, and – and I cannot think back over our time together without feeling that to leave you here for however long it takes to talk the Magnarch round would be, well, a bad memento of our friendship. The Nidro Force and I will return to Atlantis. Take your companions and the stone into some nearby cave. Light a fire."

"I'm not sitting around on a Yeti-infested mountain side all afternoon waiting for you to prise the Magnarch out of his favourite cat-house," Eric snapped. "When you want me, I'll be in the mystic city with my feet up on the fender and a mug of hot chocolate in my hands."

"Speaking of mugs," Egrah'nca said, "how are you going to explain to Ogvonda that you're expecting a few of your Atlantean chums to drop in for tea and S'nagstones? You'd better prepare a dummy, a replica of the S'nang with which to deceive your Master, whose insight being what it is, you could probably get away with a cornflake packet wrapped up in OO-gauge brick paper."

"Oh, I've already got a few ideas about that," Eric beamed. "I – "

He broke off suddenly. For a moment his own words had echoed in the drain-pipe of his consciousness. He knew at once that someone had targeted him with a long-range listening device. He smiled benevolently. "Trust me," he murmured, "I know the way their minds work. Leave it all to me. I'll see you later."

"Very well. Return to your city of tripe and custard -"

"Light and culture."

"Whatever. I shall contact you there by means of our secret agent as soon as I have fixed things up. OK?"

"Better bring some insect repellent with you," Eric said. "Lot of hairy Siberian dog-bees about, this time of year."

"I'll bear that in mind."

"You do that," said Eric. "Now, if it's all the same to you, I'll just hang about here by the precipice till you and your ugly mate have disappeared, if you don't mind?"

"As you wish." Egrah'nca bowed and in a flash of blue and green light vanished on the back of the Nidro Force from the icy slopes of Mount Meru.

A mixture of relief and terror tying itself in knots inside his bosom, Eric Maresbreath began to put his ingenious plan into operation.

"Well," said the monk Ogvonda, removing his ear-phones and rising from the control panel. "Despite the imperfections of our equipment, whose inefficiencies we are personally far too spiritual to correct, we have heard enough to know that Maresbreath intends to deceive us. What else did I expect? The fool was a stooge, no more. The mission should have been in the hands of my child, Durinda. But she - she did not survive. What other result could there be? The loon betrays us. But he does not know that I have heard something of his treacherous plans." He kicked the long-range listening device with an irritable sandal. The brass horns shuddered and clanged, the crystals tinkled, a green furry bit dropped off and was deftly caught by Ogvonda's prehensile toes. "I must get the Chief of the Secret Brotherhood of the Initiates of the Occult Sciences down here again with his socket set and remind him if he doesn't fix the bloody thing this time I shall be asking for a full refund."

Jye-Po, who had crept up behind Ogvonda with a mug of steaming brew in each hand, smiled gummily. "What concerns me, Ogvonda," he murmured, humbly offering a mug to his superior, "is the reference to a secret agent. It cannot be that we harbour a mole of the Archerons, here in our very midst."

"Tush, that is old news," said Ogvonda. He took a sip of his tea and at once spat it over Jye-Po's lilac robe, clean on that month. "So! Is this more treachery? Would you perchance infect me with an infusion of unnameable pestilence?"

"Ooops, sorry," said Jye-Po, swapping mugs. "Left, right, never sorted that out. That's my camomile and wintergreen tea. Surely there is no treachery here."

"Who do you think was responsible for melting all the Mantovani LPs? Who fed our collection of masterpieces of the birthday card to the Yetis? Who planted the device which destroyed Sadie Q Tourmaline, the Master's secretary?"

"You mean- you mean these were not accidents?"

"Well, maybe the Mantovani," Ogvonda conceded. "Might have been a mistake, storing them next to the boiler. But yes, somewhere among us lurks one who seeks to overthrow the citadel of light, to expose the throat of culture to the wolves of materialism. I have placed a double guard on the Walt Disney rooms. Now, let us concentrate on the very interesting possibilities which our Guardian of the Earth has opened up for us, shall we? A visit from the Magnarch himself will prove most amusing...."

63

While Eric dragged the almost lifeless bodies of the Captain and his beloved Empress and the infant who strangely shared his name through the wailing of blizzards into a cave, Egrah'nca and the Nidro Force did things with time and space which would have resulted in a row of dollies if the continuum had been a copy of the *Aberdeen Orrery* and appeared in a cloud of pink feathers on the floor before the throne of His Serene Highness, the Principle of Goth. By the light of burning martyrs, Egrah'nca stared up at his friend and patron, now elevated to so strangely lofty a station, and whispered:

"My Lord? Your Holiness? What does this mean?"

"My father is dead," the Magnarch replied, his voice dark with sorrow. "Caught by the Dickies."

Egrah'nca restrained the urgent need for a comedy wince.

"Eaten by Valk warriors," the Magnarch glossed. "Swallowed, regurgitated and fed to their nestlingsThe loss is a sad one and I find it hard to bear." He sobbed a little. "I had been looking forward so much to the internment. However – what report do you bring me, my old friend?"

Egrah'nca got up and edged closer to the great opal throne.

"I have come cold foot from a snowy track amid the awesome mountains of Altai," he announced, "where I left the Empress of Witches, the Guardian of the Earth, Captain Whatsisname, and The Infant Foretold by the Sage, Dacha ten Rogan of Valk."

The Magnarch suppressed a yawn. "Really?" he sighed. "Look, will you join me for lunch? I can promise you a rare treat."

"What? Oh, yes, thanks," Egrah'nca said. "No, listen. Not only did I leave the aforementioned, but something else of interest to you."

"My little friend," smiled the Magnarch, "I am not the person I used to be. My father's much lamented demise has meant a considerable revision of my roles. No longer do I lead the council of the Archerons in their tiresome affairs of state. Now my concerns in these, the last days of our once mighty Empire, are with spiritual matters, the higher mystical meditations of the Serene Principle. I am on the board of governors of several good schools and serve on various tribunals. My charity work alone consumes over a third of my waking hours. What could you have possibly left on a mountainside to interest me?"

"The S'nangstone," said Egrah'nca.

None of those present had ever before had the pleasure of watching a Serene Principle leap twenty-five feet in the air, head butt a flaming sconce and drop gibbering on his back. It would be something to tell the grandchildren, assuming they lived long enough to beget any. When the Nidro Force had righted the Magnarch, Egrah'nca said, "Yes. I have the S'nangstone."

"Where? Why have you not brought it to me? Is it safe? Is it well hidden?"

"Safe?" laughed the bear. "Where could it be safer, than in the hands of the Guardian of the Earth?"

"The Guardian of - " The Magnarch leaned very close to his small agent, an experience not unlike being eyeballed by a mad town hall, and said, "Do you by any chance imagine that along with my newfound religious interests I have acquired a sense of humour?" He paused, frowning. Hadn't his father once said something similar? "Mmm? Explain yourself, bear."

"It's really very simple," Egrah'nca said. "We have Helena Phipps. Eric Maresbreath has the stone. Eric Maresbreath wants Helena Phipps."

"So does everybody," groaned the Magnarch. "Even my late father."

"So I've set up a swap," Egrah'nca continued. "Maresbreath will render up the stone to us, if you fly Helena Phipps to the city of Shambhala forthwith."

"Impossible."

"Doesn't bother me," said Egrah'nca. "I'd rather die with Helena Phipps than live with the stone any day, but I thought you wanted the S'nang üll H'notorem. If so, it's all aboard the jolly old disc and hey for the time window at the double."

"But - but I'll have to cancel lunch."

"Oh, there's not that much of a rush," Egrah'nca said. "I mean, a couple of hours won't make any difference. What is for lunch, anyway?"

"Helena Phipps," said the Magnarch. "Marinade. All right, all right, stop shouting, I'll tell the chef to scrub it." He brightened suddenly. "I know, we'll get him to open a tin of jellied babies."

The Gnostic Frying Pan

An hour or so later, quite composed but still smelling strongly of vinegar and cloves, Helena Phipps was with a good deal of quite unnecessarily helpful handling assisted up into the passenger lounge of the Magnarch's flying saucer.

"Helena!" sighed Egrah'nca. "If only I had time to get back into my own body. However, we must fly. I have come to convey you across the aeons to the oasis of light, where your lover awaits you, Eric Maresbreath, a lord among lords in his own city. OK, Maggers baby, let's get this crate skyside, shall we?"

"When we get back," the Magnarch said, as he fastened his seat belt, "remind me to lend you a good book on Correct Forms of Addressing a Serene Principle. There are, I believe, one hundred and seven official titles but as far as I recall 'Maggers baby' has by some oversight been entirely overlooked."

"Speaking of books," said Egrah'nca, relaxing as the autopilot switched in, "did you ever get round to trying Timora Garpatheny, the occult novelist? I enjoy her stuff a lot. *Spheroids of Chraicht* was particularly fine. Just bought the new one, got it with me, actually, to read on the journey." He hefted the tome the weight of whose 431 pages had been causing the disc to slope sideways. "It's some sort of anti-clerical satire, apparently. Set in a dystopian future where nobody believes in the Demi-Urge anymore, and there's hundreds of really whacky religious cults, all of them preaching universal love and brotherhood when they've got time to spare from blowing each other up. Most of the characters just want to be left alone to buy bigger smarter 'mobiles'. Fabulous imagination,

Timora, and a lovely woman, if the picture on the back's anything to go by."

"You seem to know a lot about it," the Magnarch remarked, "given that you have evidently not yet removed the wrapper. Some say," he added thoughtfully, "that 'Timora Garpatheny' is merely a pseudonym."

"Oh yes!" Egrah'nca laughed heartily. "I suppose you think she's probably some fat-arsed Yorkshireman with a beard and a pipe."

The Magnarch sniffed. "It appears that you are spending too much time astride the future, my lambling," he said. "That was a very uncouth idiom."

"What, 'fat-arsed'?"

"Yorkshireman. And, though information is regrettably sparse, my researchers have established almost beyond question that Miss Garpatheny is a government employee."

"Never!" Egrah'nca gurgled. "A woman of romance, of high fantasy, of dreams and wild imaginings. Hard to picture her stapling vouchers at a desk in the Department of Aggravation, Viciousness and Forms."

"Almost certainly, in fact, the Prognosticator's Office. This latest mound of droppings from the sacred cow of literature, for example, *Ducklings, Scrimshaw, Sock-stretchers & Co* or whatever its ludicrous title is. My team of readers reported, before going into extensive therapy, that it is set in a recognisable but improbably distorted simulacrum of what its inhabitants generally refer to as the twenty first century. Allusions abound, for example, to Torquay. And Dylan Thomas. Although it seems that to Timora Garpatheny's inflamed consciousness Dylan Thomas is not an internationally celebrated hair-stylist but only some sort of poet. And Torquay by all accounts a rather nice place."

"I still don't see it," Egrah'nca said. "Timora Garpatheny, a civil servant in a tweed skirt and lisle stockings. Never."

"Sorry as I am to spoil your mental image, my friend, the researchers also suspect that your earlier jest was unwittingly close to the truth."

"She's from Yorkshire?"

"He's a male. I have no information about facial whiskers. Or narcotic addiction. Or the dimensions of his posterior."

"Well, it all sounds very unlikely to me," Egrah'nca insisted. "Timora Garpatheny – I seem to see her, poised on some blustery headland, tresses streaming back in the wind as her eyes scan the seas for the returning barque of her beloved, while in the humble cottage at her back the ink dries on the pages of her next multi-million diam blockbuster."

"While I," the Magnarch said, "seem to see him hunched over a tea-stained desk pretending to countersign this month's quota of dockets while secretly scribbling gibberish on stolen governmental slates with fraudulently converted governmental styli. If ever I catch up with him, I shall devour the little toad." He adjusted the hydraulic ruddervator. "Though if he's anything like his *oeuvre*, I shall find him very dry. And rather tasteless in parts."

Egrah'nca looked hurt. "The Basileian Bugle described the last book as a masterwork of asymmetrical functionality in which Garpatheny adroitly synthesises the semiotics of an imaginal futurity."

"Would I be correct in supposing that the word 'metonymy' is about to run the black flag up its masthead and attempt to board this conversation? I thought as much. When we have a convenient moment, you must tell me how you manage to find time to - "

All idle literary chit-chat ceased as the oval craft locked onto the flight path for Gorpul dül Mimpoth. The air traffic controllers were extremely reluctant to give clearance for a priority on the massive time window at the end of the airfield: not only had the Magnarch failed to submit the necessary documents, sworn oaths and so forth, the appalling instability of the window brought about by the power shortages consequent upon the loss of the stone meant that if the thing blinked out at the wrong moment the Magnarch's ship would whizz straight through and demolish the control centre.

In a hiss of superheated air the craft flashed over the rows of private discoids and the club house, heading for the time window, which at that very moment ceased to be a hungry swirling blackness and became instead a fine view of the terrified controllers battering at the locked doors of their tower.

64

Eric Maresbreath, clad now in a fetching lilac robe and quite hairless, shuffled in his toeless slippers down one of the corridors in the cavernous city of Shambhala and tapped softly at a door. For a moment he paused, half listening to the melodies of Bert Kaempfert whispering from concealed speakers in the ceiling. Then the pink door eased open and Captain Sparesbrook's brown face peeped out.

"Oh, it's you, Maresbreath," he whispered. "Come in, come in. Keep your voice down."

"How is she?" Eric enquired. He patted the head of his little namesake, who was playing on the yak skin rug with a week old Yeti cub. "Any better?"

The Captain shook his head. "Still very, very weak," he sighed. "Can't say too much in front of the child, but - Not much sign of improvement, I'm afraid. It's been, what, three days now since you rescued us from the snow. The child and I have bounced back wonderfully, but Charlotte - well, a chiffon robe and no knickers isn't the ideal gear for Siberia at 10,000 feet on a windy afternoon, is it?"

"The coma hasn't lifted?"

"Not for a moment. I've played recordings of cauldron-fire sing-songs, speeches by the Chief Black Bat, everything. They unearthed a recording of a hecatomb of refuse collectors in Angmering last Beltane for me but to no avail, to no avail." He withdrew a handkerchief from the sleeve of his kimono and blew a lusty nose. "The most we can hope for is that she - she passes away peacefully, sleeping, as she is now." He tucked the handkerchief away. "But what's the news with you, my dear fellow. Has the randy little bear returned with your lady friend?"

"That's what I came to tell you. I've just had a call from the secret agent of the Archerons. The time scanners have picked up a sighting about fifty thousand years ago and updating itself fast. It can only be an Atlantean flying disc. We must prepare ourselves."

With a thunder of riven time sheets, the Magnarch's disc had vanished into the fortuitously restored and whirling black vapours of the window. Echoes rebounded among the neighbouring council maisonettes, ageing an infant to maturity here, or reducing a senile Labrador to puppyhood there, and bringing the Protest Marchers out onto the streets again.

After a moment of incredulous silence, the air traffic controllers burst into cheers, slapping each others' hands and emitting whoops of unbounded joy, and so perished cheerfully when the first of the mega-tsunamis broke over them.

Flung wildly off course by the destabilised time window, the craft and its occupants bounced like a steel ball in a pin table off the Roman Empire, Pompeii, the Insurrection of Archimedes the Patriot and the Second Ice Age, and fell several million years down the Jurassic period, causing the rupture of the supercontinent Pangaea and melting both the polar ice-caps with its exhaust, before the Magnarch managed to get the controls back in line and adroitly swung them round the Gulf of Mexico, shook off an allosaurus from the under carriage, and powered his way back up the time lattice to about three days from Now.

While the giant ship hurtled up the aeons with its precious cargo of sensuality, whose destruction would have been so mighty a blow to the world, not to mention the Lyminge Under 20 Netball Team, conversation not unnaturally creaked back into action. In a properly ordered cosmos, one where it never rained at weekends and space viruses did nothing more deadly than souring the honey on your Sugar Puffs, the conversation might have made itself useful and run something on these lines:

Egrah'nca: But tell me, o Magnarch, for what reason do our rivals of Shambhala pursue this mysterious stone, known to some as the *lapis exillis* and others as the S'nang üll H'notorem, or S'nangstone for short. For I doubt not that they have their reasons.

Magnarch: Most true, o bear of insight and penetration. You will recall that the Stone of Supremacy, the battery which powered our civilisation, was carried away on the immeasurable grief wave of Charlotte de Maupassant, high class tart and Empress of Witches, and that without it our mighty continent will be destroyed, or will have been destroyed in years which, if we have not already overtaken them, are soon to come.

Egrah'nca: All this I do, indeed recall, o most illustrious benefactor. I clearly see why we require the return of the Stone. But what would Shambhala make of it, the wondrous rock which contains a tiny fragment of the original black hole, source of the universe?

Magnarch: I am about to reveal to you, most loquacious of toys, a state secret imparted to me on my installation as Principle. It is too late to save the continent of Atlantis. Even were the Stone returned to its sacred niche this very day (in whatever sense you choose to interpret that term) no good would come of it. Our homeland is doomed, doomed to perish in tsunami and conflagration, an unlikely but effective mix. But, hear me, friend. The fragment in the stone is not the source of the universe merely, but of the multiverse!

Egrah'nca: The multiverse? Is that not merely a neologism of little meaning but much temporary social clout in use among undergraduate physicists and the like, generally when trying to pick up student nurses at questionable college discothèques?

Magnarch: What you say is true. And yet the term has, for those who know, a great import. For you must understand that in the deep originals of time, way back at the kick off, when for whatever reason the original single particle of primeval goo, in which all of everything was compressed, exploded, what happened was this. That one single particle sped off in every conceivable direction at every conceivable time, filling the immensity of nothingness with itself in infinitely reduplicated forms.

Egrah'nca: You mean, everything in the universe, myself, you, the figure hugging garment that presses itself so firmly about the person of Miss Helena Phipps, not to mention the planet itself, the stars and even the Goat-Horror of Vharg, all these are composed of the same basic particle manifesting itself simultaneously here, there and everywhere throughout time and space?

Magnarch: Exquisitely phrased, my little lump of love. That is indeed so. But more than this – recall for a second, if you will do so without vomiting, my use of that admittedly pretentious term 'multiverse'. For a study of quantum physics would reveal to you that not only does that particle exist in the universe we know, it must also exist in the infinity of other universes which lie dimensionally adjacent to our own. An unlimited selection of possible worlds, of cosmoi like and unlike our own, but all connected by a common link – their common parent, a tiny fragment of which lies contained in the S'nang üll H'notorem.

Egrah'nca: Say no more, o purveyor of unrealisable concepts. I now need only add together the two parts of your discourse to arrive at my conclusion. Atlantis is or was or will be being destroyed. Possession of the stone is the key to the alternative universes. It would appear that neighbouring universes are very much alike. No doubt there are spheres of existence where voles or sentient hogweed rule the cosmos but the realms available to us will, it is almost certain, be congenially similar. Oh, it may be that Django Scratby is not the esteemed household name that he is to us, and hamsters will perhaps not tend to be vermillion, but the air will be breathable and much of the geography instantly familiar. Therefore we require the stone in order to transfer to a universe where the grief wave bypasses our land and the stone remains forever ours.

Magnarch: And turns Shambhala into a damp fart. Correct, amigo. While they, of course, desire the stone in order to inflict some similar indignity upon ourselves. Have you any further questions?

Egrah'nca: None, my lord. All is clear to me now as the petals of the azure humolo flower that blooms in the pastures of Tri'nth when summer dances down the hillsides of Atlantis and takes her ease among the winey woods of Twer'n. All is as transparent as the knickers of Helena Phipps. I thank you, lord, for your teachings.

However, as those who have spent a dismal Saturday trying to do the shopping while the sky hurls water at you like an excited two year old in its bath, or as the extinct race of dinosaurs would be pleased to confirm, the universe is so far from properly ordered that the actual conversation went:

Egrah'nca: Racks my guts, this time window screw up. What's the point, anyway, arsing about over half the universe just for a bit of old rock? Why don't you and me just grab the chick and head for the dawn of time? They'll never track us down.

Magnarch: If you had as much sense as stuffing, Egrah'nca, your opinion might just be worth the bother of dismissing with a contemptuous snort. Now, go back and amuse the woman while I concentrate on flying this crate.

Egrah'nca: Oh, all right. I wonder if she likes a bit of the old....

"I'm not leaving without Charlotte," the Captain said. "And then there's the child."

"Ah," said the Guardian of the Earth. "Yes. Thanks. Glad you reminded me. Yes. I'd been meaning to have a word with you about that. You

The Gnostic Frying Pan

see, in order to get us all these privileges, use of time window, bath salts, electric razors, soft toilet tissue and so on, I had to do a bit of a deal with old Jye-Po. Sweeten him a bit, you see. So I told him young Eric was one of the Dwarf Princesses of Melpobria and a bit of real hot stuff from the cat-houses of P'nor'n. So, well, she won't be going with us, as such."

"Poor creature," the Captain whispered. "Poor, poor little devil."

They watched the child toss the remains of the Yeti cub into waste bin with the rest of the litter.

"Oh, you needn't feel sorry for him," Eric said. "I reckon Jye-Po deserves all he gets, treacherous swine."

Glu'ng, glu'ng went the phone on the real walnut veneer shelf at their side.

"It's for you," said the Captain, holding out the handset.

Eric took it.

"Hallo? Yes? Oh, yes. Right. Yes. Yes. Right." He returned the telephone to his companion.

"That was the secret agent of the Archerons," he whispered. "The Magnarch's craft is only twenty two years ago and should be now in about ten minutes. We must get cracking. Sure you know what to do?"

In the control centre, the monk Ogvonda set down his telephone and smiled at his assistant. "There. I have advised the traitor Maresbreath of the imminent arrival of his confederates. It is time for us to act. You have your instructions?"

"Yes, Master."

"Now, now, my boy. Let us not be hasty. Let us not be presumptuous."

"I beg your pardon, Ogvonda."

"A loveable fault, my good Jye-Po. Now – to work!"

Back in the saucer, the Magnarch and his companions had dropped into the Shambhalan time path about seven hundred miles south west of Mount Meru. Now they were hovering over the frozen tundra; far below a tiny rider was lashing his horse round and round in circles.

"There he goes," sighed the Magnarch. "Poor old Master. He'll never learn, will he?"

"Uuuuuuh," remarked Egrah'nca, who had just stumbled into the cockpit. "Uuuuh," he added, lowering himself gingerly onto the co-pilot's divan. "Uuuuuuuh."

The Magnarch sniffed distastefully. "No need to enquire what you've been up to, you oversexed little bundle of blue and yellow nylon. I thought you left all those impulses behind you with your glands in the body bank."

Egrah'nca groaned. It may have been a laugh. "Biologists all wrong," he croaked. "Not glands." He tapped his brow with a trembling paw. "Sex. All in the astrethic mind. Pow."

"Vile," said the Magnarch. He deployed the variable sweep wings. "Quite, quite vile. And you don't even have the decency to devour the female afterwards. You just leave her lying sprawled on the carpet with her dress up round her neck and a revoltingly glazed expression on her face. It's so untidy."

Egrah'nca raised himself with difficulty on an elbow and waved a paw at the windscreen. "Meru?" he gasped.

"That's it," said the Magnarch. "I'll contact our agent."

"Who is our agent, anyway?" Egrah'nca asked.

"Some itchy old monk," the Magnarch sneered. "Attracted by the romance of the secret service, the excitement of placing plastic explosive in the vaults of authentic folk songs recorded in the field by researchers with smelly pipes, the adrenalin whisking experience of crouching in a dustbin with an illicit transmitter talking to himself – hold on, this is him now."

A golden light blinked on the PBX. Jye-Po, who had replaced the usual switchboard operator, flicked a couple of switches and passed the head set to Ogvonda. "Good afternoon, West Shambhalan Fluid Retention Service, how may I help you?" he crooned.

"Greetings, agent 69. This is code name Hungrypuppy. I am in position for landing. What have you prepared for us?"

Ogvonda flashed a particularly nasty smile at his assistant.

"I have booked you in at the landing strip," he said, "as a consignment of Our English Heritage Calendars and World of Light Classics CDs. When they come to offload you, perhaps one of you could hum extracts from The Land of Smiles for verisimilitude. Proceed to cargo bay 22. I have arranged for the stone-holder to meet you there."

The Magnarch cut the radio and glanced at his prostrate companion, who was snoring gently on the divan.

"Wake up," he roared, blasting the bear across the cockpit by the sheer force of the sound. "Get back there and do what you can to make the Phipps girl look like an illustration from a calendar. Not that sort of calendar," he added, noticing Egrah'nca's leer. "Pictures of Romantic Castle at Dawn, Rose Garden under the Summer Sun, that sort of thing. Go on. Get on with it."

65

As quiet as a dead mouse, the Captain opened the door of Charlotte's bedroom and crept into the chamber. He closed the door softly and waited for his eyes to accustom themselves to the darkness. Soon he could make out the shapes of the IKEA furnishings, the orthopaedic bed and the figure above it.

"I'm sorry to disturb you, my dear," he whispered, "but they say the saucer will touch down in two minutes time. I thought you would want to know."

Charlotte de Maupassant, Empress of Witches, allowed her eyelids to open a millimetre. She looked down at the Captain's bald head. Cross-legged and naked, apart from the ceremonial blood of weasels, she floated in the gloom two feet above the counterpane, glowing slightly. When she spoke, her voice was strained and unfamiliar. At the sound, the Captain's skin broke out in goose-pimples and small red boils.

"I am almost ready," the voice intoned, distant as the wind among the peaks of Altai. "Leave me now," she commanded. "I shall join you in a moment."

The Captain scuttled from the room and helped himself to a glass of British sherry before helping himself to another glass of British sherry and collapsing in an armchair. Wiping spilt sherry from his trousers, he sweated heavily while he waited.

The bedroom door inched open, causing him to choke on his next sherry. He rose and, smiling nervously, backed away from the pale figure which emerged, now clad in a simple black shroud. Her feet were making quite normal walking movements but disturbingly not quite in contact with the carpet.

"Damn it, Charlotte," he muttered. "Is all this really necessary? It puts the bally wind up me and I don't care who knows it."

"I must be prepared," the voice droned. "I have concentrated all my powers. Take me now."

"Now? Well, all right, if you think it's necessary," said the Captain, untucking his shirt, "though we've only got a minute or two - "

"Asinine occlude," chanted the voice. "I mean, take me now to the meeting place. We must seize Helena Phipps before the Atlanteans can double cross us. Come, we must be gone."

She floated from the room, almost losing the Captain, who was still bemused by the reference to Helena Phips, and had to undo the door before he could leave. Outside, he found her bobbing gently in the corridor and was finally obliged to grab the sash of her shroud and tow her down the passageway like a large black balloon.

"You said there would be some more baby snowman things," little Eric whined suspiciously, as her large namesake ushered her into a monkish cell on the other side of the city. There was nothing to be seen but a wooden bed, a bowl of frozen water and a couple of hundred copies of *Nude Wives of Our Dwarf Princes*. "What's the big idea?"

Eric was spared the tedious necessity of inventing some story by the sudden appearance from a secret doorway in the wardrobe of the monk Jye-Po, still with his PBX operator's head-set round his neck.

"Ah," said the monk toothlessly. "So this is the Dwarf Princess. How do you do, your Highness."

"Why do people keep saying that?" the child complained. "I keep telling you, I'm – ow!"

"I beg your pardon, Princess Ow," said Eric. "I appear to have accidentally rendered you unconscious with a blow from the back of my hand. How can it have happened? Jye-Po, be a good fellow and help me to arrange her small highness on the cot."

Jye-Po took little Eric's feet, the Guardian of the Earth seized her shoulders and together they swung her up onto the wooden shelf which served the monks of Shambhala for a bed, chopping block and chemin de fer table.

"Er, Eric," the monk said suddenly, plainly ill at ease. "Er, I don't want to appear ungrateful but, well, are you sure this is a genuine dwarf princess? I mean," he gestured at the magazines on the floor, "they generally have a bit more in the old bust department. Well, a lot more, actually. I mean, take a look at this." He held up a magazine which fell open at a splendidly underdressed dwarf princess caught in the act of trying to climb up the side of a kitchen chair. "Er, there seems to be some discrepancy." He indicated the front of little Eric's red jumper with the white cockroach pattern round the waist. "Or am I mistaken?"

"Look," said Eric, "those pictures, they're all simulated, see. Done with big tarts from the cat-houses and oversized furniture. Your real dwarf princesses, you see, as well as being insatiable nymphomaniacs, are always a bit flat chested." He could not ignore Jye-Po's look of disappointment. "In the day time," he added brilliantly. "After dusk, though, pow! It's something to with the effect of sunlight on their chromosomes."

"Oh?" said Jye-Po, unconvinced. "Only, if I'm really going to double cross that conceited old sod Ogvonda I want to be sure it's worth my while, you know."

"Course you do," said Eric. "You wait till nightfall," he promised, secure in the knowledge that by then he would be half a millennium away. "You won't have time to clean your teeth. Sorry, forgot about that. Well, you know what I mean. Must dash now. Enjoy yourself. And her. Bye, Jye-Po! Bye, Ow!"

On the bed little Eric stirred fitfully. Jye-Po prodded at her chest, then sat down on the floor with a magazine and scrutinised the pictures carefully.

They didn't look like fakes.

"I shouldn't bother with her now," the Magnarch said to the foremonk of the dock workers in cargo hold 22 as his gang rode up in their fork lift trucks. "Leave it till after lunch. Here." He flung a handful of gold coins down from the cockpit. "Have a few drinks on me."

"Right you are, squire," said the foremonk. "We'll unstuff her at half two. Come on, lads, who's up for a bevy down the Seven Stars?"

"All right, Egrah'nca," said the Magnarch, thumping with his horny fist on the crate in the middle of the passenger lounge. "It's all clear. You can come out now, the pair of you. Did you hear? I said you can come out now."

He stooped and applied an ear to the side of the packing case.

With a sigh of despair, the Magnarch unpacked them with a lash of his tail and spilt the incomparable loveliness of Helena Phipps onto the carpet, her teddy bear paramour still clasped to her bosom.

"Can't you keep your hands off that bear for a moment?" the Magnarch snapped. "The S'nangstone awaits us. Women! They think of nothing but reproduction. It's obscene."

"You're letting this Serene Holiness stuff go to your head," Egrah'nca complained as he untangled himself from the bulkhead webbing.

"Nothing to what I'll be letting go to my stomach, when this lot's over," the Magnarch threatened. "Now get come clothes on, woman, and I mean proper clothes, not some vile filmy underthing with strategic bits cut out of it. We have to go."

The monk Ogvonda paced up and down the rush strewn floor of Cargo Hold 22. He was disturbed by the inexplicable absence of his assistant, Jye-Po. Had he been wise to trust the monklet, he wondered. After all, Jye-Po had often admitted that he modelled himself entirely on his beloved master, which if he was even halfway successful would make him the second biggest traitor since Humboldt Vixpoctor, the Dumnian Judas. Ogvonda chewed his lower lip nervously.

Something big and metallic whined.

Whirling in a froth of lace and lilac robe, he found the gate of the hold sliding open to admit a twenty foot metal box in the blue and white livery of Shambhalan Container Lines. As he stared, the steel doors swung apart, allowing the fluorescent lights to illuminate the magnificent figure of Eric Maresbreath, erect in his robe[51], the golden fillet bound once more about his brow, a smile of triumphant anticipation on his face. Behind him, on a kitchen table and veiled in what may have been a shroud of rarest samite but was probably a pillowcase, seemed to stand the mysterious bulk of that object for which the princes of all continents, the priests of the Valk people and the lords of every mystic city from Shambhala to Mu would have given each other's right arm (or acceptable forelimb substitute): the S'nang üll H'notorem, that strangely shuddering rock, carved with obscene figures and said by many to conceal in its heart all that remains of the Black Hole, source of the multiverse, the mystery of whose power lay forever beyond the comprehension of mortal thought as the peaks of Mount Meru or the distant hinterlands of Grossos in the country of the Bland.

"Stop that ridiculous posturing," barked Ogvonda. "Get down here and bring that lump of stone with you. Come on, we haven't got all day."

When Eric saw that the figure awaiting him in the cargo hold was none other than the Master's trusted deputy, the monk Ogvonda, his reaction was naturally to seize the cord and lash it across the chamber to destroy his enemy. Unluckily the knot

---

[51] a consequence of dwelling overmuch on Jye-Po's magazines

The Gnostic Frying Pan

had stuck and he succeeded only in flinging himself from the container into a stack of Marks & Spencer embroidered house coats.

"Calm yourself, dear boy," smiled Ogvonda, as Eric struggled forward with the obvious intention of garrotting the monk with a nylon belt. "I can now reveal to you that I am the secret agent of the Archerons of Atlantis."

"You don't fool me," growled Eric. "Your creature, Jye-Po, has squealed. He spilt the whole plot, in exchange for what he, poor fool, imagines to be nothing more dangerous than a dwarf princess. Yes, Ogvonda, I know that you have been posing as the agent of the Archerons in order to lure the Magnarch into your trap."

"Imprudent youth," chuckled the monk, smashing Eric to the concrete with one blow of his expanding quarter staff. "That was a bluff, conceived to mislead the witless Jye-Po. What better disguise for an agent of the Archerons than the pretence of being a loyal servant pretending to be an agent of the Archerons?"

"I can think of hundreds," retorted Eric. He mopped up the blood with a corner of his lilac robe. "How do I know I can trust you?"

"You can't," Ogvonda said happily. "In my single minded pursuit of power I would not hesitate to throw you to the nearest pack of Altain were-gerbils, if I thought it would do me any good. However, you are more use to me alive, so I shall spare you now. And once you have returned to your nasty little pied a terre in Goitre Lane, you and I will have nothing further to say to each other." He laughed. "Oh yes, Jye-Po reported all your conversations to me, just as I have no doubt he reported all mine to you. A promising youth, Jye-Po, despite his lack of dentures. A man of intelligence, foresight and calculation. I must have him disembowelled. But now I hear the unpleasantly squelchy sound of an approaching Magnarch. Let us withdraw to the other side of the chamber, in case he forgets himself."

The Gnostic Frying Pan

66

Not for the first time, the narrative regrets its inability to strip off its shirt and flagellate itself with the psychotropic tendrils of the Ludorium spi'ndlro plant, whose application produced the epic poetry which is the glory of that otherwise repulsive city state. How shall it do justice to what the news readers would undoubtedly have called the iconic events which took place during that iconic lunch hour in the iconic cargo holds of Shambhala?

With a few well chosen words it would have painted the scene for you – the lofty vaulting of cargo hold 22, its walls glistening expanses of beige marble, its fluorescent tubes which hang on invisible filaments from the shadowy ceiling, its floor a whispering carpet of golden rushes. And there, as far away from the door as possible, the S'nangstone, mounted on a damask coverlet, and two equally hairless figures in lilac, one leaning on a quarter staff, the other mopping a wound on its white skull.

To them enters the indescribable presence of the Magnarch of Verox, now His Serene Holiness, the Principle of Goth, followed by a woman whose desirability is so intense that the very walls seem to lean towards her, unless that is just a side effect of thinking about spi'ndlro plants. Tucked into the bosom of her gown she carries a blue and yellow teddy bear whose expression is of an ecstasy not commonly seen on the features of such toys.

There they stand, monks and Atlanteans, facing each other across the suddenly airless hold, and between them the shrouded object vibrates with a just audible hum like a badly earthed hi-fi unit.

Seeing the nimble Helena before him, the Guardian of the Earth took a casual step forward but was restrained by the hand of Ogvonda.

"One word before we move," the monk hissed. "This object on the table – would you describe it as the real McCoy?"

"Don't worry," Eric said. He may have blushed. "I have honoured my part of the bargain. What nestles on our Ruler's wall overlooking the rather bespattered copy of the latest Timora Garpatheny is a cunning replica. This is the real stone."

"Not, then, that remarkably run of the mill fake you rigged up in the cave on Meru? I feel it would be as well to get that cleared up before we proceed."

"You spotted it was a fake, then?" Eric said with interest.

"Of course," sneered Ogvonda. "You thought to deceive us, Eric? We who know more about deceit than you do about the contents of Helena Phipps' underwear drawer?"

"Impossible!"

"When you presented us with that risible simulacrum, it was obvious at once that you had brought us a fake. For a start, the inscription on the side didn't read 'Crom ten Pogol'."

"Didn't it?"

"No. It said 'Cromwell Road Post Office'."

"Well, blame Sub-Prior Dr. McMunn, he was my tutor in Valk, the port-ridden old sot."

"Of course, we pretended to be taken in but I immediately sent Jye-Po to scour the cavern, where naturally he eventually uncovered the real S'nangstone, concealed under a heap of Yeti droppings. Realising that two could play at your little game, he at once prepared a dummy of his own, which he left in the cavern in place of the real stone. That, of course, he brought here to me. It now fills the hole in the wall of the master's study, as from time immemorial it was destined to do."

"Mmm," said Eric. "And it read all right, did it. Crom ten Pogol and all that? No reference to Post Offices?"

"Perfectly."

"Well, there you are. Perhaps old Dr. McMunn wasn't so dozy after all."

"What?"

"Knowing that you would suspect me of trying to deceive you with a fake stone, Ogvonda old thing, I cleverly prepared an example which I knew you would find defective – mis-scribed inscription, lack of low density hum and so on. Under a pile of Yeti droppings, I concealed another, a replica over which I took infinitely more care. That, Ogvonda, is what Jye-Po brought to you."

"So – you would have me believe I have swapped a fake fake for a real fake. Then where is the real stone?"

"I hid it in an abandoned Yak-spotters' hide further up the cliff. After lights out last night, I nipped off, brought the Stone into the city, and locked it safely in the container there."

"Ah, yes, I hope your manly parts have recovered from that nasty moment when you climbed over the gate, by the way? Yes, Eric," Ogvonda sneered, "I saw your clumsy re-arrival."

He seemed on the point of saying more, but a minatory cough from the Magnarch reminded him of his priorities. "Greetings, Supreme Principle! Greetings, my dear young lady. Having seen you, I quite understand Eric's readiness to exchange all the power in the universe for the inexpressible pleasures of your bed." He shook himself and added unconvincingly, "Not that I am susceptible to such temptations. Far from it. No, not me -"

"My dear Ogvonda," interrupted the Magnarch, "refreshing though it is for me to enjoy the artistry of your conversation, a very real pleasure I assure you, after the shallow sophistries which assault my ears when I am seated on the opal throne, I feel that as the workmen will not stay at the pub after closing time, we should perhaps refrain from testing the endurance of our truce. Shall we effect our exchange and be on our way. Time is of the essence. Do you not agree?"

The monk smiled horribly. "Indeed, my dear Magnarch, I do. and with one blast on this horn - " He uncurled a copper instrument from a pocket in the skirt of his robe and sounded it, "we may enjoy the final act of this comedy."

"Treachery!" roared the Magnarch. "High treachery! Egrah'nca - the Nidro Force! Summon him before doom snatches us all."

At the rasp of the monk's horn a number of packing cases stacked against the back wall had burst open to reveal that their contents, in direct contravention of the Brussels Agreement, were not plaster of Paris busts of prominent composers as described on the bills of lading, but armoured

Shambhalan warriors with slant eyes, fangs and sabres of tempered steel. Ignoring the furious thudding of one warrior who couldn't get out of his case, they charged shrieking across the rushy floor and fell upon the surprised Atlanteans.

"You swine!" gasped Eric. "Is this your loyalty to Atlantis?"

"What loyalty?" sneered the monk, spinning his quarter staff.

"You were in the pay of the Master all the time!" Eric shouted, ducking the whirling stick.

"What pay?" guffawed Ogvonda. "Do you think I care for him, the bastard who stole my only child and allowed her to die for his ridiculous purposes? No, Eric Maresbreath, my only loyalty is to the memory of my beloved daughter, Durinda Ogvonda. No more do I pretend a coldness I fail to feel. I shall seize power with the aid of the S'nangstone and cross to another universe where my child yet lives. I shall also ensure that it is a universe where you and your friends achieve existence only in the form of a number of sliced loaves on the shelves of a disreputable 8 till Late supermarket."

"You shall not have the stone!" roared the Magnarch, despatching his eighth warrior with a slash of his claws while simultaneously disembowelling his ninth with the spike on the end of his tail. He leapt across the hold. "It is mine! I have it!"

He scooped up the humming stone from its table and loped swiftly down the bay, hopping over a couple of warrior corpses and nodding farewell to Helena and Egrah'nca, who were huddled in the corner of the room between two sacks of Mills &

Boon romances. "I hope the Nidro Force isn't too delayed," he called as he passed them. "Otherwise I must admit I don't quite see how you're going to get out of this."

"No, no," chuckled the monk. He stepped over the stunned body of the Guardian of the Earth. "Let him go. Cursed as I am with an idle curiosity and a set of skeleton keys, when I observed your nocturnal ramblings, I inspected the interior of your container, my son. Deducing at once that what was wrapped in one of our pillow-cases was nothing less than the genuine S'nang üll H'notorem, I fetched the replica from the Master's office and swapped them over. What the Magnarch has is merely a dummy."

Rather relieved, the remaining Shambhalan warrior collapsed onto the floor and began to lick his wounds.

"Hysteria," said the monk Ogvonda, "though quite excusable in a man in your circumstances, Eric, nevertheless gives me a headache. Please oblige me by desisting at once."

Eric lurched to his feet and collapsed against the bosom of the aged monk. It became apparent that his entire being was shuddering not with agony but with laughter.

"Oh dear," he gasped, when speech returned to him. "Oh, my poor old Oggie. I am sorry. Really I am. Only, you see, overcome – by a fit of – conscience, last night, I - " He gurgled and groaned, almost torn apart by his amusement, "I decided to – to give the real stone to the Master and fob poor old Verox off with the fake. If you've gone and done a swap, then - "

The Gnostic Frying Pan

"What?" screamed the monk. Pausing only to kick Eric in the front of his lilac robe, he dragged the slobbering warrior to his feet. "To arms, dolt! Follow the Magnarch! Prevent him at all costs from reaching his craft. That stone must not be allowed to leave Shambhala without me. Go on, you stupid slant eyed git, get after him!"

"You might as well save your breath, old boy," drawled a voice new to the proceedings. They all turned, startled to see Captain H. 'Geronimo' Sparesbrook with the levitating Charlotte de Maupassant in tow, appear in the doorway of the cargo hold. "You see," he explained, "I followed Maresbreath there to the Master's office and, when he had gone, swapped the Stone he left behind for a replica of my own, basically the drawer of a beside cabinet wrapped in a pillow case and containing a battery razor. Obviously that is what the Magnarch is hopping up the shaft with, poor old monstrosity."

"Then where," screeched the monk, "is the S'nang üll H'notorem?"

"Well, clearly, Charlotte's got it. She's transformed it by her rather peculiar arts into a lavender scented body lotion which she's splashed all over herself. Right now she's meditating her being to a point where she'll be able to flick herself and me, oh, and young Helena there, across to an alternative universe of love, joy and peace." He beamed weakly, as though something about the prospect did not entirely appeal to him. "We just popped in to say toodle-pip, really."

"This is an outrage," fumed the monk, stamping in frustration on the hand of a dying warrior. "I demand that you order that woman to come down to the floor and restore the S'nangstone

The Once and Future Stone

to its proper shape. How dare you come in here with your babble of love and joy and other obscenities? I'll have you know - "

"Hoi!"

It is only to be expected, considering the events which have just had the temerity to occur, that the monk should be interrupted by the entrance of another figure in a lilac robe, this one distinguished by its toothlessness and the small female child clinging to its back and belabouring it with a length of bamboo cane while uttering cries of "Giddy-up! Giddy-up!"

"Jye-Po!" cried Eric, as he rolled away from the flailing staff of Ogvonda. "Cripes! Time I got out of here."

He crawled away at high speed between the lacerated corpses of the warriors to the corner where Helena crouched with Egrah'nca.

"Where's your bloody Nidro Force, then?" he snapped.

Egrah'nca coughed. "Well," he mumbled, "I seem to have somehow sort of damaged my growler." He glanced at Helena, who had gone a fetching shade of cerise. "Can't think how. Sorry."

"Great," said Eric. "Bloody great. Wonderful."

Jye-Po had by now staggered beneath his shrieking rider into the cargo hold and stood beneath the slowly gyrating Charlotte, next to the Captain.

"This," he said bitterly, "is not a dwarf princess."

"Yes it is," called Eric.

"It is not a dwarf princess," said Jye-Po. "I have studied number after number of *Nude Wives of our Dwarf Princes* and in none of them does any dwarf princess insist on playing gee-gees and demand incessant supplies of crisps. The demands of a dwarf princess are of quite another order. Also, when I returned from restocking our Magnarchical guest's larder with one or two of our local delicacies, I found the so-called dwarf princess covering my copy of the Collected Aleister Crowley with crayoned bunnies. Demonic crayoned bunnies, I admit, but that's not the point - "

Ogvonda's ugly laugh echoed round the walls. "It seems that you too have been cheated, my boy. Much, indeed, as you hoped to cheat me. If that evil woman up there had not misappropriated the S'nangstone, I should have had the greatest pleasure in packing you off somewhere very, very grim indeed. A holiday camp at the height of the season, perhaps. Madam, kindly descend from that indecorous position. I command it."

Jye-Po's smiled like a hyena with wind. "It may interest you to know, Ogvonda, that I happened to be in the Master's office last night, replacing the box of booby trapped chocolates I left there to the accidental detriment of Miss Sadie Q Tourmaline. I was also in a position to witness the arrival of the gentleman here with the witch on a string, and his departure with a certain brown humming object under his arm. Some minutes later I observed the visit of the foolish Eric Maresbreath and saw him deposit what he believed to be the S'nangstone and stagger off with the Captain's clumsy fake from the niche above the Master's desk. What may come as a surprise to you all is to learn that I then carried the S'nangstone left by Eric Maresbreath back to the container and swapped it for the Captan's fake left there by Eric under the illusion that he was aiding (or possibly deluding) the Magnarch."

"But which," they all cried, "is the real S'nang üll H'notorem, stone which contains a tiny fragment of the original black hole, source of the multiverse?"

That so many different persons should have chanced to utter exactly the same words at that moment is, perhaps, one of the few strange coincidences available in this chronicle.

Only one voice gave the answer, however, and that was Jye-Po's.

"The real stone? Well, it was of course the one which I placed in the container. The result of this salmagundi of stones, therefore, is that I have succeeded in fulfilling my duty. You see, gentlemen, and ladies, I am the real agent of the Archerons of Atlantis.[52] The Magnarch has the stone. Aiyeeee!"

The concluding exclamation was not an Atlantean cry of triumph but a fairly universal scream of agony resulting from the sudden intrusion of a razor sharp sabre into the agent's kidneys.

"Now will you giddy-up?" shouted little Eric, brandishing her gory blade.

---

[52] it appears that this statement is formally correct, although Jye-Po's understanding of his duties as an agent may not have entirely coincided with the job specification.

67

The Magnarch of Verox – but, no. Let us first of all consider the question of the traitor, Jye-Po.

Half an hour later, giggling in his cell, but not for any dwarf related reason, Jye-Po mopped the bloody wound in his back with a rag. What, after all, was a mutilated kidney compared with the success of his master plan?

The toothless monk knelt before his piles of glossy magazines and carefully shifted the front stack aside to reveal, not the back stack, but what appeared to be a block of ancient masonry with curious carvings on the side. Carefully he withdrew it from its hiding place.

The asses of Atlantis and the simpletons of Shambhala had swallowed his story and believed that the S'nangstone had left with the Magnarch in his saucer.

Jye-Po chortled to himself. Little did they know what followed when the monk Ogvonda had despatched him, like a common servant, to seek for S'nangstone in the cave.

Jye-Po, who was able to recognise the workings of a devious mind by virtue of long familiarity with his own, had become instantly alerted by the suspicious ease with which he had discovered the S'nangstone, partially concealed under a mound of Yeti droppings.

Backing out of the cave, he scanned the mountain slopes. It was not long before he made out on a ledge a couple of hundred feet above a tumbledown shed half buried in the snow. Setting his sensible brogues to the cliff face, he swarmed up the icy track.

This time the search had taken him a little longer but, at last, he ripped up a floorboard and found himself smiling at yet another S'nangstone, the twin in almost every way of the decoy in the cave below.

Giggling happily, he had heaved the chunk of ancient masonry out of the hole and carried it down to the cave, where he set it down beside the other.

Like all the monks of Shambhala, Jye-Po was a Grand Master of his Masonic Order but, unlike most members of Masonic orders, he was skilled in the use of the tools of the craft.

For two and a half hours he laboured with mallet and chisel, transforming a chuck of mountainside into the likeness of the S'nangstone. He placed his own edition of the fabled rock under the floor of the old hut, then with the pair of S'nangstones roped to his back tottered down to the city.

He first of all took the secret passage to his cell, where he stashed one of the stones, before seeking out the monk Ogvonda, to present him with a heavily edited account of his afternoon and the results of his labours.

Jye-Po beamed at the stone and cocked an ear at its faint but unmistakeable hum, the inexplicable mantra of the gulph – that field of more zero points than an Icelandic Eurosong. "To business! For now you are mine, o stone of ancient power, and I have learnt how to employ your mysteries!⁵³"

Jye-Po lifted the stone, tangled his feet in a length of blood stained rag, tripped and went sprawling. The stone crashed against the wall of the cell with some force and, shattering into several chunks, emitted what was not so much a tiny fragment of the original black hole, source of the multiverse, as a swarm of extremely bad tempered hairy dog bees.

The toothless monk had muddled up the stones. What he had so carefully hidden in his cell was Eric's superior dummy. So what he had handed to Ogvonda must have been - the real thing, the *lapis exillis*, the S'nang üll H'notorem itself...

Not long after, thanks to the hairy dog bees, Jye-Po ceased to worry about Ogvonda, the pain in his kidneys, the whereabouts of the real S'nangstone and, indeed, everything else.

Sensitive readers, those who know by heart the works of Edna Vincent Millais and can quote you whole stretches of Browning, will have seen through the narrative's guileless attempt to distract them by recounting the machinations of the ill-fated Jye-Po from the more important question of the whereabouts of the Magnarch.

---

[53] It would appear then that Jye-Po, whose decades of self-mastery had better prepared him than Eric Maresbreath for the task of distinguishing between a mystic stone and a battery razor in a pillow-case, had recognised that the Captain's fake would not for one moment delude the Magnarch, and had swapped it for what he prided himself on being a superior sham created by himself and lodged in the wall of the Master's study.

The Once and Future Stone

We are, you see, rather ashamed to admit that the Magnarch, whose magnificence we have been at some pains to point up, had completely mistaken the turning outside the cargo hold, entered the wrong elevator and got hopelessly lost among the pipes and engine casings. To compound the sadness of the situation, slowed as he was by the weight of the S'nangstone, he had been unable to shake off the remaining warrior, who was clinging to the bony plates down the Magnarch's spine with all the determination of a Bush baby in a Hurricane[54].

To make matters worse, the warrior had discovered a weak joint in the Magnarch's armoured hide and had started to prod him repeatedly with the point of his sabre.

"All right," snarled the Magnarch at last, as they piggybacked across a high level bridge which spanned a subterranean river of magma, "What's your price, warrior? A finely toasted hummingbird soufflé once a month for life? A night in the bed of the Peacock Empress of Lagronica? Name it. Only get off my back!"

The warrior, whose Atlantean vocabulary was extremely limited, uttered a couple of disgusting grunts and leant on his sword with both hands.

If circumstaces had given him a chance to talk to the lads in the hospital afterwards, the warrior would have agreed that that had been his big mistake. As soon as the fingers released their grip on his ceremonial collar, the Magnarch did his

---

[54]A chapter of the history of World War II for which the world may never be ready.

celebrated party turn - Impression of a Little Doggy who Wants his Tummy Tickled. Although much acclaimed at soirees all over Atlantis, the trick proved oddly unpopular with the warrior, who found himself being crushed under the scaly body.

When the Shambhalan field surgeons reached him, it was already too late to save the warrior's legs, one of which was still dangling from the Magnarch,.

It was also too late to stop the Magnarch. He had slipped down the rubbish chute and emerged amid a slew of cabbage leaves and candle stubs in the compost compressors on the edge of the city, just across the car park from the freight terminal, where his saucer gleamed rosily in the last rays of the sun. Hopping with his stony burden from the piles of decomposing garbage, the Magnarch crossed the car park unmolested and trampled down the gates of the terminal. A couple of overturned dock shunters smoking furiously on the tracks behind him, he smashed his way through the ranks of trailers and the stacked containers. The saucer's shining bulk was now less than 100 yards away.

The departure of Ogvonda from the cargo hold, which had ceased to hold any attraction for him once the S'nangstone had been extracted from it, left Eric Maresbreath and his companions at something of a loose end. Like guests at a party when the host has collapsed in a drunken heap under the table (identifiable as his wife) they coughed and gave each other embarrassed smiles and decided that it was probably time they might as well be making tracks.

The Once and Future Stone

For the sake of appearances, Eric and the Captain changed into the least bloody of the robes of the deceased militia, selected a couple of sabres, and escorted Helena, little Eric, Egrah'nca and the still-entranced Charlotte along the corridors of Shambhala to the chamber where the time window boiled and frothed like a cup of hot chocolate.

"What you doing up here?" the guard demanded. "Where's your dockets, then? And your pink forms? Can't let you in without a pink form. Have you had your shots - "

With a directness which will be envied by anyone who has ever had dealings with bureaucracy, Eric Maresbreath beheaded the guard and kicked open the door. The smile of adoration which enhanced Helena's already perfect face as she witness his virility would have been reward enough for any man. Little Eric's gurgle of delight as she watched the jets of blood pumping from the arteries in the severed neck was rather less appealing. She had definitely acquired some very unpleasant interests in the past few weeks.

"Well," said Eric, when they had barricaded themselves in the chamber. "I suppose this is where we all go our own separate ways. Helena and I, to Goitre Lane. Egrah'nca to Atlantis. And you, Captain, where will you go?"

"That's up to my - my fiancée here," the Captain said, smiling awkwardly. He tugged Charlotte down to ground level and shook her ineffectually. "Only trouble is, can't seem to get her out of this damn trance."

Eric smiled. "The coma you told me of, I suppose?"

The Captain nodded shamefully.

"Egrah'nca?" said Eric. "Come along, jump out of Helena's top, if you please, and see what you can do about this dear lady."

"OK," said Egrah'nca, reluctantly easing himself from his bower of bliss between the breasts of the most sensual woman in creation. He scuttled across the floor and shot up Charlotte's shroud.

With a screech of surprise, the witch woke up and tumbled to the floor.

"Egrah'nca!" she yelled. "You're a pain in the arse!"

A muffled "Pop!" sounded from somewhere under her shroud, then the teddy bear re-emerged, grinning wickedly.

"Never fails," he said, neatly dodging the fingers of little Eric. "Righto, Charlie, the gallant Captain has left to you the choice of your destination. The time window stands before you. I very much regret that you are not covered with the transmuted S'nangstone as you believed, so no alternative universe is available to you. However, you may select any period of history knitted up by the Demi—Urge in this particular cosmos. Where and when will you go?"

Charlotte raised herself unsteadily to her feet, her body trembling, her face pale, her lips dry, the whole ensemble smelling faintly of lavender. "I have seen the cat-houses of P'nor'n," she whispered, "and the gardens of Atlantis. I have watched the sun rise over the emerald lakes of Doblere. I have witnessed the rebirth of the legendary Magus of Thruarr and the arrival of the dustmen at Sparesbrook Manor. I do not care, Egrah'nca, where I go now, in this cheat of a universe, this shabby tax dodge of distress and lunacy. It is all the same to me, so long as – so long as I have one person by my side."

The Captain nodded and tried to look humble.

"Even the snail infested dungeons of Terenthor," Charlotte de Maupassant said, "would be a paradise to me with – with you, Helena Phipps. Please, I beg you, come with me. You – you could learn to love me, in time. I have several copiously illustrated guide books."[55]

---

[55] The narrative has been formally instructed by the National Health Service to include a strong warning to readers against attempting to work out all the permutations of artificial and genuine S'nangstones in this and the previous chapter, whether by computer simulation or little bits of coloured paper. In the narrative's opinion the relevant dossiers of the Akashik records, that preternatural file store on the seventh floor of the astral plane wherein all history is eternally recorded, have been chewed by astrethic mice. All we can say with anything approaching confidence is that the S'nang üll H'notorem was not in Jye-Po's cell and Jye-Po was almost certainly devoured by hairy dog bees.

68

Many might accuse the Magnarch of taking his new position too seriously, if they could have heard him as he crouched behind a consignment of hand-painted plaster gnomes and peered across the landing bay to his disc, coruscating under the loading lights. The Serene Principle of Goth was at prayer.

"Almighty Demi-Urge," he murmured, "Creator of the earth and the universe in which it throbs, hear my prayer. By thy merciful incompetence has thou led me here, unscathed, and with the S'nagstone in my clutches. Continue, I beseech thee, thy staggering ineptitude towards thy humble servant, send thine Archons[56] to strike down mine enemies, and accidentally make clear a path before me, if so it be thy artless will, that I may come safely unto my vehicle and be delivered by thy most ineffective hand from the malice of those who would thwart me. This I pray, for thy great indifference's sake. Otherwise," he added, "I might just have a word with the authorities about those account books Charlotte the Harlot left behind in Atlantis, see?"

Accompanied by a spectacular display of pyrotechnics and the sound of several different marching bands, great fissures opened up in the floor of the landing zone, leaving a narrow path

---

[56] Archons are the Seven Servants of the Demi-Urge and are not to be confused with the Archerons of Atlantis, at least if you want to avoid lawsuits and damages, not all of them financial.

between matching abysses which led conveniently from the Magnarch's hiding place to the hatch of his craft. Simultaneously great billows of yellowish smoke, tasting of chip fat and burnt peas, wallowed across the field, blinding the snipers and confusing the hordes of sabre men. With a glad cry of thanksgiving, the Magnarch hopped across the crumbling bridge and leapt into his ship as the last of the path crashed down into the steaming chasm below.

Noise, noise – worse than a three year old's birthday tea. The cries and orders, countermanded and reinstated in the same breath from the ambushers as they chopped each other up in the fog, the curses of the canteen staff whose ovens had so inexplicably exploded a few moment ago in a shower of hot fat and bullet hard peas which mowed sous-chefs and short order cooks like a gastronomic Somme, the crashing of crates that toppled into the pit, spilling sea-shell encrusted trinket boxes, volumes of Readers Digest Condensed Books, Pan Pipe CDs and souvenir postcards into the depths, all were drowned by the sudden screech of the Magnarch's engines. Nuclear light seared from the base of the hull. Slowly, with the majestic deliberation of a mediaeval monarch rising from the dinner table, the ship lifted off and ascended towards the stars.

It was at a height of exactly 27,000 feet that the booby trap concealed by Jye-Po among his selection of local delicacies exploded.

An evening mist had drifted up from the Thames and coiled in wraiths about the gas-lamps in Goitre Lane. A sex maniac, getting his breath

The Gnostic Frying Pan

back in the doorway of the funeral parlour, stared in wonder at the two figures who emerged suddenly from the vaporous curls in the ruins of the Primary School – one, presumably male, in green silk trousers, blood-red cape and furry Tam o'Shanter, a sabre still dangling from his left hand, the other the sort of woman who makes sex maniacs book a course of training at the best gymnasium in town. Hand in hand, the apparitions wandered out of the mist and strolled across the pavement. Soon a snatch of conversation reached the maniac's ears, causing him to pause as he scrabbled at his trouser buttons.

"... still think it's quite disgusting," the man was saying. "Of course, all those years in the cat-houses, not to mention the company of the perverted Andruta Tiservi, must have had their effect. But, well, to ask you to run away with her. To become her lover. Execrable."

"Aow, stop bleedin' goin' on abaht it," griped Helena Phipps. "Anyone'd fink you was scared I'd piss off with the old cow, way you go on. 'Ere, look, we're back 'ome nah, en' we. Charlie and the old geezer buggered off to, where was it?, Samarkand, and the teddy bear's taken over Jye-Po's old job. Funny 'bout that kiddie what had the same name as you, though, weren't it? You fink she'll be all right in Fifth Century Asia Minor?"

"Someone had to be the power behind Genghis Khan," the man pointed out. "Anyway, here we are, in dear old Goitre Lane at Last. I'll put the kettle on while you slip into -"

It was then that an eldritch screeching and the clatter of wings distracted the old maniac's attention from the events in his trousers. He leaned from the doorway of the funeral parlour in time to see, with what horror the narrative feels it may leave you to imagine, a ten foot Owl-thing with four human arms and a cruel beak swoop down from the murky night and hurl itself with appalling hunger at the woman's unprotected back.

At the sound, Helena turned and smiled.

"Not again!" wailed Herbert Jubb.

"Mother!" cried the unfortunate Malcolm de Maupassant, before his loathsome carapace smashed once more into the wall of the warehouse across the railway line. Unconscious in both lobes of its swollen brain, the twitching agglomeration of slime and feathers slithered down the brickwork and plopped onto the tracks just as the midnight cadaver train to Fenchurch Marshes thundered out of the mist. And so, reduced to a greyish slop not unlike blackcurrant Instant Delight beneath the wheels of the 4-6-0 mixed traffic locomotive, Roric the Viking, the Owl-thing ended its days.

"N'arf a lotta them abaht this year," Helena remarked. It was the last thing the maniac heard before the subarachnoid haemorrhage felled him, rather conveniently, on the doorstep of the funeral directors. Unaware of him, the Guardian of the Earth (retired) and his lovely darling ascended the steps of 143, Goitre Lane, entered, and closed the door on history.

"Still no sign of the porkers, I suppose?"

"Sorry, Jumbo. Absolutely neggers. Been on the blower to HQ. All I can get is a lot of bubbling noises, water splashing about, general seaside effects. Can't understand it at all."

"Some Charlie's dropped the phone in the bath, probably. Here, a few of the lads are thinking of chucking out one of the new batch of inmates for a game of Hunt the Loony later on. Fancy joining us?"

"Might well do, old sport. Wish I could just get a peep out of HQ, though. Nothing but waves and seagulls. All very relaxing it its own way but, I don't know, a bit of a worry."

69

The Shambhalan liquid explosive which detonated inside the fridge freezer in the aft quarters of the Magnarch's disc proved to be something of a nuisance. Not only did it spoil a number of a very tasty packed lunches who had been passing the time with a game of poker, it also stripped off the wall paper, scorched the upholstery in the passenger lounge, and curled up several signed photographs presented to the Magnarch by Atlantean personalities from the world of show-biz.

Slightly more seriously, it also split open the S'nangstone[57].

A tiny fragment of what some considered the original black hole, source of the multiverse, fell out and disappeared into the pile of the carpet.

Fortunately, just as so long ago Captain Sparesbrook had no difficulty in locating the hole under his own carpet, the Magnarch quickly found the precious object for, shorn of its protective coating, the splinter almost instantaneously sucked the Magnarch and his ship into itself, followed at quantum speeds by Mount Meru, the mystic city of Shambhala and everyone within it, the planet Earth (including the sunken ruins of Atlantis, Samarkand, Goitre Lane, Sparesbrook Manor and environs, Scaliselsarga-on-Sea, and a party of geriatric

---

[57] Ironically, then, it appears that when Jye-Po cried out that the Magnarch had the stone, although he believed himself to be lying through where his teeth would have been if he had any, he was in fact telling the truth.

The Gnostic Frying Pan

Spupoes who had just got off the bus in Amblebroth) and for an encore the remainder of the cosmos, all of it, including the Goat-Horror of Vharg[58], who almost got stuck.

With a sickening slurpy sort of noise the last particles of creation whirled like dust before the vacuum cleaner of the black hole and vanished. Nothingness had never been so clean.

It is a fact[59], unlike so much else recorded by the narrative, that at just after a quarter past seven on a June morning in 1922 (which, as on the morning in question we are in the middle of Siberia is not as pleasant as it sounds) a number of sane and sober witnesses, including the irreproachable passengers on the Trans-Siberian railway, are said to have observed the passage of a huge shining object across the sky. In an explosion which, in what appears to be an authentic example of backwards causation, turned herds of reindeer into burger and created exciting opportunities for architects where before there had been just a couple of smelly villages, the object disappeared, spouting a great shaft of steam and fire into the clear air. The roar of the explosion is recorded as having been heard five hundred miles away.

Some years later, a party of scientists reached the site of the explosion (near the upper reaches of the Stony Tunguska river, some miles north east of the Altai Mountains) expecting to find the

---

[58] who some suspect may well have been the Demi-Urge

[59] See, for example, Baxter, John; Atkins, Thomas. The Fire Came By: The Riddle of the Great Siberian Explosion, (London) Macdonald and Jane's, 1975. ISBN 978-0-446-89396-1.

fragments of an immense meteorite. Oddly enough, they discovered no crater, no meteorite, no evidence of impact, and yet for more than fifteen miles in every direction the Siberian forest had been flattened as though the gods themselves had come down to sprawl on the grass for a picnic.

Argument still surfaces on the Internet among scientists and fanatics of every kind about the so-called Tunguska Event. Was it a comet? A meteor, as the original investigators supposed? A spacecraft from another galaxy, crashing out of control on our tiny planet? Who can say?

Well, of course, the narrative can. While having the greatest respect for scientists (some of its best friends are scientists – hi, Norman) that wonderful body of savants who never fail to explain why something is completely impossible and then precisely how it happened, the narrative recognises that until now they have been attempting as usual to explicate the universe without being in possession of all the facts.

What those shaken witnesses might have imagined that they observed, you see, was perhaps the emergence into our own space-time continuum via a tiny fragment of the original black hole, source of the multiverse, of the Atlantean flying machine containing in indescribably compressed form the whole universe from inception to recent extinction lately inhabited by our friends the Magnarch of Verox, Egrah'nca, the Captain and the lady designated as the future Mrs. Charlotte Sparesbrook, little Eric Maresbreath, big Eric Maresbreath, Blessed Magotte and Blessed Benifons (do you remember the vicar?) the infinitely luscious Helena Phipps and her wardrobe of exotic scanties, and, oh so many others, Shambhalese, Lemurian and Dutch, now never to be named again, but everyone reduced to a quivering among the elemental particles of existence itself, as the Magnarch's ship flings them from the side of Mount Meru to the upper reaches of a cold Siberian sylvan river, where the strain proved all too much and the whole kit and caboodle translates from matter to astrethic force in an explosion of utter horror.

It is far too late now for an informative footnote on psitronic physics.[60]

---

[60] Oh, all right, then. Lay aside any sharp instruments and on no account attempt to operate heavy machinery or drive while considering the upcoming revelation.

What exactly happened that day in 1922, our time, not even the combined forces of Charles Darwin, William Shakespeare and Socrates could begin to clarify, especially as all three of them were until that moment characters in a bestselling novel by Atlantean fantasy writer, Timora Garpatheny. Some questionably confident commentators claim that without the cataclysm of that day in 1922 which they insist brought our present universe into actuality (including all of its previous history) you and I, like Darwin, would not be here. Where we would be, of course, is a nice question for metaphysicians of the old school to ponder in their cardboard boxes by Waterloo Station. The writer, who has been granted information from a source not normally available to humankind, understands that he would have been the Goat-Horror of Vharg. As in this life he is an ex-employee of the Inland Revenue, he supposes that he has come off rather badly but he has no intention of inflicting his complaints upon you.

The facts, if that is what they are, appear to be as follows. When the entirely unnecessary but standard red electric figures on the counter attached to the bomb in the Magnarch's flying disc reached 0.0099999 (some problem with the floating point arithmetic, one assumes) the subsequent explosion demolished the S'nangstone. The indescribable power source (believed by the Atlanteans to consist of a small fragment of the original black hole from which everything sprang at the moment of the 'Big Bang' but less uncertainly a psitronic intrusion from some other non-material sphere) fell out. No longer shielded by the stone, the mini-black hole behaved much like its putative parent and at once sucked everything into itself, including not only the Magnarch, his ship and at trans-luminant speed everything else in the universe, but also and perhaps significantly the copy of the latest Timora Garpatheny blockbuster which Egrah'nca had carelessly left in the cockpit. Infected by Garpatheny's 431 page fantasy opus *Darwin, Shakespeare, Socrates & Co* the singularity writhed and boiled and finally exploded, spewing forth the very reality in which you and I now live, if that is what we do. Naturally, even a genius of the order of Timora Garpatheny could not cram into 431 packed pages every detail of our astonishing universe. (A significant minority of theorists contend that it was not Timora Garpatheny's blockbuster which gave rise to our cosmological environment but the astrethic body of Egrah'nca himself. They argue, not without some cogency, that Egrah'nca's extensive exposure to the 21st Century had filled his share of the Ashkanic filing racks with sufficient information to shape our own somewhat distorted version. Others go so far as to assert that there is plenty of evidence to support the conclusion that in his spare time Egrah'nca was himself Timora Garpatheny.)

Those who have considered the matter tend to disagree wildly about how all the background is filled in but the fact appears to be that there is a transcendent omnipresent non-objective entity (TONE) which unifies all substance, guaranteeing some sort of logic and consistency in the current universe. Indeed, it has been contended that all universes, however alternative, must have emerged from that one TONE and will therefore exhibit great similarities, from the fine balance of physical constants which determine the nature of reality to the seemingly inevitable existence of Ken Russell. So, on that basis, we and our cosmos are the whole of reality now. Of what preceded us, not a wrack remains, apart from a debatable increase in background radiation in Siberia, some co-incidental sports of creation (e.g. in every possible universe there must always be a Civil Service) and a lot of drivel in shabby charity shops all over the world. Atlantis, Shambhala, the cat-houses of P'nor'n, the sess-sellers of Lemuria, the marvels of old Meru, propped up on tottery bookshelves in bedsits off the Cowley Road...

Consult a decent text book if you're still bothered about it. Otherwise take the narrative's word, as you have for so many less credible things. You see, Charlotte and the Magnarch were both in error about the precise nature of Alternative Universes. They are, shall we say, potentialities – imaginary or, as one might put it, fictional affairs. In other words, our friends have crossed by means of the S'nang üll H'notorem from their own cosmos into ours and have therefore been obliged to metempsychose into – the narrative.

Yes, dear reader, the humble narrative is itself all that remains of that glorious place where Muggoths roamed and Charlotte de Maupassant planned her plans. Flying discs, Atlantis, Shambhala, the Bermuda Triangle, the moors and chasms of Hertfordshire, Owl-things, boggarts and P'nor'n, all exist now only as the subject matter of occult literature.

And, most tragically of all, perhaps, dear reader, never will the lads' mags or the, ahem, adult channels reveal for you in all her gorgeous disarray of silk and lace and loveliness the physical presence of her for love of whom the narrative would gladly pulp itself to be recycled as the tissue on which she wipes her nose – the glory of the Lyminge Under 20s netball team, the splendid and irretrievably lost, Helena Phipps, most sensual collocation of print and paper in the universe.

Farewell, Helena! Adieu, Magnarch! Goodbye, Witches, Teddy Bears, Eric Maresbreaths. It was a good universe while it lasted. Farewell, Demi-Urge, at least you have avoided the VAT Inspectors.

And farewell, gentle reader. It breaks my heart to leave you, but we are out of the Gnostic frying pan now and into the fire of our own incredible cosmos- farewell!

                    Farewell!

                                      Farewell!

Printed in Great Britain
by Amazon.co.uk, Ltd.,
Marston Gate.